A GOOD NIGHT TO KILL

Also by Amen Alonge

A Good Day to Die

A GOOD NIGHT TO KILL

AMEN ALONGE

QUERCUS

First published in Great Britain in 2023 by

QUERCUS

Quercus Editions Ltd
Carmelite House
50 Victoria Embankment
London EC4Y 0DZ

An Hachette UK company

A CIP catalogue record for this book is available
from the British Library

HB ISBN 978 1 52941 522 3
EB ISBN 978 1 52941 523 0

This book is a work of fiction. Names, characters,
businesses, organizations, places and events are
either the product of the author's imagination
or used fictitiously. Any resemblance to
actual persons, living or dead, events or
locales is entirely coincidental.

10 9 8 7 6 5 4 3 2 1

Typeset by CC Book Production
Printed and bound in Great Britain by Clays Ltd, Elcograf S.p.A.

Papers used by Quercus are from well-managed forests and other responsible sources.

To my wonderful wife and son . . .
Everything I do is for you

2012

DAY 1

'You don't want to make
an enemy of me'

Veronika Lenkov stands by the floor-to-ceiling window in her grand office on the thirtieth floor, watching the River Thames. She's in her early thirties, but she's the de facto boss of her family's multibillion-pound group of companies, and she very much looks the part. Rupert, head of legal at the Lenkov family investment office, sits at her desk and watches her with unease.

'We could just cancel,' Rupert says. 'They're running late as it is.'

'No,' Veronika responds, not taking her eyes off the river.

Ten tense minutes pass before Rupert builds up the courage to again suggest they cancel. But before he speaks, the intercom system on the desk interrupts him.

'They're here,' Veronika's assistant says.

Veronika walks back to her desk to respond. 'Good. Let me know when they are in the meeting room,' she says in a cultured English accent, which has more than a hint of Russian.

A minute later, Veronika's assistant confirms the other party is in the meeting room. Veronika leads Rupert through a door in her office that leads into her own private meeting room. She puts on a smile and greets the three men across the table with a nod before she sits. Two of the men, lawyers in sharp suits, smile back almost apologetically, but Angus, the shabby man in the middle, scoffs.

'I'm supposed to be impressed by all this?' Angus asks in a thick Scottish accent, and gestures at the meeting room.

'Excuse Angus,' one of the lawyers quickly interjects. 'Apologies for being late. Transport issues.'

Angus rolls his eyes.

'It's okay,' Veronika says.

The door linking the meeting room to the corridor opens, and a man places a tray with shot glasses and a bottle of premium vodka on the table.

'I know this is not usual,' Veronika says. 'But considering the size of the deal and our plans for Angus Whisky, I thought it best you have a taste of the first liquor company to join our family portfolio. As I'm sure . . . well, I *hope* you are aware, we, hand in hand with Mr Vasiliev, increased the value of Vasiliev Vodka from single millions to three billion dollars in just five years.'

'I'm not drinking that Russian piss,' Angus says.

The lawyers are shocked, but Veronika remains calm. 'You will,' she says, and glares at him.

Angus is startled by her glare and hesitates. 'What?' he asks, attempting to sound defiant, but there is no confidence in his voice or demeanour. He pushes through. 'I said—'

'We will,' one of Angus's lawyers interrupts, and squeezes Angus's thigh. 'We know all about Vasiliev Vodka and the other spirit companies in your portfolio.'

'Good,' she says and nods at the man standing by the tray. 'We are going to enjoy it straight, like it's meant to be.'

The man places a carefully measured shot of vodka in front of each of them.

'To Angus Whisky,' Veronika says, and raises her glass.

'Angus Whisky,' the lawyers respond, and Angus murmurs, and they down the vodka.

The man picks up the empty glasses and leaves the room.

'Shall we get to the signatures?' Rupert says, and gestures to two contracts laid on the table between them.

'Well, err—' one of Angus's lawyers begins.

'No,' Angus interrupts.

Rupert turns to Angus's lawyers. 'What's going on? The terms have already been agreed. This ought just to be a formality.'

'I changed my mind,' Angus says.

Veronika leans back in her chair and keeps her eyes fixed on Angus.

'You changed your mind?' Rupert asks.

'Yes.'

'When, Angus? We were working on all the details until midnight last night.'

'By we, you mean you and them, eh?' Angus says, and gestures to his lawyers. 'Anyway, I changed my mind on the flight down this morning.'

'Okay,' Rupert says. 'What about?'

'You see, I'm not a fool,' Angus says, and gestures at the framed business magazine covers around the room, which have Veronika's father in a variety of poses above or underneath headlines celebrating him as a titan of business. 'I'm not fooled by this bullshit. We all know what all this is about. This is you and your father using companies that people like me built from the ground to filter your fellow Russian oligarchs' dirty—'

'Excuse Angus—' one of the lawyers tries to interject.

'No,' Angus snaps, shutting him down. 'I'm going to say my piece.'

'This is not . . .' the lawyer says, but trails off as Veronika raises her hand.

'It's okay,' she says. 'Please, Angus, continue.'

Angus laughs. 'Thank you, eh? Anyway, you are using us to clean your friends' corrupt money. The current values of your portfolio companies are not real.'

'You don't want to go into business with us, then?' Rupert asks.

'Oh, I'm not saying that. But now that it's all on the table, the number has to change.'

'There's nothing on the table,' Rupert says, struggling to bury his anger. 'Your lawyers' – he glares at Angus's lawyers, who are clearly uncomfortable – 'did their due diligence. Thoroughly. So have all the lawyers of the companies we've invested in. We run a clean ship.'

Angus laughs again. 'Certainly seems like you're a believer,' he says, and gestures out the window. 'I've got a wonderful bridge to sell you.'

'Don't . . .' Rupert begins, but stops. He turns to the lawyers. 'Are you guys not going to say anything?'

'Please, Angus, let us—' one of the lawyers tries.

'Why isn't your father here, anyway?' Angus asks Veronika, talking over him.

'Don't go there,' Rupert says.

'He's the one who's always loved my whisky, isn't he?'

Veronika's phone rings and she quickly looks at the caller ID. It's the call she's expecting. She stands and hurries back into her office to answer.

'Dad?' she says in Russian.

'No, Nika, it's Gennady,' a mature voice responds in Russian. 'It's not good news.'

'Stop, Gennady. You will not be the one to give me this news. Put my father on the phone.'

'I'm sorry, Nika, he can't talk right now.'

'He can't talk? How does he think I feel? It's my baby brother! Put my father on the fucking phone!'

'Nika, I'm sorry.'

'Gennady, you don't want to make an enemy of me.'

Gennady doesn't speak for a few moments. 'Hold on, Veronika.'

She waits for almost a minute before her father comes on the phone, and when he does, he's sobbing.

'It's Valentin!' he says. 'But unrecognisable. His body is in tatters! He's been in that river for all these years, Nika! We've been looking down at him! And there was a bullet in his skull. Just like Viktor!' He wails in agony. 'My two boys are dead!'

Veronika throws her phone to the ground in a rage, and it shatters. She shuts her eyes and silently screams for almost thirty seconds. Then she opens her eyes and walks back into the meeting room.

A charged conversation between the lawyers ends the moment she steps back in, and Rupert watches her, hoping to get a sense of the news from her demeanour. But he can't read her. She sits, and he tries to get her attention, but she ignores him.

'What were you saying, Angus?' she asks calmly.

Angus grins. 'Gotten your marching orders from the old man, eh?'

'What's your number, Angus?' she asks.

'Ah! Your man here says there is no wiggle—'

'Your number.'

'Fifty million.'

'Come on!' Rupert barks. 'That's more than triple.'

'Oh, yes. And for thirty per cent.'

Rupert is furious, but Veronika places her hand on his to calm him.

'More than triple the agreed – very fair – price for ten per cent less equity,' she says, and smiles. 'I wasn't trained in business, Angus. I was trained for something altogether different . . . something dirtier . . . more exciting . . . politics at the Kremlin. It taught me many things. My older brother, the chosen one for this *business empire*, did not want someone's empire. Wanted to do his own thing . . . in London. He came to this city. And died. So, the rest of us Lenkovs had to pack our things and come to London. And not for business, Angus. No.' She grins and whispers, '*To avenge my brother.*

'But my father lost his way, and so did my baby brother. They fell in love with all the trappings of wealth on this fine island. And even worse, my father started to feed his ego with this' – she gestures at the magazine covers on the wall – 'nonsense. I had to step up and run the family, including this business. And it turns out a lot of my training is useful. As my grandmother always used to say' – she mimics an elderly female voice – '*you must understand ALL your opposition's motives before you act.* Angus, I understand why you want thirty per cent, but fifty million is just greed.'

'No . . .'

'It is, Angus. You offer thirty per cent because when your business was struggling four years ago, you sold thirty-three per cent to a private equity firm based in the Cayman Islands.'

'What does that—'

'Patience, all will become clear, Angus. The shares of the Cayman firm cannot be diluted. You want to sell us thirty per cent, so you retain the largest share – thirty-seven per cent. I understand that. But you crossed the line with the fifty million ask. Ordinarily, I'd let it go. But not today. If you'd bothered to read the share-sale agreement with the Cayman firm, instead of being blinded by the numbers . . .' She pauses, then addresses the lawyers. 'Did you work on that deal?'

'No, we didn't,' one of them responds.

'Good. He can't blame you for this. That agreement includes a drag-along, where if the Cayman firm receives an offer for their share above a certain number, Angus will be forced to sell his shares as well. We own the Cayman firm, not that you'll ever be able to find that out. So, this was really just a formality.'

'You can't—'

'I can. I will buy your entire company for one million, and I will burn it all to the ground.'

'Hey, let's talk,' Angus pleads. 'I was just trying to bargain hard. Please.'

'Rupert, please,' one of Angus's lawyers pleads. 'We agree to the terms on the table. Right, Angus?'

'Absolutely. I'm in,' Angus says, and picks up the pen by the contract in front of him. 'Just show me where to sign.'

Rupert turns to Veronika, and she nods.

Angus's lawyer shows him where to sign, and he does. Rupert opens the signatory page of the contract in front of Veronika and hands her the pen, but she closes the pen and places it on the table.

'I want to watch it burn,' she says.

DAY 5

'Send the location'

It's 05:26 when Alan Pierce wakes up. He doesn't check the time because he wakes up for a run about the same time every day. He steps out of his large bed and takes his time to tidy it before he walks into the en-suite bathroom to get ready. Everything in the stylish bedroom is carefully considered and immaculate. Everything in the whole penthouse flat is. In fact, everything about his physical appearance is carefully considered and immaculate. Some of it comes naturally, but he also works hard at it, especially with his wardrobe, Ivy League haircut, and lean physique. He's run five kilometres every morning since he was twenty-one, and he's in his early forties now.

He runs around his quiet residential neighbourhood in Clapham, listening to his curated electronic music playlist, populated mainly by Gorillaz, Fatboy Slim and Daft Punk tracks, and he and the few other runners greet each other with a familiar smile as they cross paths. As he nears home, he drops by a local coffee shop and, almost in stride, picks up two cups of takeaway coffee and croissants that have been set on the counter for him. He blows a kiss to the middle-aged lady behind the counter, and she beams at him before he runs out of the shop.

The glass doors to Alan's building, a six-storey converted factory, open as he approaches. He skips in with a smile and finally stops running when he reaches the reception desk. He hands the coffees and croissants to the two men sitting behind the desk, and they graciously wave before he walks to the lift.

Half an hour later, Alan is dressed in a cashmere quarter-zip jumper over an oxford shirt, expensive loafers, and an even more expensive wristwatch. He sits at his breakfast bar as he eats a bowl of porridge and studies detailed financial projections on his laptop. There is a knock on his front door, and he switches on his bean-to-cup coffee machine before he answers.

He opens the door and makes way for a tall and formidable woman in her late twenties with cropped ice-blonde hair.

'Guten Morgen, Franka,' he says with his London accent, and shuts the door behind her.

'Guten Morgen, Alan,' Franka responds with her perfect native German, and they smile at each other.

He leads her back to the kitchen and continues eating his breakfast and studying the projections. Franka sets her motorcycle helmet on the breakfast bar and grabs the prepared cup of coffee from the machine. She takes off her leather jacket, revealing a pistol holstered around her left shoulder, and sits at the breakfast bar.

Alan finishes his breakfast and ejects the USB stick that contains the projections. He places the stick in a mortar on the kitchen counter and destroys it with a pestle.

'I'm ready,' he says to Franka.

Franka and Alan are in the front seats of a black Jaguar saloon; she's driving. He gets a call on a burner phone, and it's Steven, his right hand and one of the few he trusts. He answers.

'All right, Steven. Is it all set?' he asks.

'Yes, boss,' Steven confirms over the phone.

'Confirmed all the current phone numbers?'

'Yes, boss.'

'Okay. Send the location. We're on our way.'

Alan ends the call and connects his iPhone to the car stereo. He scrolls through his electronic playlist, searching for a song, but receives a blank text from 'Forest Gate'. He makes a call on his burner.

'Yeah?' Alan asks.

'You're on your way to the thing, yeah?' a young man with an East London accent asks over the phone.

'Yes.'

'Can we meet before? It's important. I'll be at the usual spot in twenty minutes.'

'Twenty minutes? I don't need you running red lights. Let's make it thirty minutes. And whatever this is, I want bullet points.'

'Sorry?'
'A summary . . . a brief one.'
'Sure thing.'
'All right.'

Thirty minutes later, Alan and Franka step into a charity shop, and the shopkeeper nods at Alan. Franka waits on the shop floor, and Alan walks into the stockroom. Hardeep, a lanky young man in his mid-twenties, steps out from behind a rack of shelving.

'Sup, boss,' Hardeep says.

'Sup, H,' Alan says, and they bump fists.

'There's some beef going on between Priyanka and Jamal.'

'Okay . . .'

'Since Krish died and Pri took over, Jamal's been sending kids to sell on our turf. Pri trying to stop it calm like . . . you know, cos these boys are youth and that. So, our mandem just knock these youth around a little and send 'em off. But different ones keep coming back every day. And more of them, too. Pri's not happy, so things might kick off at the meet today.'

'Priyanka won't do that.'

'You don't know her, boss. There's a reason the family chose her to run things.'

'Fair. But she won't fuck with my meeting.'

'All right, boss. But things will straighten out sharpish if you talk about it at the meeting, though.'

'Talk about what?'

'What Jamal's doing. There's an agreement between the collective not to fuck about and that.'

'Yeah. And I'm not part of the collective. I'm the distributor to the collective. I don't want to get involved with the business of the collective.'

'That's dangerous, fam.'

'That's the business. And this is an opportunity for you. If you steer clear when the bullets fly, your family will probably choose you to run the business this time, if Priyanka dies.'

The comment repulses Hardeep. 'Pri's my first cousin, boss.'

'These are the risks, and Priyanka is in with her eyes wide open. Best open yours, H. Anyway, thanks for the heads-up. I'll be in touch.'

'Bless, fam.'

A black Mercedes coupé pulls up in the car park of a run-down church. Jamal, a young and stocky black man with mixed heritage, hops out of the driver's seat and counts the other cars in the car park. He smirks; they're all here and waiting for him.

Jamal swaggers into the empty church hall. Six people, the heads of the largest drug-dealing organisations in London, are already sitting on comfortable chairs around a large circular table. These six and Jamal are the members of the collective, and Alan refers to each of them, when not with them, by the area of London where they base their operation. Priyanka Patel, aka Stratford to Alan, late twenties and the only woman in the room, and Tyrone, aka Kilburn, an overweight man in his late thirties who prefers to go by Snowman, are among them. Everyone but Priyanka turns to Jamal, aka Hackney, and most don't hide their annoyance. But Tyrone is amused.

'You're fucking late again, brother!' Tyrone says with a thick Caribbean accent. 'Stop your light-skinned behaviour!'

'Fuck off, man,' Jamal says in jest, and takes the empty seat beside Tyrone.

Jamal smirks as he enjoys the angry glances from the others. But he sees that Priyanka is indifferent, and this irks him. He wants to provoke her, but before he can try again, Alan walks into the hall from a side door.

'Okay, Jamal was late, so we'll get straight to it,' Alan says and sits on the last empty chair.

'Traffic, fam, and—' Jamal says.

'It's fine. You're here now, and the others have places to be.'

The interruption annoys Jamal, but he bites his tongue.

'As requested, I've made the necessary arrangements to deliver a twenty per cent increase in product to each of you next week,' Alan says, and there is a murmur of satisfaction. 'But we need to agree on an increased price first.'

'Why?' Tyrone asks.

'Simply, inflation.'

'Inflation?'

'You're fucking joking, fam?'

'Not joking,' Alan says. 'We've had the same price for a year, and since then, the Consumer Prices Index has risen by three point eight per cent.'

Tyrone laughs and nods. 'I get you.'

'Nah, I don't get you,' Jamal says.

'I'm proposing a three point eight per cent increase in price, like the Index, and each year the price will rise, or not, accordingly. And before you say anything more, Jamal, I know some of you have already increased the price of the product on the street. Not my business, I know. I just mention it to let you know – all of you – that you can easily increase your prices to accommodate your raised costs.'

'Still, fam, don't know about all that,' Jamal says.

'Fair enough. Is Jamal speaking for all of you?'

'No, he's not. I'm fine with it,' says Pete, aka Peckham, a middle-aged man with a thick Irish accent.

'I'm with Pete,' Tyrone says, and everyone else but Jamal nods in agreement.

'You want to reconsider, Jamal?' Alan asks. 'I know these decisions have to be unanimous.'

Jamal shrugs.

'Okay. We keep the same agreement, then,' Alan says.

'What does that mean?' Pete asks.

'No twenty per cent increase in your supply.'

'Wagwan, brother?' Tyrone says to Jamal. 'You already increased your prices.'

'Don't put my business out there like that, Snowman.'

'Everybody knows!' Pete says.

'No one's talking to you, pikey,' Jamal says.

'What the fuck you say?' Pete responds, and glares at Jamal.

'That's fucked up,' Callum, aka Wembley, a young man of East Asian descent, says.

'Shut up, Jackie Chan,' Jamal says.

Callum, sitting on the other side of Tyrone, shoots off his chair, and Tyrone moves almost as fast to stand between the young man and Jamal. Jamal remains seated and watches Callum without an ounce of fear.

'Relax, Callum,' Tyrone says, and turns to Jamal. 'Jamal is going to apologise to Pete and Callum by agreeing to the increase in price.'

Jamal is about to object, but Tyrone scowls. Jamal kisses his teeth and nods.

'Sorted, then,' Tyrone says, and turns to Pete and Callum. 'Yes?'

Pete nods, and Callum briefly hesitates before he nods.

'And I'm Japanese, you cunt,' Callum says before sitting.

Jamal rolls his eyes, and Tyrone fights back laughter as he sits.

'Okay, agreed,' Alan says. 'Any other business before we close?'

No one responds.

'You sure, Priyanka? Nothing to report?' Jamal teases, and grins.

Priyanka doesn't take the bait and remains calm, but she's burning with rage.

'Ah, yes,' Tyrone says. 'Not sure about this come-alone thing. I don't like to drive. And before any of you fuckers say it and I have to kill you, yes, it's because I'm fat.' He chuckles.

No one even cracks a smile, because although Tyrone likes to make light of his weight, he is very sensitive about it and his notoriously short fuse snaps indiscriminately when he thinks he's being teased about it. Tyrone's stuck at the moment when he was first teased about his weight as a thirteen-year-old child, and everyone laughed. He couldn't do anything about it then, but everyone's paying for it now.

'I understand, Tyrone. But we're trying to keep each other safe. Keep the circle small,' Alan says, and gestures to Jamal. 'And you can get your boyfriend to drive you.'

'What the fuck you trying to say, fam?' Jamal snarls.

'Fucking hell, Jamal, relax,' Tyrone says. 'It's a joke.'

'Nah, fam, man don't like them type jokes.'

'You should be used to it,' Priyanka quips.

'What you chatting, bitch?'

'Okay,' Alan intercedes. 'I won't be making any more jokes. We're . . .'

Steven steps into the room through the side door, and Alan trails off as he instantly spots that Steven is nervous.

'One moment,' Alan says to the table, and walks over to Steven.

'Michael's here,' Steven whispers.

'What?' Alan asks, and struggles to hide his anger. 'How the fuck did he get the location?'

'I . . . I . . . dunno.'

'You don't . . .'

Michael Downing struts through the side door flanked by two sturdy men – one is his own right-hand man for the last half decade, Gary, and the other is Gary's stepson, Andreas, better known as 'Dre'. All three are in shabby gym gear. Michael, formerly known as Killer Mike, Three-Bullets Mike, Five-Bullets Mike, Teflon Mike, Money Mike, and King Mike through his infamously violent decades rising through the London underworld, is now known as Councillor of East Hampstead, Michael Downing. Michael has seemingly passed on the day-to-day running of his criminal empire to Alan, his younger half-brother, as he pursues a career in politics.

'Everything okay, Michael?' Alan asks, doing his best to exude calm even as he's consumed with anxiety brought on by Michael's sudden presence. Over Michael's shoulder, he sees Franka step through the side door and position herself at the edge of the hall.

'Of course,' Michael says with a coarse London accent, which has a faint hint of Irish in it.

Michael brushes past Alan and approaches the table.

'Hello, Michael,' Pete says, and smiles. 'What are you doing here? You're missing this, aren't you?'

'Absolutely not, Pete,' he says exaggeratedly.

Michael and Pete cackle.

'Hello, Councillor. I thought you were too good for us,' Jamal mocks.

'Sorry?' Michael says, and glares at Jamal.

Michael is in his early fifties but retains his formidable presence – usually all he needs to do is glare. But his glare only excites Jamal.

'Thought you better than us now, fam. You can't be associated with the likes of us now that you trying to get to Parliament.'

'What's your name?' Michael asks.

This infuriates Jamal. 'You know my name, fam.'

'Sadly, boy, I don't.'

'Who the fuck you calling boy, fam?'

'Hey!' Tyrone says, and grabs Jamal's shoulder. 'My man's name is Jamal.'

'Thank you, Tyrone,' Michael says. 'Anyway, I'll get right to it because I know we don't have much time. I need to fund my campaign to become a member of Parliament, so our prices will increase by ten per cent.'

This staggers Alan and the members of the collective.

'I'm fucking joking,' Michael says. 'Just had a call with the suppliers. They are increasing the price by ten per cent. I'm passing that on to you, and you can pass it to the customer. Fuck's sake, most of you have already increased—'

'Fuck you chatting, fam?' Jamal barks. 'Are you trying to take man for a mug?'

'What the fuck did you say, boy?'

'Fam!' Jamal screams and leaps off his chair, but Tyrone grabs him. 'Stop calling me boy!'

'What are you going to do about it, boy?'

'You think cos you with Beavis and Butthead, I won't smack you up?'

'What's that, Dre?' Gary asks.

'A cartoon,' Dre says.

'Ah, not surprised the boy hasn't matured to adult content yet,' Gary quips.

'Are you mad, fam?!' Jamal shouts.

'There are adult cartoons out there, though,' Dre says to Gary. 'Good ones too. Anime and shit.' Dre turns to Callum. 'They're fucking good, right?'

Callum doesn't respond, just glares.

'Don't leave me hanging like that, mate,' Dre says. 'It's not racist. You're Japanese, nit? It's just like me asking . . .' Dre looks at the others in the room for an apt comparison, but he doesn't find one. 'Just like you asking me about Zeus and them.'

'Zeus . . . and anime?' Callum questions.

'Oh, fuck off, then!' Dre says.

'These are the idiots you think will stop me smacking you up?' Jamal asks Michael.

'Smack me up? You've said that twice now,' Michael replies, and gestures for Gary and Dre to stay back as he steps forward. 'Come on then, boy.'

Jamal tries to charge towards Michael, but he can't escape Tyrone's grasp. He turns to Tyrone. 'Let me go before I bust you up!'

'Leave it, brother. This not the time,' Tyrone whispers.

'Fam, get your fat hands off me,' Jamal says, and fights off Tyrone's grasp.

Jamal charges Michael and throws a right hook, but Michael blocks it and drives his forehead into Jamal's face. Jamal's nose shatters, and he recoils. Michael swings his own right hook into Jamal's stomach and knocks the wind out of him. He grabs him by the hair and drives his head onto the table. Jamal rolls onto the floor, and Michael repeatedly kicks him.

'That's enough, nit?' Tyrone says, and stands.

Gary and Dre pull out pistols and aim for Tyrone, and Tyrone sits.

'This is not right,' Callum says to Alan, and gestures to the guns. 'We agreed no weapons in here.'

Dre turns his gun to Callum and smirks.

'Put them away,' Alan says to Gary and Dre, but they ignore him. 'Fucking idiots.'

Alan walks towards Michael, and Dre turns his gun on Alan. Out of nowhere, Franka snatches the gun and snaps Dre's wrist in one motion. She trains the gun at Dre's head as he howls in pain and levels her gun at Gary. Her presence stuns both men, and it seems no one other than Alan had noticed her enter the hall. Michael is visibly furious with Gary and Dre, especially because he's not a fan of Franka.

Alan approaches his brother. 'You need to leave, right now,' he whispers.

'I'm not done,' Michael responds.

'What . . . ? '

'Boss,' Steven calls from the door.

'What?' Alan and Michael respond in unison. They immediately realise the awkwardness of their shared response, and Michael again struggles to hide his anger.

Alan quickly locks eyes with Steven and gestures for him to address Michael.

'Michael, we're starting to draw attention,' Steven says. 'We need to leave.'

'Fine,' Michael says, and turns to the table. 'Ten per cent. Take it or leave it!'

Michael, Gary and Dre storm out of the side door, and Alan takes Dre's gun from Franka before he follows.

He walks to Michael's Range Rover, parked beside his Jaguar. He hands the gun to Dre in the passenger seat and turns to Michael in the back.

'What was that?' Alan asks.

Michael laughs. 'I needed some action. I'm fucking bored.'

The response angers Alan, but he doesn't show it. 'Okay, but you could've blown the whole thing up.'

'What? Cos of Jamal? None of them like the fucker, and from what I hear, he's been due for a beating.'

It's Pete, Alan thinks. Pete's been talking to Michael. 'You can't be doing—'

'I do what the fuck I want.'

'I know. But it was your choice to pursue politics. It's put a bright light on you.'

'What the fuck are you trying to say?'

'You know what I'm saying,' Alan asserts.

'Whatever. Won't happen again . . . if you keep them *collective* fuckers in line.'

'Sure,' Alan says, although he wants to say so much more. 'About the ten per cent, we can't do that—'

'What? Who the fuck is the boss here? I want the fucking ten per cent. Are you telling me you can't get it done?'

Michael and Alan glare at each other.

'You'll get your ten per cent.'

'Of course I will. All but Pete. His price doesn't change. Don't question me.'

Alan fights to bite his tongue and nods.

'And keep Franka on a leash,' Michael says. 'Next time she fucks with any of my guys, I'll put her down.'

Michael smacks the driver's headrest, and Gary drives off.

Alan watches the car disappear into the distance, then yells, 'Fuuucck!'

DAY 7

'You used to be untouchable'

The developer of an upmarket residential property development leads Alan and other investors through the sweeping half-finished site in the Docklands. Alan's phone rings, and it's a number he doesn't recognise, but he answers anyway.

'Alan Pierce?' the female voice on the other end asks.

'Yes, who's speaking?' Alan responds politely.

'Inspector Caroline Maguire of the Metropolitan Police,' she responds with a thick Yorkshire accent.

Alan is surprised, especially because he's never heard of her. He retired from the Metropolitan Police recently enough to know of every current inspector, even the newly promoted ones, because promotion in the Metropolitan Police is a slow-moving process . . . unless you were Alan. He stays back and gestures for the group to continue without him.

'Hello, Inspector Maguire, what can I help you with?'

'Nothing serious, Alan,' she says in a friendly manner, which only makes him suspicious. 'We'd like you to come in for an interview.'

'About what?'

'I'd rather not discuss it over the phone.'

'Do I come with counsel?'

'That's totally up to you, but as I said, it's nothing serious. It's just that, as a respected former colleague, we didn't want to doorstep you.'

Alan considers for a moment. 'Sure.'

'What day and time work for you?'

'I'm free in a couple hours.'

As he expected, there is silence on the other end of the phone. Whatever's happening, he doesn't want to give them enough time to prepare.

'Today would be difficult. But we can do first thing tomorrow?'

'I'm off on holiday tonight. Would be back in a couple weeks. I'll call then, and we'll arrange a time.'

'One moment, please.'

Alan lied. There's no holiday. And if Caroline is any good, she'll know he's lying. But she can't push because that'll show her hand.

'Okay, four p.m.?' she offers.

Alan checks the time, and it's 12:30. Too much time, he thinks.

'That's cutting it close for my flight. Three p.m.'

'Okay, Alan.'

'What station are you working out of?'

'No station currently. We're temporarily renting space in Battersea. I'll text you the address.'

'See you then.'

Alan ends the call, and ponders as several alarm bells go off in his head. He needs a second opinion. He heads back towards his car and calls Nisa Fraser-Hulton, a childhood friend and leading criminal QC.

'Hello, Alan,' Nisa answers.

'Hello, Nisa. I need your advice. In person.'

'Okay, I'm on my way back to my chambers. When can you get there?'

'Thirty minutes.'

'I'll meet you at our usual spot with a coffee.'

'Thanks, I need it.'

Alan walks into Lincoln's Inn Fields and spots Nisa sitting on the grass in the middle of the park, on the phone. That's Nisa in her element – down to earth and always working. He heads towards her, and she bounces to her feet as he approaches. She hands Alan a cup of coffee and gestures for him to wait a moment as she wraps up the call. She puts her phone away, and they hug.

'Sorry about that,' she says.

'No, I'm sorry. This is all fairly sudden.'

'Let's walk,' she says, and leads the way through the park. 'What's happening?'

'Been called in for an interview with the Met.'

'Under caution?'

'I don't know. But lots of red flags. I've never heard of the officer that called. Inspector Caroline Maguire, heard of her?'

Nisa shakes her head.

'I made a few calls on the way over, and pretty much no one knows her. One contact knew the name, but had no idea she'd been transferred in from West Yorkshire Police. It's not showing up on their systems.'

'Yorkshire? Any business there?'

'No. And I don't think this has anything to do with Yorkshire. She said *they* are renting a place in Battersea. Not working out of a station.'

'Special investigation, then. I'm guessing everyone on the team is an outsider. They might be coming after Michael and trying to circumvent your many *friends* in the Met. Or they might be after you.'

He sighs. 'I know. And as far as I know, they have not called Michael in for an interview.'

'As far as you know?'

'Yes. Michael isn't being very forthcoming nowadays.'

She nods. 'Other red flags?'

'Too friendly. Said they were asking me to come in because, as a *respected former colleague*, they didn't want to doorstep me.'

'Respected former colleague,' she repeats. '"A" for effort, I suppose. But a hard red flag.'

'Yes, and she was getting orders on the call. Couldn't make a decision herself.'

'When is the interview?'

'Three.'

'That's quick.'

'I made sure of it.'

'Good. I think I should come with you.'

'That might get their backs up.'

'If they aren't already up. On the other hand, you can blame me for no commenting their questions if things get tricky.'

Alan nods.

'Text me the address, I'll meet you there. Come alone. Keep Franka off their radar.'

Alan and Nisa sit on one side of a table in what ought to be the corner office of the third floor of a recently constructed, but empty, block. They've been left waiting for over five minutes.

'I wonder how the Met affords this space,' Alan says.

Nisa shrugs, and Alan gets the cue. No small talk; they are being watched.

A middle-aged female officer and a younger male officer walk into the room.

'Sorry for the delay, Alan,' the woman says, and they sit. 'I'm Inspector Caroline Maguire, and my colleague is Sergeant Rhys Evans.'

'Hello,' Rhys says with a distinct Welsh accent.

'Hello,' Alan says, and gestures to the empty chair between Caroline and Rhys. 'Are we expecting someone?'

'Yes. But he's running late, so we'll start,' Caroline says.

Alan nods.

'I see you're here with a solicitor,' Caroline says.

'I'm a barrister,' Nisa says. 'Nisa Fraser-Hulton. But I take your point.'

'Nisa Fraser-Hulton QC?' Rhys asks, surprised.

Nisa nods.

'I've read a lot about you. You acted for the Crown in the Church of Wales sex-abuse scandal, didn't you?'

Nisa nods.

'Pleased to meet you,' Rhys says.

'Thank you.'

'Big guns, eh?' Caroline says to Alan. 'I see the private sector is treating you well.'

Alan forces a smile.

'Anyway,' Caroline says, and switches on the recorder on the table. 'I have to caution you—'

'What?' Alan says.

'You do not have to say anything,' Caroline continues. 'But it may harm your defence if you do not mention when questioned something which you later rely on in court. Anything you do say may be given in evidence.'

Alan smiles.

'Detective Inspector Caroline Maguire and Detective Sergeant Rhys Evans interviewing Alan Pierce from 3:07 p.m. Alan Pierce has counsel present. Alan, I know you've given cautions countless times over your illustrious career with the Met, so I'm going to assume you understand.'

Alan nods.

'For the tape, Mr Alan Pierce nods in the affirmative.'

The door opens, and a tall, broad-chested man with

piercing eyes and a prominent scar across his neck walks into the room.

'For the tape, Chief Superintendent Jack Moore has joined the interview,' Caroline says.

Alan watches Jack sit between Caroline and Rhys, and he has a good idea what this interview is about.

'Hello, Jack, long time,' Alan says.

'Long time, Alan,' Jack coldly responds, and gestures for Caroline to continue.

'Can you detail your whereabouts on the early hours of April 15, 2009?' Caroline asks.

'Three years ago?' Alan asks. 'I can't—'

'I advise my client to make a no comment interview,' Nisa interrupts.

Caroline turns to Alan for confirmation.

'No comment,' Alan says.

'Specifically, between three a.m. and four a.m.?'

'No comment.'

'To remind you, this is hours after Meiling Downing, the wife of your brother and employer, was assaulted outside a banquet hall in Camden. You remember that night?'

'No comment.'

'What phone number were you using that night?'

'No comment.'

'Are you still using the same phone number?'

'No comment.'

'What car were you driving on the night?'

'No comment.'

'Have you ever been to the Flower Club in Soho?'

'No comment,' Alan responds, and shifts in his chair, as he's now certain what they are talking about.

Nisa notices the subtle shift. 'Is my client under arrest?' she interrupts.

'No,' Jack responds.

'Then I'm ending this interview,' Nisa says. 'Next time you want to speak to my client, arrest him. From what I'm hearing, that's a long way off. But we get your point. You want my client to be on notice that you are looking at him for something or the other that happened between three a.m. and four a.m. on April 15, 2009. Touché.'

Caroline looks to Jack for approval, and he nods.

'For the tape, Inspector Caroline Maguire sought permission from Chief Superintendent Jack Moore to end the interview,' Nisa says.

Caroline forces a smile and stops the recorder.

'I see you didn't take up the Met's offer to pay for the plastic surgery,' Alan says, and gestures to the scar on Jack's neck.

'Not yet,' Jack responds.

'You used to be so much fun, Jack.'

'You used to be untouchable.'

Alan smiles and nods.

Alan and Nisa walk to their cars, parked in view of the Thames and the derelict Battersea Power Station.

'What was all that animosity between you and Jack Moore about?'

'Remember the kid I sent your way to apprentice?'

'I won't ever forget him. Brightest kid I ever met. How's he?'

'Good . . . I hope. Every day.'

'You hope?'

'He had something to do with that scar on Jack's neck.'

'What . . . a decade ago? The kid was involved in the Wapping Massacre? So, he's dead, then?'

'No. Well, I don't know. He didn't die that night, that's for sure.'

'The press said only Jack and his informant survived the massacre.'

Alan smiles. 'That's the official story – Jack and his team risked their lives to save their informant. Not even close to the truth. They were just supposed to clean up after an ambush. But the kid was on the other side of the ambush, so it all went tits up.'

'And how many people know this?'

'Enough.'

'How did Jack keep his job, then? And rocket through the ranks?'

'A benefactor.'

'Benefactor?'

'It happens. Anyway, I tampered with the evidence. It's all still there, but the CPS can't use it . . . and even if they are pushed for a charge, it won't hold up in court. Jack suspects I did it. To be fair, only a handful of people could've done it clean like I did. But he just can't figure out *why* I'd do it.'

'No one knows about your relationship with the kid?'

'No one in the force. But then again, the kid is not in the system at all. Not his DNA, prints, picture . . . nothing, not even his name. He has no record at all.'

'How did you do that?'

'I didn't. He's the brightest kid I ever met as well, and he's just stayed off the radar. Even the informant didn't know his name. Kept referring to the kid as *Pretty Boy*. Pissed the investigation team off to no end.'

'Right. Anything I need to know about April 15, 2009?'

'I don't know what they are talking about.'

'Stop lying.'

'I forgot about your lie detector.'

'It's more of a truth detector. Before you ask, there is a difference. In my line of work, most clients lie as default. It's key to discern the truth and work with it.'

'Fair. Well, it's best you don't know right now.'

'It's too late for that. I need to know what to prepare for.'

'The benefactor. How they can afford this space . . . it's Marat Lenkov.'

'The Russian billionaire?'

'Yep. They're looking for Marat's son.'

'I thought he died years ago in a car accident.'

'It's another son.'

'Another one?'

Alan nods. 'Yes, Valentin. And the one you're talking about – Viktor – he actually died in the Wapping Massacre.'

'What is going on?'

Alan laughs.

'This isn't funny, Alan. A Russian oligarch with one son dead and another missing. You want to be far away from this.'

'I am. Trust me.'

She shakes her head. 'The truth detector, Alan. Get your affairs in order quickly. Because they are coming after *you*, not Michael.' She steps into her car and drives off.

Alan stands by his car and stares at the power station, wondering if he'll live to see its regeneration. But he pulls himself together because he has everything within his means to ensure he does. Just needs to play his cards right. He steps into his car and calls Franka.

'Hello,' Franka says.

'I'm okay,' he responds. 'I'm going to text you an address. Delete the text once you receive it. Go there right now and tell me what you see.'

Franka drives her sports bike through quiet industrial streets south of the river. She scans the street as she drives past an abandoned garage and sees three cars parked with a perfect view of the entrance. She examines the cars, and although the plain-clothed police officers inside do their best to hide, she spots them.

Alan sits at home trying to watch the news, but he's too anxious. His burner phone rings, and he answers straight away.

'It's being watched,' Franka says, and ends the call.

Rage and anxiety threaten to overcome him as he realises that someone is talking to Jack Moore. Someone on the inside. 'Fuuucck!' he yells.

DAY 8, 05:34

'I've got all day'

I wake up and glance at my watch; it's 5:34 a.m. About thirty minutes earlier than I usually wake up, but then today's not a typical day. I consider remaining in bed till 6 a.m. . . . the rest will be helpful, especially because it was difficult to fall asleep. But I can't, I'm too excited.

I step out of my bed and head into the bathroom to brush my teeth. But I don't switch on the lights. I don't need to. I know where every item in this cottage is, and I can make my way around with my eyes closed. Which isn't as difficult as you'd think, because the cottage is minimally furnished. All of this is intentional.

I skip down the steps to the living room for my daily morning workout – eighty squats, a hundred push-ups, and a hundred sit-ups. I'm about to start the stretch routine to end the workout, but I decide to do one more set of each exercise.

I've certainly got the time and am evidently still too excited. I stretch and head to the kitchen.

I switch on the lights to prepare a cup of green tea and breakfast, which is either eggs or oats – easy and healthy. Today, it's oats. I cook the oats on the hob, then add a couple of spoons of peanut butter, a sprinkle of chia seeds, berries, and a dollop of honey. I sit by the kitchen counter and enjoy my breakfast. I used to wonder if I'd tire of eggs and oats, but it was almost a decade ago that this odyssey began, and I still enjoy every moment, from preparing them to eating them. Thank God, I suppose. Which is an odd sentiment, considering I don't believe there's a God. And even if there was a God, gratitude wouldn't be the first thing on my mind. I wash the dishes and then skip back up the stairs to shower and dress.

I part the curtains in the living room to observe the front of the house, and nothing is out of the ordinary. I switch the mode on the home security system control panel by the front door to 'away' and step out of the cottage. My Land Rover is parked just ahead, but I don't approach. Instead, I scan the remote rural street, which is surrounded by forest and has three other cottages spaced about fifty metres apart from each other. It's the crack of dawn, and everything is as it should be. I enter the car and set off.

I drive for a couple of hours, past a few other towns and cities, to the closest town that meets all my requirements. A good distance away from the cottage and London. A population large enough – so not everyone knows each other. Diverse enough – so I don't stick out. And with a relatively low crime rate – least chance of interacting with or getting recognised by the police. This is my seventh visit to the town in two years, and it's been smooth sailing.

I leave the Land Rover in a car park at the edge of the town centre and walk the rest of the way. It's approaching 09:30, and the streets are busy with cars, pedestrians, joggers, and lots of cyclists. The number of cafés struck me on my first visit, but I'm sure there are a few more now, and they are all busy. Coffee is good business, but then I shouldn't be surprised . . . any product that inherently creates a dependency is good business.

I step into a mailbox rental centre and wave at the lady behind the desk with my mailbox key visible in my hand. She gets the cue. She returns the greeting and returns to her magazine. I open my mailbox, and inside is the hardback A4 envelope I was expecting. I take a deep breath before I pick it up because I know the moment I look through what's inside the envelope, I will not stop till it's done or I'm done. But fuck it, it's time. I pick up the envelope and close the mailbox.

'Have a good day,' I say to the lady, and head towards the door.

'You too, darling,' she says with an accent peculiar to the town, a mix of various West Country sub-accents.

I walk a few minutes to the quaint bookshop beside another café, and the cheerful owner of the shop notices me when I step in. He's with a customer but takes a moment to greet me with a wide smile, and I smile back. I turn to the new release section by the entrance and spot the latest Harry Bosch novel – *The Drop*. Good. I love those, and Mrs Lewis enjoys them as well. I grab the book and browse through the other new releases.

'What are we looking for today, young man?' the bookshop owner asks, and approaches.

'I've got it,' I say, and gesture at the book in my hand.

'Good choice,' he says. 'But I see you're still looking.'

'Sherlock Holmes, eh?' I tease.

He chuckles. 'I'm more a Hercule Poirot man myself, but I can grab one of the classic Sherlock Holmes.'

'I think I've read them all.'

'Think?' he questions.

'Fair. I've read enough of them . . . and I enjoyed them. But not for today.'

'Can I suggest a book, then?'

I laugh. 'You already know the answer to that.'

'I know,' he says, and smiles. 'But it's good to be polite.'

I nod, and he picks *Bring Up the Bodies* by Hilary Mantel.

'This is special,' he says, and hands it to me.

I nod and turn the book over to read the blurb.

'You're not familiar with it?' he asks.

I shake my head. 'Seems interesting, though.'

'It absolutely is. I recommend.'

'Thanks,' I say, and gesture to two non-fiction releases that grab my attention. 'Read those?'

'Not yet. But the reviews are excellent for both. You know what? You read them and let me know what you think.'

He's a pleasant man, and a good businessman. 'Sure,' I say, and pick both books.

'That's all?' he asks.

I nod, and he leads me to the till. He scans them and tells

me the price, and I take a moment to confirm the total in my head. He offered me a discount on my second visit. I refused, and he's been trying to sneak in a discount since then. But not today. It's the right price. I pay, and he places the books in a branded tote bag.

'See you soon,' he says with a smile, and hands me the bag.

I smile back and head towards the door, but on my way out, I see the tote bag on display for sale at five pounds. He got me.

I walk to a grocery shop in a relatively quiet street on the edge of the town centre. From the outside, there's nothing exceptional about the shop that would warrant the fifteen-minute walk I've made past several other shops. But this shop not only has the softest packets of Haribo Starmix in the entire town, but a large quantity of them. I pull open the door, and a dishevelled young man barges past me as he hurries out of the shop. The young man is strung out and probably just stole something, so I ignore him and step in.

The first thing that strikes me is that the shelves aren't as fully stocked as they usually are, and then I notice the owner isn't behind the till. It's just her adult son, which is somewhat unusual, because he has a learning disability and usually doesn't run the shop alone.

'Fuck off! No discounts here,' a young man barks from behind a shelf, and a dishevelled young woman shuffles out of the shop.

I approach the till, as the Haribos are stacked on a shelf just underneath it. The lanky young man hurries behind the counter. I scan the shelf, and there are only two packets, and not where they usually are. I look up to ask the shop owner's son if there are any more, but as he turns to me I see he has a fresh black eye and bruises on his cheek. This infuriates me, and I turn to the lanky young man.

'Want something, lad?' Lanky asks, and grins. 'Come to me. My mate's a bit slow.'

'I'm not slow!' the shop owner's son shouts.

'Shut up!' Lanky barks.

'I'm not slow,' the shop owner's son mutters.

'So?' Lanky asks me.

I don't respond; I just glare at him.

'What?' Lanky asks. 'What are you doing here?'

'It's a shop. What do you think?' I say, calm.

Something about my response startles him, and he isn't sure how to respond.

'Did you do that?' I ask, gesturing to the shop owner's son's face.

'Who are you, lad?'

A door behind the till opens, and another young man covered in tattoos steps out with one hand behind his back, as if holding a weapon.

'What do you want, lad?' Tattoos asks.

'Did one of you hit him?' I ask.

'What's it to you? You're not police. Are you his social worker?'

I smile and shake my head. 'I'm not.'

'Then what is it to you if I hit him?'

'You're certainly not the lad's family,' Lanky says, and they laugh.

'You boys are amateurs, aren't you?' I say. 'Otherwise, you'd know that it's a bad thing I'm not police or a social worker.'

'How's that?' Tattoos asks.

'You boys are stupid as well, then?' I say.

'This lad's crazy, isn't he?' Lanky says to Tattoos.

'Police, social workers . . .' I say, 'they have rules to follow for these sorts of situations. Jobs to protect. Maybe families to feed. So, they can't do what they really want to do to people like you. On the other hand, I can and will do whatever I want to you, *lads*.'

They are both anxious, but Tattoos does a better job of hiding it. Maybe because he's holding a weapon, but Lanky keeps glancing at something underneath the counter – another weapon, I'm sure. But if he grabs it, he won't be the one using it.

'We don't get many of your kind around here,' Tattoos says, and Lanky sniggers. 'And I don't mean black people,' he quickly adds, correcting Lanky's assumption and seemingly wary of being seen as racist. 'I mean Londoners.'

'Yeah, Londoners,' Lanky repeats.

I nod.

'All you London lads think us lads are scraps. That we should bow before your feet. Fear you. But this is our town. Fuck off back to London before we smash your head in.'

I nod and edge closer to Lanky. I'm going to break his face the moment he reaches for the weapon underneath the counter and then I'll . . . But the thought of what I'm about to do forces me to consider the risks. I've gone almost a decade without drawing any attention to myself, and these young men aren't worth the risk.

'Where's your mum?' I ask the shop owner's son.

'Home,' he responds.

'Is she okay?'

'She's—'

'Shut up,' Tattoos commands, and the shop owner's son stares at the ground.

'Is she okay?' I ask Tattoos.

'Just fuck off!' he responds.

'Is she okay?' I ask again.

'Are you deaf?'

The shop door opens, and I glance over my shoulder to see the same dishevelled young woman from earlier excitedly burst into the shop. I glare at her, and she scurries back out.

'I've got all day,' I say to Tattoos.

'She's fine!' he says. 'I don't know what you lads do down in London, but here we don't—'

'Shut up,' I interrupt.

'Are you mental?' he snarls, and raises the blade he'd been holding behind his back.

Lanky attempts to reach for his weapon, but I slam my fists on the counter and he stops in his tracks. I stare at Tattoos, and the blade trembles in his hand. I shake my head with contempt. I pick up the two packets of Haribo Starmix and check if the sweets inside are soft. They are perfect. I place a ten-pound note on the counter and walk out of the shop.

'He's set in his ways'

I drive along the country road that leads to my cottage and notice Mrs Lewis working away in her kitchen next door. That just might have something to do with me. I park but scan my cottage and its surroundings before stepping out of the car. Everything is as I'd left it. I hop out and head inside.

I set the home security system to 'home' mode, place the A4 parcel and the packets of Haribo Starmix on the only sofa in the living room, and head to the bookshelf. I place *Bring Up the Bodies* and one of the non-fiction new releases on the shelf and pick out the two classic books Mrs Lewis gave me to read. I set the security system back to 'away' and head out.

I walk to Mrs Lewis's cottage, and we acknowledge each other with a smile through the kitchen window before we both head to her front door. She opens the door, and I'm enveloped by the rich buttery smell of whatever it is she's baking today.

'Perfect timing,' she says, and leads me to the kitchen. 'The scones are ready!'

'Scones?' I say. 'I don't think I've ever had one of those.'

She turns to me, surprised, and opens her mouth to speak but hesitates. She was about to break our unspoken rule of not asking anything about our pasts. 'Well, you'll love them,' she says, and continues into the kitchen. 'It's more a bread, so the filling is essential. I used to make my own strawberry jam, but store-bought jam will have to do.'

'Knowing you, I'm sure this is no regular store.'

She grins and gestures for me to sit beside her at the dining table, which has a platter of fresh scones, jam, and clotted cream. I sit and place the classic books on the table.

'Would you like me to prepare your first scone?' she asks. 'I'll leave you to help yourself afterwards.'

'Thank you.'

She slices the scone in half and fills it with a good amount of jam and cream before she places it on a small plate in front of me.

'Enjoy your first one before we discuss,' she says, and gestures to the books.

I have a bite of the scone, and it's delicious. But there's no way she and I will finish the near dozen scones on the table. 'This is incredible,' I say.

'I know. I tried one already,' she says, and smiles. 'So, my usual opener . . .' She gestures again to the books. 'Remarkable, aren't they?'

We spend a few hours enjoying scones and discussing the

classic books she gave me and the contemporary books I gave her.

'Super,' she says to finish the discussion, and stands. 'Let's go.'

She leads me into her living room, which is lined by impressive bookcases. I'd surmise there are almost a thousand books here, mostly classics, and she knows precisely where each book is. But that's made easier by each bookcase being dedicated to a genre, and each genre arranged in alphabetical order.

'Have you read *Brave New World*?' she asks.

'Take a wild guess,' I respond.

She chuckles. 'Fabulous,' she says, and picks out the book. 'I'm sure you'll love it.'

She strides across the room to one of her non-fiction bookcases and picks out another paperback. She hands me *Brave New World* by Aldous Huxley and *Dispatches* by Michael Herr.

'I've read this,' I say, and gesture to *Dispatches*.

'Oh, I'm sorry,' she says. 'Should've asked.'

'I'm joking,' I say, and smile. 'You never ask me if I've read the non-fiction books, so I've been waiting to say that. But you haven't picked one I've read yet.'

'I'm trying not to.'

'How? You don't know the ones I've read.'

'After spending five minutes with a person, I'd usually give myself a ninety-nine per cent chance of correctly guessing at least two seminal non-fiction books that person has read . . . if they've read any. It's a foundation block in sussing out a person's character. But you are an enigma. I've spent hours with you, and I give myself a forty-nine per cent chance of guessing one.'

'What's your guess?'

'No.'

'If you get it correct, I'll tell you another one on your shelf I've read.'

'Seems a fair bargain,' she says. *'The Art of War.'*

I chuckle and nod.

'I've still got it,' she says proudly.

'My . . .' I hesitate because I'm breaking our unspoken rule. Well, not exactly, because she didn't ask. 'The man that raised me thought it was important that I read it. Although, I'm not sure *he* did.'

She laughs. 'A soldier?'

'Police.'

She nods. 'This policeman that raised you . . . he's not your father?'

'No.'

It's apparent she has many more follow-up questions, but she's unsure whether to ask. And I remain silent to give her room to go for them, because I want to know what she wants to know about me.

'What about your father?' she asks.

Not the question I was expecting, but let's see where it leads. 'Don't know. Never knew him.'

'And your mother?'

'She's around.'

'So, this policeman was her . . .'

'No relation at all. My mother chose her boyfriend over me. So, *the policeman* took me in and raised me . . . till things got tricky with his wife.'

She pauses for a moment, considering what strand to follow. 'Tricky?'

I nod. 'His wife didn't want me around anymore.'

'Did something happen?'

'Nothing I did.'

'How old were you when they took you in?'

'Thirteen.'

'Maybe she just wanted kids of her own?'

'Not with him, though.'

She takes a moment to put the pieces together. 'She was having an affair and was worried you'd find out?'

'She knew I'd found out.'

'That is tough . . . especially for a child. How did the policeman take it when you told him?'

'I didn't.'

She's stunned. 'Why?'

'He was very good police, and it was right in front of him. He just didn't want to see it.'

'How old were you when this happened?'

'Fifteen.'

'That's incredibly perceptive for a fifteen-year-old.'

'Not for a fifteen-year-old who's been fighting to survive alone all their life.'

She nods. 'You have any animosity towards the policeman?'

'No. He did his best to continue raising me from a distance.'

'What about his wife?'

I smile. 'That's your fifteenth question, and it's the last one I'm going to answer. Is that what you really want to know?'

She smiles, shakes her head, and takes her time to prepare her last question.

'As we've determined, you're very perceptive,' she says. 'So, I'll hit the nail right on its head by acknowledging that everyone on this street, which is perfectly secluded from seclusion, is running or hiding from something, someone, or both. But you don't strike me as the type to run or hide from anything or anyone. So why are you here?'

'I am running . . . and hiding . . . from the person I'll need to be and what I'll have to do to survive when the moment comes.'

She doesn't speak as she takes in my response.

'*Beyond Good and Evil,*' I say, and gesture to the book on her shelf. 'That's another one on your shelf that I've read.'

'I wouldn't have guessed that,' she says, surprised. 'Did *the policeman . . .*'

'No,' I say, and fight back a smile. 'Not his sort of thing.'

She stares at me, and I can sense she's revising what she thought was my character and fighting the urge to ask more follow-up questions.

'So, what do you have for me?' she asks, changing the topic.

I place *Brave New World* and *Dispatches* in the tote bag and hand her *The Drop* and the non-fiction new release.

'The latest Bosch, fabulous. But I'm still waiting for *Fifty Shades of Grey.*'

I laugh. 'That's not happening.'

'We'll see.'

'It's not.'

'Let's go finish the scones,' she says, and turns back to the kitchen.

'That's not happening either. I love them, but I've had enough.'

'That's okay. I'll give the rest to Mr Ealy.'

'He wouldn't touch them, never mind eat them, if he knew I'd been anywhere near them.'

She laughs and nods.

'He scrubs Sandy—'

'Maggie,' she interrupts.

'You say Maggie, I say Sandy . . . but she doesn't listen to either.'

She laughs again. Sandy, Maggie, or whatever Mr Ealy calls her, is the cat we all share. Well, I don't know how much we *share* her. She graces the cottages on the street with her presence whenever she feels and leaves whenever she feels.

'He scrubs Sandy – or Maggie – clean whenever he knows or fears she's just come from mine.'

'I know,' she says, and laughs. 'He's set in his ways.'

'That's a euphemism for racist.'

'Absolutely.'

We both laugh.

I walk back to my cottage, switch the security system's mode to 'home', and head to the parcel and packets of Haribo on the sofa. I focus on the parcel and ponder how my life will change once I open it. Is it necessary? This isn't the life I'd have chosen growing up, but then all I wanted was calm. All I want is calm. This place is by far the calmest of the locations I've lived in this past decade . . . and honestly, my near three years here have been my calmest ever. But this isn't home and can never be home.

I walk to the bookshelf and place *Dispatches* inside it, but stop before putting *Brave New World* next to it. I walk back to the chair to pick up the parcel and place it on the shelf instead. I sit on the couch and open a packet of Haribo . . . let's see how I feel after *Brave New World*.

DAY 11

'It's terrible idea'

I spring up from a nightmare and take a moment to calm myself. Like the last two early mornings, I'm sweating, and the sheets are soaked, so I carefully step out of the bed and head into the shower.

The nightmares aren't new, and it's always a variant of the same deadly night in London about a decade ago. But my subconscious isn't punishing me for what I did that night, as savage as it was, but what I failed and continue failing to do . . . finish the job. For months after the deadly night, the nightmares happened almost every time I closed my eyes. But over time, they reduced to about once a month. They are back every night now, and more wicked . . . because of the fucking parcel.

I dress up, change the bedsheets, and take the sweat-soaked ones down to the washing machine. I grab the parcel from the shelf and head to the kitchen to pour myself a glass of water. I open the parcel and pull out a bunch of A4-sized photographs. The photographs are all of Lucas, the coward that betrayed me and set me up to die. Lucas appears in an awful state, but he's alive, in London . . . and my subconscious cannot accept that. I scan the pictures. They are all of Lucas in a car in the same location on different evenings, and sometimes with a young woman who looks miserable.

I pick a new SIM card from the parcel and glance at my watch; it's a few minutes to 4 a.m. Oleg is an early riser, but not 4 a.m. early. I'll give him a couple of hours. I could read *Brave New World* to pass the time, but I've been too distracted by the parcel to get into it. Well . . . this is going to be one long workout.

It's 06:30, and I've completed the workout, cleaned up, and had breakfast. I put the new SIM into a smartphone that I only switch on for this purpose, and call Oleg.

'Hello, my friend,' Oleg answers in his peculiar Russian accent.

'Shalom, Oleg,' I say.

'Shalom,' he responds with glee – he enjoys my attempts to speak Yiddish. 'It's always good to hear your voice. Especially speaking our Yiddish. You know you're welcome to convert anytime. You'll make a wonderful Jew.'

'Thanks, Oleg,' I say, and chuckle. 'But I'm okay.'

'You're okay,' he says, and laughs. 'I miss you, my friend. But I was hoping not to receive this call.'

I understand his sentiment. But this was inevitable. 'I've looked through the photographs,' I say.

'Good job the investigator did, no?'

'Yes.'

'Very good investigator. Used to be military police. He's a customer too . . . buys all the latest spy gadgets only Oleg can provide. Expensive gadgets too. He invests in his work; you know what I mean?'

I don't respond. I know Oleg's trying to filibuster with small talk.

'Okay then, my friend,' he says. 'You want the rest of the information?'

'Yes, Oleg. I do.'

'Are you sure you want to do this?'

'Yes, I'm sure.'

'Are you sure you *need* to do this?'

'Oleg,' I say, exasperated. But I take a moment to calm down. 'I—'

'You don't *need* to do this, my friend,' he interrupts. 'You see Lucas in those pictures? He'll be dead very soon. The investigator says the police provide Lucas, err . . . *lak-eds-cal* protection. And this is because your mutual friend Chief Superintendent Moore is losing interest in him . . . and therefore in you. Give it some more time and Moore will ditch him and forget about you. Lucas will not survive one day without that protection. And you can come back home and not worry about looking over your shoulder every second.'

As always, Oleg has a point. But I'm done waiting. I want my life back now. I want my peace of mind now. I need to kill Lucas now.

'What's the rest of the information?' I ask.

Oleg laughs. 'I thought I was going to convince you,' he says. 'I practised that little speech several times.'

I chuckle. 'It was good.'

'But still, you don't listen, eh? Being a man of principle is good, my friend. I admire it. But it's no good when you're dead.'

'I understand, Oleg. But I'm doing this. With your help, so there's very little chance of me dying.'

He laughs. 'You're looking at the pictures?' he asks.

'Yes.'

'Lucas has met that prostitute at the same location every Thursday night that the investigator has watched him for the past month. Lucas has no protection while he's there, and the street is always quiet. Perfect location. But the investigator says Lucas can change this at any point because this is the only routine he has . . . he lives a paranoid life.'

'I'll be in London on Thursday.'

'That's in . . .'

'I know.'

'You don't want to come a day before to prepare?'

I should. But there's a good deed to be done . . . and it just might be my last. 'I have something to handle here first,' I say.

'Hmm . . . did this trouble find you, or you found it?'

'Doesn't matter. I'll call you in a couple days to finalise plans.'

'I hope you do not.'

'Then I'll be dead.'

'Looking forward to your call, my friend.'

We laugh.

'I need your help with a couple of things before then.'

'Of course, tell Oleg what you need.'

'Can you arrange for me to see Rebecca on the day?'

'I can do that.'

'Thanks. And I need Topper's phone number.'

Oleg doesn't respond.

'I know you think it's a bad idea,' I say.

'It's terrible idea. I don't trust Topper . . . Tyrone . . . whatever that man calls himself nowadays.'

'Neither do I. But he's a businessman, and I'll make him a good deal.'

'I could find another buyer for you.'

'No, Oleg. You've never sullied your hands with this, and you won't start because of me. I'll be careful.'

'Okay. But what is *sullied*?'

We laugh again. 'Stained . . . dirtied,' I say.

'Ah. I understand.'

'Speak soon.'

'Take care, my friend.'

DAY 12, 05:00

'Close your eyes and count to ten'

It's 5 a.m., and a large bakery van parks by the delivery entrance of a trendy supermarket in Shoreditch. The driver picks out the supermarket's order and leaves the cargo doors open as he enters the store.

Two young men approach the van, and one remains outside as a lookout as the other hops into the cargo area. The young man heads straight to a concealed compartment and pulls a large duffel bag.

'Fucking heavy, blad,' the young man whispers as he drags the bag, but there is no response. He steps out of the van and struggles to pull out the bag. 'Fucking help me . . .'

A bullet pierces the young man's head, and he collapses.

Across the street, a strapping man sits in the driver's seat of a car, clutching a handgun as he watches the van. The man can only see the front of the van from his position, and he's anxious because his associates are taking much longer than usual to pick up the package. He spots what looks like fire on the other side of the van and hurries out of his car. He approaches the van and spots the duffel bag burning on the pavement. But before he can react, three men in tactical gear and full face masks step out from behind the van and aim their suppressed assault rifles at him. The strapping man assumes the gunmen are police and raises his hands, but he's horrified when he sees the dead bodies of his associates and considers running.

'Don't move,' the lead gunmen says with a voice modifier, and approaches.

'This is a death wish,' the strapping man says. 'You don't know whose cocaine that is.'

'Jamal's, isn't it? And you are Abey.'

This further horrifies Abey.

'We're not going to hurt you, Abey.'

'What?' Abey objects. 'Why? Jamal would think I'm in this with you, and he'll kill me and my whole family. I can't—'

'Shut up. I have a message for Jamal, and I need you to be out of here before the police arrive to give it to him.'

'Okay, still, shoot me or something. Please!'

The gunman offers Abey a small envelope, but Abey hesitates. The delivery driver steps out of the supermarket and sees the gunmen and dead bodies.

'I'm not involved, I swear,' the driver pleads. 'I'm just—'

The lead gunman shoots the driver in the head and turns back to Abey, and Abey takes the envelope.

'Close your eyes and count to ten,' the lead gunman orders.

Abey closes his eyes and counts. He peeks at six, and the gunmen are nowhere in sight, so he runs back towards his car.

Alan is asleep in his bed when his burner phone on the bed-side table rings. He wakes up and answers the phone without checking the caller ID.

'What?' he says.

'Hackney's package got jacked. And he thinks it's us,' Steven says.

'Why?'

'It happened at the pick-up spot, and a couple of his boys were killed.'

Alan gathers his thoughts. 'And the delivery driver?' he asks.

'I don't know. I'm just getting the news from Hackney, and he's going mental, so I can't ask him questions. He's calling me back right now too.'

'Give him this number. And find out about the delivery driver.'

Alan ends the call and paces as he considers the news. His burner rings, and he answers.

'This is a bitch move, Alan! Why—' Jamal screams.

'Never mention my name on the phone,' Alan scolds.

'Two of my guys are dead, fam! Why?'

'We have nothing to do with that.'

'Maybe you don't. But your brother does. And I get it, he's showing me who's boss. But why kill two of my boys? And burn the fucking package?'

'Burn the package?'

'Yes. Fucking bullshit, fam! I need that shit.'

'I'll sort it.'

Alan receives another call on his burner. It's Steven, which is worrying because Steven must know he's on the phone with Jamal.

'When are you going to sort it, fam! I need the package today! It's fucking with my—'

'I'll sort it,' Alan says, and switches the call to Steven. 'What happened?'

'Just got off back-to-back calls with Kilburn and Wembley. Same thing has just happened to them.'

'Product got burnt?'

'Yes. And Streatham is calling me right now.'

'Fuck! It's everyone, isn't it?'

'I guess. Want me to call the others?'

'No,' Alan says, and checks the time. It's just gone 05:30, so all deliveries should already be completed. 'Stop any delivery in transit. And send Kilburn my number.'

He ends the call and calls Franka on his iPhone.

'I need you here now,' he says.

'Okay,' she responds, and ends the call.

His burner rings, and he answers.

'What the fuck's happening?' Tyrone asks.

'I don't know, but we're handling it,' Alan says.

'What ya mean? I need product.'

'I know. We're professionals. We've prepared for events like this. I'll personally call you in a couple hours to make delivery arrangements.'

'Good.'

★

Ten minutes later, Alan sits in the passenger seat of his car, still parked in his building's garage. As he waited for Franka, he tried to contact the owner of an abattoir in Kent, but the owner isn't answering. Franka approaches with haste and places her helmet in the boot before she slides into the driver's seat.

'The abattoir in Kent,' Alan says. 'We need to get there fast.'

Franka nods.

The car drives along the narrow road that leads to the secluded abattoir. The journey has taken just under an hour, and Alan still hasn't been able to reach the owner.

'Fucking wake up,' Alan says as his call goes to voicemail again.

'Fire,' Franka says, and parks on the side of the road.

Alan's eyes dart ahead, and he sees smoke billowing from the back of the abattoir.

'Fuck!' he yells.

'We should walk.'

He nods, and they step out of the car. They approach the abattoir, and Franka notices that the lock to the gate is destroyed, and the front door of the building is ajar.

'Go back to the car. Come back in five minutes,' she says, and hands him the car keys.

'No.'

'Okay, behind me, stay close.'

They slip through the front door and there are no lights on in the abattoir, but Franka smoothly heads to the back door, having been inside twice before. They step through the back door, which is off its hinges, to see the burning remains of a vast amount of pure cocaine.

'They're gone,' Franka says.

'I know! Fucking two hundred kilogrammes gone!'

'I mean whoever did this. They are not here.'

Alan's iPhone rings, and it's the abattoir owner.

'I've been fucking calling you,' Alan answers.

'Yes, sorry,' the owner responds. It's obvious he's just waking up. 'Is everything okay?'

Alan struggles to contain his anger. 'I pay you for twenty-four-hour security, don't I?'

'Yes. Yes. My nephew and two others should be there.'

Alan mutes the call. 'Anyone else here?' he asks Franka.

'Dead,' Franka says, and gestures to three bodies behind the fire.

'Shit,' Alan says, and unmutes the call.

'Are you there? Are they not there?' the owner asks. 'I'm very sorry about this. I'll call my nephew now.'

'It's okay.'

'No. No. I'm grateful for everything you've done for me, and I know how precious the *cargo* is . . . and don't worry, I didn't tell my nephew. I didn't tell anyone.'

'It's okay. Really. You need to get here fast. There's a lot to do. I won't be here when you arrive, but I'll send some people to help. They'll have everything you'll need, including money.'

'What's happened?'

'You'll see,' Alan says, and ends the call.

'I don't have time to babysit'

Alan and Franka are on their way back to London, and Alan struggles to remain calm because it's clear that someone with inside information is decimating the distribution network that he's worked so hard to build. Even worse, he can't get through to Louise, his connect at Customs who ensures the shipments breeze through all the checks, and he's expecting the largest ever shipment in four days.

He calls Louise one more time, and again the number is out of reach. He calls Steven.

'Yes, boss?'

'I need you to call the Port of London and ask for Louise Fletcher,' Alan says.

'Sure, boss. And if they ask who I am?'

'They will, so come up with something sensible before you

call. If you reach her, or her secretary, tell her that her cousin, Richard, has been trying to reach her. She'll understand.'

'Okay. Everyone has been trying to reach—'

'Make the call. We'll talk about that afterwards.'

Alan ends the call and anxiously waits for Steven to call back. A couple of minutes later, he does.

'You reach her?' Alan answers.

'No. The person I spoke to said she doesn't work there anymore.'

Alan expected that. Yet he's staggered. 'Since when?'

'I didn't ask, boss.'

'Okay,' Alan says with as much confidence as he can muster. 'About everyone trying to reach me?'

'Yes, boss. They want to talk to you.'

'Including Kilburn?'

'No. Not him.'

'Didn't you tell them what I said?'

'Yes. But they still want to speak to you.'

'Fuck that!' Alan snaps. 'I don't have time to babysit. Let them know I'm out trying to fix this, and I'll call them back when I have an update. Including Kilburn.'

Alan ends the call and curses under his breath; he's one step away from pulling his hair out. Franka has never seen him like this, but she doesn't react. She focuses on the road and gives him time and space to decompress.

'We're going to pay Louise a visit,' Alan says.

Louise drinks tea as she watches daytime TV in the living room of her semi-detached home. She thought she'd be bored out of her mind with her husband at work and kids in school, but she's quickly grown to enjoy her time alone. She feared a knock on the door the first few days she was home alone, but it's not happened, so things must be moving along as planned. No rush, though.

There's a knock on her back window, and she shudders. She rushes to her front window to scan the cars on the street, and she's reassured. She steps into the kitchen and locks eyes with Alan standing by a window in her back garden. Panic over-whelms her, and she attempts to retreat, but Franka places a hand on her shoulder from behind, and she freezes.

'Open the door, Louise,' Alan says.

Louise forces a smile and opens the door. 'Hello, Alan,' she says, her voice trembling. She turns to Franka for the first time, and Franka's cold stare further horrifies her.

'Don't worry about her,' Alan says. 'She won't hurt you.'

Louise nods, but she doesn't believe a word of it.

'What's happening, Louise?' Alan asks.

'I got a job offer. And it was too good to turn down.'

'Ah, congratulations. When were you going to tell me?'

'Soon. Just wanted to dot all the i's and cross all the t's.'

'Oh, so you haven't accepted it?'

'Well, yes. No. Yes.'

'Which is it, Louise?'

'Accepted. Just not started yet, you know.'

Alan nods. 'And your phone?'

'Yeah, you know, I had to leave my work—'

'Louise, I have your work and personal number. Both dis-connected.'

'Oh yeah, I wanted to treat myself to a new phone, so I got a new contract. I was going to call you with the new number.'

Alan smiles. 'You're good, Louise. I suppose that's why we've worked so well these past years.'

'Okay. Do you want to come into the living room? Have a seat?'

'We're good here.'

'Okay.'

'And the two men in the car parked across the street will spot us in the living room.'

She attempts to speak but becomes dizzy, and Franka holds her up.

'Are you okay?' Alan asks.

Louise gathers herself and nods.

'I'd get you a glass of water, but I don't want to touch anything. In case I have to kill you and your family.'

'I . . . I . . . why?'

'Come on, Louise. Today's not the day for this dance. Just tell me the truth, and we'll leave. You have my word.'

'They knew everything I've done for you. In detail. They just asked that I take this new job, change my numbers, and not reach out to you until they told me to.'

'After everything I've done for you? You should be in prison right now. Not even approaching halfway through the fourteen years you'd have gotten.'

'I know. I'm beyond grateful. But they weren't talking police or prison. They were talking about destroying my family.'

'Who's *they*?'

'I've not met anyone else but the two outside and the two that replace them at night.'

'Not police, then?'

'No. Certainly not.'

Alan nods at Franka, and she leaves through the back door.

'What's happening?' Louise asks.

'Don't worry, I'll be out of your hair soon.'

'What if they send others?'

'Others? What do you think she's going to do?'

'I . . . I . . . I don't know. But they know where I live. Where my kids go to school.'

'So do I. And yet . . . You'll be fine, Louise.'

Louise nods.

'When did they approach you?'

'Last week.'

'What day last week?'

'Tuesday.'

'Thank you. And what's the new job?'

Louise hesitates.

'I just want to know,' Alan says.

'Head of logistics at LHQ Freight Services.'

'Congratulations. Serious bump in salary, I hope? Can't let all your years in public service go to waste.'

She nods.

'Although, I guess it probably won't happen now.'

She shrugs.

Alan's phone rings, and he answers.

'Sorted,' Franka says, and ends the call.

'But you never know,' Alan says to Louise. 'Good luck with it, though.'

Alan leaves through the back door and makes his way to his car, parked a couple of streets away. He steps into the car and Franka hands him two burner phones.

'I checked,' she says. 'No texts or outgoing calls. Only received calls from withheld numbers.'

'Fuck. Fuck. Fuck,' Alan mutters. 'Okay. We need to go to the café.'

'Built off my blood and my name'

Alan sits alone in the corner of a rustic Italian café in King's Cross, doing his best to appear calm as he drinks his second cup of coffee. He's been in the café for over an hour and has no idea how much longer he'll have to wait, but it's providing him the quiet time he needs to consider his predicament. He's sure it's the Lenkovs destroying the network as part of their scorched-earth strategy to avenge Valentin, just like they did after Viktor's death. But although the list of suspects is small, he can't work out who their inside person is.

Alan keeps information on a need-to-know basis, especially about the abattoir. Only he, Franka, and Michael knew about that. Michael is getting chattier nowadays, especially with his wife, Meiling. But Michael and Meiling would be the last people to work with the Lenkovs, because they believe the

Lenkovs are responsible for Meiling's assault outside the banquet hall in Camden three years ago.

Alan constructs a Venn diagram in his mind. The first circle is large and contains people that will happily work with the Lenkovs to destroy the network. Surrounding that circle are relatively minute ones with people that know the pick-up locations of every member of the collective, the existence of a reserve and its location, and the identity of the Customs connect. The circles do not overlap, and it dawns on him that he's working with incomplete information. He doesn't even know what he doesn't know. Moreover, it could be multiple inside persons . . .

The back door of the café opens, and a young man beckons Alan.

Alan steps into the back room, and the young man hands him a satellite phone.

'Ciao, Alan,' an elderly man in his mid-eighties warmly greets with a thick Italian accent.

'Ciao, Enzo,' Alan responds.

'Sofia will translate,' Enzo says, and continues in Italian.

'What is so urgent?' Sofia, Enzo's granddaughter, translates, and she's distinctly cold.

'About the shipment.'

'There's nothing wrong with the shipment. Everything is smooth on our end.'

'Can it be delayed? Just a few days.'

Enzo laughs, then speaks rapidly in Italian.

'It's on a ship. We can't turn around a ship,' Sofia translates, and then speaks for herself. 'We've been doing this like clockwork for years now, Alan. You must know it's on its way to you.'

'Yeah. Sorry. Just . . .'

'What is wrong, Alan? We are partners; you should let us know.'

'The ground is moving a little bit on this end, that's all.'

'A little bit?'

'Yes.'

'Anything we should be worried about?'

'No.'

'Okay.'

Enzo speaks.

'Whatever is happening on your end, Alan, your shipment is safe,' Sofia translates. 'No one messes with the 'Ndrangheta. No one. Plus, and I say this only because I'm fond of you – only Sofia and I know the ship number and cargo number. When it arrives at your end, we will tell you, and then only you, Sofia, and I will know. Your shipment will remain safe if you leave it alone and tell no one till your ground stops moving.'

'Thank you.'

'Should we expect any delays with payment?' Sofia asks.

'No.'

'Okay. We will proceed with the next shipment as planned.' Sofia ends the call.

Alan walks out of the café and considers the call as he walks to his car. It didn't go as well as he'd hoped. The 'Ndrangheta – the Calabrian mafia – are responsible for secure transport of the product from Colombia to most of Western Europe. Alan's intention was to delay his shipments until he rebuilt the network because, with no incomings, he will burn through their cash rebuilding the network and battling the Lenkovs. The organisation is legitimately asset rich – Alan puts a lot of effort into that. But he can't convert the assets to cash in time without attracting unwanted attention that will jeopardise all those assets. He will have to work fast, because he cannot miss a payment to the 'Ndrangheta. As Enzo said, no one messes with them.

Alan gets into the car, and Franka waits for instruction as he ponders his next move. It's risky, but he has to reach out to his Colombian suppliers to pause the supply chain from the source. He can't miss a payment to the Colombians, either; no one needs to be reminded of that.

Alan must reach out right away, before the business day closes, so he immediately makes a call on his personal number.

'Hello. Juan Ramos speaking,' a middle-aged man answers.

'Hello. It's Alan Pierce. I'd like a meeting at your office.'

A few beats of silence.

'Be here at 6:15 p.m.,' Juan says, and ends the call.

Alan walks into the reception of an elite law firm in the City, and Juan Ramos's personal assistant is waiting for him. She leads him through the reception without checking in and up to Juan's lavish office on the twenty-seventh floor.

'Afternoon, Alan,' Juan says, and stands. He gestures to a phone on the desk. 'I'll go grab the docs, be back in five minutes.'

Juan leaves the room.

'What's this about?' a middle-aged man with a distinct Latin accent asks over the speakerphone.

Alan approaches the desk. 'I have a situation that needs handling,' he says with confidence. 'So, I'd like to delay the next shipment.'

'No problem. I understand.'

The response surprises Alan. 'Thank you.'

'It's okay. We will find another London distributor till your situation is handled.'

The words hit like a haymaker to Alan's gut, and he is speechless.

'You must understand our position as well,' the voice continues. 'We are suppliers; we feed demand. Your situation has no effect on demand in London. In fact, every day we turn down offers from London because of our agreement with you. We have a supply network that works seamlessly. No drag. No delay. We produce and supply non-stop. We do not store. Someone else will handle your part of our network till you are ready. And I know that if this *situation* was on our end, you would find another supplier. If only for the short-term. Any other decision would be foolish. Because business is business.'

'It's okay,' Alan says. 'We continue as agreed.'

'No delay?'

'No.'

'Good.'

The call ends.

★

Franka parks the Jaguar in the garage of Alan's building and looks to him for instruction, but he is deep in thought.

'Tomorrow,' Franka says.

'Yes. Tomorrow,' Alan says. 'Going to be a busy day.'

She nods and steps out of the car, but he remains inside as he gathers his thoughts before calling Tyrone. He must keep the conversation calm, take ownership of the issue, and convey confidence that he'll sort everything soon. He steps out of the car and just before he calls Tyrone, he gets a blank text from Forest Gate on his personal phone. He ignores it; he doesn't have time for Hardeep right now. He calls Kilburn on his burner phone and heads to the artisanal shop next door.

'Aright?' Tyrone answers. 'Been expecting your call.'

'I know. Things aren't progressing as quickly as planned.'

'What that mean? No delivery today?'

'No delivery. But I give you my word, I'll make it up to you.'

'When? Your word means nothing on the street when my clientele goes to other ends for product.'

'I understand. Give me a week.'

'A week?'

'Yes. But I expect to deliver before then. We have the best product there is. The clientele in every borough knows this. They will be back.'

'Right. But I can't have my boys out there with nothing to sell . . . holding their dicks and that.'

Alan steps into the shop and walks to the bakery section. 'You don't keep any product in reserve for situations like this?'

Tyrone laughs. 'I guess we're not *professional*.'

The comment stings, but Alan doesn't react. He knew he'd have to bite his tongue, and that's why he's out in public in his neighbourhood, because that'll force him to remain calm. He bags a loaf of sourdough rye bread and walks to the fridge.

'Just talk to your brother already,' Tyrone says. 'Tell him we get it. We know who's boss. That you know who's boss. So, he can end this shit.'

The comment baffles Alan, but he recalls Jamal saying something similar in the morning, which he attributed to the heat of the moment.

He picks up a pack of jamón ibérico and considers the thought process as he walks to the checkout. Michael is infamously volatile, but Alan can't fathom why anyone would believe Michael destroyed his own network. 'He has nothing to do with this,' he says.

Tyrone laughs. 'Sure, aright,' he sneers.

Alan greets the cashier with a smile and pays. 'We'll call you with an update,' he says, and ends the call.

Alan seethes as he walks to his building, but the doors open as he approaches, which somewhat cheers him. He steps in and spots Dave, Michael's nephew from Michael's father's side, relaxing on a couch. Not good, Alan thinks. Michael is here. Alan acknowledges the men sitting behind the reception desk and walks to Dave. He approaches and notices Dave is smartly dressed and with clean dress shoes, which is highly unusual for him. But then he remembers today is Sarah's – Dave's mother and Michael's older sister – lavish sixtieth birthday party.

'Dave,' Alan says.

Dave stands. He's an imposing figure with a steely demeanour that was intensified by a recent two-year stint in prison. 'Michael's outside,' he says.

Dave makes a point of bumping Alan's shoulder as he walks past, and as he expected, Alan doesn't react. He scoffs and leads Alan to Michael's Range Rover, parked in a secluded spot a short distance away.

Dave gestures for Alan to get in the passenger seat, and Alan does. Michael is in the driver's seat and alone in the car. He's also smartly dressed.

'Thanks, Dave,' Michael says, and Dave nods.

Dave remains outside the car by the passenger door, trapping Alan in the passenger seat.

'What the fuck am I hearing, Alan? And, more importantly, why didn't I hear it from you straight away?' Michael asks. 'I had to leave Sarah's party to come find you.'

'Someone's taken down our distribution network?'

'*Someone?*' Michael barks. 'Who? And how the fuck did they take down *my* network? You talked a good game about contingency plans and all that fancy shit. What about that?'

Alan considers what question to answer first. 'They knew about everything. Including the contingency . . .'

'They? Who's they? You don't fucking know, do you?'

Alan will not give Michael another opportunity to go after

the Lenkovs. Michael's first impulsive attempt is what's led to the current predicament. The Lenkovs require finesse. Something Michael has no time or fondness for. 'Not a hundred per cent sure,' Alan says. 'And I don't want to give you any names until I'm sure.'

'I don't give a fuck about a hundred per cent. I'm Michael fucking Downing. No one would've tried this shit—'

'You chose to pursue politics.'

'*You chose to pursue politics,*' Michael mimics. 'Because I thought you were capable.'

Alan takes a moment to calm himself. 'I'm dealing with it.'

'How?'

'I'm dealing with it, Michael.'

Michael sniggers. 'You're getting confused, little brother. This shit is all mine. Built off my blood and my name. Your fuck-ups, like this colossal horseshit, affect my reputation. So, I want to know how you are dealing with it. And if I don't like it, I'll put Dave in charge. He's fucking keen to get off the bench that you put him on.'

'I spoke to the Italians and moved forward the next shipment. It'll arrive in three days. I will've rebuilt the network by then.'

'Right. I don't need you to fucking rush and build another shit network. I give you a week to set it up. I'll take care of the shipment when it arrives.'

Alan wants to object, but he bites his tongue. He'll deal with it when the time comes. As Enzo said, only he will know the cargo number on this end, and he won't tell anyone till he's ready. He considers telling Michael someone or several people are giving away inside information. But that will lead to countless deaths as Michael ravages through his organisation, searching for the person(s) responsible. And Michael would enjoy every second of his bloodthirsty inquisition.

'Okay,' Alan says. 'I'll let you know once it arrives.'

'Good. You're getting this second chance only because of Mum. Anyone else would be dead. Get the fuck out.'

Alan reaches for the door.

'Why the fuck aren't you at the party?'

'Sarah won't want me there.'

'*Sarah won't want me there,*' Michael mimics. 'Stop acting like a fucking bitch. It's not like you've made any effort since Marbella. Buy her a fucking gift. Nothing less than twenty grand. Also, your ex is there having a—'

'Hannah?'

'You have another ex-wife?'

'What is she doing there?' Alan asks, furious.

Michael shakes his head, disappointed Hannah's whims still trigger Alan. 'I don't know what she's doing there. I don't care. And I'm going to say this just one more time because I know what you're thinking, and I need you focused . . . whatever was happening when you divorced, it wasn't me. Okay? I've never had anything to do with Hannah, and I never will. But then, it's not my business who she's fucking, and it's not yours either anymore.'

'What do you mean by that?' Alan demands.

'Fucking hell, Alan! You're showing more life about this than the fucking network. Get the fuck out of the car now before I break your fucking head.'

Alan pops the door handle, and Dave steps to one side so he can get out the car.

'And,' Michael adds, 'don't you ever forget that this shit is all mine!'

Dave smirks at Alan before he hops into the car, and Alan watches them depart. If Alan didn't know better, he'd believe Tyrone is correct, and Michael set all this in motion to reassert his authority. He pulls out his phone and calls Hannah, but she doesn't answer. What the fuck is she doing, he ponders. But he'll deal with that later, because right now he needs to focus.

DAY 12

I'm sitting by the window in a café on the edge of the town centre. For all appearances, I'm drinking herbal tea and reading *Brave New World*. But I'm watching the grocery shop and waiting for Tattoos to clock off for the night. Lanky left about thirty minutes ago, and after that, the sign on the door was switched to closed. That was just after 6 p.m., which I thought was a tad early, especially because the café will be open till 9 p.m. But then that shop doesn't cater to the regular grocery shopper anymore, and they're probably out of product for the day.

A few minutes later, the lights in the shop switch off, and Tattoos steps out. I shut my book, leave the server a tip, and hurry to the electric bicycle I rented earlier. I thought I'd blend in more with the bicycle, especially in the helmet, as opposed to following Tattoos in my Land Rover. The tattooed young man closes the shutters as I climb onto the bicycle. But he doesn't head to a car like I expected. He walks away from the town centre. He must live close. I take off the helmet, step off the bicycle, and follow on foot a few steps behind until he enters a run-down three-storey townhouse, split into studios and flats.

I watch lights switch on on the first floor, and I spot him walking through the room. That's his home. I scan the building and the neighbouring buildings, and there are no cameras in sight. Okay, then.

I walk back to the town centre, return the bicycle, and head to the cottage.

DAY 13, 05:00

'Lovely to see you again'

I wake up about an hour before I usually do, but no nightmares this time. My thoughts are calm, and they've been calm since I spoke to Oleg. But I'm also excited because I've got work tonight, and I didn't realise how much I missed that. There will be danger, there always is, although more now because I'm bound to be rusty, but I spent the entire night planning for today and my more precarious day in London. I'm ready. I better be.

I work out, clean up, enjoy breakfast, and finish reading *Brave New World*. Mrs Lewis was right; I loved it. I glance at my watch, and it's just past noon. I should probably head off, but not before I pay Mrs Lewis a visit. I pick up the basket with the speciality home-made strawberry jam I bought yesterday and walk over to her cottage.

I walk past her kitchen window and glance inside. She's

not in there, and it's pristine. I knock on the front door and hear footsteps inside, walking softly away from the door before approaching even more softly. I instinctively take a step away from the door. Mrs Lewis opens the door with a smile, and I quickly scan her. She's wearing a coat that's always hung by the door, but underneath the coat, she's dressed as casually elegant as always. The cottage is also warm, and she's wearing house slippers. She wasn't expecting me today. And it doesn't seem like she was expecting anyone else, because I'm sure she's brought a weapon to the door, which is now stashed in her coat pocket.

'Come on in,' she says, with a genuine smile, and steps aside for me to enter. 'Lovely to see you again.'

'Lovely to see you too,' I say.

'Twice in a week as well. But I'm certainly not complaining.'

I chuckle. 'I brought you a gift,' I say, and gesture to the basket.

'Thank you! What is it?' she asks.

'Home-made strawberry jam from a *relatively* local award-winning jam-maker.'

'Uhh,' she says, excited, and leads me to the kitchen.

I drop the basket on her counter, and she picks out a jar to admire it.

'This isn't local at all!'

'I said *relatively*. And nothing is local to us.'

She chuckles and nods.

'Let's try it together.'

'I can't stay long.'

She's struck by the comment and wants to ask why. 'Fear not, I'm not baking scones. Toast would do.'

Before I can speak, she hurries to her bread bin. 'Thanks,' I say.

'No, thank you,' she says, and pulls the bread knife from a knife block set on the counter.

She hesitates before she slices the bread, then carefully takes off the coat, folds it, and places it on the counter beside her. I'd thought her weapon was a knife, but all the knives in the set are accounted for. It's a gun.

She places a plate with two slices of jam-covered toast between us before she sits. She picks a slice, and I pick the other one, and we have a bite simultaneously.

'Scrumptious,' she says, and has another bite.

'It is,' I say. 'And the bread is incredible as well.'

'Of course it is. I baked it.'

'Not surprised,' I say, and make a point to glance at my watch. 'I need to head.'

'Where?' she asks with concern in her voice.

The concern surprises me, and I hesitate, which increases her concern. She keenly stares at me, and I know if I lie, she'd know.

'I have something to take care of.'

She nods but doesn't speak.

'I'll be fine,' I say.

'Do you need *anything*?'

I know exactly what she means. 'I don't.'

She nods. 'Check in when you're back, okay?'

'Might be early in the morning.'
'Just tap your horn when you drive past. I'm a light sleeper.'
I nod and stand.

'Two birds with one stone'

Alan is in the middle of his morning run through his neigh-bourhood. He's powering through, but the run isn't proving to be the sure-fire escape it's been for decades, because he is consumed with thoughts of how to rebuild the distribution network quickly on the one hand, and how to best handle the Lenkovs on the other. But both hands are tied behind his back, because he doesn't know who to trust and doesn't want Michael involved.

He turns onto a quiet street and a punch to the torso blind-sides him. He loses his breath and falls to a knee, and two men drag him into the back of a white van. The van sets off, and Alan struggles to catch his breath and free himself from the tight grasp of the two men beside him.

'Morning, Alan,' someone says.

Alan recognises the voice and looks ahead to see Callum,

sitting comfortably on a bench seat. Alan tries to speak, but he's still out of breath.

'Take your time,' Callum says.

'What's this about, Callum?' Alan asks.

'I'm just trying to protect myself,' Callum says. 'I don't want to be caught in the middle of Michael and Jamal's pissing contest.'

'What?'

'I understand why Michael is doing this. He was built in the wild, where only the strong survive. Hand-to-hand combat and all that old-school bullshit. He's offended by the zoo that you created with this collective ting. Sitting around, discussing collective bargaining, inflation and all that.' He chuckles. 'That's not how this shit is supposed to run. All of us in that room are fighting for the same shit. We should be at each other's necks. At your neck. And Michael recognised that Jamal was one step away from breaking bad and coming for all of us. Including him.'

'Makes sense,' Alan says. 'But Michael has nothing to do with this.'

Callum smiles. 'You can't let the chicken know it's up for slaughter; otherwise, it'll be fucking difficult to catch. And in your case, might even claw your eyes out.'

'You're going to slaughter me, then?'

Callum nods. 'I'll make it easy if you tell me where you store the product and who your supplier is. Otherwise, I'll torture you to get the information and then deliver what's left of you to your brother.'

'Deliver me to him. Why?'

'That's what the card said.'

'What card?'

'I'm disappointed, Alan. You always knew what was going on. We all got cards when our deliveries were jacked. Simply said, "Call if you want your product". I did. The price of my product is you, dead. And if I bring you in alive, I get everyone's product. I don't need those games, so I want to make my own way. Deal with the supplier directly. But I'll play the game if I have to.'

'Either way, I die?'

'Yes.'

Alan nods in acceptance, but his mind races to find a way out. 'What's easy?' he asks.

'A bullet in the head.'

'Fair enough.'

Callum nods. 'So, who's your supplier?'

'What point is a name to you? I'll have to introduce you.'

'Shut up. You're dead in a couple hours, tops. And that'll be the hard way. No introducing. Once your supplier knows you're out of the game, he'll deal with whoever has the money. It's business.'

The van slows to a stop.

'Anyway, we're here. Are you going to tell me now? Or do I need to do some terrible things to you first.'

'Can I see what the bad things are first?'

Callum laughs and gestures for one of the men holding Alan to open the van's back door. The man opens the door, and he, the other man, and Callum are shot in the head in a second.

The men collapse, and Alan spins to see Franka wielding a suppressed semi-automatic rifle.

Alan is relieved, grateful, and even more impressed, and he can't find the words to express the overwhelming emotions. But Franka recognises them and nods at him. She reaches out and guides him out of the van.

'I expected trouble today. So, I watched you run,' she says. 'You should stop running. For now.'

Alan nods. He's still agitated by his near-death experience, so he doesn't speak in case his voice trembles. Franka enters the van to get Callum's burner phone, and Alan scans the rundown garage he was to die in.

Franka looks through the phone, and the last text is a time and address sent from an unknown number. She hands Alan the phone to read the text, and he cross-checks the number with the contacts on his burner – it's Tyrone. Alan checks the call list, and there are a lot of back-and-forth calls from yesterday. He cross-checks the numbers, and the burner phones of all the collective members are there, apart from Priyanka and Pete. There must be a meeting today at the time and address Tyrone sent. Alan smiles.

Jamal, Tyrone, and the two other collective members besides Priyanka, Pete, and Callum – Turhan, aka Streatham, and Hunter, aka Tottenham – sit around a large table in the middle of a pub in Hackney. The pub is not open for business, but it's filled with associates of the collective members, who are all armed to the teeth.

Tyrone calls Callum one more time, and there is no answer.

'I think we start. Don't think Callum is showing up,' he says, and the others nod. 'As you'll appreciate, we didn't invite Pete cos he'll just run off to Michael.'

'And Priyanka?' Turhan asks.

'I don't want that bitch here,' Jamal responds.

'And you didn't ask the rest of us if we wanted her here?'

'Fuck are you—?'

'I didn't want this meeting to turn into a bloodbath,' Tyrone intercedes. 'So, I had to choose one of them. And I thought it best to choose the one with the most manpower of all of us. Considering what we here to chat about.'

Turhan nods.

'We need to take charge of this shit,' Jamal says. 'Enough with this middleman ting. We're the ones out there taking risks with feds and next man looking to take what's ours. We can't be getting fucked about by some ex-fed and some old-school gangster out there trying to be prime minister. These niggas are some latte- and red-wine-drinking motherfuckers. They don't know what it takes to be out here on road. That's the only reason my man will pull some shit like this. Putting all our boys out there is danger. Nah!' He takes a swig of his beer. 'No doubt, I want Michael dead for the sucker punch and killing two of my boys. But this is business. Yeah?'

The others nod.

'So, what's your plan?' Hunter asks.

'Rampage,' Jamal says. 'I'm happy to handle it. But we all need to agree that Michael and Alan need to die. I don't want second thoughts when things get mad.'

'You said this is business, no? So how are you going to get the supplier?' Turhan asks.

'I'll ask before I kill them. Alan is not *hard*. He'll talk.'

'And you'll share this with us, yes?' Turhan asks.

'Sure he will,' Tyrone says. 'If you agree right now. This is a one-chance thing.'

'And if I don't agree?' Hunter asks.

Jamal chuckles. 'If you're not with us . . . you know the rest, fam,' he says.

Turhan and Hunter take a moment to consider.

'You are saying you will do this if we agree with you or not?' Turhan asks.

'Yeah,' Jamal responds. 'And if you don't, you might be next. That's how this thing goes, innit?'

Tyrone doesn't like Jamal's response, but he doesn't react.

'Are you threatening me?' Turhan asks.

'Are you not with us?' Jamal retorts.

'We're just putting our cards on the table,' Tyrone says. 'Alan has the best product. When we take him out, we will have the best product.' He gestures at Jamal and himself. 'We don't plan to share. That might make us enemies. You understand.'

Turhan nods.

'I'm in,' Hunter says.

A loud knock on the pub's front door alarms the associates, and they all pull out weapons.

'It's calm,' Jamal says to the room. 'I've got many man on watch.' He addresses one of his associates. 'Check.'

The associate tucks his gun away and opens the door just enough to see who it is.

A courier driver offers the associate a small box. 'For Jamal,' he says.

The associate accepts the box and closes the door. He walks to the table and hands it to Jamal. Everyone watches Jamal examine the box; it's light and doesn't make much of a sound when he shakes it. But then a phone inside the box rings. Jamal opens the box and removes the burner.

'Think that's Callum's, you know,' Hunter says.

'Answer it, yeah?' Turhan says. 'Put on speaker.'

Jamal answers and puts it on speaker.

'Hello, everyone,' Alan says. 'Sorry Callum can't make your meeting, but he tried to kill me this morning, and as you can imagine, he's dead now. I don't want that to happen to anyone else. So, relax and give me the week like I asked; everything will be up and running by then. And I will make it up to you.'

Alan ends the call.

'I'll give Alan a week,' Turhan says.

'Yeah,' Hunter says. 'We can discuss this again then.'

Turhan and Hunter don't trust Jamal or Tyrone, and business has been good for them, so they are happy with the devil they know.

Jamal scowls and opens his mouth to speak.

'Sure,' Tyrone cuts in first. 'We'll give Alan a week. Right, Jamal?'

Jamal nods.

Hunter and Turhan stand and leave with their associates.

'Fucking pussies!' Jamal barks once it's just him and Tyrone.

'It's okay, Jamal. Relax. We're still on track to take over. We wanted to seize this opportunity to speed things up. But Alan is smart, so we have to be smart too.'

'This isn't school, fam. And I'm tired of dealing with that white boy.'

'A lot can happen in the week. Alan knows Michael wants him gone so that'll energise him, you know. But if he takes Michael out, he becomes exposed.

He's smart and all that, but he's still an ex-fed. And for many man on road, once a fed always a fed. And Alan was a good one, still. Put a lot of Michael's enemies in prison. With Michael gone, Alan won't last the day.'

Jamal nods. 'What if Michael stops these games and just kills Alan himself?'

'Good too, brother. Michael's a warrior. He doesn't have the smarts to run the network. The shit will crumble.'

Jamal smirks.

'You still have Meiling's bracelet, right?' Tyrone asks.

'Yeah.'

'Good! Pretty Boy's coming back.'

Jamal rolls his eyes. 'The legend, yeah?'

'It's true, brother. Man is a legend on road. The Wapping Massacre is all him.'

'*Was* a legend on road. That ting was like ten years ago, innit?'

Tyrone nods. 'Still. I'll give Pretty Boy the bracelet, and Michael and 'em will go after him. And even if they kill Pretty Boy, he'll take a lot of Michael's men with him.'

'Two birds with one stone and that.'

'Two birds with one stone,' Tyrone repeats, and laughs. 'It's going to be a good week, brother.'

Jamal nods. 'Anyway, what are we going to do about Callum's territory?'

'What do you mean?'

'Who's going to take it?'

'Don't try that, brother. We already agreed. Wembley is mine.'

'Yeah, but things are getting long with Priyanka.'

'It's not my fault you picked her cos you thought she was weak.'

'She weak still.'

'Right. Handle her, then, and leave Wembley to me.'

Tyrone stands and leaves with his associates.

DAY 13, 21:00

'I've got all night'

I crouch by the bed in Tattoo's tiny studio flat. It's pitch-black, as I've closed his thick curtain, but I have a mental picture of the entire room, which was unexpectedly tidy. Although I might get a third-hand high from the overwhelming stench of marijuana if I stay in here any longer without opening the window.

I hear the key slot into the keyhole, and I stand and lean on the wall. Tattoos opens the door, and a portion of the room is lit by the hallway lights. He flicks the switch by the door, but the ceiling light doesn't switch on because I've taken out the bulb. He mutters to himself and shuts the door, and the room returns to darkness. He approaches a lamp on the bedside table, and I jab his neck with an electroshock baton. He loses consciousness on his feet and collapses onto the bed.

I empty a jug of cold water onto his face, and he wakes up,

but before he reacts, I push my captive bolt pistol onto his forehead, and he's scared stiff. I switch on the bedside lamp, and his eyes almost burst out of the sockets when he sees me. He hyperventilates, and it seems like he just might kill himself. He's more of an amateur than I thought.

'Relax,' I say, as reassuring as the moment requires. 'I understand the panic. But there's a fair chance you'll survive tonight, so I suggest you calm down and give yourself the best chance, okay?'

He nods and tries to gather himself, but he can't and glances at me with horror.

'Take your time,' I say. 'I've got all night.'

He takes his time and gathers himself enough.

'I'm sor—'

'Don't speak unless I ask you a question,' I interrupt. 'Okay?'

He nods.

'Where's the shop owner?' I ask.

'What?'

I push the captive bolt pistol harder onto his forehead. 'I'm not here for games, Rob,' I say, and he's shocked that I know his name. 'I'm not a magician, Rob. You have a couple council tax letters on your kitchen counter you should probably take care of soon.'

He nods, as if taking in my advice.

'Can you see what I have on your head?' I ask.

He looks at the captive bolt pistol, and it's not what he expected, so he focuses on it but still doesn't know what it is.

'Do you know who Cormac McCarthy is?' I ask.

He shakes his head.

'I thought as much, but didn't want to presume. But you have quite a DVD collection here, so you might've seen the movie adaption of his novel . . . *No Country for Old Men*?'

He nods.

'Anton Chigurh . . . the villain played by Javier Bardem. Remember him?'

He nods and glances at the captive bolt pistol again. He now has a good idea of what it is.

'Good. This only has one cartridge. So, when I pull the trigger, it won't be to scare or hurt or torture you; it will be to kill you. So, when I ask a question, you answer straight away and truthfully, and I might not pull the trigger. Do you understand?'

He nods.

'Where's the shop owner?'

'She's my ma. She's at home. I wouldn't ever do anything to hurt her.'

I wasn't expecting that.

'I swear, I'm not lying,' he says, and nods towards his jacket. 'Check my phone. There're pictures and all.'

I know he's not lying. 'Why are you selling whatever you're selling out of her shop, then? And, more importantly, why did you hurt your brother?'

'No. No. That wasn't me . . . well, yes, I'm selling gear out of the shop, but I didn't touch my brother. I wouldn't, and I wasn't even there when Brad did . . .'

'Brad?'

'The other guy in the shop.'

Hmm . . . Brad struck me as more of a follower. 'And you just let Brad get away with doing that to your brother? That's your operation, isn't it?'

'No. It's not. Ma's cancer's back, and she's fighting, but she can't really do much else. And my brother's trying, but you know . . . So, I tried to make some extra money to help. Got Brad to introduce me to his older brother because everyone knows he's got the link. But they took over the fucking shop. There's nothing I can do.'

'Do you owe them money?'

'No. Brad takes all the money home when we finish selling the gear every day. His brother keeps saying they'll give me something soon . . . but nothing yet. *They* owe me.'

I take the captive bolt pistol away from his head. 'Where do Brad and his brother live?'

He stares at me, confused.

'Yes, Rob. I was just fine killing you a second ago, but now I'm going to sort your mess.'

He opens his mouth to speak but hesitates. 'Thank—'

'No,' I interrupt. 'I'm not doing this for you. Just tell me the address.'

He does, and it's close.

'Peanut's got a real gun, though,' he says, and gestures at my captive bolt pistol.

'Peanut is Brad's older brother, then?'

He nods.

'Anyone else in the house?'

'The three brothers. Peanut's the oldest, and Brad's the youngest.'

'Have you seen this *real gun*?'

'Yes. It's a Beretta handgun. Peanut's always flashing it about in the house. That's why I don't like going there.'

'You know where he keeps it?'

'Somewhere in his room upstairs.'

'Thanks,' I say. 'Now, sleep.'

I jab his neck with the electroshock baton, and he loses consciousness.

I watch the terraced house from the back of an abandoned car across the street. I've watched for over an hour, and there is activity in the house. But there is also an empty parking space in front of the house, behind Brad's car, which I'm sure belongs to one of the brothers. I'll wait till they are all home.

A few minutes later, a new Range Rover approaches, blaring music at a volume that would've been infuriating to the neighbours during the day. I can't imagine the fury it's triggering at near 1 a.m. A burly man hops out of the car with a large gym bag and slams the door shut before he strides into the terraced home. It must be Peanut. Now, I'll wait till they fall asleep.

It's 03:45 as I approach the terraced house. I repeatedly bang the door like the police would in a pre-dawn raid, and as I expected, there is frantic activity inside. About thirty seconds into the door banging, the middle brother opens the door, and he's furious.

'Fuck you rats want? We've done nothing!' he says, and looks over my shoulder, expecting to see more police officers.

'Don't know about your rodent problem, but I'm here to have a word with Brad and Peanut,' I say. 'But you're welcome to join us as well.'

He glares at me, confused. 'What? Who the fuck are you, lad?'

'Exactly. Brad asked me that last week and I'm here to let him know.'

'Are you . . .'

Brad hurries to the door and anxiously whispers into his brother's ear.

'What you mean, gone?' the middle brother asks him. 'Peanut brought it in . . . I saw it.'

'You're talking about the gear in Peanut's gym bag?' I ask.

'What?' the middle brother barks. 'Where the fuck is it?'

I shrug.

I hear footsteps race down the steps, and Peanut approaches his brothers. 'Money's gone too,' Peanut tries to whisper, but he's too agitated to speak in a hushed tone. He turns to me and forces a grin. 'Come on in, lad.'

I step in, and before my foot hits the ground, Peanut punches me in the jaw. The heavy right hook stuns me and cuts my bottom lip, but I keep my balance, barely.

'Where the fuck is my gear and my money?' Peanut demands.

I'm furious, but I bury it and remain calm. 'You lot only had one free hit,' I say. 'I'll put down the next that tries.'

Peanut pulls out the Beretta and points it at my head. 'What now?' he barks. 'What the fuck are you going to do now, nigger?'

I sigh. 'That is always lurking under the surface in these

interactions. But I prefer that you've brought it to the surface. Now we know you're a fool and a racist.'

'I will fucking shoot you!'

'No, you won't.'

'You think voodoo is going to work here, nigger?'

'That's twice. I really don't want to kill you, Peanut. I'm trying hard not to do that anymore. But if you say it one more time, I will not hesitate.'

'Where's the gear and the money?' Brad asks, almost pleading.

'It's in Peanut's car,' I respond.

'Go get it, Brad,' Peanut says.

'The car's not outside,' I say.

'What do you mean?' Peanut asks.

Brad looks out the window. 'It's not there,' he confirms.

Peanut is overwhelmed with rage. He lowers the gun to my belly and pulls the trigger, but there is no gunfire. This shocks him. He pulls the trigger again, but still no gunfire.

'I told you, you won't shoot me,' I say.

He pulls the trigger again, but no gunfire. And his brothers anxiously watch him.

I pull the Beretta's bullets out of my pocket and toss them to the ground. 'You're a heavy sleeper,' I say. 'All of you are, to be fair. Must run in the family.'

Peanut attempts to swing the gun towards my chin, but I jab his chest with the electroshock baton, and he collapses.

I turn to Brad and the middle brother. 'You want to talk about getting your gear and money, or you want to fight?' I ask. 'At this point, I'm happy with either.'

'Where's the gear?' the middle brother asks, somewhat calm.

'In the car, like I said . . . and I'll tell you where that's parked in a minute. But first, you need to stop selling on my turf.'

'What turf?' he asks.

'Ask Brad. He knows.'

'The shop?' Brad asks.

'That's just a shop . . . but on my turf.'

The middle brother glares at Brad.

'I didn't know anyone was selling around there,' he pleads to his brother and me. 'I asked around . . .'

'You expect me to put my name on the street, so you boys can pay me a visit like I just did you?'

Brad nods. He's embarrassed and worried that his brothers will beat him up when I leave.

'But then, I understand you boys are small-time with big dreams,' I say. 'So growing pains are expected. Next time ask the right people.'

Brad and his brother nod.

'Give me your phone,' I say to Brad.

Brad hesitates, but his brother glares at him, and he pulls out a smartphone and a burner.

'The burner,' I say. 'And call your number, so it's the first one on the log.'

Brad does and hands me the burner.

'I didn't touch your gear. But I took a tax from the money for selling on my turf. And I'm going to take another tax for Peanut being a racist.'

'How much?' the middle brother asks.

'How much do you think is fair?'

'What?'

'How much tax do you think is fair for being a racist? A percentage.'

'I don't know . . . ten?'

I shake my head.

'Fifteen?' he asks.

'No. I took forty per cent for selling on my turf . . . so use that as a gauge.'

The revelation threatens to overwhelm him. 'That's already more than half.'

'I know. Racism is fucked, isn't it?'

He nods. 'Twenty?' he asks.

I take a moment to watch him squirm. 'I'll take another forty.'

'What?!'

'What?' I challenge. 'You don't think being a racist is worth that?'

'I didn't say that. But come on, lad. That's just twenty per cent left.'

'I can take it all. And the gear.'

'No. No. Take your tax,' he says, dispirited.

I nod and turn to Brad. 'Why did you hit the shop owner's son?' I ask.

'I . . . I didn't do it,' Brad lies, and it's not convincing. 'Rob did it!'

'Who's Rob?'

'The other guy. With all the tattoos. He's the lad's brother. He did it. Had nothing to do with our business. I promise.'

'The lad's brother did *that* to him?'

'You just wait to see what we're going to do to him,' the middle brother mutters, and gestures to Brad.

Brad looks so scared that I wouldn't be surprised if he's peed in his pants. I'll leave his brothers to deal with him.

'Where can I find Rob? Right now.'

'I'll text his address to the burner,' Brad says.

I nod. 'I won't call about the car's location till I'm done with Rob, so if you tell him . . .'

'He won't,' the middle brother says.

I nod. 'One last thing,' I say. 'If you boys ever sell on my turf again, I'll kill you all in your sleep.'

I walk out of the house.

I pay Rob another visit to tell him I've sorted his mess and to get his mother's address. But I don't tell him about Peanut's money or what I intend to do with it. I then stop by his mother's home and leave the money with a note on her dressing table before heading back towards the cottage. And yes, I text Brad the location of Peanut's car. I'm a man of my word.

DAY 14, 07:50

'That's the way, my friend'

The lights are on in Mrs Lewis's kitchen as I drive towards my cottage. I'm sure she can hear my Land Rover, but she asked that I check in, so I tap my horn as I drive past. I park and head straight up to bed.

I wake up and glance at my watch; it's 13:57. A good six hours. I should go on more all-night adventures, I guess. I work out, clean up, and enjoy lunch – lentil dal and pittas – before I switch on the smartphone to call Oleg.

'My man,' he answers.

'Hello, Oleg,' I respond.

'You sorted the trouble, yes?'

'Yes.'

'And you're okay for London in two days? Don't want to take some time . . .'

'I'm okay, Oleg. Thanks for asking.'

'You're a problem, you know?' he says, and laughs. 'You leave me here praying that you sort your problem, yes, but that you get some little injury to prevent you from coming to London. Oy vey!'

We laugh. 'I got my lip cut, though.'

'Ah,' he dismisses. 'I should see the other guy, no?'

I laugh.

'Anyway, I've arranged your meeting with Rebecca. She chose to meet in her place, so I guess she misses you too,' he teases.

'Stop it, Oleg!'

He laughs. 'I'll text you her address after this call.'

'Okay, thanks.'

'I have Topper's number too,' he says, and stops.

'Do you want me to beg?'

'That'll be nice,' he says, and chuckles. 'But no. I repeat that it's terrible idea. But you have leverage. From what I gather, there are supply issues across the city. Topper needs what you have. So, negotiate accordingly.'

'Thanks, Oleg. I appreciate the information.'

'No need to thank me, my friend. I'll text you Topper's number. He's expecting your call today.'

'I'll call him right after this.'

'What are your plans for London? I have some other business to handle during the day, but I'll be free in the evening . . . and I'll take you to the Lucas location.'

'That works. I'll get the last train in tomorrow night. Handle business with Topper first thing in the morning, see Rebecca, and then meet you. I'm not travelling with a weapon, so I'll need a handgun with a suppressor.'

'I'll have it.'

'I'm not travelling with this SIM. So, I'll get one in London and call you.'

'We should have a code, so I know it's you.'

'My voice will be the code.'

'No . . . you say "hello, saviour".'

I laugh.

'I'm serious, my friend. They have this technology nowadays that can fake your voice.'

'Why would anyone want to fake my voice?'

'Why are you buying a new SIM in London? Cautious, no? You say the code.'

'Okay, saviour,' I say, and chuckle.

'That's the way, my friend,' he says, and laughs.

'Speak soon.'

'See you soon.'

Oleg ends the call, and a second later, a text arrives with Topper's number and Rebecca's address. I call Topper, and it rings once before it's answered.

'Who this?' Topper asks with a thick Caribbean accent, which is odd because the last time we spoke over a decade ago, he didn't even have a faint one.

'It's me, Topper.'

'You, brother. Man thought you were dead and that. Where you been?'

'I can't talk for long. But we can catch up in person in two days. Right now, we talk business. Okay with you?'

Topper laughs. 'Sure thing, brother. How much you got?'

'Twenty-five kilograms of pure premium grade.'

'If it is what you say it is, and I will test it, half a mil.'

I don't respond. I don't particularly care about the money, but the price was more than double that a decade ago, and it has only increased since then.

'Not happy with that?' he asks.

'You know I know what it's worth. I also know there is a lack of supply in the city. But I'm not looking for full value. So, name a price we're both happy with, or I'll call the next guy.'

'I thought you called me because we're old friends and that,' he says, and laughs. 'It's wild out here, me no lie. It's best to only deal with people you trust. Plus, this is a big money thing. Not many man got the deep pockets like me. But they will say they do for sure. And when it's time to pay up, shit turn to disaster like before. You get me, brother?'

I get him, but he pushed a little too hard, which tells me he really wants this deal. 'Name a price we're both happy with,' I say, calm.

'You're cold, brother,' he says, and forces a chuckle. 'One mil, cash.'

'Okay.'

'Okay?'

'I'm happy with that.'

'Bless. When we meet, then?'

He's eager. 'In a couple days, like I said. The morning, preferably.'

'Nine? Ten?'

'Around then works.'

'Will have to be my place, then. I won't—'

'That's fine with me. I'll call you just before eight a.m. for directions.'

He hesitates. I'm sure he's wary about how quick I decided to meet at his place because he knows what I'm capable of. 'Aright,' he says. 'I'll expect your call.'

'Till then,' I say, and hang up.

Now I've got just over twenty-four hours to finish *Dispatches*. Here's hoping it's fun.

'See you soon'

I approach Mrs Lewis's cottage and spot her in the kitchen, placing a tray of pastries on the dining table, and I smile. I knock on the door, and when she opens it, I'm enveloped by the smell of butter and cinnamon.

'That smells amazing,' I say.

'Cinnamon rolls,' she says, proud. 'Taste amazing too.'

'Oh, I'm sure!'

'I see you suffered a little damage,' she says, and gestures to my burst lip.

'Can't make an omelette without cracking a few eggs, I suppose.'

She chuckles. 'I suppose.'

And that's the last mention of my night away. She gestures for me to lock the door and follow her into the kitchen.

'What would you like to drink? Lemonade or mint tea?

And don't worry, I've reduced the sugar content of the lemonade.'

'Mint tea.'

She shakes her head. 'You're never going to get over that one time I was heavy-handed with the sugar.'

'No . . . it's not that. I just prefer something warm.'

'Liar. Anyway, I'm having lemonade, and I'm adding more sugar to it.'

We laugh, and she adds a heap of sugar to the jug of fresh lemonade. I approach the counter, pick a cup out of the cabinet, and pour myself some fresh mint tea from the pot. She glances at me and smiles because I've never felt comfortable enough to do that before.

We sit at the dinner table, enjoy too many scrumptious cinnamon rolls, and discuss our books. She wasn't surprised by how much I was gripped by *Dispatches* and enjoyed *Brave New World*, but she was surprised by how keen I am to read more sci-fi books, which made her change her mind about the next fiction book she'll give me. She loved *The Drop*, and although she disagreed with a few of the author's points, she enjoyed the non-fiction book I gave her.

We drift to her living room for her to select the next books. This time, she picks a novel without asking me if I've read it, but asks about the non-fiction book.

'Have you read *Travels in the Interior Districts of Africa*?' she asks.

'No.'

She hands me *The Left Hand of Darkness* and *Travels in the*

Interior Districts of Africa. 'I think you'll enjoy both,' she says, and smiles.

I hand her *Bring Up the Bodies* and the second non-fiction new release I got from the bookshop. 'I assume you've read the first one,' I say and gesture at *Bring Up the Bodies.*

She smiles; she has.

'I think you'll enjoy both,' I say, and smile.

We walk to her front door.

'Same time next week?' she says, and unlocks the door.

I hesitate, and she can tell I'm uncertain.

'Something else you need to take care of?' she asks.

'Yes. Leaving tonight.'

'Check in tomorrow morning, then.'

'I won't be back then.'

'Check in when you're back.'

'I'm . . . not sure when that will be.'

I can see the concern in her eyes, but she remains calm. 'Not making an omelette this time, then?' she quips.

'No,' I say, and smile.

'Not hiding from the person you need to be any longer, but running towards it, then?'

I nod. 'For one day. I'll be back.'

'See you soon,' she says, and hugs me for the first time.

'See you soon.'

'We stick to our promises'

Veronika sits at her office desk, studying the financial statements for a company the Lenkov family investment office is looking to purchase. There is a knock on the door, and her assistant steps in and hurries to her.

'There's an Alan Pierce here to see your father,' her assistant whispers.

The news confounds Veronika. 'Does he have an appointment?'

'No. He just walked in.'

'Is my father going to see him?'

'I think so. He's been waiting for about fifteen minutes.'

'He's been here fifteen minutes?'

'That's what I was told.'

Veronika is furious that her father, Marat, hasn't informed her of Alan's presence and doesn't hide it. 'Thank you,' she says. 'Cancel my meetings and hold any calls till I come back.'

Veronika leaves her office and strides to Marat's. She tries to open the door, but it's locked, and she glares at Marat's secretary at a desk opposite the door.

'Is my father in there?' Veronika demands.

Her father's secretary nods. 'He's with Gennady . . . they asked not to be disturbed.'

'Call them now and let them know I'm here.'

The secretary picks up the intercom and calls.

Gennady, Marat's right-hand man, answers. 'What?' he barks.

'It's Veronika,' the secretary says. 'She's here.'

There is a pause as Gennady relays the information to Marat. 'Tell her to come back later,' Gennady says.

Marat's secretary glances at Veronika; she's not telling her that. 'I don't think I can,' she whispers.

'What?' Gennady asks.

Veronika walks to the secretary's desk and snatches the intercom receiver. 'Open the door now,' she says to Gennady in Russian, and slams the phone down.

Veronika walks back to the door, and Gennady opens it as she approaches. She steps in and storms past him to Marat, sitting in the lounge area of his grand office.

'You weren't going to tell me?' she demands in Russian.

'We're taking care of it. But of course, I would've told you eventually,' Marat responds.

'Eventually? When is that?'

Marat doesn't respond.

She gathers herself. She wants to be involved and doesn't

want her temper to jeopardise that. 'How are we taking care of it? He's been waiting fifteen minutes.'

'We know,' Gennady says, and prepares two glasses of whisky. 'I've reached out to my man in their organisation to find out why Alan is here. We're waiting for him to call back.' He gestures to the whisky. 'Want one?'

'No, thank you.'

Gennady hands Marat a glass. 'Alan is either brave or crazy.'

'He's crazy,' Marat says, and drinks. 'He will pay dearly for this.'

Gennady nods and is about to speak, but his phone rings. It's the inside man. Gennady answers and puts it on speaker.

'Sorry for the delay,' the inside man says. 'Couldn't speak.'

'Alan is at our London office. He wants to see my boss. Why?'

'Really? I don't know. Things are going crazy out here, so there's not much communicating going on.'

'Okay. What do you know?'

'Nothing new. No . . . there's a shipment arriving tomorrow.'

'That's something. What's the shipment number?'

'I don't know yet. Only Alan knows for now. He'll tell Michael when it arrives because Michael wants to sort it himself.'

'We can work with that.'

'Okay. But, err . . . you know we agreed to leave Michael out of this.'

Gennady is about to respond, but Veronika gestures to put the call on mute. She's furious. He mutes the call.

'Why would we agree to leave Michael out of it?' she asks. Gennady turns to Marat.

'I want that bastard to watch us destroy everything he's built,' Marat says. 'I want him to watch us wipe out his entire family one by one, then we'll kill him.'

Veronika wants to object. She understands her father's desire for Michael to suffer before they put him out of his misery, but that's a lot of time for things to go wrong. Her brother, Viktor, underestimated the London underworld, and she fears her father is underestimating one of its great warlords. But she nods in agreement.

Gennady unmutes the call. 'Yes, we did,' he says.

'Well, everyone seems to believe Michael is doing all this.'

The reasoning behind that belief perplexes Gennady, Marat, and Veronika, and they ponder what motive *everyone* ascribes to Michael's destruction of his network. Gennady and Marat shrug; they don't much care. But the thought sparks an idea for Veronika, and she fights back a smile.

'That's not our doing. We stick to our promises.'

'Okay.'

'Call me when you have the shipment number,' Gennady says, and ends the call. 'I think Alan wants a truce before the shipment comes in tomorrow. It's his last chance to survive.'

Marat nods and walks to his desk. 'Bring Alan Pierce up to conference room one,' he says into the intercom. 'Make sure he's comfortable.'

★

Alan sits in the middle of a luxurious conference room enjoying a cup of coffee, and he's awed by how good the coffee is. The door opens, and Gennady holds it open for Marat and Veronika to enter. Alan greets them with a nod as they sit directly across from him.

'Hello, Alan,' Marat says. 'Good to see you again.'

'Good to see you again, Marat,' Alan responds and turns to Veronika. 'And you, Veronika.'

Veronika gives a polite smile.

Alan turns to Gennady. 'And you as well, but I don't think we were properly introduced last time.'

'Gennady,' Gennady responds. 'Good to meet you too.'

'So, to what do I owe this pleasure?' Marat asks.

Alan smiles. 'Are we going to dance around the subject? I'm sure this room is incredibly secure.'

Marat, Veronika and Gennady do not respond. They simply stare at Alan.

Alan has a bite of the shortbread set in front of him, and again, he's awed. 'Wow,' he says. 'This is great.'

'Thank you,' Marat says. 'It's from a company we invested in. Incredible quality.'

'The coffee too,' Alan says. 'Amazing.'

'Thank you. We invested in that company as well. I'll have someone get your address before you leave, and I'll send you plenty.'

Alan chuckles at the suggestion of giving his address for some coffee and biscuits, but they don't respond. Marat is serious. 'Sure,' Alan says.

'Okay. I'm sure you appreciate we're busy people. So, why are you here?'

'I know you are coming after our network, and someone is providing you inside information,' Alan says. 'I just don't understand why.'

Alan's audacity to claim ignorance infuriates Marat, but he doesn't react. Neither do Veronika and Gennady.

'As we said last time, we had nothing to do with Viktor's death. And we have nothing to do with whatever you have Jack Moore investigating either.'

Marat is overcome with rage by Alan's denial, and it shows, but for only a fleeting moment.

Alan notices but continues speaking as if he didn't. 'Jack is a dick. But he's very good at his job and has an excellent team working for him. In time, they'll find out we had nothing to do with this. But by then, you'll have us off the board. Whoever is providing you information is just trying to get you to do what no one else has been able to. You're being played. And I'm here to let you know that before we get desperate. Desperate people do terrible things, even to people in ivory towers.'

Marat stands and walks out of the room, and Gennady quickly follows.

'Brothers, eh?' Veronika says.

The comment confuses Alan, and he ponders what she could mean by it. Fuck it, he'll ask. 'What's that?' he asks.

'Sibling rivalry, you know. We had a good life in Russia before Viktor decided to come to London to play your games because father chose me to run the company. That jealousy got him killed, and now we are all here paying for it.'

'I'm sorry to hear that.'

'It's okay. This is our life now. And London is not too bad,' she says, and smiles. 'But you should talk to your brother. Before it's too late.' She stands. 'Please finish your coffee and biscuits. Someone will come in a moment to get your address. And I understand if you don't want to give your home address. Any address will do. Take care of yourself.'

'Thanks. You too.'

Veronika walks out of the room, and Alan smirks. Good effort, he thinks, but he's not biting. Hopefully, they do.

DAY 16, 11:10

'It's my job'

Alan sits on a sofa in his living room. He's trying to watch the news, but he can't focus and keeps glancing at the satellite phone on the coffee table in front of him. As always, Alan switched the phone on at 11:00 for a thirty-minute window, to wait for Enzo's call about the shipment's arrival. And he's not the only one – Gary has called his burner phone three times already, and he's ignored every call.

Franka sits at the coffee table reading *White Teeth* by Zadie Smith, her most challenging English-language novel yet. Franka's pleased with her progress, because when she arrived in London six years ago, she couldn't read a word of English and wasn't comfortable speaking the few words and phrases she knew. She glances at Alan and senses his anxiety, although he's doing his best to remain calm. She's skilled at reading people; there is no language barrier for that.

Alan's personal phone rings for the umpteenth time, and he picks it up to end the call, but he doesn't because it's Hannah. He'd called her again right after Callum attacked him, and she didn't answer, as has happened the last few times he's called, but he left a very emotional voicemail. He regretted the voice-mail as soon as he left it, but thought it would've triggered her to call. But that was three days ago. He answers.

'Hey, Hannah,' he says.

'Hey, darling,' she says. 'Are you okay?'

'Yeah . . . yeah.'

'That was a rather . . . *odd* voicemail.'

'I know. Just . . . things were crazy at that point.'

'Sounded like a near-death experience . . .'

'No. Just . . . no. I'm okay.'

'You sound okay. But I hope Michael isn't working you too hard.'

Alan forces laughter.

'I'm serious,' she says. 'Go on holiday. Trust me, things won't fall apart without you.'

'I plan to . . . just not right now.'

'Not right now,' she says, and laughs. 'Sounds like you need one *right now*.'

'You seem pretty keen on me going on holiday. Want to come with?'

'Err . . .' She hesitates. 'This is busy season for the shop . . .'

'I understand. Was just teasing.'

They both force laughter.

'I heard you were at Sarah's sixtieth . . . didn't know you were tight with her.'

'Yeah, well, I didn't know either. But they invited me.'

'They?'

'Yeah. The family.'

'The family? Like . . . Michael?'

'The family, Alan. Your family. And I expected to see you there.'

'Oh, come on. You know Sarah wants nothing to do with me after *Marbella*.'

'Get over yourself, Alan. Sarah was distraught. You came back alive. Charlie – her pride and joy – came back in a coffin. You should reach out soon. Because the longer this goes on, people will start to think you have a guilty conscience.'

'I have nothing to feel guilty about.'

'I didn't say you did, did I? I'm just saying the more you avoid her—'

'I'm not avoiding her. She doesn't want me around. She never did.'

'Okay. Well, I don't know that.'

'You do.'

'Sure. So, then you don't want me to have anything to do with her and Dave either?'

Dave? Alan thinks. Fuck does Dave have to do with it? But he dismisses the thought. 'I'm not saying—'

'Alan, I was just calling to see if you're okay. And you are.'

'Hey, no need to end the call—'

'I'm in the shop, Alan. I have to go.'

Hannah hangs up, and Alan curses himself underneath his breath. But in the next moment, the satellite phone rings, and he answers.

'Ciao, Alan,' Enzo says.

'Ciao, Enzo,' Alan responds.

Sofia tells Alan the ship and cargo number, and Alan makes a coded note of it on his iPhone.

'I hear things are not sorted on your end,' Enzo says in Italian, and Sofia translates.

Alan hesitates; he doesn't know how to respond to that.

'We hear everything, especially when it comes to our partners. Usually, I would offer help. But we have been asked to sit this one out.'

'Sorry?'

'It is as I said.'

Alan is confounded, but he plays it cool. 'Okay,' he says. 'I understand.'

'Good. I will say this because I have said it already. Do not let anyone else know about this cargo and do not touch it until you are sure your tribulations are over. Good luck, Alan. I hope you survive this.'

'Thank you, Enzo.'

'If we don't receive payment, I'll assume you're dead and don't mind us destroying what's left of your organisation,' Sofia adds. The line goes dead.

'Fucking Lenkovs,' Alan mutters, and his iPhone rings. He checks the caller ID, and it's Michael. The immediacy of the call concerns Alan, and he turns to Franka. 'Is this room clean?' he asks.

She nods.

Alan answers.

'Come to the council office right fucking now!' Michael roars, and immediately hangs up.

Alan takes a deep breath and tries to contain his anxiety, but his left hand trembles. He notices and clenches his fist to stop it. It's the first time that's happened, and it angers him.

'Let's go,' Alan says to Franka, and jumps to his feet.

Alan and Franka are on the way to Michael's office in the East Hampstead Council Planning and Building Development department, where Michael is chair of the planning committee. Franka notices Alan's left hand trembling as she drives, but he seems unaware of it – he's deep in thought, trying to devise a way to avoid telling Michael the shipment's cargo number.

'Do you want to play some music?' Franka asks.

Alan snaps out of it. 'I thought you hated my music,' he teases, and connects his iPhone to the car stereo.

'I'm getting used to it,' she responds, and smiles.

Alan plays 'Insomnia' by Faithless and bumps along to it.

'Come on,' he says. 'Join me. This might be your last chance to dance with me.'

'I won't let that happen,' she says.

He can tell she means every word, but she won't be enough to stop it if Michael wants him dead.

'Thank you,' he says, heartfelt.

'It's my job,' she responds without emotion.

'I kn—'

His iPhone rings, cutting out the music; it's Michael. Alan's furious at the persistent calls and answers through the car's stereo because it'll force him to be fearless.

'Where the fuck are you?' Michael roars.

'Trying to sort the shipment—' Alan says.

'Pass that shit to Gary,' Michael interrupts. 'I need you here now. Some fucker's just tried to sell the bracelet to Farrukh!'

2009

4 APRIL

'It's not worth it'

Michael, Gary, and Dre are in the balcony seating outside a large private box in Arsenal's Emirates Stadium, revelling in the last few minutes of Arsenal's win over Manchester City. Alan sits alone inside the box, uninterested in the match's result as he devises a way to leverage this opportunity.

The Lenkovs invited them to watch the big match in their box and have spared no expense to ensure the experience is memorable, down to an endless supply of each person's choice of food and drink. The Lenkovs want something, and they want it bad. Having friends like the Lenkovs will be tremendous for Michael's organisation.

Michael, Gary, and Dre enter the box and head straight for beers. Alan wants to stop Michael, because he'd prefer his half-brother keep a clear head, but Michael usually handles his alcohol well. Right on cue, Michael roars in elation and pours beer over Gary, and Alan worries Michael might not handle euphoria mixed with alcohol quite as well. But he *is* in a good mood, so that'll help.

Gennady enters the box and attempts to get Michael's attention, but Michael ignores him. Gennady steps forward to take a more direct approach, and Alan rushes over to intercept him. He knows Michael reacts badly to approaches by people he doesn't know, and Gary and Dre will follow Michael's lead.

'Hello,' Alan says, and reaches out to shake Gennady's hand.

'Hello, Mr Pierce,' Gennady says, and shakes Alan's hand. 'Marat and his daughter, Veronika, are waiting outside, and they'd like to meet you and Mr Downing alone.'

'Okay. Give me a moment,' Alan says, and approaches Michael. 'Marat wants to meet you and me, alone.'

'Why?'

'What do you mean?'

'Why just us?'

'I don't know. But if that's what Marat wants . . .'

'Why should I care what Marat wants?'

'Because Marat's going to ask you for a favour that will be very beneficial for you. Why else would he invite us? And I'm sure Gary and Dre will enjoy roaming around the stadium with their VIP access.'

Michael nods, conceding the point. 'Gary,' he calls, 'you and Dre step out for a bit.'

'You sure?' Dre asks.

'Does it look like I'm not sure?'

'Sorry, boss.'

'Whatever. Come back in ten.'

'Make it fifteen,' Alan adds.

'Ten it is,' Gary says.

Gennady holds the door open for Gary and Dre and follows them out of the box.

'What the fuck you think he wants to talk about?' Michael asks.

'I have an idea, but I'm not sure.'

'Good. You do the talking, all right? I'm not in the mood for this.'

Alan nods; that's what he was hoping for.

The door opens, and Marat and Veronika enter the box.

'Evening, Michael,' Marat says, and approaches Michael. 'I hope you had a wonderful evening.'

'Of course, Gooners won,' Michael says, and shakes Marat's outstretched hand.

'Yes! Always a good evening when the Gunners win,' Marat says, and turns to Alan.

'Right, how long have you been a supporter, then?' Michael asks.

Marat turns back to Michael. Marat's angry but hides it well. 'Since Arshavin signed in January, of course,' he says, and smiles.

Alan chuckles, but Michael doesn't react.

Marat turns to Alan, and they shake hands. 'Nice to meet you, Alan,' Marat says.

'Nice to meet you, Marat,' Alan says.

Marat sits beside Veronika at a nearby table and gestures

for Alan and Michael to sit across from them. Alan sits, but Michael grabs a beer and sits on the counter. Michael's impertinence irritates Marat and amuses Veronika, but neither show it.

'I have a favour to ask of you, Michael,' Marat says.

'Sure,' Michael says.

'I've been told nothing happens in this town without your knowledge, so I will assume you know that my son, Viktor, died in what is referred to as the Wapping Massacre—'

'We had nothing to do with that,' Michael interrupts, and takes a swig of his beer.

'I know you had nothing to do with it.'

'Yeah, it was a fucking shitshow.'

Marat bites his tongue and continues. 'For years, I have funded investigations through official and unofficial channels and have gotten nowhere. So, I'm asking for your help, and you can name your price.'

Alan fights back a smile. 'What help, exactly?' he says.

'If you don't already know, I want you to find out any information you can about this *Pretty Boy* . . .'

'You want me to get my people to rat?' Michael says.

'This will be done through unofficial channels. The information—'

'That's still ratting, mate,' Michael interrupts.

Marat takes a moment to calm himself. 'I understand why—'

'You understand. So you're asking me to get my people to rat.'

'If you want to put it that way.'

'I'm not putting it no way. That's the way.'

'Okay!' Marat snaps.

This infuriates Michael, and he squeezes the beer bottle almost to breaking point.

'Let's be frank, Michael,' Marat says, and gestures to Alan. 'Providing information to the police is not new to you.'

Michael grins, and it's feral.

'As you can tell, what you are asking is a contentious point for us,' Alan intercedes. 'So, what are you offering in return?'

'That's up to you.'

'A billion quid, then,' Michael quips.

'Okay,' Marat responds, deadpan.

Alan and Michael can't tell if he's being serious.

'Sorry?'

'That's what you want, yes?'

Alan turns to Michael, and Michael scoffs.

'This is bullshit,' Michael says. 'Same as your fucking dead son, you come to my town and think you can do whatever you like without coming to me first. You think there are special rules for you billionaires? In places like this, yes. But not where your dead son decided to dip his toe. And not where you've been trying to investigate for years. I'm fucking sure you were told to talk to me the minute you started. But no, you thought you could do it yourself. Now what, eh?'

'It seems you are refusing my request.'

'Fuck you, and I suggest you get the fuck out of the room before I smash this bottle on your head.' Veronika laughs, and Michael glares at her. 'What the fuck are you laughing at?'

The door opens, and Gennady and three bodyguards in suits step into the room.

'This is our box,' Marat says. 'I suggest you leave now before I have them throw you out and ban you from ever visiting this stadium again.'

Michael looks at the bodyguards with excitement; he's up for the fight.

'Okay,' Alan says, and stands. 'It was good to meet you, finally.'

'Likewise,' Marat says.

Alan walks to the door without turning to Michael because he knows it'll force Michael to follow. Alan's lack of fight disappoints but doesn't surprise his brother. Michael scans the bodyguards; he would love to show the Lenkovs what he's made of, but not today. Soon, though. He follows Alan to the door and feints at a bodyguard, and all three reach for guns holstered around their waists.

Michael feigns fright and cackles.

Michael's Bentley pulls away from the Emirates Stadium. Gary drives, Dre is in the passenger seat, and Alan and Michael are in the back. Michael seethes, and everyone else in the car is silent as they give Michael time and space to calm down.

'You've been going on about the legitimate companies you've been working on, right?' Michael asks Alan.

'I don't know about going on—'

'You fucking been on about it. Right, Gary?'

'Yes, Michael. He's been going on about it.'

Alan curses underneath his breath.

'Yeah. I want you to use one of the companies to purchase the box next to those fuckers.'

Alan hesitates. 'Sure. But that'll be for next season. The boxes will be sold for the rest of this season.'

'Okay. Fucking Marat won't be alive to see it. But his cunt of a daughter will.'

Alan considers Michael's words. 'What do you mean Marat won't be alive to see it?'

'You know what the fuck I mean.'

'I don't.'

'Do you, Gary?' Michael asks.

Gary nods.

'Dre?' Michael asks.

'Yeah, boss,' Dre answers. 'Marat will be six feet under.'

'Exactly.'

'No,' Alan says. 'We're not doing that.'

'Are you telling me what to do?'

'I'm telling you it's a suicide mission.'

'I'll call Osama then.'

Gary and Dre burst into laughter.

'It's not fucking funny.'

'Get Franka on it, then. Decorated German Kommando and all that.'

'No. It's a suicide mission.'

'Even better,' Michael says, and chuckles.

Gary and Dre laugh.

'We're not doing this,' Alan insists.

'*You're* not doing this,' Michael says.

'It's suicide for all of us,' Alan says. 'Marat's a Russian

billionaire with vast international connections. He's every-where in the business press. The ramifications of his death will be monumental. The scrutiny from the police, the press, the government . . . international too, will be beyond anything we've witnessed. Ten times worse than what happened after Viktor's death. Lots of people that were thought untouch-able – your peers and rivals – are in prison off that scrutiny.'

'That was good for me. It created a void that I filled.'

'Because I put them away.'

'Fuck are you trying to say?' Gary asks.

Alan doesn't acknowledge Gary. 'We'll be the void this time,' he says.

'We still have friends in the police.'

'So did your peers and rivals. But they didn't have family with the means to do anything at any cost to protect them and put *their* rivals away.'

The car falls silent, but Michael is agitated.

'I put you in there!' Michael says. 'I made you—'

'I wasn't the only one you put in, Michael. But I was the only one that soared through the ranks, without a whiff of suspicion, and the only one you could rely on to sacrifice everything for you when the time came.'

Michael glares at Alan and wants to pummel him, but that won't change the fact that Alan is correct – he was invaluable as an asset in the Met.

'It's not worth it,' Alan says.

'To you. Marat disrespected me. He has to pay for that.'

'I understand. But—'

'But nothing. He's Russian, isn't he? I bet he has many enemies.'

'People might even think it's the Chechens,' Dre adds. 'They're beefing—'

'Shut the fuck up,' Alan barks.

Dre spins to Alan. 'I'll fucking spark you from here, you cunt.'

Alan glares at Dre, and Michael and Gary laugh.

'No one's sparking anyone,' Michael says. 'I can tell you're passionate about this one, Alan. So, you'll sit on the bench for it.'

'*It* shouldn't happen.'

'Don't . . .'

'I'm telling you this as your brother and, on paper, the person responsible for your security as you set out to become a legitimate power broker – a member of Parliament – don't do it.'

Michael nods.

14 APRIL

'You should go before he shoots someone'

Alan sits in one of the opulent living rooms of Michael's secluded mansion in the outskirts of London. He's waiting for Michael and Meiling, who are scheduled for a walk-through with the event planner of the charity ball Michael has organised for tonight. The ball is a huge deal for Michael, because it's his coming-out party as he launches a bid to become an MP. But this walk-through certainly isn't a huge deal for him, because it's scheduled to begin in ten minutes and the journey into Camden will take at least an hour at this time of day.

Meiling walks into the room, casually dressed and with no make-up, but she's as stunning as ever. 'Morning, Alan,' she says. 'And before you say anything, no, it's not my fault. I've been ready for almost an hour now. It's your diva brother.'

'Morning, Meiling,' Alan responds. 'What's he doing?'

'Who knows. He'll be down when he's ready. Want anything to eat?'

'No, thanks.'

'Is Franka here?' she asks, excited.

'Yeah. In the car outside?'

'Outside? C'mon!'

'Sorry. I was hoping I'd be in and out,' he lies – Meiling doesn't know Michael doesn't want Franka anywhere near her, and certainly not in his house.

'Yeah. But you've been here over an hour.'

Alan shrugs. 'Still hoping, I guess.'

'Whatever,' she says. 'Has she eaten? Would she want anything to eat?'

'I don't know.'

'I'll take her something,' Meiling says, and hurries out of the room.

Alan can see why Michael grew jealous of Meiling and Franka's relationship, but it's also clear to see it's an honest friendship, and Meiling doesn't have a lot of that in her life since she got with Michael.

Alan's personal phone rings – a withheld number, but he answers anyway.

'Hello,' Alan says.

'Hello, A,' a woman responds, and Alan recognises her voice.

'Hello, X.'

'This isn't a friendly call. I've just stepped out of a briefing with Interpol about two of Eastern Europe's most prolific assassins arriving on our shores last night and vanishing off our radar. These boys work in a pair and cost a lot of money with a large up front in cash, so they are only used for very big jobs by big players. I know your brother has a big party tonight, so I just wanted to let you know. Just in case.'

'Thank you. Are they Russian?'

'No. Ukrainians. Have any problems with Russians or Ukrainians?'

'Not that I know. But I'll check just to be sure.'

'Good. Take care, Alan.'

'Take care, X.'

Alan ponders, and Michael bounces into the room holding one of Meiling's large handbags.

'Where's Meiling?' Michael asks.

'Don't know,' Alan responds, and stares at the handbag, which seems full to the brim.

'Well, let's fucking go,' Michael says.

Alan nods and follows Michael. Michael calls out for Meiling as they walk through the house towards the front door and, as Alan expected, Meiling doesn't respond because she's outside.

'She's outside, boss,' a young man says, and opens the front door.

'What?' Michael says, and speeds up.

Michael steps out onto his expansive driveway and spots Meiling and Franka enjoying a conversation by Alan's car.

'I fucking told you to keep that cunt away,' Michael mutters to Alan.

Alan shrugs and walks towards his car.

'Meiling!' Michael calls.

Meiling turns to Michael and gestures for him to wait, and Alan fights back a smile. Alan approaches and hears Meiling and Franka jovially chatting in German.

'You should go before he shoots someone,' Alan says to Meiling.

Meiling rolls her eyes. 'I'll see you at the venue,' she says to Franka in German, and heads towards Michael.

Alan climbs into the passenger seat and watches Michael hand Meiling the bag, which is much heavier than Meiling expects. She attempts to ask him why it's so heavy, but he walks off towards the car. Meiling's about to open it to check, but Michael turns around to stop her and ushers her to the car. Alan's suspicion grows.

The cars set off towards Camden, and Alan calls Kash – his name for the man in charge of the clean cash – on his burner phone.

'Hello, I need three hundred grand in fifties in a couple of hours.'

'Sorry, boss, but the big boss cleaned me out of fifties a few hours ago,' Kash responds. 'Can this wait till the evening?'

'Don't worry. I'll find another way,' Alan says, and ends the call.

He curses under his breath. Michael has brought in the assassins for Marat. Not good. Not good at all.

The convoy of three cars parks in front of a banquet hall in Camden, and Alan quickly steps out of his car to hurry towards Michael's. Meiling storms off towards the hall with the bag as he approaches, but Michael is just stepping out of the car.

'I need to talk to you, right now,' Alan whispers to Michael.

'We'll talk when I say we talk,' Michael responds, and walks towards the hall. 'And we're fucking late, aren't we?'

Alan follows and attempts to speak, but Michael places a hand on his chest and turns to him.

'And stay out here,' Michael says. 'I don't need you bringing this shitty vibe in there.'

Michael walks towards the entrance flanked by two men, and Gary and two other men wait by the door. Michael greets Gary with a fist bump, and Gary leads him into the hall. The other four men stand guard at the entrance.

Alan paces around outside the hall as he waits for Michael to come out. He must convince Michael to end the contract with the assassins before he makes the first payment, because then it'll be too late. And time is of the essence, because Meiling is carrying the cash around and Michael hates to have that much cash around him.

Alan knows Michael's schedule for the day — he set it up, and it doesn't give Michael or Meiling the opportunity to meet assassins. Plus, Michael wouldn't meet assassins in the day — too much opportunity to be spotted. So the meeting must be after the charity ball, or during the charity ball — which will provide Michael an alibi if things go south.

Alan's pacing has taken him to the corner of the building, and he hears a side door open and slam shut. He assumes it's an employee entrance but goes to check it anyway. He turns the corner and spots Meiling lighting a cigarette by a fire exit, and he quickly retreats. He turns to Michael's men at the entrance – they clearly didn't hear the door and have no clue that she's outside.

Alan watches Meiling. She's alone in the desolate side street with the bag, and she takes her time to smoke. He can tell she savours the moment alone, and he understands because she rarely has a moment to herself. From the moment she started dating Michael – while he was still in his first marriage – he's ensured someone has eyes on her every minute, even in the house when he's not home. Michael is without a doubt a jealous man, which has something to do with it, but he has a justified fear that she's a prime target for the vast collection of enemies he's amassed through his infamously violent decades in the London underworld.

Alan likes Meiling; she's been nothing but good to him and made Michael a less bad person to be around. But this is an opportunity Alan can't pass up, and he'll have to be very careful. Alan walks away and calls Owen James, an old colleague at the Metropolitan Police who he recently helped to get promoted to Detective Chief Inspector, on his burner. Owen answers immediately.

'That was a quick pick-up,' Alan says. 'You're not in, then?'

'No, off today, gaffer,' Owen responds.

'Good. I need you to arrange something for me. It's urgent. I need two people with no connections to the big players and limited police records – if anything, small drug offences and theft crimes – for a snatch-and-grab job tonight. But a very delicate snatch and grab.'

Owen doesn't respond.

'I'll pay you and them premium and a half,' Alan says.

'No, it's not that,' Owen says – it's a lie; that's why he hesitated. 'I was just thinking of the right guys.'

'Okay. Call me back when it's arranged.'

Alan walks back to the entrance and waits for Michael.

Michael, Meiling and Gary step out of the hall, and Alan approaches his half-brother.

'I need to talk to you, Michael,' he says.

'Some other time,' Michael replies, and continues towards his car – he suspects Alan knows about the assassins and doesn't want to have that conversation again because he's not changing his mind. He will kill Marat . . . and might kill Alan as well if Alan continues to pester him about it.

'I need money,' Alan says.

Michael stops and walks back to Alan.

'I know I could just take it, but it's a large amount and I'd want your permission,' Alan says.

'How much are we talking?'

'Three hundred grand.'

'Uh. That is a lot. What for?'

'It's personal, Michael.'

'*It's personal, Michael,*' Michael mocks. 'It's my fucking money.'

'It's personal. And that's all I'm saying about it.'

'That's why you're acting jumpy?'

'I'm not acting jumpy.'

'You fucking are, Alan.'

'Okay. Can I take it?'

'I warned you to keep your cock in your pants. But then I know it's not Hannah, so thank God you're over her.'

'How do you . . .' Alan snaps, but quickly regains his composure.

'Still not over her, then,' Michael says, disappointed. 'That's going to get you killed.'

Alan doesn't respond.

'Take one fifty, and fucking negotiate. Abortions aren't ever worth that much,' Michael says, and walks off to his car.

Alan doesn't need the cash; he has more than enough for the job. But the conversation will provide cover when Michael interrogates Kash about who Kash told about this morning's withdrawal. He calls Kash.

'I need one fifty in fifties soon as you can,' Alan says.

THE NIGHT OF 14 APRIL

'If we survive the night,
I'll make it worth your while'

The black-tie ball is an absolute success for Michael. Everyone who RSVP'd showed up and is having a wonderful time, and the donations and auctions have raised over £250,000 for charity so far. The event programme is over, and the real business has begun as the crowd mingles with the help of an endless supply of champagne. Michael is in the middle of it all, working the crowd of politicians, minor celebrities, sportsmen past and present, and influential local business owners with ease, and he looks the part in his black tuxedo.

Alan and Meiling are the only two people not having fun in the palatial hall. Alan is doing a good job of hiding it as he mingles, but always with an eye out for Michael and Meiling. He's anxious that his gamble isn't going to pay off, because Meiling hasn't moved from her seat since she arrived. But he can see that she's getting increasingly angry watching Michael work the crowd for close to an hour without even a glance at her. Not that she's jealous; she's just lonely and tired of women's envious glares and men's lecherous stares.

Alan heads to the free bar and orders a glass of Baileys with ice. He watches Michael as he waits for his drink, and he's impressed. He didn't know Michael had this charm in him, but then Michael has been preparing for tonight for almost a year, and he almost always achieves what he sets his mind to.

Alan enjoys his drink and devises another way to stop Michael's attempt to murder Marat. If he can't stop the contract from being activated, he could try to get the Ukrainian assassins arrested. It won't be easy, because these assassins have evaded Interpol for nearly a decade and are already off the Met and SOCA's radar. Alan considers tailing Michael to the meet and then following the assassins. But the thought makes him smile; he's no spook. Franka is, though . . .

A young woman further along the bar smiles at him, and it dawns on him she thinks he was smiling at her. He looks away from her; he can't have that distraction tonight. But then it doesn't have to be tonight . . . they can just talk tonight. He turns back to her and spots Michael and Meiling talking, and although Michael is trying to put a happy face on it, it's not a happy conversation. He continues watching them, and just like that, Meiling storms out of the hall towards the fire exit. It's on, and Alan would appreciate a distraction to hide his anxiety, but the young woman on the other side of the bar isn't there anymore. 'Fuck,' he mutters, downs his glass of Baileys, and gestures for another one.

Alan doesn't touch the second glass and struggles to contain his anxiety as he waits. And the more time passes without the commotion he expected in the aftermath of the snatch and grab, his mind spirals further. What if the guys Owen sent didn't show up? Or they did, but tired of waiting and left? What if they got caught? What if Meiling fights back? Ah, shit . . . Franka was teaching Meiling self-defence for a few months before Michael stopped it because Meiling was enjoying it too much. Maybe she continued the classes elsewhere. And she is fucking fearless.

Alan spots Dre burst into the hall in a suit that's several sizes too small, and he's frantic as he searches for Michael in the crowd. It's happened, but it doesn't look good. Alan rushes out of the hall. Only two of the six men Michael had stationed just outside the entrance remain, and both are consumed with fear.

'What happened?' Alan asks.

'Fucking hell, Alan, we're dead,' one responds. 'But nobody told us there was another . . .'

'What are you talking about?'

'It's the boss's girl.'

'What happened to her?'

The man hesitates and gestures to his hand. 'Her hand . . . gone, boss.'

'What? Where is she?'

'Still there.'

'Where?'

'Round the corner.'

'Is that where the others are?'

'No, they're chasing after one of them.'

Alan hurries around the corner, and it's silent. Not at all the commotion he was expecting. He walks along the desolate side street past one of Michael's men, who is despondent, his head in his hands like there's been a death, and Alan's heart pounds out of his chest. Two large men standing guard part as Alan approaches, and he sees Franka crouching over Meiling. Meiling is alive, thank God, but her once vibrant eyes are dead and heavy. She's sitting on the pavement, and you can tell she's been crying, but she's done with that and has moved on to rage.

Franka is topless, wearing just her bra. Her leather jacket covers Meiling's shoulders, and her t-shirt is wrapped around Meiling's left hand, but blood is seeping through it.

'Where is the towel?' Franka shouts. 'And where is the ambulance?'

Alan recognises the pain in Franka's voice and takes off his jacket to offer to her. But before he does, one of Michael's men runs over with a towel. Franka unwraps her t-shirt to reveal Meiling's left hand cut off at the wrist. Franka wraps the towel tight around the exposed wound, and Alan – still in shock – searches the ground for Meiling's hand.

'They took it,' Meiling says, deadpan. 'Because of the fucking bracelet.'

Rage consumes Alan – not only did Owen's guys not follow

his explicit instructions, but they were also greedy and went for the bracelet.

The diamond bracelet is astonishing, but Meiling hated wearing it because it drew attention from people, including Michael's boys, who would never earn its worth in their life-times. But that's why Michael loved it, and he forced her to wear it every time there was an occasion. That'll end now. That and every other thing he forces her to do. She's in the game now, and she's going to own it.

'How many were there?' Alan asks.

'Two.'

'Describe them.'

'They were wearing masks.'

'Did they speak?'

'The taller one had on a Tony Blair mask. He did all the talking. Nothing particular about his voice . . . well, he's a native. And articulate. The stocky one with the Gordon Brown mask didn't talk . . . he just muttered after he took my hand.'

Alan nods. He needs to handle this quickly and will need Franka's help for that, but he can't fully involve her because she can't know he's responsible. Alan crouches next to her.

'Stay with her,' Alan whispers. 'Make sure she's safe. I'll call if I need you.'

Franka reaches into her jacket for Alan's car keys, but Alan stops her.

'Keep it. I'll take another one. Can't use my car tonight,' he says and turns to Meiling. 'I'll find them for you, Meiling. I promise.'

'Alive,' she says.

Alan nods and approaches the man still with his head in his hands.

'You're driving one of the Mercedes, right?' Alan asks.

The man nods.

'Is it clean?'

'Yeah, Gary rented them for the night.'

'Okay. Give me the keys.'

The man hands Alan the keys, and Alan rushes to the cars parked in front of the hall. He unlocks a Mercedes saloon, but before he steps in, he sees Michael charge out of the hall towards the side street, followed by Gary and Dre. This is going to be a long night, Alan thinks. And his last night if he doesn't fix this sharpish. He gets in the car and drives off.

He calls Owen.

'What's up, gaffer? My lads do well?'

'Where are you?'

'At the drop. Waiting for—'

'I'm on my way. If either of them show up, keep them there till I arrive.'

'If?'

Alan ends the call and heads for the drop.

The Mercedes's headlights are off as Alan drives to a secluded field surrounded by dense trees. He spots Owen leaning on the boot of his car and parks beside him. He realises he doesn't have a weapon on him and checks the glove compartment. It's empty. Fuck. He sees Owen approaching and steps out.

'Gaffer, I know! I'm fucking sorry!' Owen says.

'You told them my instructions, right?' Alan asks, and scans their dark surroundings.

'Of course. I don't—'

'They're not here.'

'Well, only one showed up.'

'And where is he?'

Owen walks to his boot and opens it to reveal the stocky man, dead with three bullets in his chest.

'You did this?' Alan asks, surprised.

'Yeah. He didn't want to stay. Wanted his money, otherwise he'd keep the bag. I tried to talk to him, but he's not really a talker. Came at me with his cleaver.'

Owen is armed, so Alan must be careful with him. Alan nods and searches the dead body for the bracelet.

'The bag is in the car,' Owen says. 'All the money's there.'

'I don't care about that. Where's the bracelet?'

'What bracelet?'

Alan spins to Owen. 'You didn't talk to him at all?'

'Well . . . I don't speak Russian.'

'He's fucking Russian?'

'Yeah. You said people not connected to the big players. Boris isn't. He knows nobody . . . well, knew nobody.'

Alan prays Meiling doesn't have a better recollection of Boris's mutter, because she's good with languages and accents. And a Russian's involvement in her assault will give Michael all the cause he needs for a full-frontal attack on the Lenkovs.

'He didn't speak any English?' Alan asks.

'Barely.'

'How did you deliver my instructions?'

'Other lad speaks Russian. And don't worry, he's not Russian. Just an Oxford dropout.'

Meiling had mentioned the lad was articulate — her assessment under pressure was good . . . hopefully not too good. 'He didn't have a hand, by any chance?'

'A hand in what?'

'A hand — a severed human hand.'

'A fucking hand? Fuck no! What the bloody hell happened?'

'Your two lads might have lit the match that'll burn London to the ground . . . or, at least, will get both of us killed by the morning if we don't fix this now.'

'Sure, I'm in!' Owen says.

Alan hesitates, because Owen smells like he's been drinking, but he needs all the help he can get.

'This isn't your car, I'm guessing?'

'Fuck no.'

'All right. We burn it with the cash inside.'

'That's almost 400K!'

That's a precise figure. Owen counted it. 'I know. Those notes cannot ever surface. But don't worry. If we survive the night, I'll make it worth your while.'

Owen nods.

'I'm guessing your other lad isn't showing up.'

'Not if they chopped off someone's hand. He's never seen that much action. But I know where he might be.'

'Okay. Let's light this up and go find him.'

14 APRIL, 22:00

'Not Jeff . . . Jeffrey'

Alan parks in front of a large semi-detached house in an affluent South London neighbourhood. He scans the house – there are no cameras outside, all the lights inside are switched off, but there is a car parked in the driveway.

'That's a big house; you sure she's alone?'

'Yeah. The lad's sister is married and has moved out, and the father committed suicide last year. Was facing prison for fraud . . . couldn't handle it, I suppose.'

Alan nods. 'I'll follow your lead,' he says.

Alan and Owen walk to the front door, and Owen knocks loudly several times. Lights switch on upstairs, and Alan hears footsteps coming down the stairs and approaching the door.

'What do you want?' a woman asks from the other side of the locked door.

'It's the police, Mrs Mantle. We're here for Eric,' Owen

says, flashing his warrant card up to the peephole briefly, but obscuring his name and photo.

There is a quiet moment as Cheryl Mantle considers her response.

'Eric's not here,' she says.

'He should be here every night for nine p.m., Mrs Mantle.'

'I know,' she says. 'He's always here, but not tonight.'

'Open the door, Mrs Mantle. We're going to search the property for him.'

'He's not home.'

'Open it now, or I'll call somebody to break it in.'

'I will, but I'm alone. Can you please call a female—'

'Open it now!' Owen roars.

Owen's tone angers Alan, but he doesn't react.

Cheryl opens the door; she's in her late fifties, wearing a night-robe, and it's clear she's been sleeping. She attempts to speak, but Owen barges past her into the hall. Alan greets her with a nod and steps in.

'Eric!' Owen shouts.

Cheryl shuts the door. 'I told you he's not home, and please keep your voice down.'

'Where's his room?' Owen asks.

'Upstairs on the right. Please follow me.'

'No, you stay down here.'

'I can't just—'

'You think I'm going to steal something? I'm police, not one of your son's criminal associates.'

'I'm not saying—'

'Then stop talking,' he says and turns to Alan. 'Stay here with her. In case he's down here somewhere and tries to run off.'

Alan nods, and he and Cheryl watch Owen march up the stairs. Cheryl turns to Alan to complain, but Alan doesn't acknowledge her and continues to stare up the stairs. They can hear Owen turning Eric's bedroom upside down, and the noise upsets Cheryl. Then a door slams and Owen seems to be marching along the upstairs landing.

'No! That's my room down there!' Cheryl cries, and attempts to hurry up the stairs.

'Don't,' Alan says.

She stops, turns to Alan, but then something breaks in her bedroom, and she hurries up the stairs. Alan curses underneath his breath. Owen's aggressive approach infuriates him. Owen was on his CID team for a few years, and he never noticed this behaviour. But then Owen was a junior on the team, and never led questioning before leaving to join Gang Crime Command. Owen's developed bad habits; habits that will be exposed now that Alan's helped him get back into CID as a DCI. But not until Owen railroads a good number of suspects, and the thought of that makes Alan's blood boil.

'Back downstairs, now!' Owen roars.

Cheryl scurries down the stairs, crying, and Alan wants to console her, but he won't intervene. Owen marches down the stairs and barges past Cheryl to search the rest of the house. Cheryl follows Owen into the living room and watches in horror as Owen turns over her furniture.

'Eric's not here, I swear! He doesn't stay here. He stays with Kayla, his girlfriend.'

'Where?' Owen asks.

'In Brixton somewhere . . . one moment, I'll get you her address.'

She hurries towards the stairs.

'Where are you going?' Owen snaps.

'To get my phone.'

He nods, and she hurries up the stairs.

'She'll probably try calling him as well,' Owen sniggers. 'She can try . . . but I made them leave their phones with me so their movements couldn't get tracked in an investigation. I left them in the car to burn.'

Owen is proud of himself and looks to Alan for acknowledgement, and Alan nods.

'I know the girlfriend, too,' Owen continues. 'And I have an address, but I want to confirm with Mrs Mantle. And we'll also find out if she's lying or not.'

'She's not lying,' Alan says.

'I know,' Owen sniggers again.

Alan bites his tongue.

Cheryl hurries back into the room wearing reading glasses and writes the address in a notepad on her desk. She tears off the page and offers it to Owen. Owen snatches the paper, reads the address, and nods at Alan.

'Thank you for your cooperation,' Owen says, and walks towards the front door.

'Can I please have your badge numbers?' she asks.

'Why?' Owen barks.

Cheryl recoils with horror. 'I'm sorry.' She stumbles over her words.

Owen shakes his head and leads Alan out of the house.

Owen and Alan step into the car, and Alan can't hold back anymore.

'That was unnecessarily aggressive,' Alan says.

'What do you mean?' Owen asks, and chuckles. 'I thought we're trying to stop London *burning to the ground*?'

The comment inflames Alan's anger, but he stays calm. 'Fair point. I'll lead with the girlfriend.'

Owen shrugs and drives.

Alan and Owen approach the door of a small block of flats above a shop, and Alan buzzes Kayla's flat. A moment passes before Kayla responds.

'Who is it?'

'The police,' Alan says. 'We're sorry for the late visit, Kayla, but we are looking for Eric Mantle.'

Kayla doesn't respond.

'His mum gave us this address and said he stays with you. We need to talk to him right away.'

Kayla still doesn't respond.

'Eric was involved in an armed street robbery earlier tonight, and his accomplice assaulted the victim – a young woman. There are several witnesses, and from what we are gathering, Eric and his accomplice had a falling-out right after the assault and went their separate ways. His accomplice has gone on to assault three more young women tonight, and we fear he'll continue till we stop him. We need Eric's help.

'I won't lie to you, Kayla; Eric is going to be recalled to prison as a result of the robbery. But if he helps us, we'll make sure the CPS don't add any further charges.'

The story impresses Owen, but he doubts it'll work.

'He's not here.'

'Thank you for that, Kayla. But as you can imagine, we'd expect you to say that even if he is with you, so we'll need to come in to search.'

'Second floor, door is on the right.'

'Thank you.'

The door opens with a buzz, and Alan and Owen step through.

'He's definitely not here, then,' Owen says.

Alan ignores him and heads up the narrow steps to the second floor, where Kayla is waiting for them.

'Come in,' she says, and steps aside.

Alan and Owen step into the small studio flat.

'As you can see, he's not here,' Kayla says, and shuts the door. 'I couldn't hide a mouse in here.'

Alan smiles and gestures for Owen to look around. Owen searches underneath the mattress, seat cushion, and the single wardrobe – Eric is not here.

'We're not exactly in a good place at the moment,' she says. 'Eric didn't spend the night here last night and I haven't spoken to him today, but he always comes back. Can I call him?'

'Sure,' Alan says.

She calls, but it doesn't ring. 'It's not ringing. Is he okay?'

'We don't know, Kayla. That's why we need to find him soon as possible.'

'He's probably getting high with his pretentious boarding school friends,' she scorns.

'Where would that be?'

'A bunch of them share a house round here. Think they're *urban*, living in the posh bit of Brixton.'

'You know the address?'

She nods and reads them the address from a text message on her phone.

'Which of them is closest to him?'

'Jeffrey. Not Jeff . . . Jeffrey.'

'Thank you.'

'If he calls you, tell him to call Officer James straight away,' Owen adds.

She nods, and Alan and Owen leave.

14 APRIL, 23:00

'The eyes never lie'

Alan and Owen approach the front door of a terraced house on a quiet street in Brixton. Alan knocks twice, and a few seconds pass before the door opens.

'How much . . . ?' a young man with a topknot and a full beard asks as he opens the door, but he stops when he sees Alan and Owen. 'What do you want?'

The stench of weed that pours out of the house surprises Alan, and he almost coughs. 'We're the police . . .' he says.

The young man shuts the door in their faces, and Owen steps back to kick it in, but Alan stops him. Whoever the young man is, he's much more than pretentious; he's privileged, so they'll have to tread carefully. Alan knocks again, and another young man opens the door.

'What do you want?' the shirtless young man demands,

with even more confidence than the previous young man, and a hefty dose of disdain.

'We're the police . . .'

'I heard. What do you want?'

'We're looking for Eric M—'

'He's not here,' Shirtless says, and slams the door shut.

Alan sighs and steps aside, and Owen grins as he steps forward. He bangs the door over and over till Shirtless opens up. But Owen doesn't let him speak and barges past him into the house. Alan follows.

'What the fuck are you doing?' Shirtless asks, and grabs Alan.

Alan glares at him, but Shirtless is not afraid. Owen continues towards the music and voices coming from a room off the hall, and Shirtless hurries ahead to grab him.

'Don't you fucking touch me!' Owen barks, and flings Shirtless into the room.

Shirtless crashes onto the guy with the beard and topknot who first answered the door, who's now relaxing on a bean-bag, and smashes into his nose. Topknot screams in pain and his nose streams with blood, and there are shouts of protest mixed with cries of alarm by the others in the room.

'You lot, fucking calm down!' Owen says.

Alan scans the room – two young men and two young women, in addition to the two guys floundering on the bean-bag. They look like university students, all stoned, and one of the guys and a girl are still enjoying a giant spliff.

'Put that shit away!' Owen demands.

They ignore him and continue to pass the spliff between them. Owen slaps it to the ground.

'Fuck, man,' the young woman protests, and tries to pick it up.

'No one bloody move!' Owen says.

They don't move, but their glares take on an air of defiance.

'Is this all of you in the house?' Owen asks.

'You can't do this,' Shirtless asserts.

'But I am, aren't I?' Owen says.

'You don't know who I am,' Shirtless says. 'I'll have your fucking badge for this.'

Owen laughs. He grabs Shirtless by his dishevelled hair, and he attempts to struggle but Owen easily drags him to his feet. 'Let's go look around the house, and you tell me all about yourself and how you'll have my badge.'

Shirtless tries to fight off Owen's grasp, but he can't, and Owen leads him out of the room.

The others stare daggers at Alan but stay where they are, and Alan fights back a smile because they won't hurt a fly – not physically, at least. He walks around the untidy open-plan living area, subtly examining every inch, and when he steps into the kitchen, one of the young men stands to protest. Alan locks eyes with him, and the young man doesn't speak. Alan gestures for him to sit, and he does. Alan takes out his phone, tapping away as he flicks his gaze from the screen to the kids across the room.

Owen shoves the shirtless man back into the room and shakes his head to tell Alan that Eric isn't in the house.

'Which one of you is Jeffrey?' Owen asks.

They don't respond.

'C'mon, I don't have all night,' Owen says.

'I'm Jeffrey,' one of the young women says.

'I'm Jeffrey too,' the other girl says.

'Me too. But—' another young man says.

'Shut the fuck up!' Owen says. 'All right, show me some ID.'

'No,' Shirtless says. 'We're not doing that, and there is nothing you can do about it.'

'You sure?'

'Yes,' he says, and stands. 'Do something. Hit me.'

Owen is itching to do just that, but he holds back.

'Fucking pig,' one of the young women sneers.

'What did you say?' Owen demands, and scowls.

'Maybe he doesn't understand,' Shirtless says, and oinks.

The others join in and oink with glee. Alan can see Owen is boiling over, but he doesn't intervene. Owen slaps Shirtless, and the young man falls. The others stop oinking, and Shirtless wipes the blood seeping from his burst lip before he stands.

'I was hoping you'd do that,' he says. 'Cos now you're finished. You don't know who my mother is, do you?'

'I do,' Alan says. 'The Right Honourable Dame Fiona Slaughter. Heard a lot about her. Fair judge, by all accounts. And you are Thomas Slaughter.'

'Yes, and—'

'You are Theo Davenport,' Alan says to Topknot, whose beard is caked with blood from his nose. 'Your father's a hedge fund manager, and your mother is a partner in a big City law firm with' – he gestures at the young woman that called Owen a pig – 'Clara Monet's father.' He gestures to the young man who attempted to protest when he stepped into the kitchen. 'You're Jeffrey "not Jeff" Garcia, and both your parents are doctors.' He turns to the other girl, who'd tried to pick up the giant spliff Owen knocked down. 'You're Paris Oswald . . . and listen to this' – he turns to Owen – 'her mother is *Zaza*.'

'Zaza . . . like, "Feel the Groove" *Zaza*?' Owen asks.

'Yes. The Disco Queen herself.'

'Uhhh . . . Mr Oswald's a lucky man.'

'Fuck you, pervert,' Paris scolds.

Owen chuckles.

'And saving the best for last,' Alan says, and focuses on the last young man, who's barely said a word. 'You're Daniel Jackson, and your parents are . . . regular working folk. And this makes sense because although you're fighting hard not to show it, you understand that the future you and your parents have worked so hard for you to achieve is in the balance tonight. The eyes never lie . . .'

'How the fuck do you know all this?' Clara demands.

'Oh, it's not magic,' Alan says and waves his phone. 'I spotted one of Jeffrey's letters on the counter, and Facebook and a quick Google search did the rest. But here is the magic – I'm telling you right now that in less than five minutes, the rest of you will be begging Jeffrey to tell me everything I need to know.'

'Fuck you!' Thomas says.

'Okay. Here we go. I know you sell weed out of this house . . .'

'That's a fucking lie. You're going to plant some weed on us, you dirty cops.'

'Calm down, Thomas. Theo gave it all away when he greeted us at the door. And I know where your stash is. You see, Theo – and I'm not picking on you, Theo – but Theo hasn't moved an inch since we got in, not even to get something to wipe his nose or clean the blood off his face . . . because he's sitting on your stash.' He turns to Owen. 'Please kick young Theo off the bag and open it.'

'Don't fucking touch—' Theo says.

Owen kicks Theo off the bag and zips it open to reveal lots of little bags of marijuana.

'Thank you very much,' Alan says, and bows. 'We shall call the drug squad in a minute.'

'That's for personal use,' Paris says.

'Oh, I'm sure Dame Fiona Slaughter can see to that, and Mrs Davenport or Mr Monet could find you a high-priced colleague to argue it . . . sure. But that's not why you lot sell weed, in *Brixton*, with no fear.' He turns to Owen. 'Romeo still runs the weed down here, right?'

'Oh yes.'

'And Romeo's ruthless. He won't have some rich kids selling on his turf, no matter who their parents are. But here you are – without any security, without any fear. You have Romeo's protection, and not because you're selling for him, because I imagine you smoke as much as you sell. But because – as I said earlier – the eyes don't lie.'

Alan walks into the kitchen. 'From the moment we stepped in, Daniel hasn't been able to keep his eyes away from this area . . . right around the fridge here.' Alan theatrically inspects the appliance, before yanking it away from the wall.

'What are you doing?' Thomas pleads.

'Shut up!' Owen barks.

Alan runs his palm along a small section of the wall behind the fridge. He finds the spot he's looking for, and smiles.

'Fucking stop,' Thomas pleads.

The others look on the verge of tears as Alan pulls the fridge further into the room and pops open a small door hidden behind it, to reveal countless tightly wrapped packs of marijuana stacked on top of each other.

'Well,' Alan says, 'I don't think Dame Fiona can fix this. Do you, Thomas?'

Thomas and the others are speechless.

'This is at least fourteen years in big-boy prison for all of you. But that's not the real problem, is it? I'm not the best at maths, but this is at least three million quid's worth of product. Romeo would not be happy to lose it. And we'll make sure his friends in the police know that we only called this in because you refused to tell us where to find Eric Mantle. He'll have to kill all of you then . . . and he'll probably try to collect his debt from your parents. Which will be a problem for the Jacksons.'

Owen grins. He enjoys watching them realise how fucked

they are . . . and for most of them, it's probably their first time, too.

'So, Jeffrey,' Alan says. 'Where can we find Eric Mantle?'

The others turn to Jeffrey, their expressions begging not only for Jeffrey to answer but for him to have the correct answer.

'I don't know where Eric is, but if he did something that's going to get him recalled to prison or that's put his life in danger, he'll make sure to spend some time with his true love before he gets caught.'

'We already visited Kayla . . .'

'Kayla's not his true love. It's some fancy prostitute he fell in love with when he spent the night with her on his eighteenth birthday. And she plays along with it . . . long as he pays.'

'Do you know her name?'

'Yeah, Megan. But that's not her real name. And I know where she works.'

'Where does she work?'

'Pleasure Mansion in Mayfair.'

Alan smiles – that makes things easier.

15 APRIL, 00:00

'The shoes, darling'

Alan pushes the buzzer on the side door of a nondescript mansion block in the heart of Mayfair and looks up to the camera over the door, so his face can be seen clearly. This is the staff entrance of Pleasure Mansion, so Alan knows there'll be a lot of running around and pondering inside as to why he is using this door.

A minute passes before the door unlocks, and a large man opens it.

'Hello, Sultan,' Alan says, and steps in.

'Hello, Alan,' Sultan says, and puts a hand across the door to stop Owen from coming in. 'I'm sorry, Madam says only you. Especially because he's a copper.'

'How does she know that?' Owen asks.

'I asked the same thing,' Sultan says and chuckles. 'The shoes, she said.'

Alan and Owen look down at Owen's shoes, and Alan smirks. 'He's with me, Sultan. And this is not police business.'

Sultan nods. 'She said you'd say that, and I should let him in if you did.'

Alan chuckles, and Sultan lets Owen in.

'She's in her office. I'll take you up,' Sultan says, and shuts the door.

He leads them to a small lift at the end of the hallway and uses a key card to open it. He allows Alan and Owen to enter before he does, and he uses the key card again before pushing the sixth-floor button. The door opens on the sixth floor, and Sultan leads Alan and Owen to a large door at the end of the hall. He unlocks it with his key card and opens it.

Madam sits behind an exquisite wooden desk in the middle of the room and greets Alan with a warm smile. Alan returns the gesture before he and Owen step inside.

'Thank you, Sultan,' she says. 'I'll call when they need to leave.'

'Pleasure, Madam,' Sultan says, and closes the door.

'To what do I owe this visit?' Madam says, and gestures for Alan and Owen to sit on the chairs across from her desk.

Alan and Owen sit. 'I need to know if one of Megan's clients is here right now, has been here, or is coming later tonight.'

Madam is unhappy and takes a moment before she responds. 'I imagine you told Sultan this wasn't police business.'

'It's not.'

'Sounds like it, Alan. Especially as you've brought a copper along with you.'

'I've never lied to you, and I won't start today. Yes, Owen is a copper. But this is not police business. I don't want to say too much other than that, but this matter is very delicate and very urgent.'

Madam nods. 'What's this client's name?'

'Eric Mantle.'

She smiles. 'I thought as much.'

'Is he here?' Owen asks.

She glances at Owen like he's an undisciplined student and speaks to Alan. 'He's been nothing but trouble since his dad passed. His dad was a member and brought him here for his eighteenth birthday . . .'

'What a fucking present that is,' Owen says.

She ignores him and continues. 'He never makes a booking – just shows up each time, demanding to see Megan. We would've banned him by now, but Megan has a soft spot for him, and I'm sure he pays her a little extra. And yes, he's been here tonight.' Owen opens his mouth to speak, but she raises a hand to shut him up. 'In fact, you just missed him. He left because Megan is busy and didn't want to see anyone else, but he will be back. He always comes back. Plus, he's already paid to make sure she doesn't take another appointment for the rest of the night.'

'Thank you. Is there a room where we can wait?'

She types on a laptop on her desk. 'I'll put you in a room on the same floor. Alan, you know the rules. No violence in the building.'

Alan nods. 'Thank you.'

★

Sultan leads Alan and Owen to a door on the third floor and unlocks it with a key card, which he passes to Alan before he opens the door. He steps aside for Alan and Owen to enter what looks like an elegant hotel suite.

'We'll buzz the phone when he arrives. And Madam says the drinks are on the house, but only up to a grand limit because, and she said I should say this, she fears Owen might overindulge himself.'

Alan expects Owen to feel insulted, but instead, he's amused.

'How bloody right she is,' Owen says.

Sultan nods and leaves.

Alan and Owen sit on the sofa in the small living area.

'Fucking hell, Alan. This place is glorious. You come here often, then?'

Alan smiles but doesn't respond.

'You a member? How much does that go for?'

'Eyes on the task, Owen.'

'Sure, sure,' Owen says and pauses. 'But still . . . hook me up, mate.'

Alan forces a smile; he could see that coming a mile off.

'We'll talk about it later.'

'So, you're a member, then?'

Alan struggles to hide his anger. 'I didn't say that. And that's the end of that topic.'

'Sure, sure . . . until we talk about it tomorrow, yeah?'

Alan nods, and Owen bounces to his feet and walks to the fridge with a pep in his step. He opens the fridge and whistles.

'Quite the selection,' Owen says. 'What do you want?'

'A beer,' Alan responds.

'Which beer? There are all kinds here . . . and I haven't heard of half of them.'

'One of those, then.'

Owen picks two beers, opens them, and walks back to the sofa. He hands Alan a bottle and sits.

'The Madam said no violence in here,' Owen says, and takes a large gulp of the bottle. 'So, what are we going to do with Eric?'

Alan sips the beer. It's subtle and light. He makes a mental note of the name. 'Talk to him. I need to find the bracelet before we do anything to him.'

'What if he doesn't talk?'

'He will.'

'You've got some magic for him as well?'

Alan laughs.

'That was fucking great, though. You haven't lost your touch at all.'

'Thanks.'

'You miss it, don't you?'

'It?'

'Being a copper . . . and not just any copper, you were a star . . . best arrest and charge record for years. That's why I was surprised you left. Everyone was.'

Alan doesn't want to talk about his exit from the police because it still burns him. But he does miss it. Every day. He was great at every part of the job, and his peers respected and admired him. When he retired, he was just a DCI, but he ran his own show and was allowed to because of his unprecedented success. And he was listened to . . . his voice carried weight. But now, he has none of those things. Michael's men look at him with suspicion because of his career as a copper, which doesn't bother him. But Michael promised to be hands-off and listen to his counsel. Instead, he gives him zero autonomy and doesn't listen to him. Above all, Michael expects him to be grateful for the position. Fucking bullshit.

Alan won't be telling Owen any of that, though. 'It was the right time,' he says.

'Oh, so it was your choice, then? Cos the word is that you were pushed out . . . and given a full pension.'

Alan fights back a smile because Owen isn't subtle, and he knows what's coming next. 'It was my choice.'

'Ah, okay. Because the word is that they found out Michael's your brother. And they haven't been able to pin a charge on Michael for years. So, two and two together, and they blamed you.'

There it is. Alan knew Owen was going there. 'I can see why people would think that. But it was my choice,' he says.

'Because that's the only choice they gave you?'

Not subtle, but he's sharp, Alan thinks. 'Did I ever tell you about the kid my ex and I raised for a few years?'

Owen shakes his head.

'Well, this kid was brilliant. Always beat me at chess, and we started learning together. After the hundredth loss, I asked him how he always won. He said he wasn't winning. He was surviving. And to do that, it wasn't enough to think two, three steps ahead . . . it's chess, every above-average player does that. You need to prepare for all eventualities, especially those you fear the most. That way, the last move is always your choice.'

Owen is impressed, but he doesn't dwell on it and ploughs on. 'What does the brass think of you working for Michael now?'

'It's all legitimate. On paper, I'm the head of security for a property development company that's aggressively expanding. There were job adverts and everything, and I wasn't the only ex-copper that interviewed for the gig. A few active ones did too. And regardless of what we know, Michael is a wealthy property developer without a criminal record seeking to enter politics. There are a few of those around.'

'They still don't know Michael's your brother?'

'I don't care.'

Owen laughs. 'You miss being a copper, though. I've seen it in your eyes all night.'

Alan shrugs.

'What do we do about food? Cos I'm hungry,' Owen says.

'What do you want?'

'Do they have kebabs out here?'

'They'll fix you one,' Alan says, and makes a call from the phone on the table. 'I want a kebab.'

. . .

Alan turns to Owen. 'Beef or chicken?' he asks.

'Chicken. I like it spicy too.'

'You heard that?' Alan asks over the phone.

. . .

'Thanks,' Alan says, and ends the call. 'It'll be up in twenty minutes.'

About twenty minutes later, there is a knock on the door, and Alan walks over to open it. A beautiful young woman in lingerie rolls a food trolley into the room and places a plate of kebabs on the table. She smiles at Owen, who is ogling her, and turns to Alan.

'Would you like anything else?' she asks suggestively.

'No, thank you,' Alan responds.

'Okay,' she says, and walks towards the door.

'Fucking hell,' Owen protests. 'Why the fuck didn't you ask me?'

Owen's tone irks her, and she turns to him. 'Because you're not the one paying,' she says.

'How the fuck do you know that?' he asks.

'The shoes, darling,' she says, and walks out of the room.

This time Owen *is* offended and struggles to hide it. 'I guess if we survive tonight, the first thing I'm going to do tomorrow is buy new shoes,' he says, and forces laughter.

Alan laughs too, until his burner phone rings. He checks the caller ID, and it's Michael's burner.

'Yeah?' Alan answers.

'Where are you?' Michael asks.

'Trying to find the fuckers.'

'I know. Put that on pause. I need you right away.'

Alan worries Michael knows he's behind Meiling's assault. 'Is everything okay?' he asks.

'We're on the move. Where the fuck are you, so we'll know where to meet?'

This eases Alan's worry, because if Michael wanted to ambush him, he'd have the location ready. 'West End,' Alan says.

'We're about Greenwich. So, we'll meet outside Dre's dad's restaurant in Bermondsey in twenty-five minutes?'

'I'll be there.'

'Everything okay?' Owen asks through a mouthful of kebab.

'Yeah. I need to leave for a bit.'

'What if Eric shows up?'

'Keep him here till I'm back.'

'What if I need to move him?'

'What do you mean?'

'Not like his body or anything, just take him somewhere to calm down.'

'You're on your third beer.'

'I'm fine to drive, Alan.'

'Sure. But no more,' Alan says, and tosses the Mercedes keys to Owen. 'I'll get a ride.'

Alan grabs the phone on the desk to call Madam.

'You okay, Alan?' Madam asks.

'I need to leave for a bit, but Owen's staying, so I'll need a quick ride to Bermondsey.'

'I'll call you a taxi.'

'Thanks.'

'I don't trust Owen to abide by the rules if you're not around. I want your number, and I'll call you when Eric arrives.'

'Fair,' Alan says, and gives her his burner number.

'Sultan will buzz when the car arrives.'

'She doesn't have your number?' Owen asks. 'I thought you were a member?'

Alan ignores the comment. 'They don't trust you to follow the rules when Eric arrives, which I know you don't give a fuck about. But you want to become a member, so prove them wrong.'

'I'll behave.'

'I'll be back in an hour. Keep him here till then. Sultan or one of his boys will help if you need it.'

Owen chuckles. 'I won't need help.'

'It's always banking hours in the Caymans'

Alan steps out of a taxi a few buildings away from Dre's dad's Greek restaurant and spots Michael's car ahead, parked between two Mercedes filled with his boys. Alan walks to Michael's car, and a back door opens as he approaches. He steps in, and Michael speaks before he shuts the door.

'I need you to find someone quickly,' Michael says.

'Okay. Who?'

'He's wounded but can't go to a hospital, and he's not from around here, so his options are limited.'

'I need more than that.'

'He's Ukrainian.'

It's one of the assassins, Alan thinks. 'That's not enough, Michael. Name? Description? Where was he last seen?'

'Talk, Bam-Bam,' Michael says to the man sitting in the passenger seat.

'Yes, boss,' Bam-Bam says. 'Err . . . he's taller than the other one, but not exactly—'

'Other one?' Alan asks. 'What is going on? If you need me to find someone fast, I need the complete story.'

The man in the passenger seat hesitates and looks at Michael for instructions.

'I got these two Ukrainian hitmen – the best, supposedly – to come sort Marat.'

'Marat?'

'Don't interrupt me again,' Michael scolds, and glares.

Alan nods.

'But these Eastern Bloc motherfuckers stick together. Because either they or the fixer tried to play me.'

'How do you know this?'

'They asked for a million, which I thought was fair, considering Marat's profile. But they wanted half up front in cash tonight. Only they and I knew I'd be holding that amount of cash. Meiling had the cash in her bag, and she said them fuckers came for the bag.'

'I spoke to her . . . she didn't say those fuckers were Ukrainian.'

'I didn't say *they* were Ukrainian. They knew about the money, though.'

Alan could interrogate the thought process further. For one thing, how would they know Meiling had the money in her bag? But he doesn't want Michael's fury to focus on someone else tonight. He nods.

'I sent eight proper men to the meet to kill the fuckers. Only Bam-Bam came back. One Ukrainian's dead, the other's hurt . . .'

'How hurt?' Alan asks Bam-Bam.

'I thought he was dead. He's the first one we hit, and he dropped. But when the shooting stopped, I went over to check, and he was gone. But there was a ton of blood where he dropped.'

'You checked with the fixer?' Alan asks Michael.

'He's dead. I handled that personally.'

'Okay.'

'Is he connected?'

'Yes. Ukrainian mafia.'

'That's—'

'I know. That's why we need to find this hitman before he talks, and we have to slaughter the Ukrainian mafia.'

Alan bites his tongue. That sort of irrational confidence is what's led to this situation, but it's also what led Michael to the top of the London underworld. 'I think I know who to call,' Alan says.

'Stop with the modest shit. I know you do. That's why I called.'

The retort angers Alan, but he ignores it and makes the call on his burner phone.

'Who's this?' a coarse voice answers after a few rings, and it's apparent he was sleeping.

'Alan,' Alan responds. 'Sorry for the late call, Sly.'

Sly sparks into life. 'No problem, Alan. What do you need?'

'Thanks, Sly. If a member of the Ukrainian mafia in town on a work trip gets hurt and needs to stay off the grid, where would he go?'

'Ivan . . . he's their man in London.'

Alan mutes the call. 'What's the fixer's name?' he asks Michael.

'Ivan.'

Alan unmutes the call. 'What if Ivan is off the board?'

'Well, then it depends. How bad is he hurt, and where did it happen?'

Alan mutes the call again. 'Where was the meet?' Alan asks Michael.

'By the pier in Greenwich.'

'Where was he hit?' Alan asks Bam-Bam.

'I'm not sure. I thought it was the head when he went down.'

Alan unmutes the call. 'He's badly hurt, and it happened in Greenwich.'

'Greenwich . . . if it's very bad . . . like critical, it'll have to be Virgil.'

'Virgil? Why him?'

'Virgil's mum is Ukrainian. And as you know, Virgil is a grafter, but he doesn't get much respect or work from the Ukrainian mafia because he doesn't speak the language well, and he's black. But if it's critical, he's the only one connected around Greenwich.'

'Thanks.'

'You need his contact?'

'No, I've got it.'

'Anytime, Alan.'

Alan ends the call. 'He might be with Virgil,' he says to Michael.

'I heard. You know where Virgil stays?'

'I could find out, but Virgil's smart. If he's with the Ukrainian, he won't be home or anywhere we can find him.'

'So? We still have to look.'

'I think we should call Virgil. He's an opportunist. If he has the Ukrainian, he'll be keen to make a deal.'

'If he isn't, he'll know we're looking.'

'That's my point. Virgil already knows someone's looking. But when he knows it's you, he'll deal.'

Michael nods, and Alan calls Virgil.

'Who's this?' Virgil answers.

'Alan,' Alan responds.

'Michael's Alan?'

'Yes, Virgil. And you do have a way with words, don't you?'

'I know, matey,' Virgil says – he speaks with a lyrical delivery. 'I've been expecting this call . . . but not from you guys. You run a tight ship over there, and this here is a major, *major* fuck-up.'

'Again. Smooth talker, you are.'

'Just saying it how it is, matey.'

'I take it he's with you.'

'Yeah. He is.'

'Has he called home?'

'Not yet. He's badly wounded. Keeps drifting in and out. But every time he wakes up, he demands a phone call . . . I can't keep pushing it and acting like I don't understand the ungrateful idiot.'

'Let's make a deal, then.'

'What's the offer?'

'Name your price. We'll pay.'

Virgil laughs. 'Of course you will. A quarrel with the Ukrainians will cost a lot . . . not just money. And it's just me in the way of that right now. So, I'm thinking . . .'

'A number, Virgil.'

'I'm working it out . . . I had a number in mind before you called. But you lot are the top of the food chain, so that number shoots up . . . way up.'

'Be careful, Virgil.'

'Oh, I'm always careful, but thanks for your concern, matey,' Virgil says, and takes a moment to think. 'One million is fair. And I want to roll with you guys. I'm tired of scrapping on the fringes.'

'The latter, done. But one million? C'mon, Virgil.'

Michael's eyes widen when he hears the number. But he nods to approve, which surprises Alan.

'Take it or leave it, Alan. The idiot's awake; I can hear him blabbing in the other room. One phone call is all it takes, and you'll be in a war for decades.'

'And what happens to you? Because the Ukrainians won't *see* you any differently.'

Virgil chuckles – he understands precisely what Alan means. 'I'll be fine,' he says. 'I've survived this long.'

'By minding your Ps and Qs and not going up against us. You won't survive till morning.'

'If you can find me.'

'I'll find you. That's a promise, Virgil.'

The conversation ceases as Virgil considers his next move, and Michael gestures for Alan to mute the call. Alan does.

'Fucking agree to it.'

'You don't want to accept Virgil's first offer. He'll—'

'Fucking do it.'

Alan nods and unmutes the call.

'Seven fifty, then,' Virgil says before Alan speaks.

'Okay.'

'Okay?' Virgil responds, surprised. 'I guess I should've gone for nine hundred.'

'Maybe.'

'I'll text you the account to wire the seven fifty to. And when I receive it, I'll let you know where we are. Or I could finish this idiot as my first job for you, on the house. But I'm sure you want to handle this yourself.'

'It's past midnight, Virgil. How do you expect us to wire the money now?'

'It's always banking hours in the Caymans, Alan. Call back when it's done.'

Virgil ends the call.

'He wants the money now,' Alan says to Michael.

'Is that possible?'

Virgil's text arrives, and Alan takes a moment to read it.

'Yeah. Might be at a premium, though,' he says, and Michael scowls. 'But I know you don't care about that right now.'

'Then don't mention it!'

Alan nods. 'I'll make the calls.'

It takes less than five minutes for Alan to wire the money to Virgil, and Virgil calls back moments afterwards.

'I have the money,' Virgil says.

'I know,' Alan replies.

Virgil chuckles. 'I must say, I'm surprised, Alan. Didn't you consider I might just take the money and run? Or ask for more?'

'No.'

'Really?'

'You're part of the side now, aren't you, Virgil? We trust our people.'

'Yeah, but still . . .'

'The address, Virgil. We can continue this chat in person if you want.'

Michael's car is parked in the middle of a quiet residential street in Greenwich, and Michael and Alan scan the street. Alan's burner phone rings, and he checks the caller ID, expecting it to be Virgil, but it's not; it's Madam. Alan ignores the call and puts the phone on silent mode. Hopefully, Owen handles it till he gets back.

'That Virgil?' Michael asks.

'No. Franka,' Alan says. 'Think we need her?'

Michael doesn't respond and watches Dre approach his window. He lowers the window, and Dre leans in.

'The street is quiet. But I've put the boys in good positions, just in case.'

'And the house?' Michael asks.

'Dead. No one's moved in there.'

'Okay, let's go.'

Michael and Alan step out of the back seats, and Gary steps out of the driver's seat. Bam-Bam tries to step out of the front passenger seat, but Dre stops him.

'You've done enough damage tonight, mate,' Dre says. 'Stay here and watch the car. I'm sure you can handle that.'

Dre walks away before Bam-Bam can respond, and he leads Michael, Alan and Gary to the address Virgil sent. Alan scans the Victorian terraced house, and his burner vibrates, but he ignores it and focuses on the task at hand. Michael tries the front door handle, and the door is unlocked. Gary gestures for Michael to wait for him to enter first, but Michael opens the door and enters the house, and the others follow.

Virgil sits in darkness on the stairs just in front of the door. 'Hello, Michael,' he softly says, so as not to startle them.

'Where is he?' Michael asks.

'Basement,' Virgil says.

'Can he speak English?'

'From what I hear, yes. But he hasn't spoken any English since I've been with him tonight.'

Michael nods and turns to the others. 'Stay here. I'm going down alone,' he says, and turns back to Virgil for directions.

'Door's just further down under the stairs,' Virgil says. 'Try to keep it down . . .'

Michael glares at Virgil, and Virgil instantly stops speaking. Michael walks towards the basement door.

'Hello, Alan,' Virgil says. 'Nice to see you again.'

Alan nods.

'You must be Gary, and you Dre,' Virgil says to Gary and Dre, and they both nod. 'Heard a lot about you. Nice to finally meet you.'

'Good things, I hope?' Dre asks.

'Depends, I suppose. But it's all respectful.'

'Fuck does that mean?'

'They fear you guys, that's all.'

'That's good!'

'I told you, it depends. Me? I'm a businessman. Can't have people scared of me.'

'Well, my business is making people terrified. And business is good!'

Alan glances at Dre with derision. 'Whose place is this?' he asks Virgil.

'Some old pensioners,' Virgil responds. 'I have a few on rotation. I pay for their cruises and use their houses as a base while they're away.'

'They don't ask questions?'

'No. Part of the deal. And I always make sure everything is as it was before they left.' He smirks. 'I told you you wouldn't find me.'

Alan's burner vibrates again, and he ignores it again, but the incessant calls worry him.

'How much do you bench, Dre?' Virgil asks.

'Two twenty kilograms PB at the moment,' Dre is quick to respond, and he's proud of it. 'You?'

'That's very impressive, Dre. Nothing like that for me. I'm getting old, stopped all the heavy stuff years ago.'

'That's lazy talk, mate. Michael and Gary are early fifties and pushing one forty.'

'Is that so?' Virgil asks Gary.

Gary nods; he's also proud of it.

'Impressive,' Virgil says, and turns to Alan with a smirk. 'What about you, Alan? How much you bench?'

Alan ignores the question because, unlike the others, the painful groans coming from the basement worry him. 'Can the neighbours hear that?' he asks Virgil.

'I don't know,' Virgil says, and shrugs. 'But I'm not going to be the one to interrupt Michael.'

Alan walks to the window and peeks out – the street remains quiet, and there is no sign that anyone's heard.

'Everything quiet out there?' Gary asks.

'Yeah,' Alan says, and walks back to the others.

'So, how much do you bench, Alan?' Dre asks, and barely keeps a straight face.

Alan takes a moment to respond, because the screams have stopped. 'Strength training isn't my thing,' he says.

'No shit,' Dre quips.

'But I've got the likes of you to do the grunt work for me, so I'm good.'

Virgil laughs, and Dre glares at him, but it doesn't stop

Virgil. 'It's going to be fun working with you guys,' Virgil says.

Michael walks out of the basement door and shakes his head in disappointment.

'He couldn't understand English?' Gary asks.

'He understood every word I said and called me a stupid motherfucker half a dozen times. But he didn't say much else. He's a soldier. Died with his head up and chest out.'

Michael walks out of the house, and Dre follows.

'Alan,' Virgil calls, and hurries off the stairs.

Alan turns back to him.

'What's next for me?' Virgil asks.

'I'll send a couple of people over in an hour or so to clean up the basement. They'll give you a burner with all the phone numbers you'll need already saved.'

'Including yours?'

'I'll call you on the burner tomorrow, and we'll talk the finer points.'

'Good. And I got ideas—'

Gary steps forward and swings a hammer onto the back of Virgil's head. Virgil's eyes roll backwards, and he frantically staggers before he crashes onto the stairs.

'Boss's orders,' Gary says.

Alan nods. He knew this was inevitable – Virgil would always have this over them, and Virgil has shown himself to be a disloyal opportunist. But he didn't expect it to happen now. 'We could've at least got some value out of him for the seven hundred and fifty grand,' Alan says.

'I know! But Michael don't give a shit about that,' Gary says, and approaches Virgil's lifeless body. 'You think he's dead?' he asks.

'Probably,' Alan responds.

'That's no good.'

Gary smashes Virgil's head until the hammer gets stuck in Virgil's skull.

'Now?' Gary asks.

'Probably,' Alan says.

'Ah, fuck off, mate,' Gary says, and tries to pull out the hammer, but it doesn't budge.

'Leave it,' Alan says.

'No. My prints are all over it.'

'That's the least of your problems. With the way you were swinging that hammer, your DNA is all over this place. The clean-up team will take care of it.'

Gary nods and walks to the door, but Alan doesn't follow.

'You coming?' Gary asks.

'No. Get one of the other cars to wait for me. Need to tie up some loose ends.'

'Need some of the boys with you?'

'No. Just the car and a driver.'

Gary nods and walks out of the house. Alan pulls out his burner and calls Madam back.

'Are you okay, Alan?' Madam asks. 'I've been calling.'

'I'm sorry. Been occupied. Eric is there?'

'Yes.'

'I'm on my way. Did you let Owen know?'

'I had to when I didn't hear from you. Owen's heading back now.'

'Heading back?' Alan can't keep the surprise out of his voice.

'He left.'

'Okay, thanks. I'll be there in twenty-five minutes.'

Alan hangs up and calls Owen, but it goes straight to voicemail. Alan curses underneath his breath and hurries out of the house. Headlights flash from a car parked just ahead, and Alan climbs into the passenger seat.

'Nice to meet you, Alan,' the driver says. He's nervous.

'What's your name?' Alan asks.

'Steven.'

'*V* or *p h*?'

'V.'

'Nice to meet you, Steven,' Alan says. 'Where in London are you from?'

'Hendon.'

'How did you get with us? Who hired you?'

'I used to drive Flex around before he died. Since then, haven't been getting much work. But Gary needed people with licences and no record to drive tonight, so I got the call.'

Alan likes that Steven isn't closely affiliated with anyone and hasn't gone out of his way to climb up the ladder since Flex died. 'Can I trust you?' Alan asks.

'Yes, Alan.'

'Okay. You're going to drop me off somewhere, but if you ever get asked, you say you dropped me home.'

'Okay.'

'What question should you ask right now?'

'Where's home?'

Alan smiles; Steven's sharp. 'Stick with me, Steven. And you won't be driving much longer.'

'Man's an addict. He'll be back soon'

After Alan leaves Pleasure Mansion, Owen waits for five minutes before he redials Madam from the phone on the desk.

'Hello, Owen,' Madam answers, and she's cold.

'I need to leave briefly. Take my number down and call me
if Eric arrives before I get back. Are you ready?'

'Yes.'

He tells her his number and asks her to say it back to him, and
she does. 'I won't be far, so I'll be back in a jiffy once you call.'

'Okay,' she says and ends the call.

Owen laughs to himself and leaves the room.

Owen parks outside a drug house in the heart of Hackney. He
switches off the safety of his gun and tucks it in the waistband
of his trousers before he steps out. He knocks on the door and
waits a few seconds. He can hear loud music inside the house,

and considers knocking again, but a teenage boy opens the door.

'Jamal is expecting me,' Owen says.

The boy nods and steps aside.

'Is Jamal in there?' Owen asks, and gestures to the living room, which sounds like there's a party going on.

'No. Upstairs,' the boy says, and walks past Owen into the living room.

Owen walks up the stairs, and a burly young man gestures to a door at the end of the hall. Owen walks over and tries to open the door, but it's locked. But before he knocks, the door opens. Owen steps into the dark room, full of young men smoking weed and playing FIFA.

'Over here,' Jamal says.

Owen spots Jamal sitting alongside a young man with dyed red hair on a long sofa in the corner of the room. Both men are counting a large amount of money. Owen approaches, and Jamal gestures for the red-haired guy to stand up.

'Let the officer sit, Tunde,' Jamal says.

Tunde – the red-haired guy – gets up and steps aside, and Owen sits.

'I see business was good today,' Owen says, and gestures to the money.

'Business is always good, fam. What do you want?'

'I'm here to clear my debt and give you some information that'll earn you much more.'

'Your pockets don't look fat. Can't be no twenty-three grand in there.'

Owen pulls out Meiling's bracelet with a flourish and hands it to Jamal. Jamal is speechless as he admires it; he knows nothing about jewellery, but he can tell this bracelet is worth more than twenty-three grand.

'Where you get this, Owen?'

'You don't need to worry about that. Just be careful who you sell it to.'

'Careful? Where you get this, fam?'

Owen shakes his head. 'You want it or not?'

'Okay. I'll take it. And the information?'

'I know where you can grab over three million worth of weed. But you'll need to act quick because it'll get moved.'

'I don't do that grab thing no more. And weed isn't my thing. But I can pass you on to a man that does.'

'No. I'm only dealing with you.'

'I don't want it, then.'

'Three million worth?'

Jamal nods. 'We good.'

'It'll be a simple job . . .'

'You do it, then. Or you meet my man that does. I don't want to hear about it anymore.'

'You're moving up in the world fast, Jamal. It feels like yesterday when you were out selling on the street.'

Jamal shakes his head. 'I thought you'd know better, Owen. Time moves differently in this game. That there was a lifetime ago.'

'Yeah. I understand. But I was just imagining telling that kid that in three years he'll be scoffing at three million.'

Owen's persistence angers Jamal, but he doesn't react, which surprises Tunde, listening in as he stands next to the sofa.

'We're done, Owen,' Jamal says. 'You want some gear? Want to join the party downstairs? Or you want some personal time with one of the girls in the rooms?'

Owen considers the options, but his phone rings, and he checks it. He doesn't recognise the number but reckons it's Madam. 'Hello,' he answers.

'Eric is here,' Madam says simply, and ends the call.

Owen switches off the phone and leaps to his feet. 'Debt is clear, yeah?' he asks Jamal.

Jamal nods, and Owen hurries out of the room. Tunde sits back down beside Jamal and continues counting the cash, but Jamal picks up the bracelet and admires it. Jamal glances at Tunde, sensing he has questions.

'Speak, Tunde,' Jamal says.

'Why didn't you press the fed to find out where he got the bracelet from?' Tunde asks. 'It'll be difficult to sell if we don't know.'

'We're not selling it. I have a feeling this thing is more valuable than money. We'll find out everything we need to know about it from the fed. But not now. Whatever he's up to right now is making him high on life. We won't get anywhere . . . and might lose him.'

'You cleared his debt, though, so we might lose him anyway.'

'No, Tunde. Man's an addict. He'll be back soon. And he won't be high on life then. We'll press him. All the way.'

'You'll know it if you see it'

Steven parks outside Pleasure Mansion, and Alan tries to call Owen again, but Owen's phone goes straight to voicemail.

'Is there a gun in here?' Alan asks Steven.

'Yes,' Steven responds, and pulls out a handgun from underneath his seat.

'Give it to me,' Alan says.

Steven hands Alan the gun, and Alan tucks it away.

'Should I come in with you?' Steven asks.

'No. Go home. I'll be fine.'

Steven nods, and Alan steps out of the car. He walks to Pleasure Mansion's staff entrance and rings the buzzer, and a minute later, Sultan opens the door.

'Sorry about this,' Alan says, and steps in. 'Is Eric still here?'

'Yeah. Owen's with him,' Sultan says, and leads him to the lift.

'Owen's here?'

'Yeah, he got back about ten minutes ago.'

Alan grows suspicious, but he doesn't show it. The lift opens, and Alan and Sultan step in.

'How was Eric when he arrived?'

'Normal, which isn't a good thing, because he's always on edge.'

Alan nods, and the lift opens on the third floor.

'I'll take it from here, Sultan. What room is it?'

'Second door to your right.'

'I'll call if we need anything,' Alan says, and steps out of the lift.

Sultan nods and stays in the lift as it closes.

Alan knocks on the room door and waits a few seconds before Owen opens it. Owen appears anxious. Alan steps into the room and spots Eric and Megan naked and lifeless on the blood-soaked bed. Both their throats have been slit by the jagged edge of a broken bottle in Eric's right hand.

'I met them like this,' Owen says. 'I'm so sorry I left, mate.'

Alan struggles to hide his fury and searches Eric's clothes, set neatly by the bed. But he doesn't find the bracelet.

'What are you looking for?' Owen asks.

'The bracelet,' Alan responds, and approaches the bodies. 'Have you seen it?'

'Oh, no, I haven't seen it,' Owen says. 'But what does it look like?'

'You'll know it if you see it.'

Alan checks Megan's wrist, and she's not wearing it. He

resigns himself to the fact that the bracelet is not here and takes a step back to scan the bodies and the area around the bed.

'What's wrong?' Owen asks.

'Nothing. We have to call Sultan and Madam.'

'She'll be fucking pissed. So do we need to get ready . . .'

'No. It looks like a murder-suicide, so it's not on us. Would've happened tonight, anyway. Although, yes, we should've stopped it.'

Alan calls Madam from the phone on the desk.

'Hello, Alan,' Madam answers. 'How bad is it?'

'It's best you come have a look.'

She ends the call.

'Madam and Sultan wouldn't get violent,' Alan says. 'So, whatever happens, however volatile it may seem, you stay calm. Do not bring out your weapon. And let me do the talking.'

Owen nods.

The door opens, and Sultan and Madam enter the room. They spot the bodies, and Sultan is shocked, but Madam is stoic.

'It was over before Owen got here,' Alan says. 'I'm guessing he wasn't keen on going back to prison.'

Madam focuses on Megan and struggles to hide her sorrow and fury.

'How do you want us to handle this?' Alan asks. 'We can get the police involved, or I can clean it up for you.'

'What's the clean-up going to cost me?' she asks. 'And what happens to Megan's body?'

'It won't cost you anything. And you decide what happens to her body.'

Madam nods and leaves the room, and Sultan follows.

'That went better than I expected,' Owen says.

Alan ignores him and makes a call on his burner. 'I need a clean-up team at Pleasure Mansions soon as possible.'

. . .

'Make it a priority,' Alan says. 'And tell them to ask for Sultan when they get there. He'll have the instructions.'

Alan ends the call and turns to Owen. 'Let's go.'

Alan and Owen step into the Mercedes, still parked in front of Pleasure Mansions.

'That's your first time doing that, isn't it?' Alan asks.

'Doing what?' Owen asks.

'Faking a suicide.'

'Sorry, what?'

'Stop, Owen. I knew the moment I walked in. Just tell me what actually happened.'

'Alan, I didn't do it.'

'Okay, Owen. You made one mistake. When a person slits their own throat as deep as you did Eric's, they don't have the strength to pull out the knife, bottle . . . whatever. It stays in the neck or falls to the ground. They certainly don't have it in their hand.'

Owen sighs. 'Fuck, Alan,' he says. 'Nothing gets past you.'

'What happened in there?'

'He freaked out once he saw me. Grabbed the bottle and came for me. I overpowered him and tried to keep him down.

But Megan tried to be a hero and smashed the bottle on my head, and I just reacted. It all went to shit after that.'

Alan nods. He knows that's not the truth, but that's as close as he's going to get to the truth tonight without putting a gun to Owen's head with the intention to kill. And Alan won't kill a copper, no matter how dirty they are.

'We survived the night and stopped London burning to the ground, though,' Owen quips.

Alan forces laughter. 'How do you want the money I promised?'

'How much are you talking?'

'Trust me, you won't be disappointed.'

Owen grins. 'Seventy per cent in an account and the rest in cash.'

'It'll have to be an offshore account.'

'Sure!'

'Okay. I'll send someone to you tomorrow evening with the cash and details of the account.'

'Sweet!' Owen says, and can't contain his excitement. 'You want to come party right now? I've still got the money I was supposed to give Eric and the Russian when they completed the job. We can have a lot of fun with that!'

Alan doesn't want to party with Owen, but his iPhone rings before he can politely refuse. He recognises the number and answers.

'Hello, X,' he says.

'Do you guys have anything to do with this?' the female voice demands.

'With what?'

'Valentin Lenkov.'

'What?'

'Marat Lenkov's son.'

'I know who he is. What happened to him?'

'He was kidnapped right outside a club in Soho, and his boyfriend was shot dead on the street.'

'When?'

'Ten minutes ago.'

'It wasn't us.'

'Nobody else but you guys have the balls for something like this.'

'It wasn't us.'

'It better not be. Because if it is, you'll lose a lot of friends. Plus, I suggest you guys use your considerable influence to find who did it and get the boy returned home . . . or heads will roll. On my end and yours!'

The call ends, and a mixture of panic and fury threatens to overwhelm Alan. He knows it's Michael, but he hopes it isn't.

'You're going to have to catch a taxi or something, Owen. I need to be somewhere sharpish.'

'Can I help?'

'No.'

'Just call if you need me; I'll be right there.'

Alan nods, and Owen steps out of the car. Alan watches him walk away and calls Michael, but Michael doesn't answer. He calls Gary, and Gary answers straight away. But before Gary speaks, Alan hears the painful cries of a desperate man.

'You okay, Alan?' Gary casually asks, like the cries aren't happening.

'Is that Marat's kid?' Alan asks.

Gary doesn't respond.

'Gary, is that Marat's kid?' Alan demands.

'We are at the garage on East Lane,' Michael says. 'Come see for yourself.'

Michael ends the call, and Alan drives.

'Do something. I dare you'

Alan strides past a couple of Michael's men guarding the entrance to the garage and walks into a room full of cars at different stages of repair and many more of Michael's men idling.

'Where are they?' Alan asks one of the men, and the man gestures to a door at the end of the room.

Alan approaches the door and hears screams from inside the room. He knocks hard several times, and Gary opens it a crack to see who it is. Alan spots Valentin Lenkov, blindfolded, tied to a chair, and beaten half to death.

'Fuck is going on?' Alan mutters.

'Come in,' Gary says, and opens the door.

'No! All of you get the fuck out here, now!'

Alan's tone shocks Gary. 'What?' he asks.

'Get the fuck out of there. Now!'

'Okay,' Michael says from inside the room.

Michael, Gary, and Dre, who's still wielding the bloodied wrench he's used to batter Valentin, walk out of the room.

'What the fuck is going on?' Alan screams at them.

Gary turns to Michael, and Michael isn't reacting to Alan's scathing tone, so Gary follows his lead. But Dre is furious.

'What sort of inept bullshit is this?' Alan scolds. 'Why the fuck would you kidnap that kid in the middle of Soho? Why would you kidnap the kid at all?'

'His dad probably paid them fucking Ukrainians to double-cross us . . .'

'Probably? You lot pull a stunt like that on *probably*? Fucking hell, aren't there any brain cells—'

'Don't fucking chat to me like that!' Dre barks.

Gary checks Michael again, and Michael remains calm, so Gary stays calm.

'And how long did it take you to realise that his dad isn't involved?'

'I'm still working—' Dre says.

'Shut the fuck up!' Alan says. 'It should've been obvious when you were kidnapping the kid and he had no security with him, no? Cos no one will be anywhere near a move like tonight on Michael Downing's wife without making sure their loved ones are in hiding far away from London AND protected by mean fuckers armed to the teeth till the mayhem that follows is over. Certainly not a fucking multi-billionaire with holiday homes across the world. You lot might be dumb as fucking rocks, but it's not your first rodeo, so you ought to know this. Michael worked it out a while ago, and that's why he's fucking bored right now waiting for you lot to realise.

'But no. The next genius idea is to torture the kid. Try some Abu Ghraib CIA shit you watched on YouTube. What's the kid said? Other than begging for his life?'

'I'm not done.'

'You *are* fucking done! Don't you get it? Or have all the steroids killed your brain cells?'

'I will crush you!'

'Shut up, you dumb cunt!'

Dre charges towards Alan, and Alan pulls out his handgun and raises it to Dre's head. Dre stops, but Alan approaches him and pushes the gun into his forehead.

'Do something,' Alan says. 'I dare you. Give me a reason not to put a bullet through your head.'

Gary grabs his gun and turns to Michael, but Michael grins and watches Alan with pride. Gary lets go of his gun and watches, hoping Dre behaves because it looks like Alan is eager to shoot.

'You're not going to do anything?' Alan asks.

Dre shakes his head.

'You're done with the kid?'

Dre nods.

Alan lowers the gun and glares at Dre, as if taunting him to make a move. Dre is full of rage and considers charging, but Alan looks away from him to Michael.

'We're done with Valentin,' Michael says. 'Done for tonight. Send the boys home. I'm off to be with my wife.'

Alan nods and walks into the room.

'He can't let the kid live,' Gary says to Michael.

Michael nods.

'Want me to stay to make sure it's done?' Dre asks.

'He'll do it,' Michael says. 'We've broken him. He's done acting like a copper.'

Gary nods.

'Stay and do whatever he asks,' Michael says to Dre, and leads Gary out of the garage.

Alan scans Valentin – every part of him has been battered by the wrench. Alan crouches next to him, and Valentin flinches, which causes him more pain.

'It's okay, Valentin,' Alan softly says.

'I don't know anything, I swear,' Valentin begs.

'I know you don't,' Alan says and unties one of his hands. 'This was a mistake.'

'Thank you. Thank you so much.'

'It's okay,' Alan says, and unties his other hand. 'But I have to ask you something very important.'

'Okay, anything.'

'I need your promise that you're going to forget anything that leads your people back to us.'

'I promise!'

'It's not going to be easy,' Alan says, and unties his feet. 'There are things you might not know that might cause you to rethink your promise.'

'No, I won't.'

'We killed your boyfriend.'

Valentin hesitates and tries to hide his grief. 'I . . . I promise.'

'I believe you,' Alan says, and unties his feet. 'But your father will want to avenge this. I need you to convince him not to. But if you can't, tell him we all spoke Ukrainian.'

'Yes. Yes, I will.'

Alan helps Valentin to his feet, but Valentin struggles to stay up, so Alan supports him and guides him out of the room. 'I trust you, Valentin. But I can't take your blindfold off. You understand, don't you?'

Valentin nods. Every step hurts, but each step is a step closer to home, so he pushes through, hopeful that the nightmare is over.

'I'll have someone drop you outside St Thomas's Hospital and hand you your phone. Don't speak to him and keep your blindfold on, and everything will go smoothly.'

'Okay.'

The plan invigorates Valentin, and he quickens his steps. But he trips over his feet and falls to his knees, and Alan shoots him through the head.

'Take care of the body,' Alan says to Dre.

'All right,' Dre responds. 'I'll call the cleaners.'

'No. You take care of the body.'

'Why me? We've got—'

'Well, they're all fucking busy because you lot have been going around killing folk like it's the Wild West. And this can't wait. So, get it done, yeah?'

Dre nods, and Alan walks out of the warehouse.

Alan steps into the Mercedes and calls Franka.

'Hello, Alan,' she whispers.

'How's Meiling?'

'Good. Sleeping.'

'Good. I need your help, Franka.'

'I'm not leaving her alone.'

'Michael is on his way. But you should probably leave before he gets there.'

'No. I leave when he's here. In the room.'

Michael will not like that, but Alan knows nothing he'll say will convince Franka to leave Meiling. It's not a safety thing, because many of Michael's boys are hovering around the hospital. Franka just wants a friendly face there for Meiling when she wakes up. Alan understands that. And maybe Michael will too.

'Okay,' Alan says. 'I'll wait for you.'

15 APRIL, 05:00

'Done'

Owen is naked and asleep on the floor of his untidy living room, next to a naked young woman who's also asleep, and another sprawled on the sofa behind them. They are in the crash that follows an alcohol- and cocaine-fuelled orgy.

Franka tiptoes through the room and crouches to inject the contents of a small syringe into Owen's neck. She watches Owen's breath become faint and then stop. But she continues watching for another minute before she checks his pulse. He's dead.

Franka steps into the passenger seat of the Mercedes, parked a few streets away from Owen's house.

'Done,' Franka says to Alan.

Alan nods and drives. It's been a long night, but all loose ends are tied . . . he thinks . . .

2012

'I want to punish him and then kill him'

Alan and Franka walk through the reception of the council building, and Alan spots two of Michael's personal guards presenting as civilians in the reception area. Alan greets the receptionist with a smile and uses his ID card to get past the turnstile – on paper, he's employed by the council as head of security. The receptionist lets Franka through after him.

Alan and Franka take the lift to the third floor, which houses the Planning and Building Development department. Franka waits in the reception area with another of Michael's personal guards, and Alan heads to Michael's office.

Alan knocks on the door once before he steps into Michael's large office – it was originally the conference room until Michael converted it. He walks past the room's lounge area, which has a golf putting mat, battered dartboard and a minibar, and approaches Michael's desk. Michael erupts from his chair.

'I'm going to fucking murder the bastard,' Michael says. 'His family. His friends. I'm going to eat him.'

'Eat him,' Alan repeats and sits on the desk. 'Try to calm down. And from what you said earlier, it shouldn't be this geezer you're after. He can't be that stupid to sell your bracelet to Farrukh. Sheikh Farrukh, for fuck's sake, if he knows the consequences. But he might know who we're after.'

Michael nods. 'Farrukh has the geezer's number,' he says. 'Think you can track it?'

Alan doesn't like that suggestion, because he wants to control every element of the search to ensure the person with the bracelet doesn't speak to anyone but him. He's about to reject the suggestion, but Michael glares at him, and it's clear it's not a suggestion; it's an order. This angers Alan and he wants to reject the suggestion even more, but he knows Michael will chase this some other way, which won't end well . . . for one of them.

'I know who to call. But I need to switch SIM cards to a secure one in the car,' Alan says, and walks towards the door. 'I'll be right back.'

'I'll pay anything,' Michael says.

Alan stops and turns to Michael. He wants to remind Michael they don't have the funds for 'anything' because they are stretched trying to get the distribution network rebuilt and the shipment sorted. But it doesn't seem like Michael is worried about that at all, which Alan finds odd because Michael is fixated on his reputation and standing in the London under-world. And the longer it takes for the network to be rebuilt, the more Michael's reputation erodes, allowing someone else to build up the courage and manpower to fill the void, which will lead to a war on another front for their already overex-tended organisation. Alan bites his tongue and walks out of the office.

Alan and Franka get into Alan's car, and Alan swaps the SIM card on his personal phone to a new SIM he picks from his glove compartment. He considers not making the call and going after Farrukh himself. But he senses Michael is desperate to find the person quickly, so Michael will immediately out-source the job to one of the elite private investigation firms that tout their ability to locate and apprehend in record time. That will take the search far out of Alan's hands. He calls a former colleague, now in counterterrorism in MI5, and the call goes straight to voicemail, as he expects.

'It's AP,' Alan says. 'Call me back on this number soon as you can. It'll be live for five minutes.'

Alan ends the call and settles in to wait, but a withheld number calls his personal phone right away, and he answers.

'Hello, AP,' the male voice says.

'Hello, Pat,' Alan responds.

'This must be urgent.'

'Yes. Can you track a number for me?'

'Yes. If the number is active — that is, on a call — it'll be straightforward. I'll track it down to a precise location in minutes. If not, no problem, but it'll take much longer . . . maybe a few hours.'

'We can get the number on a call.'

'Perfect.'

'How soon can you set up?'

'It's MI5, AP. We're always set up.'

'Thanks. We'll get the number active and call you back in five minutes.'

'That won't work. I need to make the call from my end. So, I'll call you, and you call the number.'

'I don't have the number. Someone else does.'

'That's fine. I'll call that person.'

'Okay,' Alan says, and reads out Farrukh's number from his contact list.

'What's his name?'

'Sheikh Farrukh.'

Pat laughs. 'That's ideal. Might even be able to keep this official. Who is he, and what does he do?'

'Officially – owns a successful jewellery shop in Marylebone. Unofficially – the go-to fence in London for high-value stolen jewellery and watches.'

'I can work with that.'

'I'll prep Farrukh and then call you, so we keep your interaction with him to a minimum.'

'Very good. And let Farrukh know to keep the number active for as long as he can. Helps with precision.'

'I will.'

'And if anyone at your end asks, I'm a Met officer from the Yard.'

'Okay.'

'This is a big risk for me, AP. But I trust you'll make it worth it,' Pat says, and ends the call.

Alan walks into Michael's office, and Michael leaps off his chair. Alan drags a chair to the desk and sits. He gestures for Michael to sit down, but Michael doesn't, so he doesn't speak. Michael curses underneath his breath and sits.

'Spoke to an old mate in counterterrorism,' Alan says. 'He can track the phone.'

'Fucking bloody hell!' Michael yells, and punches the desk as he leaps to his feet. 'That's what I'm talking about!'

Alan nods and waits for Michael to calm down. 'But it's going to cost you,' he says.

'Sure, money won't be an issue here. How's it going to work?'

Alan gestures for Michael to sit, and Michael immediately does. 'I'll let my mate at the Yard know when Farrukh's ready,' he says. 'My mate will call Farrukh on a secure line. Farrukh conference-calls this geezer, and my mate tracks the geezer's phone. The longer Farrukh keeps him on the phone, the better.'

'Good, good, sounds like a fucking plan.'

'Okay. Call Farrukh.'

Michael snatches his phone off the desk and calls Farrukh. It rings several times before Farrukh answers.

'Hello, Mr Downing,' Farrukh says.

'This is what's going to happen,' Michael instructs. 'Some-body will call you in a minute. You conference-call your fucking friend on the number he gave you. The copper will be tracking your friend, so keep him on the phone for as long as you can. If your friend gets spooked, it's on you, and you'll pay for that. I fucking swear, you will.'

'Copper?' Farrukh asks. 'Are you sure . . . ?' He stops; he knows it's a bad idea to question Michael.

But Michael is confused; he's sure he didn't say it was a copper, he wouldn't make such a mistake. He turns to Alan and sees the disapproving look on his face, which confirms he did say it. He scowls, and Alan buries the disapproving look.

'How long am I supposed to keep him on the line?' Farrukh asks, attempting to move the conversation along.

'I don't fucking know. Just keep him on the line,' Michael says and ends the conversation.

Michael stands and stomps around the room as they wait for Pat to call back with an update, and Alan is surprised Michael isn't using this opportunity to talk about the shipment or the status of the network. Maybe Michael is working on a solution and doesn't want to involve him, Alan thinks. And that's bad, because you don't get made redundant in this job; you get killed. He con-siders broaching the topic, but he doesn't have an update on the network and doesn't want to give away the shipment's location. He needs more time to fix the network, and Michael's distraction with the bracelet will afford him some. But, if it comes to it, the shipment's location will follow him to the grave.

Alan's phone rings, and Michael spins to him. Alan checks

the caller ID, and it's a withheld number. He nods, and Michael rushes over to him before he answers the call.

'Yeah?' Alan says.

'We have him. Docklands,' Pat says.

'Good,' Alan says, and gives a thumbs up to Michael.

Michael grins, and Alan notices the beads of sweat on his forehead. In fact, Michael is sweating profusely. Odd, Alan thinks. But then, Michael has been stomping around the room for approaching ten minutes.

'Obvious problem, though,' Pat says.

'What's that?'

'He's in a block of flats called Cannon House. It's seven floors, lots of flats. No way we can know what flat he's in.'

'Shit, right.'

Michael's grin switches to a worried glare.

'You want me to send a couple officers there?' Pat asks.

'Thanks, but no. You've done more than enough, Pat, we'll handle it from here.'

'Okay, mate.'

'Thanks again.'

'Anytime, AP. But you owe me one. A massive one, too.'

The comment angers Alan, and he has to fight the urge to respond. He ends the call and nods to Michael.

Michael hurries behind the desk and pulls out a silver Colt Anaconda revolver hidden underneath the table. 'Let's go get this fucker!' he says.

'Why the fuck do you have that in here?' Alan chides. 'Put it away.'

'Fuck off! I'm keeping it,' Michael says, and instinctively points the gun at Alan. 'And don't fucking talk to me like that.'

'All right, calm down,' Alan says, and gestures for Michael to lower the gun.

Michael realises he is pointing the gun at Alan and lowers it.

'We won't get there in time,' Alan says. 'And you can't be anywhere near this.'

'Fuck that.'

Alan fights the urge to shake his head. 'You know we can't just kill this guy, right?' he says.

'I know. I want to punish him and then kill him.'

'First, we need to find out who he works for. Then you can kill him.'

'Yes, right.'

'As I said, we won't get there in time, but I know the right people for this. They'll get to him quick, and they'll bring him to us.'

'Who?'

'The Shetty brothers.'

'Those fucking mugs? No, this is too delicate for them.'

Alan knows it is. The Shetty brothers are good enough to grab the man with the bracelet, but nowhere near good enough to get any answers out of him. 'Probably,' he says. 'But they live close enough in Peckham. And for the right price, we can make sure they act appropriately.'

'Okay, but I want Tony in this as well. He lives around there last I knew . . . in Canning Town.'

Alan raises an eyebrow; he strongly dislikes that idea for several reasons. 'The chef . . . Stutter Tony?' he asks.

'Yes, Tony.'

'I know you haven't forgotten what happened last time. Tony can't work with people.'

'I trust Tony. Just make the calls, Alan. And make sure they understand how delicate the situation is.'

'Wait . . .'

'No! That's what I want. Fucking get it done already!'

Alan is furious, but he remains calm. 'Okay,' he says, and nods. 'Do we even know how this geezer looks?'

Michael calls Farrukh and gets a description — a Londoner, black guy, about six feet, in a black jacket and carrying a black duffel bag. The description surprises Alan, because he struggles to comprehend how this black Londoner came to possess the bracelet and why he's attempting to sell it now. But he doesn't believe in coincidences, so this must be connected somehow, and he will find out before the day's over.

Alan calls Stutter Tony, who has an infamously short fuse, especially with people who mock his stutter, and offers double Tony's usual rate up front to deliver the man with the bracelet alive. Tony snatches the offer, as Alan expects, because Alan hasn't sent any work Tony's way since the last job went extraordinarily tits up, and Tony doesn't exactly have a day job. Alan also offers a substantial bonus if Tony tolerates Tariq and Khalid, the Shetty brothers — in other words, a bonus if he doesn't kill them during the job. Alan then calls the Shetty brothers and implores them to follow Tony's lead and not mock or laugh at his stutter.

Alan stands. 'I should head over . . .'

'No,' Michael says. 'You stay till they grab him. I want live updates till the shit is done. Then we head off together.'

'You can't be anywhere near this, Michael.'

'Fucking hell, Alan,' Michael says, and smacks the table. 'I keep telling you this, but you're not listening. Stop telling me what to do.'

'I'm not telling you what to do, Michael; I'm just advising you.'

'Are you fucking kidding me, Alan?' Michael says. 'Advising?'

'I'm just saying . . .'

'I advise you to shut the fuck up. Grab a fucking drink and sit down.'

Alan doesn't respond for a moment, then chuckles, and the defiance angers Michael.

Michael stands, ready for a fight. 'Are you—'

'Relax . . . I was just wondering if you had any red wine in here . . . but then I remembered you're a fucking barbarian.'

Michael laughs and sits. 'Fuck off!' he says, and gestures to the minibar. 'I've got cider in there for you fancy fucks.'

'Fancy? Cider?' Alan questions, amused. 'I guess that'll have to do.'

Alan walks to the minibar to grab a cider, and they drink in silence for almost thirty minutes before Michael demands that Alan get an update. Alan calls Tariq – the older Shetty brother – but he doesn't answer. This worries Alan. He calls Tony, and Tony answers but doesn't speak.

'Tony?' Alan says.

'Yes,' Tony responds.

'Where is Tariq?' Alan asks. 'Why isn't he answering his phone?'

Tony doesn't respond.

'Tony . . .' Alan says with authority.

'Tariq's gone.'

'Gone. What do you mean, "gone"?'

'Gone gone.'

Alan is furious but remains calm. 'And Khalid?'

'Here, searching f-for the brace . . . let!'

'You haven't found it? Isn't the geezer there?'

'Yes. But—'

'Is he alive?'

'Yes. But still can't f-find the bracelet!'

'Okay, Tony, I'm on my way. I'll be there in fifteen minutes. What's the flat number?'

'Six . . . zero . . . four.'

'Okay, thank you. And, Tony, don't kill anybody else until I arrive, okay?'

Tony grunts and ends the call.

'What the fuck happened?' Michael asks.

'What I thought would happen if I wasn't—'

Michael kicks the desk. 'Shut the fuck up with that hindsight nonsense. What happened?'

'Tony killed Tariq . . .'

'Do I look like I give a fuck about those boys? Does he have the geezer?'

'Yeah. But they can't find the bracelet.'

'Are they sure it's the right man?'

'That's what I'm going to check.'

Michael considers if he should go with Alan, but decides not to. 'Call me soon as you get there.'

'Sure,' Alan says, and leaves the room.

'A rare and majestic beast'

Franka turns onto the street where Cannon House is located and notices a Range Rover parked in the middle of the road with its driver-side door wide open.

'Does that concern us?' she asks.

'I don't know,' Alan responds.

As they get closer, they spot a police car parked in front of the building.

'That might concern us,' Alan says.

They drive past and park at the end of the street as the sound of sirens gets closer. Two police cars tear down the street and stop at Cannon House.

'That definitely concerns us,' Alan says.

They watch officers hurry out of their cars into the building.

'Should I go check?' Franka asks.

'No. We'll give it ten minutes, and if Tony or Khalid don't call, I'll call someone who'll know what's going on in there.'

Five minutes pass before Alan's phone rings, and he excitedly checks the caller ID, but it's Michael. He ignores the call, and Franka raises her eyebrows in surprise. She hides a smile because it's high time Alan ignored his brother. Another five minutes pass, and in that time, a couple of ambulances and three more police cars have arrived outside the building.

'They are either all dead or arrested,' Alan says. 'But I'll confirm.'

Franka nods, and Alan makes a call on his burner.

'Hello, A,' the female voice answers.

'Hello, X,' Alan responds. 'Do you know anything about what's happening in Cannon House by Canada Water?'

'No. But hold on.'

Alan holds for a few minutes.

'Four men dead. One has been identified as the husband of the only survivor.'

'What's his name?'

'Jamie Pepper.'

'IC3?' Alan asks, using police radio code for black.

'No.'

'Any of the other deceased IC3?'

'No. Two IC4s and one IC1,' she responds, using the police code for South Asian and white.

'And has the wife made a statement?'

'Not yet. But she made the call. Said the two IC4s and the IC1 tried to rob her and her husband. They're still trying to work out what happened after that. Supposedly, the scene is very graphic. I'll call back when I have more details.'

'Thank you,' Alan says, and ends the call.

He can't make sense of the information. Why would Tony and the Shetty brothers go after this Jamie Pepper when he clearly told them the target was black? But, on the other hand, he can see how things became 'graphic' in the flat. It's what he feared once Tony killed Tariq, because Tony is a man mountain, and Khalid isn't much smaller.

'Let's go,' Alan says. 'This is going to be a long day.'

Franka drives, and Alan calls Michael.

'What's happening?'

'Not sure. But Tony and the Shettys are dead, and this geezer is nowhere to be found.'

'Who the fuck is he?'

'I don't know.'

'Fucking find out, then!'

Alan doesn't respond.

'Find this fucker! Fast!' Michael says, and hangs up.

'I'm hungry,' Alan says to Franka. 'Let's get something to eat.'

Alan and Franka sit by the window in a Japanese restaurant in Fitzrovia. They've finished a sushi lunch, and Alan drinks green tea as he ponders his next move. He needs to find the person with the bracelet to close that chapter, but not at the expense of rebuilding the network. But the more he thinks about it, the more unlikely the coincidence seems – the bracelet turning up could be somebody trying to distract them. Successfully. Measure twice, cut once . . . He needs to confirm it really is Meiling's bracelet, and the description of the man with the bracelet. He needs to see Farrukh.

Alan and Franka approach Farrukh's Gold, an unremarkable jewellery shop on a dead-end street in Marylebone. Alan looks through the glass door – the shop floor is empty. He rings the doorbell, and there is no response for almost a minute. He attempts to ring again, but Franka stops him.

'Something's not right,' she says, and gestures to a half-open hidden door behind the counter.

'Yeah. Not right,' he says.

Alan tries to open the front door, but it's locked, as he expected. He calls Steven.

'Yes, boss,' Steven answers.

'Who handles Sheikh Farrukh's security?'

'One moment, boss,' Steven says, and doesn't speak for a few seconds as he tries to find out. 'Cape Securities – the South Africans.'

'Hmm . . .' Alan mutters. Cape Securities are outstanding. Alan considered hiring them for Michael's personal security, but Michael didn't want outsiders. Cape Securities should already know things are not right here, but then, they aren't here yet. 'Give me their number.'

'I have the number for the head of their London team.'

'Gerrie?'

'Yes.'

'That's what I want. Text it to me,' Alan says, and ends the call. 'Let's head back to the car,' he says to Franka.

Alan calls Gerrie once they're back in the car.

'Hello. Who is this?' Gerrie answers with a strong Afrikaner accent.

'Alan Pierce.'

'Good day, Mr Pierce.'

'Good day, Gerrie. And I remember asking you to call me Alan.'

'I remember that. But it's been almost a year. I didn't want to be presumptuous. Have you reconsidered our offer, Alan?'

'This is about another matter. You handle security for Farrukh's Gold in Marylebone.'

'You know I can't confirm or deny that.'

'I know. I wasn't asking you to. I was stating it as fact. I'm outside the shop right now, and something is not right inside. How does it look on your end?'

'What do you mean something is not right?'

'The hidden door is open, and there is no one on the shop floor.'

Gerrie doesn't speak, because that is certainly not right.

'I'll be expecting you in less than five minutes, as you advertise. I'm in the black Jaguar parked outside,' Alan says, and ends the call.

Four minutes later, Franka gestures to a sturdy man in an expensive suit approaching the Jaguar from behind. Alan recognises Gerrie, and he and Franka step out of the car.

'Hello, Alan,' Gerrie says, and they shake hands.

Gerrie greets Franka with a respectful nod, and she reciprocates.

'I wasn't expecting you to show up personally,' Alan says.

'I was close by. And you're correct. The live feed from the shop is dead on our end, but none of the silent alarms have been pushed,' Gerrie says, and gestures over Alan's shoulder. 'They'll find out what's happening.'

Alan turns to see six sturdy men in expensive suits unlock the shop door and enter in tactical formation. Alan, Franka, and Gerrie watch the entrance, and less than thirty seconds later, one of the men returns to the door and gestures for Gerrie to approach.

'Would you like to join?' Gerrie asks Alan and Franka.

'Thanks,' Alan responds.

Gerrie leads them into the small and uninspiring shop. 'What's the situation, Lieutenant?' he asks the man at the entrance.

'This way, Major,' the lieutenant says with an equally strong Afrikaner accent, and heads through the hidden door into a small hallway. 'That's Mr Javad.' The lieutenant gestures at the dead body of a middle-aged man by a vault-like blast door at the end of the hallway. 'Hasn't been dead for long. Less than an hour. And there are no signs he was forced to open the door.' He stops at Javad's body and points to the two bullet holes in his head. 'Very skilled shooting. Entry points could not be closer together. Same as inside.'

He leads them through the blast door into a vast room filled with lavish jewellery. 'That's Sheikh Farrukh,' he says, and gestures to an elderly man slumped in a chair behind a desk.

Gerrie, Alan and Franka step over to the desk, and see the clean bullet wound in Farrukh's head.

'Skilled shooting, indeed,' Gerrie says. He walks back across the room to receive a report from one of his team, then rejoins Franka and Alan.

'You seem to be taking this well,' Alan says. 'It's going to be bad for your business.'

'A little bad in the short term, I imagine. But ultimately very good, because it's been difficult to get clients to believe the threat is high enough for our comprehensive package.'

'Comprehensive . . . that sounds expensive.'

'Yes. But we don't pull prices from the air. We have models that determine the price for each client. And it is worth it. The comprehensive package is to secure the premises or asset, have eyes on it 24/7, and respond to any threat in less than five minutes – Secure, Monitor, Respond. We offer other packages, where the client picks any two out of the three options, or just one, like Farrukh did. Farrukh went for Respond, which meant we didn't have operatives here to secure the shop and act as a deterrent, and we only monitor the live feed from his cameras when we are alerted. I understand he didn't want us seeing his clients.'

'Your clients will believe the threat after this.'

'Yes. But I'll have to massage the story a little, because whoever did this is a different beast altogether. This beast did not force entry or leave any trace. She must be disarming to convince Javad, who is very cautious, to let her into the shop. And then convince Farrukh, who is even more cautious, to let her in here through the blast doors. She is exceptionally skilled. One shot through the head is all it took for Farrukh, and two shots in an extremely tight grouping did for Javad. No wasted bullets. She is clinical. Javad was already on the floor, probably unconscious, when she shot him. Not greedy — she wasn't interested in any of the shiny merchandise prominently displayed to tempt you to touch and trigger the silent alarm. From what we can tell, she took nothing. Other than what she was here for, because we don't exactly have an inventory.'

'How do you know it's a woman?'

'Oh, we don't know. The cameras' central unit is destroyed, the backup drive is gone, and we only get the live feed on our end. Can't rewind. But this is a rare and majestic beast, so the female pronoun is fitting.'

Alan nods, and Franka hides a smile.

'It could also be two people. At most. Because that's the maximum Farrukh will let in here.'

'But that's less majestic?'

'Not at all. Two people are naturally more threatening . . . so it'll take much more to convince Javad and Farrukh. Are both exceptionally skilled and clinical? Neither was greedy? Neither left a trace? You understand.'

'I do,' Alan says, and scans the room. 'So, what happens now?'

'We'll take care of it. There are arrangements in place.'

'You guys have everything covered.'

'We do our best,' Gerrie says, and glances at Franka before he speaks. 'I have to ask, Alan. What were you doing here?'

'You think we did this?'

'No,' Gerrie responds, and gestures at Franka. 'Although I know your associate is a rare and majestic beast.'

Franka cracks a smile, and this makes Alan happy.

'I wanted to speak to him about something.'

Gerrie nods and remains silent, allowing for Alan to fill the silence with more information. But Alan doesn't take the bait and enjoys the silence. He knows precisely what Gerrie is doing, because he employed the tactic a lot as an investigator and more than a few times since. Gerrie ought to know better.

'Seems someone got to him first,' Gerrie says, breaking the silence.

'Seems so.'

'Let me walk you out so the men can get to work.'

Gerrie accompanies Alan and Franka to their car. Alan is surprised Gerrie, the consummate salesman, hasn't offered the services of Cape Securities to deal with his current predicament. Alan is sure Gerrie knows all about it; Gerrie endeavours to know where the danger is, because that's where the money is for Cape Securities.

'Can I ask you something, Gerrie?'

'Of course. The issue is whether or not I answer.'

Alan nods. 'You know what's happening with us, don't you?'

'Yes.'

'Why haven't you offered your services? You were very keen three years ago.'

Gerrie doesn't respond.

'You've been asked to sit this one out?'

Again, Gerrie doesn't respond, and he and Alan stare at each other, waiting for the other to break the silence.

'I can't confirm or deny that,' Gerrie says.

Alan nods and steps into the car, and Franka drives. Alan takes a deep breath – the Lenkovs are so many moves ahead of them. He needs help. He needs a master strategist with a formidable reputation who thrives in adversity . . . a rare and majestic beast. Where the fuck is Pretty Boy?

'That's a problem, isn't it?'

Franka is driving through Clapham towards Alan's home when Alan gets the phone call he's been expecting.

'Hello, X,' he answers.

'Hello, A,' the female voice responds. 'The wife is making a statement as we speak, but that's not what has perked up the investigating officers. It's who she is – Rebecca Pepper, maiden name Reynolds. Damian Reynolds Junior's daughter . . . Israel Reynolds's niece.'

The Reynolds family, led by Damian Reynolds Snr, built one of the first yardie gangs in London. Their influence has waned over the years, especially when the clear leader of the next generation of Reynolds, Damian Reynolds Jnr, died in a car accident at twenty-three years old, a few years after Damian Snr died of cancer. Israel has kept the fire burning as much as he can, concentrating their territory to a collection of tower blocks in the same council estate in Hackney. Israel is well respected, but more for his diplomacy than his viciousness. So much so that when Jamal was gunning through his opposition on his inevitable path to taking over the drug trade in Hackney and the surrounding areas, Israel and Jamal struck a deal for Israel to keep control of the tower blocks but buy product exclusively from Jamal.

'I didn't know Damian had a daughter,' Alan says.

'Neither did we. But it's not exactly a secret; she's just never showed up on our radar. Until now.'

'How's she holding up?'

'That's the thing. Like a normal citizen who just witnessed her husband's death.'

'So, you don't think she's involved?'

'Not sure. Could be a coincidence, but . . .'

'We don't believe in coincidences.'

'Exactly. We'll know more after her statement. Especially after we corroborate it with the other surviving victim's statement.'

'There was someone else in there?'

'Not exactly. Ahmed Khan, the concierge of the building. We found him unconscious in a storage cupboard behind the reception desk with several fingers chopped off. He's not stable enough to make a statement yet, but the officers think it'll happen soon.'

'Rebecca doesn't know of this surviving witness, I suppose?'

'No. The SIO is very good. DCI Neera Whitaker . . . you might know her by her maiden name, Shah.'

'I know Neera. Straight arrow, though. No lever to pull there if I need a favour.'

'Don't worry about that. Leave it to me.'

'Thanks, X. And about the car parked in the middle of the road outside the building?'

There is a pause in conversation as X looks through the information in her possession. Franka parks in Alan's space in his building's garage, but she and Alan remain in the car.

'Don't have anything about that yet,' the female voice says. 'You think it's related?'

'No coincidences and all that.'

'True. I'll find out.'

The call ends, but before Alan and Franka step out of the car, Alan's burner rings. It's Steven.

'Everything okay, Steven?' Alan answers.

'Kilburn is dead,' Steven says.

'What? How?' Alan asks.

'Someone stormed the Fortress—'

'What?' Alan interrupts. 'Stormed the Fortress?'

That shocks Alan even more, because Tyrone's base in Kilburn is known as the Fortress for a reason. The entire street is a no-go area without an invitation, even for members of the collective. The Met have even warned their officers not to approach the area.

'That's what I'm hearing, boss.'

'Someone . . . so not the police?'

'Not the police. And no one knows who right now.'

Alan ponders. Could it be Jamal? His aggressive expansion

was curtailed by his membership in the collective, and he and Tyrone were very close. Alan knows there are no real friends in this game, though, just people that share a common interest . . . for however long that lasts, and the collective is on its last legs. But if it was Jamal, he'd make sure everyone knew it was him soon as it was done. Could it be Priyanka? It seems too aggressive for her, and her beef is with Jamal, but as Hardeep said, Alan really doesn't know her. Alan's personal phone rings, and it's his friend calling back.

'Find out and call me back,' he says to Steven. He ends the call on his burner and answers his personal phone. 'Hello, X.'

'Hello, A,' the female voice responds. 'Rebecca has made her statement, and the SIO doesn't believe the team has anything to hold her on.'

'The SIO believes the statement?'

'She doesn't have a reason not to. It's comprehensive, consistent with her 999 call, what she said to the first officers on the scene, and the evidence gathered at the scene so far. These three men burst through the door posing as a pizza delivery, and knock her out. A fight in the living room wakes her, and she finds herself tied up in her bedroom with one of the men dead by her feet. Her room has been ransacked. She struggles to untie herself, and the fight is over by the time she manages it. So, she locks herself in the bedroom and calls us. She only came out of the room when the first officers arrived. That's when she saw her husband dead in the living room, which had also been ransacked. She doesn't know when her husband returned from work or why . . . because she didn't call him.

She also has no idea what the men were looking for. As far as she knows, her husband doesn't keep cash at home and has no criminal involvement. We checked; he doesn't.'

'It is comprehensive. But not true.'

'Is there something you should be telling me? Are you involved?'

'Yes.'

'Talk.'

'Still ongoing. And it's delicate, so I can't say much right now. But we sent those men in with clear instructions.'

'Why use them? All three have long criminal records that signal they don't follow instructions . . . regardless of clarity.'

'They do when I'm involved.'

'Not today.'

'Seems so. But Rebecca is lying. Which station is she in, and when is she being released?'

'She's not being *released*. We never held her. She's given her statement voluntarily and is simply waiting for an officer to return to the station with some of her belongings, because her home is being closed off as a crime scene for the foreseeable. Why are you asking?'

'I need to talk to her urgently.'

There is silence on the line.

'I know she's not going home because it's a murder scene,' Alan continues. 'And if she's smart, and so far all signs point in that direction, she'll be going somewhere very public, where no one can come for her without being spotted a mile off. I need to see her before she gets there.'

X still doesn't respond.

'I will not lay a finger on her. Just let her know who she is dealing with, and I'm sure that'll make her tell the truth, either to me or the investigating team. Either way, a win for you. Because if she tells me, I'll handle what needs handling quickly and delicately, and pass the necessary information to you for the investigating team to close the murders before the end of the night.'

'Grundy Street police station.'

'Thank you,' he says, and mutes the call. 'Limehouse,' he says to Franka, and she drives. He returns to the call and unmutes it. 'Have you heard what happened to Tyrone Cousins?'

There is silence for almost a minute, but Alan knows his friend is finding out.

'What the fuck is happening?' she demands. 'He's one of yours. Did you have anything to do with this?'

'No. We—'

'Because this only continues to be mutually beneficial if you hold up your end of the bargain,' she asserts. 'And from what I'm reading, it's a massacre. More than a dozen dead, including Mr Cousins. That's almost twenty bodies already today. This is not keeping crime down. The stakeholders on my end will be very unhappy.'

'I understand. We had nothing to do with it.'

'And you don't know who did.'

'Not yet.'

'That's a problem, isn't it? How are you supposed to keep the crime under control if you don't know who's doing it?'

'How am I supposed to do that if you don't let me know that people capable of such a massacre are in our town? I rely on your intelligence. And last I checked, I have the most violent and capable criminal gangs, according to your intelligence, already in my collective. None of them did this.'

There is silence.

'That's true,' she says.

'And we haven't addressed the elephant in the room,' Alan says. 'The Lenkovs.'

'The Lenkovs didn't do this.'

'But you know what they are doing?'

'That doesn't concern us.'

'How's that? If they keep pushing, there will be bodies dropping across the town.'

'That will mean you failed to hold up your end of the bargain. And you'll have more to worry about than the Lenkovs.'

'Wh—'

'Stop digging,' she interrupts. 'The Lenkovs aren't a new threat. I warned you about them years ago. There was an obvious solution then, and I'm sure that remains the solution today.'

What obvious solution? Alan thinks. But he can't ask because it'll force her to question the man she believes he is – the man he portrays himself to be – one that can spot an obvious solution in his sleep.

'Can I get pictures from the scene in Kilburn?' he asks.

'Sure,' she responds. 'I'll send you Rebecca's statement too. And call me when you're close to Grundy Street.'

DAY 16, 21:00

'You see the lass?'

A minute out from Grundy Street station, Alan's phone rings again. It's X.

'Hello, X,' he answers.

'Hello, A,' she responds. 'Where are you?'

'Close. A minute away.'

'Okay. Rebecca has left the station, but she's been driven by an officer, so I've arranged for the officer to drop her off in a quiet side street. PC Shannon is an exemplary young officer, so although we left her no choice but to comply, I'm sure she struggled with the decision. Don't make her regret it.'

'I won't.'

X tells him the name of the side street and ends the call. Alan passes the location to Franka and manoeuvres into the back seat.

Minutes later, Franka turns into the side street, and she and

Alan spot a young woman dressed in an oversized jumper and tracksuit bottoms on the pavement. The clothes are police issue – provided after taking her clothes for forensic testing. It must be Rebecca, and to Alan's surprise, she is unusually calm as she watches the car approach. Alan already knows she's going to be tough.

Franka parks beside her, and Alan is struck by how stunning Rebecca is, even in the oversized clothes. He opens the back door, and Rebecca climbs in to sit beside him without hesitation. She shuts the door, and Franka locks it, but Rebecca still doesn't flinch.

'Hello, Rebecca Pepper,' Alan says. 'Forgive me, but I'll get straight to it because I've got somewhere to be. I read your statement. It's bloody good. Very believable and covers all the bases, really. But someone is missing from it. I need to know who he is and how to find him.'

'I don't know what the fuck you're talking about,' Rebecca says.

'Okay. I'll give you this to consider. Ahmed Khan, your building's concierge . . . I hear he's getting better rather quickly, and he'll be ready to make a statement soon. What do you think is going to happen to you when the police find out your version of events is very different from his? And that you just forgot to mention this mysterious man in a leather jacket?'

'You sent those fuckers, didn't you?'

Alan doesn't respond, and she stares, stoic.

'I can help you with Ahmed,' he says. 'I just need you to call your friend.'

'Sure,' Rebecca says, and points the sharp end of a headless electric toothbrush at Alan's neck.

Rebecca's speed surprises Alan, but he remains calm, and Franka doesn't even react because she's been pointing a pistol at Rebecca through her seat.

'Franka, don't shoot,' Alan says, and Franka nods. He turns to Rebecca. 'Put that away. You're not going to hurt me, and I don't intend to hurt you. Not here. Not now. Because then I'd have to hurt the righteous PC Shannon. That'd be disappointing . . . and foolish. And I don't do foolish. Unless I'm forced to.'

'I know you're not going to do shit to me,' Rebecca says, and pulls the toothbrush away. 'I know who you are. I know your mob. But you don't know me. I just wanted to give you a quick taste. So you know who you're dealing with. And that I don't scare easy. Then we can have a proper conversation.'

'Fair.'

'Your mysterious man is no friend of mine. He got my husband killed for whatever shit you guys are into. And I don't have his number . . .'

'That's okay. I do.'

'Good for you. But I'm not sure he'll be eager to speak to me. I promised him I'll kill him the next time I see him. That's why his name is not in my statement. He's mine to deal with. Which brings me to you and your mob . . . stay the fuck out of my way.'

Alan laughs. He nods at Franka, and Franka unlocks the doors. 'Okay, Rebecca,' he says. 'Enjoy your hunt.'

Franka drives, and Alan watches Rebecca through the rear-view mirror until they turn into the next street.

'I like her,' Franka says.

Alan looks at Franka in the rear-view mirror, and she's smiling. He smiles as well because Franka's smile is warming.

'I like her too,' Alan says, and manoeuvres back to the passenger seat. 'But she's going to be trouble.'

Franka nods in agreement.

Alan is about to speak, but he receives a blank text from Forest Gate on his personal phone. Alan won't be ignoring Hardeep anymore, after Hardeep tried to alert him about the cards the collective members received after getting their deliveries burnt. Alan calls him straight away.

'You heard about Tyrone?' Hardeep asks, excited.

'Yeah,' he answers.

'It's Pretty Boy!'

'Pretty Boy? What? How do you know this?'

'Tyrone had a few girls in the Fortress today working on new product. None of them was touched during the attack, and one of them, who's actually one of Priyanka's girls, said she heard Tyrone say the man who brought the product earlier in the day was Pretty Boy. She saw the same man leaving after the attack.'

Alan's excitement fades. The story has all the beats of previous instances attributed to Pretty Boy – a righteous kill of someone or some group previously thought untouchable with no 'civilians' harmed, even those who supposedly witnessed the killings. But in all those instances, it wasn't Pretty

Boy. Some were police raids, some were even set up by Alan, and the others were just gangland killings where the killers were happy to use Pretty Boy as cover. Pretty Boy's reputation has grown with each of these incidents, and today he's regarded as the bogeyman of the London underworld . . . all in his absence.

'Did you get a description of Pretty Boy?' Alan asks.

'Oh . . . no. Haven't spoken to the girl directly. Just you said I should call if I heard any news on Pretty Boy.'

'I know. And thanks. But this is third-hand, then?'

'What?' Hardeep asks, not understanding what third-hand means in the context.

'Who did you hear this from?'

'Priyanka. She spoke to the girl. I don't even know who the girl is.'

'Can you get a description?'

'I can try.'

'Thanks, H.'

'No problem.'

Alan ends the call and calls Steven straight away.

'Yes, boss,' Steven answers.

'I'm hearing this is Pretty Boy. Is that what you're hearing?'

'Err . . .' Steven hesitates. 'Yes, but I was trying to confirm because there have been a lot of false alarms.'

'I understand. What have you heard so far?'

'Some of Noriega's runners—'

'How old?'

'The runners?' Steven asks, and realises it's obviously the

runners Alan is asking about, so quickly answers. 'Twelve, thirteen years old, I think.'

Alan sighs. He's tried to convince the collective members to stop using minors to sell the product, and most listened . . . apart from Tyrone. It was all business for Tyrone, and kids cost less, especially the young ones. And Noriega, Tyrone's cousin, was the worst culprit. Although, to be fair to Noriega, he's been selling for Tyrone since he was eleven, so it's probably normal to him.

'Go on,' Alan says.

'A few of the runners said Noriega was bragging about driving Pretty Boy to the Fortress to see Tyrone this morning. Noriega even took a detour just to bring the so-called Pretty Boy to the crack house he and the kids work out of. To show off, I guess. But the man came back later and left with Noriega in Noriega's car. And from what I'm hearing, Noriega is dead in the car, parked right in front of the Fortress.'

'Description?'

'That's the problem. It's all over the place. Some of the kids are lying . . . just want to be involved, you know . . . say they saw "Pretty Boy". It's hard to know who actually saw this man. They all say he's black, though.'

Alan takes a deep breath. Both Hardeep's and Steven's sources can be considered unreliable, but they are two distinct sources. More than enough to launch an investigation back in his copper days. Plus, it's Pretty Boy's birthday today, and he always had an oddly dark sense of humour. Alan wouldn't be surprised if Pretty Boy saw no better way to celebrate his birthday than executing an impossible mission or dying in the attempt. However, Alan can't think of a motive, and Pretty Boy always has cause.

'Keep working on it,' Alan says. 'And try talking to the girls Tyrone had working on product at the Fortress today. I hear they weren't harmed.'

'That's what I'm hearing. Might take a while to find them, though. Because they all scattered after the attack and are trying to stay hidden to avoid the police.'

'I . . .' Alan hesitates because his personal phone pings repeatedly with texts of pictures from the Kilburn attack. 'I trust you'll find them.'

Alan ends the call and studies the pictures. It's a massacre. Tyrone has been ripped apart by what looks like a shotgun blast. He scrolls through the pictures to one of Noriega, and it's exactly as Steven heard it. Dead in his car with . . .

'Down!' Franka screams.

Alan ducks, and Franka speeds up to avoid a van that bursts out of an adjacent street towards the passenger side of the Jaguar, but the van still clips the rear of the car. The car veers violently, and Alan smashes into the door, but Franka deftly corrects the car's motion and evades a Ford Focus that screeches to a halt right in front of them. She applies the brake and turns the wheel, so the driver's side faces the van and the Ford Focus. And even before the car stops, she fires a shot that pierces through the windscreen of the Ford Focus and hits the driver in the neck. She fires another shot that hits the passenger in the crown of his head as he attempts to duck.

'Stay down,' Franka commands, and leaps out of the car.

A man hurries out of the back seat of the Ford and hides behind the door. But before he aims his assault rifle at Franka, she shoots him in the ankle and he falls, exposing his head, and she shoots his head.

She darts to the pavement as two men jump out of the back of the van with assault rifles. She shoots the younger one through the knees, and he collapses. The older man quickly aims in her direction, but she's not there. He frantically searches for her as his associate clutches his knee and screams.

'Shut up,' the older man commands with a Scouse accent, and leans against the van. 'Chunkz, you see the lass?' he asks the driver.

Chunkz is hiding in the footwell and doesn't respond, but even if he had, the second man wouldn't be able to hear him over his associate's screams. The older man considers advancing, and peeks towards the Ford Focus. He sees the others are dead and curses underneath his breath. He's not going to die in fucking London, he thinks. He tries to pull open the driver's door, but it's locked. He turns to jump into the back of the van, and he's face to face with Franka. Before he can react, she shoots him through the forehead, and he collapses beside his companion, whose throat has been slit open.

Franka knocks on the driver's door, but Chunkz doesn't respond. She uses the reflection from a parked car to look into the front cabin of the van and sees a chunky man hiding in the footwell. She uses the reflection to aim and shoots the man twice in the back of the head. She reloads her pistol and checks the back of the van, but it's empty. She approaches the Ford Focus, and the three occupants are dead. She puts her gun away and walks to Alan's car.

'It's over,' she says.

Alan raises his head. One side of his face is bruised from the impact with the door, and his right arm is hanging awkwardly. His shoulder hurts like hell. He looks around and recognises the desolate street but knows it's not on the route home, which confuses him.

'They'd been following us since we got to yours earlier. At first, I thought it was the police, but they were awful at following us, so I knew it wasn't. They'd almost made their move a couple of times, so I led them here. A quiet place to handle it.'

'Why didn't you tell me?'

'They would've known. They were watching.'

Alan understands her thought process, but he still would've liked to know, so he could've been prepared. 'Okay,' he says. 'But tell me next time.'

She nods. There will be a next time, she's sure of it. And she will do the same thing again if that's what's required to keep him alive. 'You should quickly check if you recognise any of them,' she says. 'A lot of noise; someone would've called the police.'

Alan tries to open the door, but his right shoulder is too painful.

'Need help?' she asks. 'Your shoulder's dislocated.'

'I know. I'm fine. Lucky I'm a lefty,' Alan says, and opens the door with his left hand.

Alan cradles his left arm and hurries to check the faces, as Franka rummages through their pockets for their phones. Alan doesn't recognise any of them, and they head back to the car.

Franka drives and gives Alan the phones.

'That one first,' she says, and gestures to the older man's phone. 'He was their leader.'

'Okay,' Alan says, and picks up the older man's phone. 'We need to go see someone about my arm, though.'

'How bad is it?'

'I don't know; that's why I need to see someone.'

'I'll check when we get to your home. If not broken, I can help.'

Alan nods and looks through the phone. There are several outgoing and incoming calls, all from today, with most of them occurring in quick succession during the evening. He checks the inbox, and there are two text messages. The first is in a code he can't decipher, but the second message reads:

You already accepted the job. Can't pull out now. M won't be happy.

'"M",' Alan reads, and shifts in his seat. He quickly checks the sent items, and there are two text messages. The first text reads:

Just seen target. You didn't tell me it was him.

The second text reads:

I'm not pulling out. Just need to hear from M direct. Need to make sure M giving the go-ahead on this. Need assurance will be no regrets or second thoughts that lead to problems for my people.

Alan quickly scrolls to the call log to see if there was a call from the number in the texts. There is. It's the first call, hours before any of the back-and-forth calls in the evening. He types the number into his burner phone and calls. It's Gary's burner.

DAY 16, 23:00

The heightening sounds of approaching sirens wake me. I open my eyes, and I'm on the ground, surrounded by burning pieces of Lucas's car. I look ahead to what's left of the car, and it isn't much; the explosion has obliterated it. Lucas is dead. But at what cost?

I try to stand, but I can't feel my legs. I try to push off the ground, but I can't feel my hands either. I try to look at my arms, but I can't feel my neck. Fuck, I can't feel anything. I close my eyes and concentrate on moving my fingers and toes, but the sirens are distracting. I scream as panic overwhelms me, and adrenaline charges through my body. I feel my limbs.

I leap to my feet and attempt to run, but my legs are unsteady, and every step is excruciating. I power through the pain and limp as fast as I can away from the flashing lights . . .

'Some of us have families'

Alan sits by his kitchen counter, holding a pack of peas up to his face and watching Franka wrap a sling around his right arm. He's impressed by how quickly she diagnosed his dislocated shoulder, pushed it back into the socket, and prepared the sling from a comprehensive first aid kit she'd stored in his kitchen months earlier. He had no idea the first aid kit was in his home, which makes him wonder what other things Franka has kept in the flat in case of an emergency.

But Alan doesn't dwell on the thought too long because he's still stunned that Michael put out a contract on his life. He shouldn't be too surprised, he tells himself, because Michael is infamously ruthless and had told Alan in no uncertain terms to fix the network or face the consequences. Michael gave him a week to fix it, but Alan surmises that his delay in providing the shipment's details or any worthwhile progress has led Michael to lose faith in him.

When Alan left the police, he knew the only way to survive and thrive in Michael's organisation was to make himself indispensable. He saw the opportunity to build the delivery network and ran with it, putting every fibre of his being into making it a success. And it was exceptionally financially successful — bringing in more money each year than Michael had made in the decade before the network. This made Alan believe he'd become too important to kill, because he was at the centre of every strand of the network, and without him, it would crumble. But money isn't what drives people like Michael. It's power. And Alan's growing importance must've been encroaching on Michael's power. It's obvious in hindsight. Michael is the only other one that knew all the information the Lenkovs used to destroy the network. But Alan stupidly discounted Michael as the inside man, because he thought no one would willingly lose that amount of money. Alan couldn't see the motive, but Callum, Jamal and Tyrone could. Because they would've done the same thing. Taken out the contender before he became a genuine contender. It's a cruel pursuit; you have to be ruthless to get to the top, and even more ruthless to stay there.

Alan considers his next move. He can run, but he wouldn't get far. He could fight, but Franka can't take out all comers, although he knows she'll die trying. He'll need men loyal to him, but no one in the organisation except Steven will back him against Michael, which is partly his fault because he kept his circle very close and sometimes couldn't hide his disdain at their criminal actions. Just as much as they couldn't hide their disdain for his past as a decorated police officer. Alan could've still paid for their loyalty, as fleeting as that would be, but that option vanished when the network did. Cape Securities and the few other elite private security firms working in the space would've been ideal as well, but he's sure they've also been told to stay out of it.

'Done,' Franka says. 'How does it feel?'

Alan shrugs, and Franka can tell he is disheartened. She's also been thinking about the attack, but she sees one more option – delay. They have the attackers' phones and can communicate delays with Gary, giving Alan a few days to rebuild the network or consider his next move carefully. She's been waiting for Alan to see the option, but she can't wait any longer.

'We have their phones,' she says.

Alan smiles, understanding exactly what she means. He grabs the older man's phone and reads the previous texts to Gary. He composes a text:

Close, but no chance today. On tomorrow.

He takes a moment to read the text, then edits it.

No chance today. Tomorrow.

He shows Franka the text, and she nods. He sends it, and a moment later, Gary responds:

Okay. Keep us posted.

The quick response excites Alan and Franka, but fury soon buries Alan's excitement. Keep *us* posted! Fucking cunts, he thinks. Whatever happens over the next few days, he's going to make sure Gary and Dre take their last breaths.

'You can go home,' Alan says.

'No,' Franka says. 'I'll sleep on the couch.'

Alan wants to object, but she glares at him. 'Okay, sure,' he says. 'Don't want to make an enemy out of you as well. Because you evidently don't miss.'

She smiles. 'And you won't see me coming.'

Alan laughs. 'You've spoken more today than you've ever done. You come out of your shell when the battle rages.'

'My English is just getting better.'

'I should expect you to be a chatterbox by next month, then. Unless that's only reserved for Meiling?'

She forces a smile because she knows there is much more to the question – he's questioning her ultimate loyalty.

Alan is about to prod further, but his personal phone rings. It's Michael. Like clockwork, he must've heard the hit isn't happening tonight. He answers.

'What the fuck, Alan?' Michael barks. 'You haven't found this geezer?'

Alan bites his tongue because he now understands why Michael was rushing him all day to find whoever tried to sell the bracelet. Michael wanted to exhaust all of Alan's connections and resources before he died. Now he knows he has at least one more night to push, so he is pushing.

'Alan?' Michael barks. 'Are you fucking ignoring me?'

'No,' Alan says. 'I haven't found the geezer.'

'What the fuck have you been doing all day?' Michael barks. 'And you haven't passed the shipment to Gary either. Has that turned to shit too?'

The question puts Alan on the back foot, and he doesn't respond.

'You're all fucking finished, aren't you?' Michael teases, and chuckles. 'I'll get Dave to give you a call. It's about time . . .'

'Calm down,' Alan asserts.

'Calm—?'

'I was waiting to hear from the copper from earlier today. He's tracking the phone, but it takes longer when the phone's not on a call.'

'Oh,' Michael says, excited. 'And?'

'He's just messaged me. I'll call him back, and—'

'I'm coming this time. None of that bullshit from earlier.'

A thought strikes Alan, and he smirks. 'Very well,' he says, speaking his mind.

'What? Who the fuck are you talking to? I've fucking warned you . . .'

'Sorry. I'm sorry, Michael.'

'No, I'm sorry. I let you get too big for your boots. But we'll handle this later. Just call your copper friend and call me back with the fucking location.'

Michael ends the call, and Alan smirks again.

'Everything okay?' Franka asks.

'I think I know what to do. And I'm going to need your help.'

She nods.

'But I need to make this call first.'

He swaps the SIM on his personal phone to a new one he picks from underneath a loose-leaf tea tin. He calls Pat, and it goes straight to voicemail, as he expects.

'It's AP,' Alan says. 'Call me back on this number soon as

you can. It'll be live all night, and I'll call back every five minutes until you do.'

Alan and Franka wait, and as it approaches five minutes, Pat calls back.

'Hello, Pat,' Alan answers.

'What is this, AP?' Pat asks, angry. 'Some of us have families.'

'I'd apologise, Pat. But you'd see right through that.'

Pat chuckles as the comment softens him. 'What do you want?'

'I know you're tracking the phone number from earlier.'

'I'm not.'

'You are, Pat. That's the reason you left the Met for MI5. You're a natural snoop.'

'Should I be offended by that?'

'No. It's actually a compliment. You know what you're good at, and you found your path.'

'You're sweet-talking me. That's not good.'

'It depends.'

'On what?'

'If you're keen or not.'

'Okay. What do you want?'

'I need the location of the phone,' Alan says. 'And please don't say you aren't tracking it.'

'What I did for you earlier was a big risk. This is an enormous risk.'

'But there is a reason you're still tracking the number. You were expecting this call.'

'Yes. Earlier, when I saw the phone leave the block of flats. And maybe sometime afterwards . . . during work hours. But this is almost midnight. I'm at home.'

'Being at home doesn't change anything for you, Pat. I know you have access from home.'

'But I'll need to explain why I'm accessing from home at near midnight.'

Alan bites his tongue. He knows Pat is looking at the track as they speak. 'I'll make it worth your while.'

'What's that mean? Are you going to talk numbers?'

'I'm not. But you can. What do you want?'

'What do I want?'

'Yes, Pat,' Alan says, burying his frustration.

'I don't know . . . you make an offer, and we can negotiate.'

'I won't negotiate. Say your number, and the answer is yes.'

Pat squirms, unsure how to respond. 'Err . . . 75K?'

The modest number shocks Alan. 'Sure, 75K. It'll be in the regular account by the morning.'

'Okay,' Pat says. 'I'll send you a link that opens to a secured browser with the active track. Soon as you're done, you destroy the SIM and the phone. I mean crush it, then burn it, then crush the ashes again, and toss it far away from anywhere you regularly visit.'

'I will.'

'And don't call me for at least six months.'

Alan is sure that has nothing to do with ensuring this doesn't get traced back to them. 'Sure.'

'Okay,' Pat says, and pauses for a moment. 'You have a problem, though.'

'What's that?'

'The phone is on the move. And it's very fast.'

'In a car?'

'Doesn't seem like it. But that's your problem now,' Pat says, and ends the call.

Alan's phone pings with a text the moment the call is over. He clicks the link in the text, and a browser opens to a blinking blue dot on a very detailed map. As Pat described, the dot is moving very fast through the map, and Alan expands the scale to see that the blue is outside London, and heading further out. Alan contemplates his next move, and his left hand trembles. He clenches it into a fist and wraps his right hand around it, hoping to stop the trembling, but it doesn't. He looks at Franka and doesn't need to say a word before she nods to reassure him, and the trembling stops. He grabs his burner and calls Michael.

'Who's this?' Gary answers.

'It's Alan,' Alan responds. 'Give Michael the phone.'

'Why are you calling with—'

'Give Michael the phone.'

'Yeah?' Michael says.

'We have the track.'

'Fucking right, you do.'

'It's on the move. Fast. Heading out of town.'

'I thought Farrukh said the geezer was a local?' Michael says. 'I'll kill the fucker first thing tomorrow.'

Someone has beat you to it, Alan thinks. 'We could wait till the guy stops or follow him,' he says. 'What do you want to do?'

'We're ready on this end, so we move soon as you get here. We're at the warehouse in Wembley.'

'I'll be there in fifty minutes.'

'Good. But call Kenji before you leave. I put him on standby after your fuck-up earlier today, cos we're not playing around anymore. First, you apologise to the old man for the delay . . . a proper one, too. Then tell him to meet us in the warehouse, and that transport's sorted.'

Kenji is the leader of what can only be described as a troop of supremely skilled modern-day ninjas. Kenji and his troop are mercenaries of the highest order. But they only work twice a year at most, because of their price, Kenji's mercurial nature, and the fact that although you'll never see them coming and won't hear it happen, everyone, including the police, knows it's them once the job is done because of the unmistakable katana wounds. Alan is shocked Michael would get Kenji involved in this. For several reasons, but mainly the cost for such a relatively unremarkable matter – one geezer stupid enough to attempt to sell Meiling's bracelet to Farrukh.

'Sure,' Alan says.

'And bring Franka,' Michael says, and ends the call.

Michael specifically asking for Franka to be involved surprises Alan. Michael is either looking to make a statement tonight, or he's one step ahead. Fuck it.

'They're in the Wembley warehouse. But we can't drive the Jag there because people might ask questions about the dent. It's too late . . .'

Franka raises her motorcycle helmet. 'I have another one in the boot of the car.'

Alan smiles. 'What about this?' he asks, and gestures to his arm in a sling.

'You'll be fine,' she says. 'I'm a careful driver.'

'Okay, then,' he says, and nods. 'Need to make a call first.'

DAY 17, 01:00

'It all got too much for you, didn't it?'

Franka speeds through Wembley on her sports bike, and Alan is behind her with his right arm wrapped around her waist. She drives into a derelict industrial park and slows as they approach the warehouse, which appears empty from the outside. Alan steps off the bike and rings the buzzer, and a few moments later, an electric garage door slides open just enough for the bike to fit in.

Franka drives into the warehouse and parks by the door. Alan walks in after her and is stunned by how busy the vast warehouse is. It looks like a military base.

'You okay, Alan?' the young man tasked with operating the garage door asks.

'Sorry?' Alan responds, and glares at the man.

'Your arm,' the young man responds.

'Oh,' Alan says. 'I'm okay. Thanks for asking.'

'No problem,' the young man says. He hands Franka a car key and gestures to three black BMW X5s with tinted windows. 'The boss said I should give this to you; the one in front is yours.'

Franka nods.

'He wants to see you,' the young man says to Alan, and takes a moment to gather himself. 'But not her.'

Alan glances at Franka, and she nods. 'Where is he?' Alan asks.

'The red door on the other side,' the young man says.

Alan nods and walks through the warehouse. It's filled with excited young men, and he fights to hide his disdain for their pointless excitement. He knocks on the red door once and steps into what appears to be a war room. Michael sits at the head of a desk in the middle of the room, surrounded by Gary, Dre, and Dave.

'What the fuck happened to your arm?' Dre asks. 'Were you trying to bench-press or something?'

Dre sniggers at his own joke, and the others sat around the table laugh as well.

'Yeah,' Alan responds, deadpan. 'Slipped off my wrist and hit my face.'

'What?' Dre asks, surprised. 'Seriously?'

Alan nods.

Dre glances at the others across the table, and they are laughing at him now. 'Fuck off,' he says, and acts like he never believed Alan.

'What happened?' Michael asks.

'Went for a run to clear my head; got hit by a bicycle.'

As Alan expected, the men at the table laugh with a hefty dose of derision.

'What happened to the other guy?' Gary asks.

'Nothing. Wasn't his fault.'

Michael shakes his head with contempt, and the others laugh.

'Anyway,' Alan says, and gestures at all the activity in the warehouse. 'What's this all about?'

'Someone's making moves,' Michael responds. 'Took out your man, Tyrone.'

'With extreme prejudice,' Gary adds.

'Exactly,' Michael continues. 'So, we're on a war footing.'

Alan nods. He considers telling them that Tyrone's death is to their benefit because Tyrone and Jamal were leading the effort to take over the network. But despite all the Pretty Boy theories, Alan doesn't know who did the killings, so it'll come across as conjecture. And Michael couldn't care less about the network. He destroyed it to get to the situation he wanted all long – chaos. It's where he shows his worth, how he reasserts his power. Michael hasn't looked more in his element in years.

'When was I going to be told about this?'

There is a knock on the door before Michael responds, and a young woman sticks her head in.

'Kenji's here, boss,' she says.

'Put them in the cars like we spoke about,' Michael responds. 'We'll be out in a minute.'

'Okay, boss,' she responds, and shuts the door.

'Anyway,' Michael says to Alan. 'Battle isn't really your

thing. More the network and all that. Speaking of . . .' Michael smacks Dave in the back. 'Dave's off the bench. He'll call you tomorrow morning, and you'll introduce him to the Colombians and Italians.'

Alan glances at Dave, and Dave smirks – Dave's been waiting for this moment since he got out of prison two years ago.

'Don't worry,' Dave says. 'You're not being put on the bench. You'll help me set up the new network.'

'No problem,' Alan says, deadpan.

'It all got too much for you, didn't it?' Michael asks. 'My fault.'

Alan nods and glances at the other men. They're all enjoying the moment.

'We shouldn't keep Kenji waiting,' Alan says.

'True,' Michael says. 'Can I see the track?'

Alan pulls out his phone, which has the browser with the track open, and slides it across the table to Michael.

Michael studies the browser. 'The geezer is moving fast,' he says.

'On a train, most likely,' Alan says.

'I thought this geezer was a Londoner?'

Alan shrugs.

'Fuck it.' Michael shrugs too, and slides the phone back to Alan. 'You're in the lead car, so we're following your direction. Don't fuck it up.'

'Again,' Dre adds, and sniggers.

Michael glares at Dre, and Dre stops sniggering.

'Take care of the boys and girls till we get back,' Michael says to Dave.

Dave nods, and Michael, Gary, and Dre stand. Michael leads the way towards the X5s, and there is a hush of reverence as he walks through the warehouse.

He opens the back seat of the last X5, and Alan spots Meiling calmly sitting in the back seat before Michael shuts the door. What the fuck is she doing here? Alan ponders. But then it all makes sense.

Michael and Meiling have been on the rocks since the night of her attack. In truth, Meiling has been on the rocks with everyone since that night. The attack changed her; all her infectious vibrancy is buried under an intense and unfulfilled desire for revenge. She and Alan haven't spoken for over a year because he's had nothing to report, especially after promising to find the men from that night. Alan's not sure of Meiling's relationship with Franka either, because Franka doesn't speak about it. Michael's going all out to win back Meiling's affections and bring back the vibrancy that made her the life of every party.

Gary and Dre step into the front seats of the same X5 as Michael. One of Michael's men climbs into the driver's seat of the second X5, and Alan spots Kenji in the car's passenger seat. Alan walks past the lead X5, where Franka waits, to the young man tasked with operating the garage door.

'Did she stay in the car the whole time?' Alan asks.

'Who?'

Fair question, Alan thinks. 'Franka – the lady I came with.'

'Yeah.'

Alan nods. 'And the boss's wife?'

'Yeah. She's been in the car for almost an hour.'

Alan is relieved Franka doesn't know Meiling is in the third car, and he won't mention it. 'Thanks,' Alan says, and pats the young man's shoulder.

Alan gets into the passenger seat of the lead X5, and finds three of Kenji's troops in the back seat. Sturdy men with steely eyes, wearing balaclavas to hide their identities, because Kenji's troop supposedly keep regular lives outside of being ninjas. Alan greets them with a nod, and they nod back. He looks around for an ideal spot to put the phone for Franka to see the tracker as she drives, but there is none.

'Ready?' he asks her.

'Yes,' she responds.

'Okay,' he says, and gestures to the browser. 'I'll direct you.'

Franka nods, and Alan gives a thumbs up to the young man by the garage door. The young man opens the door, and Franka leads the other two cars out of the warehouse.

DAY 17, 03:00

'Take care of him'

Franka leads the convoy of cars slowly and with their head-lights off through a semi-rural street surrounded by forest, and finds a good spot away from any lights for the cars to park in darkness. Alan scans the four remote and modest cottages ahead, then fixes his gaze on the one furthest along the street where the blue dot has been static for almost an hour. He's doubtful this is the right location, but this is where the tracker has led them. He turns to Franka, and she shrugs – she shares his doubt.

Alan steps out of the car and walks to Michael's side of the last car, and his half-brother lowers the tinted window.

'That's the house,' Alan whispers, and gestures to the detached cottage where the blue dot is.

Michael leans forward for a better look. 'You sure?' he asks.

'Yes. According to the trace.'

'Really? You're sure?'

Alan takes a moment to bury his annoyance. 'Yes, according to the trace,' he repeats.

'I don't get it. What's a geezer from round 'ere doing fucking around all the way in London?'

'I don't know. But we'll find out soon enough.'

Michael sits back and turns to Meiling, and Alan notices her attire for the first time. She's dressed in black, with a wide-brim hat that covers her face. She's dressed for a funeral.

'Baby,' Michael says to her. 'This is the place.'

Meiling nods and raises her state-of-the-art prosthetic left hand. She moves the fingers, and the mechanism is mesmerising, but it's slow and lacks the rhythm of real fingers. She raises her right hand and twirls the fingers. 'Kill him,' she says, cold as ice.

'You heard her,' Michael says. 'You make sure they cut him up real good. I want all his limbs ripped apart. And you bring me his head, Alan. I want his facking head.'

Alan nods and walks to the passenger side of the second car. The window is down, and Kenji scans the street. Alan nods to tell Kenji it's time and walks to the lead car. He taps the back window, and Kenji's three ninjas hop out. Another three ninjas hop out of the back seat of the second car, but Kenji takes his time to step out. Kenji is an ageless wonder. He's supposedly in his mid-seventies but just as sturdy as his ninjas.

The ninjas huddle around Kenji, and when he puts on his balaclava, all seven become indistinguishable. They approach Alan and bow, and he bows too.

'Anybody you see in there,' Alan whispers, and points to the cottage, 'kill. No mercy. And bring me his head.'

The ninjas pull out katanas and charge towards the cottage; they don't make a sound.

Alan turns to Franka and doesn't need to signal; she knows it's time. She steps out and walks to him.

'Take care of him,' Alan says and gestures to the driver of the second car. 'And come to the back. I'll be waiting.'

Franka walks to the second car, and Alan walks to Michael's side of the last car. Michael lowers the window and leans out, and Alan bends to be eye to eye with him.

Alan reaches into his blazer and is about to speak, but Meiling bursts out of the car. Alan pulls out a suppressed handgun and shoots Michael in the head before Michael even reacts. He fires a shot towards Meiling as she races towards the treeline, and it hits her somewhere around her neck and shoulder, but she keeps running and plunges into the forest.

Alan turns his aim to Dre in the passenger seat as Dre and Gary frantically pull out their guns, but Franka shoots them both in the head before Alan can pull his trigger. He turns his attention to the forest, and Franka approaches to scan the car. Michael, Gary and Dre are dead.

'Who was that?' she asks, and gestures to the forest.

Alan considers lying, but there's no need for that anymore. Meiling is probably going to bleed out in the isolated forest. 'Meiling,' he says, and turns to Franka.

Franka nods, emotionless.

Even if it was just a tiny crack of emotion, Alan expected a reaction, but Franka is blank. He imagines Meiling is not the first friend Franka has lost in battle.

Franka turns to the cottage. 'Something's not right,' she says.

He follows her gaze to the cottage, but nothing looks 'not right' to him. It is silent, but Kenji's ninjas are renowned for working in silence. 'What's not right?'

'It's too quiet.'

'That's what they are known for.'

'To the—' she hesitates as she thinks of the right word '—untrained, they are silent.'

Alan nods and watches the cottage but still can't spot anything. 'Give them another minute,' he says.

A minute passes, and the house is still silent. It shouldn't take this long for seven men to slice off one man's head. 'Okay. Something's not right.'

'Wait in the car,' she says. 'I'll go check . . .'

'No. I'm coming.'

'Okay. You go through the front door. Knock first, like a good neighbour would. I'll go through the back.'

Alan nods, and Franka darts through the field towards the back of the house. Alan holds his gun behind his back and walks to the front door. As he approaches, he sees the door is halfway open. He sneaks up and peeks in, but he can't see anything because it's pitch-black inside. And he can't hear anything either. He slides through the open door, and someone sticks a gun to the back of his head and shuts the door.

'Drop the gun,' a female voice says.

Alan recognises the voice – it's Rebecca. He does as she instructs and places the gun on the floor.

'Not laughing now, are you?' Rebecca asks. 'And where is your stunning driver?'

'Didn't bring her. Thought the ninjas—'

'Alan?' a male voice says.

Alan recognises that voice, too. The hallway lights switch on, and Alan turns towards the voice – it's Pretty Boy. They stare at each other and smile.

'Happy birthday,' Alan says.

'Didn't peg you as country folk'

'That was yesterday,' I say to Alan. 'But thank you.'

'You know this dickhead?' Rebecca asks.

'He's my son,' Alan says.

Alan turns to watch Rebecca do the calculation in her head like everyone else does when Alan says it. But Rebecca isn't having any of it.

'Fuck off!' she says to him, and turns to me. 'Whoever the fuck this dickhead is to you, he's working for Michael Downing and that—'

'Worked,' Alan interrupts.

'What? You quit since we met a few hours ago? Fuck are you doing here, then?'

'Trying to kill two birds with one stone. Michael is dead in the car outside.'

'That's a lie. He's your brother. You're slick and all, but you don't have that in you.'

I agree. The Alan I know, the Alan that raised me for all those years, doesn't have that in him. But it's been a decade, so . . .

'Michael probably thought that too,' Alan says. 'But he tried to kill me. So, I did what I had to.'

Well, that's fair, I suppose.

'Lower your gun,' Alan says to Rebecca. 'I need to reach into my pocket to grab my phone and make a call . . .'

'No,' Rebecca says.

'Trust me, I do. I need to call Franka, my driver, and stop her from slipping in here and killing both of you before any of us even knows it's happening.'

'She's welcome to try,' Rebecca says.

'You don't want that. Trust me. She's a decorated German commando; she'll do it in her sleep.'

Rebecca glances at me, and I gesture for her to lower her gun, but she still hesitates.

I trust Alan, but I can tell Rebecca never will. 'It's okay,' I say to her. 'Trust me.'

Rebecca lowers the gun, and Alan quickly makes the call.

'Stand down,' he says into the phone. 'It's my son.'

'Is that supposed to be funny?' Rebecca asks.

'Just wait, and watch Franka's eyes when she studies both of us.'

Alan scans the bodies of the two ninjas in the hallway, and I can tell he's surprised we handled them.

'Are they all dead?' he asks.

'What do you think?' Rebecca retorts.

'Just, these . . . *ninjas* are first-rate mercenaries . . .'

'Not fucking around with swords in a gunfight, they're not,' Rebecca quips.

I fight back laughter, which makes my body ache all over. It's been a long day and even longer night, and I need to rest. And to be fair to these supposedly first-rate ninjas, once their element of surprise is gone and you see them coming, it doesn't matter how skilled they are. Bullets move faster.

A tall and formidable woman, who must be Franka, strides into the room, and just as Alan said she would, she looks at Alan and me to work out if he is, in fact, my father. But she takes less than a second to conclude he's not.

'I knew she was sharp,' Rebecca says.

Alan smiles. 'Meet Franka,' he says.

'Nice to meet you again, Franka,' Rebecca says.

'Nice to meet you too,' she responds.

I greet Franka with a nod, and she nods back. She came in through the back door, so I wonder if she met Oleg and his ex-wife, Katerina. But if she did, either she or them would be dead. And if she killed them, I'd put her down right where she stands. I put my finger over the trigger of my gun, but before I ask Franka anything, I spot Rebecca reading a text. Rebecca turns to me and nods to reassure me.

'Is this where you've been living this past decade?' Alan asks me.

'Not all of it. Past three years, yes.'

'Didn't peg you as country folk.'

I smile. 'I didn't either.'

'How did you get the bracelet?'

'Topper . . .'

'Topper?'

'Tyrone . . . Snowman, whatever he calls himself nowadays, he gave it to me.'

'That's why you killed him.'

I nod.

'You killed Farrukh as well?'

I hesitate, still unsure Farrukh's death was necessary. 'I tried to sell him the bracelet, but he set me up,' I answer. 'He left me no choice.'

'Your girlfriend helped you?' he asks, and gestures to Rebecca.

'You know you killed my husband today, right?' Rebecca responds, with feeling.

'That wasn't my choice. That was Michael's.'

'Blame the dead guy, yeah?'

'You believe he's dead now, then?' Alan quips. 'I'm not blaming anyone. Just stating the facts; I'll leave the emotions to you. The bracelet belonged to Michael's wife, and Michael really wanted it back. Plus, he wanted to know who set up the attack on his wife three years ago. Vicious shit. They took her hand and the bracelet,' he says, and turns to me. 'Evidently wasn't you. But it doesn't matter anymore.'

'Matters to me,' Franka says.

There is gravity and pain in Franka's response, which evokes a moment of silence from the rest of us. I glance at Rebecca and can tell the way she feels about Franka – respect.

'What's your next move, then?' Alan asks me.

I stare at him with a raised eyebrow. It's a leading question, and he knows me well enough to know that I'd appreciate it if he got to the point straight away. Especially today. Especially now.

'Just that you can't stay here tonight. There are bodies all over the place . . .' Alan says, and gestures to the two dead ninjas. 'Where are the others?'

'About the house,' I respond. 'They all dropped the moment they stepped foot inside.'

Alan can't hide his shock. 'Just the two of you?'

'Yes,' Rebecca responds before I can. 'He's Pretty Boy, after all, and I'm bloody Rebecca Pepper.'

I smile. Rebecca has a way with words. And there must be a reason she doesn't want Alan to know Oleg and Katerina were involved. Maybe they said so in the text, or she just doesn't trust Alan.

'I've got somewhere to lay my head till morning. I'll think of next moves then.'

'Come with me back to London,' Alan says.

'No,' Rebecca interjects. 'Don't trust this dickhead. You've only made new enemies today, and the police are still—'

'That's it, isn't it?' Alan interrupts. 'That's why you're avoiding London. You don't fear these *enemies* . . . you just don't want to be put in a position where you have to hurt police, and you know you'd have to if they came for you, like the last time. But I'll sort the police thing. Even Rebecca can tell you how much influence I have there. Come back home.'

He's correct. I don't fear these enemies, but I'm tired of the killing. And in London, they will keep coming, and I will keep killing. There's only so long you can tell yourself it's self-defence, or noble, for your peace of mind.

'Thanks, Alan,' I say. 'But I'll stay away.'

'You can't, though,' Alan says. 'Stay away. You see, everyone thought you were dead. Including me. Maybe not Rebecca . . .'

'I did too,' Rebecca adds.

'Exactly. So, no one came looking. But now they know you're not, so you're not exactly safe anywhere. Because some of the people looking for you have even more money and resources than Michael. And he found you. You can't keep running for ever.'

Alan is convincing, and he added that last sentence to provoke me. I'm exhausted, and I know Alan won't let up. There is much more to why he wants me in London which he isn't saying, and he won't say unless I steer him ever so gently . . . but that's not for tonight.

'Okay,' I say.

'Good,' Alan says, and doesn't hide his relief well enough. 'There's a clean car outside. We'll use that. And I'll call clean-up to take care of the bodies in here and out there before sunrise. We need to move fast. Is there anything you need to pack?'

'No. I'm ready.'

Alan smiles. 'You've not let yourself get attached to anything you can't walk out on in thirty seconds flat if you feel the heat around the corner, then?'

I smile back, because I get the reference. 'Exactly.'

'What the fuck?' Rebecca asks.

'You've never seen *Heat*?' Alan asks.

Rebecca rolls her eyes. 'I need a ride back to London,' she says, and gestures to Alan. 'And I'm not travelling with this dickhead.'

'Take my car. It's clean,' I say, and she nods.

'Call me before noon,' she says, and turns to Alan. 'Or I'll come gunning for you.'

Alan chuckles.

'Not you, though,' Rebecca says to Franka. 'I like you.'

Franka cracks a smile, and Alan stops chuckling. There is a thread to pull between Alan and Franka, and Rebecca will find it and pull it. Unless I ask her not to . . . softly.

'Speak later,' I say to Rebecca, and gesture to my car key on a table by the front door.

'Speak later,' she responds.

Rebecca bids farewell to Franka with a nod, and Franka nods back. But she doesn't acknowledge Alan before she grabs the key and leaves.

'I think she likes me,' Alan says, and chuckles.

'Give me thirty seconds,' I say, and hurry up the stairs, feeling every step.

'Nothing much could've changed since then'

Franka drives a new Jaguar saloon through the bustling City towards the Lenkov family investments office, and Alan couldn't look more confident in the passenger seat as he enjoys 'Right Here, Right Now' by Fatboy Slim booming out of the stereo. He gets a call on his burner, and it's the lead of the clean-up team he sent to take care of the scene inside and outside the cottage.

'We're done, boss,' she says, a note of doubt in her voice. 'But there is a problem.'

'What problem?'

'The . . . err . . . *ninjas* . . . there are only six of them.'

'Are you sure? We counted seven before we left.'

'Yes. All the other bodies were exactly where you said they were. But there was only one at the back entrance. We checked everywhere for the body . . . followed every trail. But couldn't find it.'

Curiosity overcame Alan at the cottage, so he checked the identity of the dead ninjas before they left. He didn't recognise any of them, and, to his surprise, only one other ninja besides Kenji could be considered to have Japanese heritage. They were from all over the world, and there were two women. Proper London ninjas, Kenji had assembled. And speaking of Kenji, his body was one of those at the back door. Alan hopes to Christ it isn't Kenji's body missing.

'Body at the back door, old geezer?'

'No. Young. Late twenties, maybe.'

Fuck, Alan thinks. That's just . . . no, he won't let that spoil his mood. 'Okay,' he says. 'What about the other thing?'

'That's, err . . .'

'Get to it.'

'The forest is large and dense. We've been searching for hours, but now it's daylight we're starting to draw attention from the locals. We cleaned up a large pool of blood where she fell, but we're not sure what direction she went. Although, based on the amount of blood, she won't have survived for more than thirty minutes, especially in an agitated state – she would've been frantic. There are no homes for miles in either direction through the forest, except the cottages, and we have no trail coming out of the forest towards the cottages. Long story short, her body is in the forest. We can come back tonight to find it.'

'Do that,' he says, and ends the call.

★

Veronika is on a conference call at her desk, but she's not an active participant, so she's also working through her emails. There is a knock on the door, and her assistant steps in and hurries to her but waits for Veronika to get off the call before speaking.

'It's on mute,' Veronika says, and gestures to her headset.

'Alan Pierce is here,' her assistant says.

Before Veronika responds, her phone rings, and it's Gennady. Veronika takes off the headset and answers the call.

'Alan is here,' Gennady says in Russian. 'Your father is hosting some investors in his office. So, I'm on my way to your office to discuss.'

'Okay,' Veronika responds in Russian.

She types a quick direct message to her team and leaves the call.

'Cancel all my meetings till lunch,' she says in English to her assistant. 'And let Gennady in as soon as he gets here.'

The assistant nods and leaves the room, and almost immediately, Gennady walks in.

'I've reached out to my man,' Gennady says in Russian, and marches to her desk. 'But I think this meeting is going to be good.'

'Why?'

'I spoke to my man yesterday. He said Alan's time at the organisation is ending fast because he can't rebuild their distribution network, and there are payments due for the supplier and the transport. I think Alan is here to make a deal.'

'What about the shipment?'

'No details on that yet. I think that's Alan's last card, and he's waiting to play it at the right time. But what good is a shipment of cocaine if he can't distribute it? If he offers it, we bargain hard.'

She nods; she disagrees with Gennady's assessment of the situation and his plan. Her detailed opposition research on Alan tells her he's someone that will do whatever it takes to win. Not a planner per se, but one who won't hesitate to do the unthinkable if the situation calls for it. That sort of person doesn't show up unannounced to a meeting with a limp card. She'll sit back and allow things to play out, because she still holds the joker.

Ten minutes pass, and Gennady's man hasn't responded. Gennady sends him another text, and they wait for a couple minutes, but there is no response.

'Maybe busy,' Gennady says.

Veronika nods, and they continue waiting.

Another ten minutes pass before Marat walks into the room, and he's anxious.

'Sorry about that,' Marat says in Russian. 'I tried to wrap it up soon as I could. Are we ready?'

'I'm still waiting for my man to call back,' Gennady says.

Marat doesn't hide his disappointment. 'What's happening?' he asks Gennady.

Veronika stands and leads Gennady and Marat to the lounge area of the office. Gennady restates to Marat his assessment of the situation and his plan, and although he tries to portray confidence, it's clear to Veronika his confidence is waning.

'Call the man,' Marat orders.

Gennady calls, but the phone is switched off. That's never happened before.

'Call again,' Marat orders.

Gennady does, and the phone is still switched off.

Marat is furious, and Gennady is embarrassed.

'I don't think we should keep Alan waiting much longer,' Veronika says.

Marat nods in agreement.

'What time last night did you speak to your man?' she asks Gennady.

'Just before midnight.'

'Nothing much could've changed since then,' she says, not believing a word of it.

Gennady nods, not believing it either but knowing they can't wait much longer.

Veronika walks to her desk and calls her assistant on the intercom. 'Bring Alan Pierce to my meeting room, and make sure he's comfortable.'

Alan sits in a meeting room that's luxurious but somehow more modest than the conference room he was in last time. But the treats are the same. He enjoys the delicious coffee and shortbread as he waits.

A door opens, and Veronika leads Marat and Gennady to seats directly across from Alan.

'Hello, Alan,' Marat says. 'Good to see you again.'

'Hello, Marat. Good to see you as well,' Alan says, and turns to Gennady. 'And you, Gennady.'

Gennady nods but doesn't speak.

Fair enough, Alan thinks. He greets Veronika with a polite smile, and she returns the gesture.

'I see you're enjoying our coffee and biscuits,' Marat says.

'Yes. They're even better than I remember. If you're still offering, I'm happy to drop my address.'

'Of course.'

'What happened to your arm?' Veronika asks.

'You should see the other guy,' Alan quips.

The joke falls like a lead balloon.

'Car accident. But I'm okay,' Alan says.

'Yes. You appear very full of life for someone recently in a car accident. Near-death experience open your eyes to the many wonders of the world?'

Alan chuckles. 'Wasn't that bad an accident.'

Veronika nods.

'To what do I owe this pleasure?' Marat asks.

'I'm going to assume this room is just as secure as the other room, especially as it's attached to Veronika's office.'

Veronika fights back a smile – Alan is showing off. He must be in a very good mood.

'It is,' Marat says.

'Okay. Whatever it is you were doing, it's over,' Alan asserts.

Gennady shifts in his chair, which Alan notices, and smiles at him.

'What are you talking about?' Marat asks.

'Let's stop playing games, Marat. This is fucking done, all right?'

Alan's tone infuriates Marat and Gennady, and he sees it.

'That was a bit strong,' Alan says. 'I apologise. Just had a long week. Thanks to you. But it's finished now.'

'Why?' Marat asks. 'Maybe for you, not for me.'

'What the fuck?' Alan asks, exasperated. 'What do you have against me?'

The question almost knocks the wind out of Marat. 'You killed my son.'

'Fucking hell,' Alan says. 'We already said we didn't do it. And last I checked, you were sure it was Pretty Boy.'

'Oh, I'm sure Pretty Boy killed Viktor, and you killed Valentin.'

The certainty of the accusation stuns Alan, but he doesn't show it. 'Why would I do that? Anyway, last I heard, he was missing . . .'

'Valentin is not missing. He's dead. And you killed him.'

'I can see why the person you had feeding you the information you used to destroy my distribution network would tell you that. I imagine he thought you needed the right motivation, but, as far as I know, Valentin is missing.'

Marat chuckles. 'You are an excellent liar, Alan. And if I hadn't seen the body myself, I might even believe you.'

Alan wasn't expecting that development. But, again, he doesn't show his surprise.

'You think Valentin's body disappeared like the bodies of your enemies?' Marat asks. 'That's what I feared as well. But the river brought him back to us.'

Alan expects his left hand to tremble, but he glances at it, and it's still. If he could, he'd kill Dre all over again. That incompetent cunt. 'I had nothing to do with that,' he says, calm.

Marat shakes his head. 'You will never stop lying. So, this will never stop.'

'Well, your inside information is finished. Actually, there's no need for us talking around the issue. You stupidly let yourself get played by Michael. All that inside information he was feeding you was just for you to take me out as a contender to his throne and for chaos to reign, so he could remind everyone why he's the king. I killed him, and I'm going to restart the network. Stay the fuck out of my way.'

Marat and Gennady can't hide their shock, as Alan expected. But Veronika doesn't react, which isn't surprising to Alan either because she never gives anything away.

Marat stands up and leaves the room, and Gennady quickly follows.

Veronika and Alan stare at each other, and he's waiting for her to leave as well because he owns this room. He owns this town now. But she laughs, which surprises him.

'What was it?' she asks.

He doesn't understand the question.

'I think it was . . . "keep *us* posted",' she says.

The revelation stuns Alan, and he can't hide it.

Veronika bursts into laughter. 'It was, wasn't it?' she says. 'I thought so. I was trained to always know a person's motives before you deal with them. Not just their motives dealing with you, but their motives in general . . . their ambitions, you could say. Probably a better translation, actually. And yours were easy. I spotted it the first time we met at the stadium. You thought you'd have handled that meeting better. And you would've. You think you'd run your network better without Michael's interference, and you would. So, I knew just a little push is what it would take. I sent some amateurs I knew Franka would deal with easily in your direction. And I knew you'd take the phones, so I cloned Gary's phone number and left the breadcrumbs for you to find. I actually didn't expect you to text. I was going to text around midnight asking for an update. But you're sharper than I thought.

'And more decisive as well. I'm impressed you have killed your brother already. Thank you very much.'

Alan is on the verge of boiling over.

'Ultimately, it was a stupid decision. You couldn't see that the only reason you were in that box at the stadium was that you were Michael's brother. The only reason you ran the biggest cocaine distribution network in London was that you were Michael's brother. The only reason anyone in the criminal world listens to you or shows any respect is that you were Michael's brother. And most important, the only reason you're not dead is that you were Michael's brother. I'm surprised you didn't notice the contempt his men have for you, a former top copper, who has put a lot of people – some of their friends too, I'm sure – in prison. And that's just your brother's men. The people you expect to lead now.'

Veronika laughs.

'Think about all the other gangs. Just imagine how they would be salivating when they know Michael is dead and you're' – Veronika cackles – 'in charge. Alan, Alan, Alan.' She shakes her head. 'Stupid, stupid, stupid.'

Alan glares at her like he wants to dive across the table and strangle her, and she grins.

'Okay, I'll stop torturing you now. Because I'm starting to feel bad. You're not giving anything back; you just look like you want to cry.'

'People that underestimate me usually end up dead,' Alan says.

'I didn't underestimate you. I believed you had it in you to kill your brother. That's the opposite of underestimating. Gennady and my father underestimated me. I don't know if you could tell, but they were shocked that you killed your brother. It's completely messed up their plans. When I tell them I was the puppet master, they will be even more shocked.'

'I'm no one's puppet,' Alan says.

Veronika laughs. 'Do you honestly believe that?' she asks, and scoffs. 'I don't care. What's important to me is that we are almost even. I've lost two brothers. You've lost one. But you only had one, and you killed him . . . so that counts more than one. Not two, though. What do you think?'

'Are you done?'

'I didn't call this meeting. You did. Are *you* done?'

Alan stands.

'If you're not dead by then, Chief Superintendent Jack Moore will be in touch about your arrest for Valentin's murder in a couple days,' Veronika says. 'I suggest you get your affairs in order. I don't think prison will suit you, so I suggest you run. But wherever you end up, we will find you and kill you.'

Alan walks towards the door.

'Please don't forget to leave your address with my assistant so we can send you the coffee and shortbread.'

Alan walks out of the room, and Veronika laughs.

DAY 17, 11:00

'The lady that gave birth to me'

An alarm from my phone wakes me, and I'm in the dark in a large unfamiliar bedroom. I leap off the bed and flinch in pain because I moved too quickly; I'm still sore, everywhere. The bedroom is silent, and I listen for any sounds beyond the bedroom door, but nothing; it's also silent. I part the curtains to peek out of the floor-to-ceiling window. I'm on the top floor of a block of flats. I look around to find my bearings and spot Battersea Power Station in the near distance. I'm in West London.

I open the curtains for daylight to fill the room and spot a note on the bedside table beside my phone . I approach it and recognise Alan's handwriting.

I set the alarm for 11 because I don't need Rebecca hunting me down. There are clothes in the wardrobe, but I don't think you'd be a fan of them, so I'll drop in around noon with clothes that are more your style.

I laugh because I'd love to see what Alan thinks my style is. I continue reading.

Don't worry, I'll ring the buzzer when I arrive. I've seen how you treat uninvited guests. There's food in the fridge, but call me if you want something else. We changed the SIM in your phone because that's how Michael found you, and I've added my number to your contacts.

So that's how Michael found me. With Alan's help, I'm sure. Farrukh gave them my number; he's the only one that had it. I feel less guilty now about killing him, but no less about his son, Javad.

I pick up the phone and call Rebecca.

'Who's this?' she answers.

'Me. Stopping you from killing Alan.'

'For today.'

I chuckle.

'How do you know him? And why does he keep calling you his son?'

'Long story. But he and his ex-wife took me in for a few years after Jess kicked me out.'

'Who's Jess?'

'The lady that gave birth to me.'

'Your mother.'

'I don't think she'd be happy with that title. She always preferred Jess.'

'Whatever. I'll be calling her your mother and try stopping me.'

'I won't dare.'

'How old were you when this happened?'

'Why?' I ask. 'It's not important.'

'I saved your life last night. So, you answer my questions. For ever.'

I laugh. 'You didn't tell me that was the bargain.'

'I know you're *the* Pretty Boy, but you didn't have much of a choice last night.'

I shrug; she's probably right. 'I was thirteen.'

'Your mum kicked you out when you were thirteen?' she asks, fuelled with rage.

'I suppose you'll start calling her Jess now.'

Rebecca isn't amused. 'I want to ask why she did it, but there is no good reason.'

'Well, it was either me or her boyfriend. And he came with strings attached – drugs.'

'That is . . . fucked.'

'Yeah, but I fucked him up royally before I left.'

'You were thirteen . . .' she says, and pauses. 'But then, I'm not surprised.'

'That's how I met Alan. Jess called the police and reported an assault. Alan, then in uniform, arrives with his partner and they don't understand why the crazy lady is accusing her thirteen-year-old son of assaulting her thirty-year-old boyfriend when it's clear it was mutual combat. As mutual as it could be between a thirteen-year-old and a thirty-year-old wired crackhead . . . before I grabbed the knife. Alan took me in after that.'

'I suppose Alan was a good man once.'

'He's always been good to me.'

'Okay. But I don't trust him, and I know you think it has a lot to do with Jamie, and it does. But Oleg doesn't trust him either, and Oleg has had your back longer than any of us.'

That's true about Oleg, and Oleg hasn't been wrong so far.

'I'll be cautious,' I say. 'Speaking of cautious, I'm not going to call Oleg with this SIM, so can you tell him I'll be at his shop in a few hours?'

'I will.'

'Speak soon.'

'Why?' she asks. 'I care about you, but that doesn't mean I forgive you and you can call me for a chat.'

'I understand.'

'But call if you need me,' she says, and hangs up.

I spot my jacket neatly folded on the other bedside table beside *The Left Hand of Darkness* and *Travels in the Interior Districts of Africa*. And whoever folded it set my golden pistol – a birthday gift from Oleg – on top of it. I grab the gun and eject the clip to confirm it is full; it is. I reinsert the clip and check there is a bullet in the chamber; there is. I walk out of the room to explore the flat . . . cautiously.

The three-bedroom, two-storey penthouse is exquisite. But more importantly, it's empty. The flat belongs to Alan. The clothes, and particularly the shoes, in the walk-in closet are very much his style, just many times more expensive than I remember. But it's also clear that no one has lived in the flat, and the only people that have been inside are the people who service it.

I open the fully stocked fridge and spot eggs, butter, peppers, and tomatoes. Perfect. I prepare a large portion of scrambled eggs, add a hefty sprinkle of dried chilli, and enjoy breakfast with some green tea. I wash the plates and pans before I realise there is a dishwasher right underneath the sink, but then, I haven't used one in years.

I consider having a shower, but I check the time – it's 11:51; Alan will be here soon. I decide to check if any of my escapades yesterday have made the news, but before I switch on the television, there is a buzz from the intercom. Alan's early.

I walk to the intercom and Alan waves at me through the large monitor, but he's not outside; he's in a room.

I push the button to speak. 'Where are you?' I ask.

'Downstairs,' he says. 'By the private penthouse lift. I let myself in with my card, but as I promised, I've buzzed. I can use my card to call the lift, or you can push the blinking blue button.'

I scan the intercom system for the blinking blue button, and 'LIFT' is written clearly underneath it. I chuckle. 'You thought I wouldn't be able to find the button that says "lift"?' I ask.

'Well, you have been living in the forest for a decade.'

'Fuck off,' I say, and push the button.

I sit by the kitchen island, which has a perfect view of the lift. It opens a few moments later, and Alan steps out looking as smooth as ever, even with his arm in a sling. I hadn't paid attention to his hairstyle last night, but it's precisely the same as it was a decade ago . . . with every strand in its place. He loves himself, and I always liked that about him.

'You like the place?' he asks, and approaches.

'It's very nice,' I answer. 'Yours?'

'Yes and no,' he says, and drops a large bag full of clothes on the island before sitting beside me. 'I've got a few of these spots around London, just in case.'

'A few of these?' I ask, and gesture around the flat.

'Yeah. Well, we . . . I own the buildings,' he says with relish.

I nod; I don't need to know any more.

He spots the washed plates in the dish rack. 'You've eaten, then?' he asks.

'Yeah.'

'Good. I have your clothes,' he says and pushes the bag to me. 'Go on. Check how much I know you.'

I look through the clothes and trainers, and unsurprisingly, they are *my style* – a pair of plain t-shirts; fitted jeans; white low-top trainers; and a mac coat – but much more expensive than anything I'd ever purchase myself. It all feels like quality, although I don't recognise any of the brands except the Nike trainers. He hasn't lost his attention to detail.

'You still know me pretty well,' I say.

'Good,' he says, and smiles proudly. 'I was going to get another leather jacket as well, but you seem attached to the one you have. That's all you brought with you. And the books. What's with that?'

'What's with what?'

'The books.'

'I'm reading them.'

'But there were lots of other books on your shelf.'

I nod. 'Speaking of . . . I need your help with that. Is the clean-up done?'

'For now. They'll be back tonight to finish up.'

'And my next-door neighbour is all good, yes?'

'Yes. From what they could tell, all your neighbours are alive and well.'

'From what they could tell?'

'It's not like they could drop in to check.'

'I didn't ask about anyone else. I only asked if the lights in my next-door neighbour's kitchen switched on at six a.m.'

'They did.'

'Thank you. I need them to drop all the books in front of my next-door neighbour's door. Cover them with a tarp or something, so they don't get wet. They should not knock on the door. Plus, I need them to buy a copy of *Fifty Shades of Grey* and place that on top of the other books.'

He nods. 'Although I'm shocked you don't have a copy of that book already,' he teases.

We laugh. This seems like the perfect time to gently steer him into telling me why he wanted me in London so keenly.

'What's going on, Alan?' I ask.

He stares at me as if contemplating how much of the truth to reveal.

'The Lenkovs are coming after me,' he says.

Well then, I guess I don't have to steer him.

'Why?'

'I killed their son.'

'Why the fuck would you do that?'

'That's rich coming from you. You killed the other son. The one Marat really cared about.'

'Fair. But I had no choice.'

'What exactly happened?'

'You don't believe the story your colleagues fed to the press?'

'They haven't been my colleagues for years now. And neither you nor Viktor was in that story, so it was obviously bullshit.'

'The press ate it up, though. The Wapping Massacre,' I say, and nod. 'That's going to follow me for ever, isn't it?'

Alan nods and doesn't speak. He wants me to answer his question.

'It was a set-up,' I say. 'I was working with Sean Pounds – well, Andrea Florenzi is his real name if the press got that right. He got a large delivery of pure cocaine and was looking to sell it. Lucas, Jack Moore's precious informant, according to the press, was working with Sean as well and introduced us to Viktor. Wealthy Russian looking to get into the drug business. What could go wrong? But Viktor never intended to pay for the cocaine. He and Lucas had a side deal to take Sean and me out. But things didn't go their way . . .'

'That's putting it lightly. Seven people died, including three officers, and Jack Moore barely survived . . . you almost slit his throat wide open.'

'They left me no choice,' I reiterate. 'I don't exactly regret it, but it's not a proud moment either. And I've been running ever since.'

'I can help with that.'

'You said.'

He stares at me, expecting gratitude, but I know the help isn't free. He wants something, and he'll tell me when he's ready.

'What happened to the other brother?' I ask.

'Valentin,' he says. 'It was the night Michael's wife got attacked. Michael thought Marat had something to do with it, so he kidnapped Valentin from the middle of Soho. They tortured him. Don't know what they were trying to get out of him. By the time I got there to stop the torture, it was too late. There's no way we could've returned him without turning London into a battlefield. So, I put him down.'

'How do the Lenkovs know you did it, then?'

'Michael told them.'

'Why?'

'He wanted to use them to take me out. I was running the drug distribution network, for Michael, and I guess the financial success led Michael to question his position.'

Okay, that makes some sense. But a person like Michael wouldn't use someone else to handle that . . . especially if he thinks his power is being challenged. He'd kill Alan himself, in public. I'll interrogate that later.

'Do they know Michael is dead?' I ask.

'Yes.'

I'd imagine the Lenkovs are happy with that because Michael

is a scrapper . . . and has earned the respect and loyalty of the London underworld. I don't know if Alan has.

'What's your next move?' I ask.

'I need your help.'

'For what?'

'To handle this.'

'This . . . ? Be explicit, Alan.'

'You're Pretty Boy. People think of you as the bogeyman of the underworld.'

'I've been away for a decade.'

'I know. But others don't. They think Pretty Boy has been lurking in the shadows . . . watching and killing those that step too far out of line. Ask Rebecca what people whisper about Pretty Boy. And what you did yesterday to Tyrone only adds to it. His fortress was supposedly impenetrable, but Pretty Boy destroyed it.'

'Right,' I say. 'I guess that name's stuck, then?'

He laughs. 'Yeah,' he says. 'Pretty Boy is a legend.'

'Legend is right. Because it's lies.'

'Most of it, yes. But bookended by the Wapping Massacre and Tyrone's fortress . . . you did those. And those are incredible by themselves.'

Alan is really trying to butter me up, but he ought to know that's only going to raise my suspicions.

'Okay, Alan. What do you want from Pretty Boy?'

'Help kill the Lenkovs and rebuild the distribution network.'

I don't respond. The Alan I knew wouldn't ask me to kill

anyone. But power corrupts, and absolute power corrupts absolutely.

'The Lenkovs will soon know you're alive and were in London yesterday,' Alan says. 'And the moment they do, they will use every resource they have to hunt you down before you go to ground again . . . and they are very, very resource-rich. I'll be on the back burner, but they have enough resources to hunt me too. We need to meet that head-on. Your presence will rally the troops, and your beautiful mind will help us outfox the Lenkovs because, in truth, they are a few steps ahead.'

I want no more deaths on my conscience. But I have to stop running sometime. Viktor came after me, and that's when the killing started. Seems his father will have to be the last for the killing to end. But only as a last resort. There must be a way of ending this without more bloodshed, but I don't think Alan is interested in that. If there is, I'll find it.

'And I'm not saying I won't do this for you anyway,' Alan continues. 'But I'll make all the evidence the police have putting you at the Wapping Massacre disappear. And I'll make Jack Moore disappear as well. That way, when this is over, you can walk away a free man.'

Can . . . no. I *will* walk away a free man. But we'll cross that bridge when it comes.

'Say something,' Alan asks.

I nod.

'Good,' he says, elated.

'But why would your *troops* believe I'm Pretty Boy?'

'Have you looked at yourself in the mirror?'

I raise an eyebrow, wondering where he is going with the question.

'You look like you're someone special,' he says. 'I told you that years ago. You own the space.'

'Calm down, Alan. I already agreed to help.'

He laughs, and I smile.

'Plus, no one is crazy enough to claim to be Pretty Boy considering all the killing, righteous or not, that has been done in your name.'

'Righteous?' I ask.

'Yeah. Every unexplained killing for the past decade with a moral bite, no matter how tangential, has been credited to you.'

'Okay,' I say, mildly astonished – well, not so mildly.

'I know. People love Pretty Boy, but it's a lot of killing, so you've acquired a lot of enemies.'

'And you want me to step out of the shadows into that?'

'Yeah. Because more than the love or the hate, there is the fear. None of these lot will come after you after what you did to Tyrone . . . especially when they know Michael's army surrounds you.'

I nod. Walking away a free man will not be easy, but I'll make it work.

'And on a more practical level,' Alan says. 'There's a description of you going around from your activities yesterday. Even those that haven't heard the description will not question you in the room, but they'll ask around afterwards, and it'll be confirmed.'

'What room?'

He smiles.

DAY 17, 13:00

'The life and times of a warrior king'

I'm in the back seat of Alan's Jaguar as we approach a warehouse in Wembley. Franka focuses on the drive, and Alan, sitting in the passenger seat, seems to be going through what he'll say to the troops over and over in his head.

A garage door slides open, and Franka drives into a vast warehouse filled with eager young men and women. There is a palpable sense of anxiety as they watch Franka park the Jaguar by the entrance. Alan steps out of the car, and, again, the disappointment is palpable. The troops were expecting – hoping – it was Michael. Franka remains in the car, and I step out, and everyone watches me, consumed with curiosity.

I follow Alan through a red door to a back room, and I recognise the man holding court there. Dave. Time hasn't been good to Dave.

'I've been trying to call you,' Dave snarls at Alan. 'Where

the fuck . . .' He spots me over Alan's shoulder and is over-whelmed with panic, as I expected.

Alan notices Dave's panic and pounces. 'You were saying?' Alan goads.

Dave shakes his head; he has nothing more to say.

'You sure you don't want to discuss taking over the net-work?' Alan asks, and turns to the others in the room. 'That's what he was chatting to you lot about, no?'

They don't respond, but their silence says enough.

'All right,' Alan says. 'You lot step out and gather everyone. I'll be out in a minute to talk to them.'

The others leave the room.

'Where's Michael?' Dave asks, anxious.

'He's dead.'

The news hits Dave like a truck, just as I imagine it'll hit the others.

'What happened?' Dave asks.

'One battle too many,' Alan says. 'The life and times of a warrior king, I suppose.'

Dave looks on the verge of tears.

'None of that shit right now,' Alan says. 'There'll be time for it, but we need to be strong for him. We need to be strong to finish this fight.'

'Who did it?' Dave asks.

'Let's go outside,' Alan says. 'I'm sure the boys and girls have been waiting for news.'

Alan leads us out of the room, and everyone in the ware-house has gathered just outside the door. They are anxious.

'Michael died last night,' Alan says, and it seems the news knocks the entire warehouse sideways. 'As you'd expect, Michael didn't die in a fist fight or gunfight. We were set up. Lured to a fucking cottage in the middle of nowhere where Meiling's bracelet was supposed to be. Michael knew it was a set-up. But as you all know, he never backed away from a fight . . . and with Gary, Dre and Kenji's ninjas, he felt ready for anyone in there. But when they entered, the cottage exploded. The coward's way to fight. But that's the Lenkovs for you. They don't want to get their hands dirty. Think they're too rich for us. But still want to take our city.'

I scan the boys and girls, and it looks like they believe Alan, but his speech isn't doing much to lift their spirits. It's not the words, I suppose, but the man delivering them.

'We need to take the fight to them. Get their fucking hands dirty. But Michael was worried you lot won't follow me into a fight, and I don't know why,' Alan quips, and there is muffled laughter across the warehouse. 'But then you saw what happened to Tyrone yesterday . . .'

'That wasn't you, that was Pretty Boy,' a young man in the crowd shouts.

'I know. But why would Pretty Boy destroy Tyrone? And why now?'

There is a murmur through the crowd.

'Pretty Boy is one of us. Working in the shadows. It's time he steps out to lead us into this fight.'

Alan steps aside and gestures for me to step forward.

Okay . . . more than a bit dramatic, and he didn't tell me this 'reveal' was his plan.

The crowd watches me as I step forward, questioning, expecting, and hoping. But all I see is young men and women that'll likely lose their lives in a fight that shouldn't concern them. Drugs will filter into this town one way or the other. Kings will rise and fall. It's the way of the circus. Their deaths will ultimately be meaningless.

'Go home,' I say, and this stuns everyone in the warehouse – especially Alan. 'Have a good sleep, spend time with the ones you care about, and wait for our call . . . Because when you get it, you're in this fight 24/7 till we kill them all, or they kill us all.'

The warehouse falls silent, but the atmosphere is electric, and Alan grins. But those calls will never happen if I have anything to do with it.

'We're done here,' Alan whispers to me, and leads me towards the car.

I look around for Dave before I follow, but Dave's gone. Hmm.

Alan and I step into the Jaguar, and Franka drives out of the warehouse.

'That's a lie. And you know it'

Franka and Alan drop me outside the penthouse apartment building. Alan was unusually vague about his plans for the rest of the day, and I wouldn't have cared otherwise, but now I'm intrigued. But I'll follow up later because I need to see Oleg. Alan mentioned there was a clean car in the garage for me, and I worry it might be something flash as I enter the building and go up in the private lift to get the key. It's keys to another Jaguar; I didn't know Alan was such a fan.

I step into the private garage, and it's a saloon identical to Alan's current car. Luxury, but somewhat modest. Certainly not flash. I step into the car and drive, and it's a smooth ride.

I walk into an independent grocery store in the heart of Notting Hill, and the young man behind the till recognises me and directs me to a door at the end of the shop floor. I thank him with a nod and head to the door, and it opens as I approach. I step through into a small hallway that leads to another, sturdier door, which opens the moment I shut the first door; it's Oleg, and he's smiling at me.

I smile back, and we hug. He leads me into the vast room that serves as his office and storage for some of the merchandise he sells, which he keeps securely hidden away because it's mostly weapons.

'How are you feeling?' he asks, genuinely concerned.

'I'm okay.'

He gestures to a long sofa that faces a large television showing a live feed from the security cameras inside and outside the shop. 'Please sit,' he says.

I sit, and he sits beside me.

'Are you sure you're okay?' he asks.

'Yes. Thank you for saving my life last night.'

'That was Rebecca,' he says. 'I wouldn't have known it was happening unless she called.'

I nod. 'And thank Katerina from me as well.'

'I will,' he says. 'I think Katerina feels she stills owes you one more.'

'Why?'

'She was pregnant when you helped. Can't you remember? That's two people you saved.'

'Saved might be a stretch. You guys had it covered.'

'That's a lie. And you know it.'

I shrug. 'Anastasiya's your daughter as well, and you've saved my life a lot more than twice.'

'Katerina and I are not married anymore. So, her debts are her debts.'

I laugh.

'And that is not me saying it . . . that is Katerina. You know her.'

There is a buzz, and Oleg turns to the screen. I follow his gaze and spot Franka at the back door. Fuck! She followed me.

FRANKA

'If she did, she'd be dead, wouldn't she?'

It's the summer of 2007. Meiling and Michael are in the VIP section of a bustling club in Mayfair, and Meiling is having the time of her life. It's the first time in a long time they've been out to a club, and the first time they've come alone without carloads of his men inside and outside the club, which, as you can imagine, just kills the vibe.

Tonight, Meiling is a vibe all by herself. And Michael is enjoying it. He does feel out of place, but he's not anxious like he usually is when he and Meiling are in public. Michael doesn't fear for his safety; he believes he can handle himself in any environment and is always eager for a good fight. But he worries some coward might attack Meiling to get to him. And that thought keeps him up at night.

'Umbrella' by Rihanna and Jay-Z comes on, and Meiling

almost jumps out of her skin with excitement. She grabs Michael and attempts to pull him to the dance floor in the main room, and he refuses, but, to her great surprise, he gestures for her to go on without him. She passionately kisses him and hurries to the dance floor.

Meiling dances like no one's watching, screaming the lyrics with the entire club until the song is over, and then she heads to the busy bar. A bartender spots her and rushes over like she was instructed by the club's manager, but Meiling gestures for her to attend to the people ahead of her. She dances by the bar and waits her turn, which comes quicker than she expected, so she checks to see everyone ahead of her has been attended to; they have. She orders a strawberry daiquiri, and the bartender takes her time preparing an excellent one with top-shelf rum.

A young man Meiling recognises from inside the VIP room appears next to her at the bar.

'What are you doing with the old man?' he asks her.

She waves her large engagement ring in his face.

'He's already locked you down,' the young man says, and laughs. 'Cheeky sod. But I would if I was him.'

She doesn't respond and smiles at the bartender as she places the strawberry daiquiri in front of her. The bartender glares at the young man, and he assumes it's his cue to order, but before he speaks, she walks away to attend to someone else.

'What's her beef?' the young man asks Meiling. 'Does your old man own the club or something?'

'No,' Meiling says. 'She just knows how close you are to

getting this cocktail, which she worked very hard to prepare, poured over your head.'

'Okay,' he says. 'I was just trying to have a—'

Michael grabs the young man's head from behind and smashes his face onto the bar. The young man falls, and Michael kicks him repeatedly in the ribs. Another young man charges at Michael, but he's intercepted by a bouncer who pulls him to the ground and pins him. Three more bouncers run over, and they carry the two men out of the club like little boys.

Meiling glares at Michael, and he shrugs.

'I was handling that,' she says.

'He wasn't listening, was he?' Michael responds.

'I've been handling people like that chancer for years before I met you,' she says. 'Don't act like I'm helpless.'

He shrugs, and she walks away in a huff.

She heads to the smoking area and curses underneath her breath when she remembers her cigarettes are in her purse inside. She's not used to the new indoor smoking ban yet. She spots a girl picking a cigarette from a full pack, and it's not her brand, but she asks for one. The girl recognises Meiling as the one dancing like no one was watching, and gladly gives her a cigarette. She helps Meiling light it, and they chat about their fun nights so far.

A tall woman steps out of the club, and Meiling notices her through the corner of her eye because the woman is holding a fresh pack of Meiling's favourite cigarette brand. Meiling glances at the woman to check if she seems approachable, and she is taken by how stunning she is.

'Look to your right,' the woman shouts in German.

Meiling understands, and turns to her right to see the young man Michael beat up approaching. He grins at her, but she's not afraid. She's going to kick his balls the moment he's within reach, but the tall lady appears out of nowhere and drives the side of her palm into the young man's throat. He recoils, and the tall woman knocks him out on his feet with a straight punch. Then she races across to the other side of the door and grabs the hand of the young man's friend just before he drives a knife into the back of one of the bouncers that threw him out. She snaps his wrist, tosses him to the floor, and drives her elbow into the back of his head. He loses consciousness before the bouncer he was about to attack or anyone besides Meiling notices his presence.

Meiling watches in awe as the tall woman walks back to her, unconcerned with the chaos erupting behind her as the bouncers notice the man unconscious on the floor beside a large knife.

'I'm Franka,' the woman introduces herself, and offers Meiling the pack of cigarettes. 'It's yours. I don't smoke,' she says in German.

'I'm Meiling,' Meiling says in German, and accepts the cigarette.

'I know,' Franka says. 'How good is your German? Cos my English is bad.'

'It's good,' Meiling answers fluently. 'How did you know I speak German?'

'Alan told me. Also told me your cigarette brand. And that you like to step out alone for a cigarette once in a while.'

Meiling chuckles. They weren't alone after all . . . but she doesn't mind this badass at all. 'You're my bodyguard?'

Franka nods. 'But don't worry, most times you wouldn't know I'm there until you have to.'

'I could've handled him,' Meiling says, and gestures to the unconscious young man in front of them.

Franka nods and rolls the young man over to reveal a small bottle in his hand. 'Acid,' Franka says. 'I could not take the risk.'

The bottle of acid stuns Meiling, but she's reassured by Franka's presence.

'Thank you,' Meiling says.

'It's my job,' Franka says. 'But you're welcome.'

Meiling smiles, and Franka smiles back.

Michael bursts out of the club, followed by a few bouncers. He spots Meiling is safe and is relieved. Franka greets him with a nod, but he dismisses her with a wave, and this infuriates Meiling. Michael notices Meiling's fury and forces a smile at Franka.

'Let's go,' Michael says. 'I heard there was a knife.'

Meiling places a soft hand on Franka's shoulder to thank her and then walks to Michael. Michael hurries Meiling towards the car, and she turns back one more time to smile at Franka before she disappears down the next street.

Meiling and Franka's bond continues to blossom for the next six months. They spend a lot of time together because, beyond Franka's close-protection duties, Franka teaches Meiling self-defence, before progressing to offence because Meiling is a fast learner. Meiling also attempts to teach Franka English, which doesn't progress past a few key words because Meiling prefers speaking with Franka in German.

Michael is initially happy with the arrangement because Meiling stops complaining about being lonely. But that changes because Meiling and Franka spend too much time together; more time than he spends with his wife. When they are around him, he doesn't even know what they're talking about, because they mostly speak German.

The last straw comes when Meiling asks to go on a holiday with Franka. Meiling loves a holiday, but hasn't been on one for years because Michael is always busy and doesn't want her to travel alone or with friends without his security. But he doesn't exactly trust his security around Meiling, because he's seen the way the young men stare at her. Michael says no to the holiday. And Meiling gives him the cold shoulder for a few days before he makes it worse by saying, in Franka's presence, 'When we won the bloody war, we should've made all them Nazis speak English!'

Franka doesn't understand half of what Michael said, but she heard Nazi, which is enough. Meiling is furious and doesn't speak to Michael for three days, which prompts him to call Alan.

'Franka needs to go,' Michael says.

'What did she do?' Alan asks, but he knows precisely why Michael wants her gone. Everybody has noticed how friendly Franka and Meiling have become. And they also know how jealous Michael can be.

'I didn't say she did anything. If she did, she'd be dead, wouldn't she?'

'But you said she was perfect.'

'I want her gone.'

'Michael, she's a fucking unicorn. She's everything you asked for . . . a woman, speaks German, and a fucking decorated commando.'

'*Fucking decorated commando,*' Michael mimics. 'I didn't ask for Brigitte Nielsen, did I? Or some bloody lesbian who's sweet on my wife.'

Alan doesn't respond. He knows the suggestion is ridiculous, but sometimes it's pointless trying to reason with his brother's jealous nature.

'You send her back to Germany, or she dies in the line of duty,' Michael says. 'Your choice.'

'I'll take her on,' Alan says. 'The distribution network is picking up, so I could use her.'

'Good,' Michael says. 'And keep her the fuck away from me and Meiling!'

The day after, Alan approaches Franka with an improved offer to become his personal protection – he says he needs her, as he's starting to move in more dangerous circles, but Franka knows the real reason. She's a master at body language, so she didn't need to understand English to know Michael was unhappy about her relationship with Meiling. She tried to tell Meiling this would happen, but her friend believed Michael would recognise their relationship was nothing other than platonic.

Franka doesn't take long to accept Alan's proposal. He's always seemed like a decent man, the job would keep her around Meiling, and she still has a pension to fund. Franka was discharged from the Kommando Spezialkräfte for an action she, her team, and the military chain of command knew was a good deed. But it went against the diplomatic and economic agenda of the German ruling party, so she had to face the consequences. She didn't regret her actions or the consequences, because they confirmed to her she couldn't let others decide what is good or bad. That would be her choice to make.

She offered her services to the highest bidder, fully aware the people who were interested or could afford them aren't seen as the best of people. But neither were her previous employers. The bids came in, and Alan's wasn't the highest, but she felt the job – protecting a young, spirited woman married to a leading London gangster – would be the most rewarding for her, especially in the aftermath of the actions that led to her dismissal. And it was very much that, while it lasted.

Working for Alan proves rewarding as well, not just because he is indeed as decent a man as could be in his situation, but because they build trust in each other. Their current situation has forced Alan to become more ruthless, which is understandable and necessary for him to survive. But, last night, she was forced to question her trust in him.

Franka observes the warehouse from the driver's seat in the lead X5, ready to light the entire room on fire and kill whoever she needs to kill to ensure Alan gets out alive if Michael makes a move, or avenge Alan if she's too late. But she also notices everyone repeatedly glance towards the last car in the convoy and speak in hushed tones around it. There is somebody important in the car, and it isn't Michael because he's in the room with Alan. And the ninjas haven't arrived yet. It's Meiling.

Franka keeps observing, and when Michael, Alan, and the others step out of the room, she studies them for a reaction. And Alan confirms it's Meiling with his response when Michael opens the back door of the last car. Franka expects Alan to head straight to their car to inform her, but he goes to speak to the young man at the entrance. And the young man gives away what he and Alan are talking about with his eyes, because he looks in Franka's direction and then in Meiling's direction. Alan wants to know if Franka knows Meiling is there. Alan doesn't intend to tell her. And he doesn't for the entire ride to the cottage.

Alan doesn't trust Franka enough not to jeopardise or abandon the mission to save Meiling, and Franka is hurt by the lack of trust. Franka would never interfere with the ulti- mate purpose of the mission – kill Michael, Gary, and Dre for revenge and to give Alan a clear path to rebuild the network – but she easily could've saved Meiling as well. And Alan knows that. But he wants Meiling dead, which serves no purpose.

When they arrive at the cottage, and Alan steps out to speak to Michael, Franka drafts a message on her burner to Meiling's number, which she knows by heart.

Schau nach rechts.

It means 'look to your right'. Meiling will immediately know it's from Franka, and hopefully it will trigger Meiling to run. But Franka doesn't send it just yet. She waits till the ninjas run off to the cottage and the time for her and Alan to execute their mission approaches.

As Franka expects, Alan sends her to quietly kill the driver of the second car while he distracts Michael, Gary, and Dre. Franka sends the text as she approaches the driver, quickly snaps the driver's neck, and turns back to Michael's car. Meiling bursts out of the car towards the forest, just as Franka hoped. But Alan shoots Meiling just before she disappears into the trees. The shot hits Meiling's shoulder, and she tumbles into the forest. Franka is furious but notices Gary and Dre in the front seats of Michael's car, reaching for their guns. Franka doesn't understand why Alan would bother with Meiling before taking care of Gary and Dre. But her instincts kick in, and she shoots Gary and Dre in the head before either raises their gun.

Franka notices Alan scanning the area of the forest where Meiling fell, so she hurries to the car to distract him. Meiling's a fighter, so a bullet to her shoulder won't stop her running. But Alan will catch up if he goes after her, and he looks intent on killing her. Franka guesses she'll stop that happening if she asks who he shot heading towards the forest. She expects him to lie, which will stop them pursuing Meiling. But to her surprise, he admits it's Meiling and shows no remorse. This situation has changed him — she's seen it happen to many others in the heat of battle. They are never the same afterwards. She might have to put him down now if he chooses to pursue Meiling into the forest, but she notices the silence coming from the cottage. There are more important things . . . for now.

Franka sends Alan to the front door, and she heads to the back of the cottage. But as she carefully makes her way along the side of the building, she spots a window with its glass detached. She peeks through the window. There are two dead ninjas just inside – they didn't make it far at all. She approaches the edge of the house and peeks towards the back entrance, and there are two dead ninjas just inside the open back door. The open door is an invitation, and the dead bodies left by the door are a deterrent. Whoever is inside is very good and isn't interested in just killing; they are just as happy if you leave them alone. But she can't, because they have Meiling's bracelet or, at least, know who attacked her that night.

Franka scans the bodies, and it's clear there were two shooters because of their position. She crouches and stays almost attached to the walls of the building as she sneaks towards the back entrance. But she hears a conversation happening inside and stops. She recognises Alan's voice, and it doesn't sound distressed. She then recognises Rebecca's voice, but not that of the third person – a man. She listens, and although she can't make out the words, it's a calm conversation. She also notices steady breathing from two people at either side of the back entrance who are not in the conversation.

Franka's phone vibrates, and it's Alan, so she answers.

'Stand down. It's my son,' Alan says, and ends the call.

Franka needs to act fast.

'I need your help,' Franka says with just enough volume for the two people at either side of the entrance to hear.

There is silence for a moment. 'What do you want?' a woman with a Russian accent responds.

'My friend is hurt in the forest. I fear she will die there if you don't help her.'

'Why don't you go help her?'

'My boss, Alan, shot her.'

There is silence again.

'Why do you trust me to help?' the woman asks.

'Alan says his son is inside. I know he doesn't have a son, but I know who he is talking about . . . *Pretty Boy*. If you're a friend of Pretty Boy, I trust you.'

'Okay,' a man with a Russian accent says from behind Franka.

Franka heard him approach but didn't react in case he reacted, and she was forced to kill him. She turns around to the man.

'I'm Oleg,' he says, and reaches out to shake her hand.

'I'm Franka,' she says, and takes it.

A woman steps out the back door and approaches them. 'I'm Katerina,' she says. 'What is your friend's name?'

'Meiling,' Franka responds.

'We'll find her,' Katerina says.

'She'll be scared and hiding. Call out to her and tell her to look to the right. She'll know I sent you.'

Katerina nods.

'What's your number?' Oleg says. 'We'll call when we find her and let you know where to come see her.'

Franka nods and gives Oleg her number.

'Don't tell your boss about us, yes?' Oleg asks.

Franka nods.

'London is my home'

Oleg lets Franka in and quickly fills me in on what happened last night.

'And she knows I'm here?' I ask.

Oleg nods. 'She says she trusts you.'

Fair enough.

Franka walks in through the back door and greets me with a nod, and I reciprocate the gesture.

'Thank you,' she says to Oleg.

'It's okay,' Oleg replies. 'She lost a lot of blood. But she is strong; she will survive. I don't think you should wake her up, though.'

Franka nods again.

'Follow me,' Oleg says, and leads her towards a door on the other side of the room.

'Wait,' I say, and pick Meiling's bracelet from my pocket.

I walk to Franka and offer the bracelet. 'I was going to give you this anyway when I thought Meiling was dead, because it sounded like you care about her. But now she's alive, and there's no one better to give it back to her.'

'Thank you,' she says, and accepts the bracelet.

Oleg opens the door to a room that resembles a state-of-the-art sick bay, and Meiling is unconscious on the bed, receiving medicine through an intravenous line in her wrist. Franka steps inside the room, and Oleg closes the door to give them privacy.

Oleg walks back to me and gestures for us to sit.

'Alan is going off the rails,' Oleg says. 'I didn't trust him before, but certainly not now that he's snatched power from his brother.'

I concede Alan is going off the rails, but I trust him, and I'll get him back on.

'And he won't survive this,' Oleg says. 'Michael's men won't follow him.'

There it is. The obvious reason Alan needs me, and I know Oleg won't be happy.

'I . . . well, Pretty Boy, rallied the troops, and . . .'

'You did that?' he says, and shakes his head. 'You're a lot more sentimental than you think. But then I know this.'

'Ah, shut up,' I tease.

'It's true. But, my friend, this will get bloody very quick. I beg you to stay away.'

'It's the Lenkovs. They're coming after me as well.'

'Yes. But they've been coming and couldn't find you. I

will sort out another location. Maybe outside UK. It's easier nowadays.'

'I wasn't going to stay away for ever, Oleg. London is my home. Not theirs. If anyone is to leave, it should be them.'

Oleg smiles, but then shakes his head. 'You are too fearless, my friend. I love it.'

We laugh.

'I'm not going to convince you to leave, yes?' he asks.

'No. Plus, I've given Alan my word.'

'You and your principles,' he says, and chuckles. 'These people break their word when they need to all the time . . . I told you, there are very few of you left around.'

'Let's hope enough to stop London turning into a war zone.'

Oleg shrugs.

'I'm going to need your help,' I say.

'No problem, my friend. What do you need?'

'Not sure yet,' I say. 'But I'll let you know soon as. And don't worry, I'll make sure Alan doesn't know you exist.'

Oleg nods.

'Speaking of which,' I say. 'I need a secure phone.'

'No problem,' Oleg says, and bounces off the sofa.

He opens one of the many safes hidden around the room and picks out a phone and a charger. He hands me what looks like a regular smartphone, but I know there has to be more to it, otherwise it wouldn't be in a safe.

'Okay,' I say, and gesture at the phone. 'Tell me about it.'

Oleg grins; he enjoys this part too much. 'Nothing special. Just the latest smartphone. But it cannot be tracked. If someone tries, you will receive an alert letting you know and giving you the person's location. You will also have the choice to counter the track – track who's trying to track you – or send a fake location of your choice to the person, and then move this location however you like. Lead this person to where you want.'

'Nothing special?' I ask.

He shrugs, and we laugh.

'I told you, my friend. I have it all.'

I nod. 'Including a sick bay.'

'Sick bay?' he asks, seemingly having never heard the term.

'Emergency room,' I say, and gesture to the room Meiling and Franka are in.

'Ah,' he says. 'That's what it's called?'

'Err, sort of,' I say. 'What do you call it?'

'Oleg's clinic,' he says with pride.

'That's much better,' I say.

We laugh, but the door to Oleg's clinic opens, and we stop. Franka steps out, and over her shoulder, I can see that Meiling is still unconscious. Franka gently shuts the door and approaches Oleg and me. She shows no emotion, but I know it's buried away.

'Are you okay?' I ask.

She seems shocked by the question. 'I've been better,' she says, which I imagine is as much emotion as she will give away. 'Can you keep her till she recovers?' she asks Oleg. 'I have money. I'll pay.'

'Don't insult me,' he says. 'I like to help good people. I will

let our friend here know when Meiling regains consciousness, and I'm sure he will find a way to let you know soon as
possible. Other than that, call me whenever you want for an
update.'

'Thank you,' she says.

'I need to ask for something,' he says.

She nods.

'I know you will follow your boss into this fight with the
Lenkovs. You are a soldier; you are used to following orders
you don't like, from superiors you don't like. Our friend here
is going to follow your boss into this fight as well because he
gave his word.'

She glances at me, and I can tell she respects the principle.

'I need you to watch out for him, for me,' Oleg says.

I chuckle. 'I'm okay, Franka,' I say.

'I will do that,' she says to Oleg.

'Thank you,' Oleg says.

'No need for that,' she says. 'I like to help good people.'

She smiles, and Oleg and I smile back.

'See you soon,' she says to me.

'See you soon,' I respond.

'Talk soon,' she says to Oleg, and walks out of the back
door.

'You hungry?' he asks me.

I nod.

'Good.'

'How is any of this relevant?'

Alan leans on his Jaguar outside the makeshift police station in Battersea and watches Nisa's car approach and park beside him.

'What is so urgent?' Nisa asks, and steps out of her car. 'I had to leave a legal clinic for this, Alan. And those people really need help.'

'They found Valentin Lenkov's body, and they plan to arrest me for his murder.'

'Okay,' she says, unfazed. And this time, she won't ask Alan if he has anything to do with it. 'What evidence do they have?'

'Nothing.'

'Nothing? But they are going to arrest you?'

'It's not really about a conviction. I don't think I'd make it to the hearing.'

'The CPS has to agree to charge, so what will the investigating team present to the CPS? And don't tell me the CPS is in on this too. You are fairly high-profile . . . there has to be evidence that stands up to some scrutiny.'

He shrugs. 'They don't have the murder weapon. It's destroyed. And they have no credible witnesses.'

Destroyed murder weapon . . . lack of *credible* witnesses, she repeats to herself. Alan did it. But she'll ask why some other time . . . when this is all over.

'And I have an alibi,' he adds.

That makes little sense. He did it, so he can't have an alibi. 'Let's hear it,' she asks.

Alan and Nisa sit on the same side of the table in the same interview room as ten days earlier, waiting for the officers. But this time, they don't have to wait long. Jack Moore leads Inspector Caroline Maguire and Sergeant Rhys Evans into the room. They sit across from Alan and Nisa, and there are no pleasantries before Caroline starts recording.

'Chief Superintendent Jack Moore, Inspector Caroline Maguire, and Sergeant Rhys Evans interviewing Alan Pierce with his counsel Nisa Fraser-Hulton QC present. The time is 4:13 p.m.,' she directs at the recording device, and turns to Alan. 'We gather you want to make a statement.'

'Yes,' Alan responds.

'And legal counsel is happy with this?' Caroline asks Nisa.

'Yes,' Nisa responds.

'Go ahead,' Caroline says.

'Last time you asked me to detail my whereabouts in the early hours of April 15, 2009, specifically between three a.m.

to four a.m. I made no comment on the advice of counsel, but I've heard through the grapevine that you've found Valentin Lenkov's body, and you are looking at me for that.' Alan pauses. 'That's a serious crime, so I need to clear my name before this gets out of hand. I have an alibi for those hours. I was in the A&E of University College Hospital, and I'm sure you'll see me on the CCTV.'

'You're well aware that NHS trusts don't keep CCTV recordings that far back.'

'Sure,' Alan responds. 'But if you check the CCTV on the streets around the hospital, I'm sure you'll see my car arrive with an ambulance just before ten p.m. on April 14, 2009, and leave around five a.m. on April 15, 2009.'

'We'll check,' Caroline says.

Alan knows the CCTV wouldn't show him in the car. It will show Franka driving the car, but as the back windows are tinted, they'll have to take her word that he was in the back seat. Not that they'll believe her, but it'll add a dent to the version of the night they are trying to prove.

'Also, I have several witnesses willing to make statements that I was in the hospital. I initially wasn't keen to ask them, and you will know why when I give you their names, but after I told them you were trying to railroad me for a murder, they were more than happy to make a statement and eager for you to contact them. Gary James, Andreas Goutas, Meiling Downing, and Michael Downing.'

Jack shifts in his chair at the mention of Michael, and Alan spots it. The Lenkovs must've told Jack that Alan killed

Michael, but he hasn't told his investigating team. How can he? It's not exactly public knowledge at the moment. Alan pulls out a sheet of paper with handwritten contact details for the names he mentions.

'Yes. That's my half-brother, a suspected gangster, his wife, and two of his closest friends. But there are many more people willing to make a statement if those names aren't enough.'

Rhys takes the paper, and Caroline leans away from Alan. Both are starting to question the strength of their case and the information they are working with. It's time for Alan to pounce.

'I did my research on both of you,' Alan says, and gestures to Caroline and Rhys. 'The best of the best Leeds has to offer, and the best of the best Cardiff has to offer. I bet Chief Super Moore brought you down to London for a highly confidential case aimed at stopping gang crime in the capital. Bet he didn't tell you that the only reason this is secret is that you're working directly for Marat Lenkov.'

Jack is angry but forces a smile, and Caroline and Rhys are curious.

'Yes, the father of the victim. How did you think your investigation could afford this building overlooking the river? I know the Met has more budget than the forces you both came from, but c'mon! Weren't you intrigued to find out who owns the building? It's Battersea View Developments. Which is owned by this shell company that's owned by another shell company, but ultimately owned by Lenkov Family Investments Limited. I know there are a fair few shell companies in between, but you lot are the best of the best . . . aren't you? These are things you should investigate.'

'How is any of this relevant?' Jack asks, and reaches across Caroline towards the recorder.

'Oh, no, don't stop the recording now, Jack. I'm not finished.' Jack pulls away from the recorder.

'I just wanted these fine officers to have the full picture before they tarnish their stellar careers on this stitch-up.'

'We'll confirm your alibi,' Caroline says.

'Thank you.'

'Are you done?' she asks.

'Yeah.'

Caroline stops recording.

'I'm sure you've heard Pretty Boy is back?' Alan asks Jack.

The news stuns Jack — he hasn't heard, but he also doesn't know if Alan is telling the truth. Caroline and Rhys turn to Jack, having no clue who Pretty Boy is or his connection to Jack. They read from Jack's reaction that Pretty Boy is important to him, and not for a jolly reason.

'I guess not,' Alan says, and turns to Caroline. 'Anyway, I look forward to your call clearing this whole mess up.'

Alan and Nisa walk out of the building and head to their cars. Nisa is pissed and just wants to get out of there, but Alan is so delighted with his performance that he doesn't notice her annoyance. Nisa enters her car without saying a word, and that's when Alan realises she's unhappy.

'Are you okay?' he asks before she shuts her door. 'I thought that went really well. Didn't you?'

'It went well,' she says coldly, and shuts her door.

'Oh, come on, what's wrong now?'

She lowers her window. 'I need to get back to the clinic.'

'Okay,' Alan says. 'But can we discuss next steps first?'

'Discuss?' she asks. 'We didn't discuss what happened in there. I was just there for decoration while you play your games with Jack Moore. Don't call me again unless you get charged.'

'Relax, Nisa.'

'Relax?' she asks, and glares at him.

'I don't mean it—'

'I thought so,' she interrupts, and drives off.

DAY 17, 20:00

'It's not their fight'

I step into the penthouse flat and the only thing on my mind is going to sleep. But just before I get to the bedroom, the intercom buzzes. I walk to the screen, and see a woman waiting at the front entrance of the building. She appears harmless but has a presence to her.

'Who are you?' I ask.

'A friend of Alan's. You might have heard him refer to me as "X",' she says. 'But don't bother asking him because I haven't told him I'm paying you a visit.'

'What do you want?' I ask.

'I think it's best we have that talk inside.'

I let her into the building, and she makes her way to the private lift without guidance and buzzes again. I let her into the lift and walk to the kitchen island to wait. The lift opens, and she strides out towards me; she's calm. I gesture for her to sit anywhere around the kitchen island, and she picks the seat closest to me.

'Nice to meet you, Pretty Boy,' she says. 'I've heard a lot about you.'

I nod. I'm not getting into that. 'Want something to drink?' I ask.

'Sure. I'd like tea.'

I remember the cabinet stocked with a large variety of tea and head over to it. 'Anything in particular?' I ask, and step aside for her to see the options.

'Okay,' she says, astounded by the variety. 'I thought I went for the straightforward option. Is there mint in there?'

'Yeah,' I say, and grab two individually wrapped bags of mint tea.

I put on the electric kettle and grab two teacups as the water boils.

'You're having one as well?' she asks.

'Yes. I hear it helps you sleep.'

'Never tested that myself. But you'll let me know if it works for you.'

I nod and prepare the teas. I walk back to my seat and place a cup in front of her.

'Thank you,' she says.

'No problem.'

'You're not going to ask who I am?'

'No. If you want to tell me, you will.'

She nods. 'Very well. I'm a bit like you. I like to keep my identity to myself. But it's only fair you have a name for me because I think you might be hearing a lot from me. Although you probably won't see me again. It's better that way.'

'I'm guessing "X" is off the table.'

She smiles and nods.

'Well, it's your name,' I say. 'You decide.'

'"Mint". How's that?'

'Works for me. And it's better than Pretty Boy.'

'Absolutely not. I was intrigued the first time I heard it a decade ago, and have been looking forward to meeting you since. You haven't disappointed. You're also polite, which isn't on the list of your many virtues. I'll be sure to add that to the legend.'

'You're police.'

She rocks her hand slightly. 'Close enough,' she says.

'What does that mean?'

'Let's just say I haven't arrested anyone in over a decade. But my job is to keep London safe.'

I nod.

'And from what I hear, you have London's best interests at heart as well.'

I don't respond. But I can tell she's getting closer to why she's here.

'We received information that Michael was preparing his troops for war and were all ready to raid that warehouse and arrest the lot of them to prevent the city descending into chaos. But then you arrive and send everyone home.'

'It's not their fight.'

She smiles and sips her tea. 'I agree,' she says. 'And the

people I ultimately work for believe you're the one we need to contain the gang crime in London. We can't stop the illegal drug trade. The horse left the barn a long time ago on that one. We appreciate that, but we won't ever stop trying. We can't . . . no politician will be courageous enough to campaign on legalising drugs, and that's where we get our marching orders. But we also need people like you to help keep the violent crimes to a minimum. And you're brilliant, so I'll just put this on the table . . . the motives of the stakeholders on my end aren't entirely altruistic.'

I sip my tea and don't speak.

'It's good tea, isn't it?' she asks.

'Yes,' I say.

'I knew that'd make you speak,' she says. 'There is a meeting in an hour, and my superiors would like you to attend. Alan would be there, and I asked him to bring you, but he refused my request. I suppose he doesn't want to make the same mistake Michael did.'

I know what she's talking about, and she's also telling me she knows Michael is dead.

'I'm here to invite you personally,' she says. 'I even have a car waiting outside to take us.'

'I'll pass,' I say. 'But thank you for considering me.'

'Loyal as well,' she says, and smiles. 'I'll be sure to add that to the legend too. Is there a number I can contact you on?'

'Sure,' I say, and give her the number of the *very* smart phone Oleg gave me earlier in the day.

'I'll call you soon,' she says, and finishes her tea. 'I know this has been a tad odd, but it really has been a pleasure to meet you.'

'Likewise,' I say, and reach for a handshake.

She shakes my hand, and I walk her to the lift.

'I wouldn't tell Alan about this meeting if I were you,' she says, and steps into the lift. 'He's still finding his footing as the *king* and might make a rash decision.'

I don't respond, and the lift door closes. That was more than a tad odd. And more to come, I'm sure. I finish my tea and go to bed.

DAY 20, 11:00

'Fuck inflation'

I'm sitting at a round table in a large meeting room of a private members' club in Soho, which is supposedly neutral territory. Alan sits beside me, and the rest of the chairs are occupied by members of the 'collective' who I've just been introduced to – Priyanka, Turhan, Hunter, and Pete. Each has a couple of associates inside the room who are visibly armed. They weren't going to come to the meeting otherwise. And Franka stands behind Alan, watching them all.

The four collective members at the table try to project nonchalance, but they are anxious at my presence. And some of their associates aren't even trying to hide it – their eyes are fixed on me like I'm a dragon that'll breathe fire and burn them to ashes at a moment's notice. It's amusing, and I struggle not to smile.

'Thanks for coming,' Alan says. 'First, I apologise for taking a few days to put this together. But with everything that's happening, I needed to come to the table with something real.'

The collective members nod in acceptance.

'I'll make this as brief as possible,' Alan continues. 'The bad news first. Yes' – he gestures at me – 'Pretty Boy demolished Tyrone and his fortress. But you all knew it was coming. He was trying to destroy what I built. We have no issue with anyone at this table. So, you don't need to worry about that.'

'I'm not fucking worried,' Pete says.

'I understand, Pete. I used the wrong words there, and I apologise.'

Pete nods.

'What about Jamal?' Priyanka asks. 'He was just as involved as Tyrone.'

'I know. And that's the *bad* news. I've reached out to him . . .'

'Why?' she asks.

'I think it's better for Jamal to be in the tent pissing out than out pissing in.'

'I can handle him,' she says. 'And he won't be pissing anywhere when I'm done.'

I fight back a smile. She's confident in every word. I like her.

'I know. But that might end up another long and drawn-out battle that'll only bring more police attention to our business. And we need to get up and running quickly.'

'You're ready to kick off delivery again?' Turhan says.

'Yes. That's the good news. But we'll get to that in a minute. I just want all of us to agree about Jamal first.'

Turhan nods.

'What makes you think Jamal will come back?' Hunter asks. 'He's already trying to take over Tyrone and Callum's territories. Why would he stop now?'

'He needs product, and we all know he's keen to make a deal when he wants to.'

'Are we just supposed to allow him to take Callum and Tyrone's territory?'

'We're not allowing him to do anything,' Alan says. 'And from what I hear, he's facing serious opposition from what's left of Tyrone and Callum's crews. But I don't see why we should interfere, either. The territory has been available for a few days, and neither of you showed interest. So, I'm guessing you're happy to let the chips fall where they may.'

Pete sniggers. 'Fuck are you chatting, mate?' he chides. 'Of course we were keen. At least, I was. We just didn't have the product, so what use was the territory?'

'What use is the territory to Jamal, then?' Alan retorts.

'Fuck him, he's young and stupid—'

'Do you have a point?' Alan cuts him off.

This stuns Pete.

'You said you need product to take the territory,' Alan says, stern. 'But the young and stupid Jamal is trying to do it without product. So, do you have another excuse? Or can we move on?'

The room falls silent, and Pete doesn't know how to respond. He's astounded. I'm guessing Alan hasn't spoken to him like this before. Hello, Pete, meet the new Alan.

'Okay. We move on,' Alan says. 'I've arranged a meeting

with Jamal tomorrow. He wasn't keen to meet me, but he is keen to meet Pretty Boy.'

That's news to me, but I don't react.

'I imagine you lot prefer Pretty Boy in the meeting as opposed to me,' Alan says, and smiles.

Hunter and Turhan chuckle, but Priyanka and Pete do not react.

'If you guys – and girl – want,' Alan says, 'we can negotiate Jamal pulling out from the other territories. As you remember, we got him to stop his expansion last time.'

'Yeah,' Turhan says. 'But you sold him product at five per cent below our rates for nine months.'

'I know. We all agreed to that.'

'That might be what he's doing now,' Hunter adds. 'Throwing his facking toys out of the pram for a better deal. No!'

'Okay. Things have to be unanimous here. So, a reduced rate is off the table for Jamal. But you still want us to negotiate him pulling out? We don't need to use the carrot,' he says, and gestures to me, 'when we have the stick.'

Turhan, Hunter, and Pete nod, but Priyanka doesn't respond.

'Priyanka?' Alan asks.

I can see in her eyes that she doesn't want Jamal back in, but she nods anyway.

'Good,' Alan says. 'Now, the good news. As an apology, the first four deliveries will be at a ten per cent discount.'

This news delights the collective members.

'The first delivery will be in two days . . . very early morning, as usual. And you will get calls with the details a few hours before. So it might be a sleepless night for you, but it'll be worth it.'

The collective members nod in approval.

'Wait,' Turhan says. 'This ten per cent discount . . . is it just us going back to the previous price for four deliveries before we return to the price Michael jacked up by ten per cent last time? Cos that's . . . ?'

'No,' Alan says. 'Michael's price is done. We stick to the increase pegged to the inflation rate, as agreed.'

This surprises Pete, and it seems I'm the only one that notices before he hides his expression.

'Three point eight per cent, then?'

'I trust you to know the number, Turhan.'

Turhan smiles.

'That's it, we're finished,' Alan says. 'Thanks for coming.'

The collective members and their associates leave the room as quickly as they entered. Except Pete and his associates, who don't move.

'What, Pete?' Alan asks.

'First, what's this about a three point eight per cent increase?' Pete asks. 'Michael and I agreed my price wouldn't change.'

'I know,' Alan says. 'But from now on, everyone's price, including yours, is pegged to inflation—'

'Fuck inflation. That's not—'

'Shut up, Pete. I'm talking.'

'Who the fuck do you think you're talking to?' Pete asks, enraged. 'If not for Michael, I would smack—'

Alan slaps Pete, and Pete almost falls off his chair. Pete's two associates reach for their guns, but Franka points her gun at them and shakes her head before they pull their weapons. They hesitate and turn to Pete for instruction, and he gestures for them to relax.

'Aright, Alan,' Pete says. 'Aright.'

He walks out of the room, and his men follow.

Franka glances at me, and I can tell she doesn't like the new Alan very much.

DAY 20, 11:30

'You know nothing'

Franka drives us away from the private members' club. Alan, in the front, glances at me in the rear-view for the second time in under a minute.

'I'm okay, Alan,' I say.

'I'm sorry about that. Pete's just been an annoying fuck for too long now, and I need to set him straight. Especially—'

'It's okay, Alan,' I interrupt. 'Franka had it covered. But what's this about me meeting Jamal tomorrow? We didn't discuss that.'

'I know. But it wasn't exactly my choice.'

'Whose, then?'

'The person setting it up.'

'Who's that?'

'You'll see very soon,' he says to me, and turns to Franka. 'Let's head to his.'

Alan connects his smartphone to the stereo and plays

'Runaway' by Kanye West. I love the song. I love the entire *My Beautiful Dark Twisted Fantasy* album, but I know Alan isn't a big fan of the genre.

I lean forward. 'Is this what he usually listens to?' I ask Franka. 'Or is he just playing it because I'm here?'

'He's just playing it because you're here,' Franka responds, and we laugh.

'I thought you'd be a fan of Kanye West,' Alan says.

'His work is genius. But I couldn't care less about him.'

'You couldn't care less about anyone,' he says. 'But me, of course.'

He laughs, and I indulge him with a smile.

Fifteen minutes later, Franka parks outside the penthouse, and Alan and I step out, but she remains in the car.

I walk to the driver's side. 'What are you doing?' I ask her.

She hesitates and glances at Alan. 'There's no threat inside,' she says. 'So, I'll stay outside to watch.'

I open the door. 'You're not staying outside. And before you say anything, I'm sure we'll feel much safer with you around. Not outside.'

'I agree,' Alan says.

She nods and steps out of the car.

We step into the reception, and Rebecca is sitting on one of the sofas.

'What's she doing here?' I ask Alan.

He ignores me. 'I hope you haven't been waiting long,' he says to Rebecca.

'No,' she says, and stands. 'Was just a couple minutes ahead of you.' She turns to me. 'I see you're happy to see me.'

'Always,' I respond. 'But what are you doing here?'

Rebecca ignores me and turns to Franka. 'Lovely to see you again, Franka,' Rebecca says.

'Same,' Franka responds.

'You didn't tell him?' Rebecca asks Alan and gestures to me.

'I thought it was better you did,' Alan answers.

She nods. 'All right, let's see this penthouse.'

The private lift opens, and I lead everyone towards the kitchen island.

'Want anything to drink?' I ask.

'A good host,' Rebecca quips, and admires the penthouse decor.

'Okay,' I say. 'Want anything?'

Franka shakes her head.

'Red wine,' Alan says.

'Same,' Rebecca says.

'I have no idea where that is,' I say.

'Shit host,' Rebecca quips.

'Fuck off,' I say.

Alan laughs. 'My fault,' he says, and pulls out a wine storage cabinet concealed in the wall. 'I didn't exactly give him the tour.'

'And it's hidden,' I say.

'There are other things hidden in the wall,' Franka says.

'That's the tour I want,' I say.

'Me too,' Rebecca says. 'Sounds like that'll be fun.'

'Might have to be another time though, cos we need to rush out,' Alan says, and pours red wine into two glasses. 'Need to get things ready for the delivery.'

'No problem,' I say.

'You're a fucking killjoy, Alan,' Rebecca adds.

Alan laughs. 'Trust me, I'm not,' he says, and hands Rebecca a glass of red wine. 'I'll make sure Franka gives you the tour soon.'

'Whatever,' she says, and sips the wine. 'Wow . . . this is good.'

'I knew you'd like it. From a family vineyard in Burgundy. There are four more in the cabinet,' he says and gestures to me. 'And as far as I know, he doesn't drink, so it's all yours.'

Rebecca nods.

'Okay, then,' I say. 'Now that we've let the bougie ones in the room have their moment, what are you supposed to tell me, Rebecca?'

She rolls her eyes. 'I set up the meeting with Jamal,' she says. 'It's at one of my uncle's tower blocks in Hackney.'

'Your uncle?' I ask. 'Why would Jamal agree to that?'

'My uncle is Israel Reynolds,' she says, and allows that to sink in.

I know Israel Reynolds — everyone in the game knows the family — but I didn't know Rebecca was his niece.

'Jamal and Israel have been in business for a couple of years now, and there is trust there. Jamal listens to him, so he'll mediate as much as possible. And he'll provide the security as well.'

'Are you happy with that?' Alan asks.

I nod.

'I'm coming with you,' Rebecca says. 'And I don't want to hear anything about that. If I'm not coming, it's not happening.'

I nod again.

'Good,' Alan says. 'I'll leave you to discuss strategy or whatever. But we're happy to continue distributing to him at the previously agreed price . . . with the same ten per cent discount as the others.'

'And about his expansion to Tyrone and Callum's territories?' I ask.

'I don't really care about that . . . it's not key for us.'

'It is for your collective members, though.'

'Not enough to allow us to sweeten the deal with Jamal. Come on, do they expect you to beat him up till he agrees?'

'How much do you usually deliver to him?' I ask.

'Why?'

'He needs more product to feed the new territories. I'll make sure we agree to no more than his usual delivery . . . even considering the disruption.'

Alan nods. 'I'll send the numbers for the past six months tomorrow morning.'

I nod.

'See you in a bit,' he says.

'See you,' I say.

Rebecca nods at him and blows a kiss to Franka.

Franka smiles and nods at me, and Alan leads her into the lift.

The lift doors close, and I wait a few moments before turning to Rebecca. 'Why are you doing this?' I ask.

'Someone has to watch your back,' she says, and refills her wine glass. 'It was supposed to be you and Alan. And we both know I'm much more useful if things go wrong in there.'

'Fair. But it's not your fight.'

'You made it my fight when you gave him your word.'

Oleg has spoken to her. I appreciate them both more than they know. But maybe they do, and that's why they keep risking their lives for me. I can't afford to lose Rebecca to this fight, though. I fear I'd take it very badly and plunge this town further into chaos.

'We'll be fine,' she says, as if reading me. 'I'm Damian Reynolds Junior's only kin. Israel can't let me die on his watch. The security will be fucking tight. Much tighter than it would've been with you and Alan.'

I nod. That's true.

'I'm going for a tour of this stunning place,' she says.

'Oh, yeah . . .'

'Not with you . . . you've only been here a couple days. You know nothing.'

'Fuck off, then.'

'Fuck you, then,' she says, and walks off.

I chuckle and put on the kettle. I pick a bag of green tea from the tea cabinet as I wait for the kettle to boil.

'Come here,' Rebecca calls from upstairs.

'What?'

'Come here!'

I huff and walk up the stairs.

'In here,' she calls.

I follow her voice to a bedroom, and she is naked on the bed. I hesitate.

'What?' she says. 'You were happy to fuck my brains out when Jamie was alive. But now that he's dead, you've developed a conscience?'

Something like that, I think. But I won't dare say it.

'Come here,' she says.

I take off my t-shirt and walk to her.

DAY 21, 23:00

'Curiosity killed the cat, innit?'

I drive into the council estate that houses Israel's tower blocks, and a young man immediately recognises the car. He waves for me to stop, and Rebecca gestures for me to comply. I do, and he approaches the passenger side of the car, so I reduce the volume of the stereo – playing 'All of the Lights' by Kanye West – before I lower the window.

'We got a spot for you,' he says to Rebecca. 'Follow me, yeah?'

She nods, and he leads the car to an empty parking spot in front of one of the tower blocks, which I'm sure would otherwise be occupied at this time of night.

Rebecca and I step out, and music booming louder than I thought possible from a car engulfs us. We turn to the music, and there are three cars across the street full of young men glaring at us. That must be Jamal's boys trying to intimidate us, but I'm preoccupied with how good the song is.

'Don't worry about them boys,' the young man says. 'They can't step foot this side.'

'We're not worried,' Rebecca says. 'But thank you.'

'What's the song?' I ask.

'Giggs, "Look What the Cat Dragged In". It's hard, fam.'

I nod. It is.

The young man points to another two young men standing at the entrance to the tower block. 'They'll take you up,' he says.

Rebecca and I walk to the men, and one of them leads us into the tower block, where three more young men guard the lift. The men greet us with a nod, and one of them calls the lift. As we wait, I study my surroundings to evaluate the threat level and Rebecca's and my chances to survive and escape if the need arises. They're not very good, because the other lift in the tower block is out of service, and there only seems to be one way out, which is the way we came in.

'Are mandem having a party outside or something, Nando?' the largest of the men guarding the lift asks.

The man who let us in shrugs. 'Allow it, Kofi. Them boys just want trouble, is all.'

'Taking the piss, fam,' Kofi says, and turns to me. 'Yeah, boss?'

I nod. 'Hard song, though,' I say.

'Yeah, fam,' Kofi responds. 'Giggs is hard and that.'

Finally, the lift arrives, and Nando pushes the button for the twelfth floor – the top floor.

We arrive, and Nando leads us to two men standing in front of an open door. One is much older than the other.

'Thanks, Nando,' the older man says.

Nando nods and walks away.

'Hello, Rebecca,' the older man says with a familiar tone.

'Hey, Mo,' Rebecca responds, and kisses him on the cheek. 'Long time.'

'I know. But good to know you're doing good,' Mo says.

'I'm not sure about that, Mo. I lost my husband a few days ago.'

'I didn't know you were married,' Mo says. 'My condolences.'

I guess I'm not the only one she didn't tell. I don't react, but Rebecca glares at me anyway, knowing exactly what I'm thinking. But I don't acknowledge her glare.

'Everything bless?' Mo asks me.

I nod.

'Any weapons?' Mo asks us both.

We shake our heads.

'Okay. I trust you,' Mo says, and gestures to the young man beside him. 'But Jamal's boy here . . .'

'My name's Tunde, fam,' the young man interrupts. 'I told you already.'

'Calm down, Tunde fam,' Mo teases, which infuriates Tunde. 'Tunde fam is going to search you. Don't worry, I searched Jamal and his boy upstairs—'

'His name is Bash,' Tunde interrupts.

'I'm an old man, innit?' Mo teases. 'I don't hear very well anymore.'

Tunde rolls his eyes and approaches to search me, but I glare at him, and he stops in his tracks. Mo and Rebecca laugh. I didn't intend to show Tunde up; it was just a natural reaction to him approaching me without proper notice. I raise my arms to invite him to search me, and he does.

'Don't fuck about,' Rebecca says, and raises her hands.

He pats her down carefully and nods.

'You really didn't bring weapons?' Mo asks.

We nod, and Mo picks a tray from inside the house to show us two handguns and a knife.

'We're not worried,' Rebecca says. 'But I guess they are.'

Mo smiles and steps aside. 'Up the stairs. First door on your right,' he says.

Rebecca and I step through the door, and I take in our surroundings. Someone other than Israel lives here. Someone very tidy. But there are no options to escape; the only way out is through the front door, but there's a kitchen, and there'll be weapons there.

Rebecca leads up the stairs and opens the first door to our right. Israel sits at the head of a dining table, and Jamal and Bash, an enormous young man with arms bigger than my head, sit to one side. No weapons are allowed in the room, but Jamal's brought a human weapon. Rebecca is amused by Bash and glances at me with a smirk before we sit on the chairs across from Jamal and Bash. I scan the room for something I can use to fight Bash, because a fist fight probably won't go my way. There are two sturdy glasses in front of him and Jamal, filled with what looks like whisky, or brandy maybe. That might do.

'Nice to see you, Rebecca,' Israel says. 'You look well.'

Israel doesn't seem to know Rebecca was married either, or that Jamie's dead. And she doesn't mention it this time. 'Thanks, Uncle,' she says. 'You look well too.'

'Thanks. Cutting down on meat. Been good for me,' Israel says, and turns to me. 'Pretty Boy?'

'Yeah, it is,' Jamal jumps in. 'Just got it confirmed. You remember Shadow from round Noriega? Skinny boy with scary eyes—'

'And about fifteen years old?' I ask, not burying my contempt.

'Yeah, but Shadow's a grown man. Got bodies on him, you know. He's in one of the cars downstairs . . . he confirmed you were the one that did Tyrone. The Pretty Boy.'

I nod.

Israel stares at me and seems impressed. 'You okay?' he asks. 'Want a drink or something?'

Before I can respond, Jamal jumps in again. 'I know they call you Pretty Boy, but I honestly didn't expect you to be a fade and some earrings away from being a sweet boy,' he says, and Bash chuckles. 'I thought the name was a joke thing. With all the shit you've done, I expected you to be bigger . . . meaner . . . and ugly like Bash.'

Bash laughs.

'Fucking hell,' Jamal says. 'I'm disappointed in Tyrone.'

'Want a drink?' Israel asks me again.

'I'll have what they're having,' I say, because I want to know where the bottle is and have a glass in front of me.

This surprises Rebecca, because she knows I don't drink, but she also knows there's a reason. 'Same,' she says.

'You sure it's not too hard for you?' Jamal teases.

'Is that what Bash asks your mum every night?' Rebecca retorts, which stuns Jamal.

'Okay!' Israel intervenes. 'No more of that, yeah?' he demands.

'He started it,' Rebecca says.

'No more!' Israel shouts. 'We're here to talk business. That's it!'

Israel turns around to pick two glasses from a cabinet behind him and picks a bottle of Hennessy XO cognac from below his chair to fill the glasses. That bottle will certainly do.

'Thanks,' I say, taking the glasses and placing one in front of Rebecca.

'You see,' Israel says. 'You lot can be polite. So, who's going to kick off?'

'I'm happy to,' I say.

Jamal nods.

'We're prepared to accept you back into the collective on the previously agreed terms.'

Jamal grins and shakes his head. 'No,' he says.

'Okay,' I say. 'What's your counter?'

'Fuck your counter.'

'We're here to make a deal. You need product, and we're willing to sell you the best product in the country at the best rates in the country.'

'I don't fucking need product,' Jamal says, and laughs.

I can tell from his demeanour that he's telling the truth. He has product. So, what are we doing here? I glance at the bottle by Israel's feet and prepare myself to grab it when the moment arises.

'That collective thing is bullshit,' Jamal says. 'Just that white man trying to control man's progress like they've been doing for years. Never again, fam. And you can run tell him that, Uncle Tom!'

'Relax with that kinda talk, Jamal,' Israel says.

'You're familiar with *Uncle Tom's Cabin*, then?' I ask, and the room falls silent.

'What are you talking about?' Jamal asks.

'The book,' I say. 'You read it?'

He chuckles.

'Thought so,' I say. 'You use these words, but you don't really know what they mean. Yet you expect them to have an effect on me.'

'Uncle Tom is an Uncle Tom, innit?' Jamal says.

I nod. 'I suppose so. But I can tell you prepared your little speech. Least you could've done was read up on the history of the punchline. Especially if you're delivering it to me. But I suppose you're not curious.'

'Curiosity killed the cat, innit?'

I laugh. 'I think it's best you stick to preparing your lines.'

'Fuck you, fam!'

'That's much better.'

'I will fucking end you, fam!'

'You can't,' I say, and gesture at Bash. 'He has a fair chance. But he can't either.'

Bash grins.

'Okay,' Israel says. 'Are we going to talk business? That's why we are here, innit, Jamal?'

Jamal doesn't respond and glares at me.

'Doesn't seem like it,' Rebecca says.

'I understand what you're talking about, Jamal,' Israel says. 'I do. But Alan has the best product in the country, like my man said, and we need that product. Let's see if we can negotiate less strings attached to the product. No more control. Just buyer and seller.'

Jamal doesn't respond, and I shake my head with contempt.

'What?' Jamal barks.

'This is not the right place or time for this, but you put it on the table. You're here throwing around the term "Uncle Tom", which says to me you have some pride in our race. Want us to support each other and progress. You, me, Israel, Rebecca, Bash . . . we're in this life for many reasons, but mostly because there was a lack of opportunity to be anything else of substance. We're in now, and we can try to get out, but it's fucking hard. Whether for money, power, love, revenge . . . or principle . . . we keep coming back. But here you are, in a position of power, bringing black kids as young as fifteen into this shit to do your dirty work. And for what, Jamal? So one of them can be you in ten years and then die or end up in prison soon after?'

'What are you chatting, fam?' Jamal asks, defensive. 'They're out there on road, anyway. But they want to work, so I put them to work. Put money in their pockets. More money than—'

'Shut up,' I interrupt. 'I've seen your numbers, Jamal. Last year alone, you made over thirty million pounds in turnover. I don't know what your overheads are, but they will certainly leave you enough money to build a community centre or two. But no . . . you'd rather spend it on your stupid watch, your stupid chain, and your shoes . . . and let's not even talk about your clothes or your belt.'

Jamal is so consumed with rage that he doesn't speak, and I know it's just about time to grab the bottle.

'One last chance to talk business . . .' Rebecca says.

'Shut the fuck up, bitch!' Jamal screams. 'Men are talking, yeah?'

'Oi!' Israel shouts. 'No need for that, Jamal.'

'No need for you!' Jamal barks.

Bash grabs Israel's head and snaps his neck, killing him instantly. I toss my glass at Bash, and it bounces off his nose before I dive to grab the bottle.

Rebecca tosses the contents of her glass at Jamal just before he jumps at her, and he hesitates long enough for her to smash the glass into the side of his face.

I grab the bottle and swing for Bash's head as he lunges at me. The bottle shatters on his forehead, but he powers through and shoves me across the room. Blood gushes from his forehead to his eyes, blinding him, so I pounce. He abandons wiping his eyes as I approach and throws a wild punch that hits me on the shoulder as I attempt to grab a shard of glass. The power of the punch sends me scurrying, but I quickly regain my footing. My palm bleeds, but I have the piece of glass. Bash continues to wipe the blood from his eyes, but he can't keep up with the stream gushing down from his forehead. I rush him, and this time I dodge his wild swing and drive the glass into his liver. He swipes me to the floor but falls to his knees in the same motion. I grab another shard of glass and repeatedly stab his throat till the glass snaps off in his neck.

He drops like a log, and I turn to Rebecca and Jamal. Rebecca is on top of Jamal, strangling him with his bloodied thick chain. I step closer, and Jamal already appears lifeless. His face is almost unrecognisable from the battering Rebecca has delivered with the chain. Rebecca looks untouched, apart from the splashes of Jamal's blood on her body. She stops and checks for a pulse.

'Is he dead?' I ask.

She nods and stands, but then stamps on his throat to crush it. 'Now . . .'

I gesture for Rebecca to stop speaking, because I hear footsteps on the stairs.

'Is everything—' Mo starts.

There is a gunshot, and I hear Mo collapse and fall down the stairs. Tunde.

We hear Tunde cautiously walk up the stairs, and we tiptoe to hide at either side of the door.

'Jamal?' Tunde calls.

Silence.

'Bash?' Tunde calls.

Silence.

'Yeah, fam,' Tunde says. 'Go tell Israel's mandem to come up here to take care of Pretty Boy cos he done killed their boss, yeah?' . . . 'I think Jamal's dead. Yeah. But the plan still live though, yeah?'

That's not good. Both sides will be coming after us. And Tunde smartly made the call close to the door, so we hear and get desperate.

'Pretty Boy,' Tunde calls. 'Jamal's dead, yeah?'

I don't respond.

'RIP, Jamal,' Tunde says. 'We're going to throw a big one for you, King.'

Rebecca tiptoes to Israel's body and finds a small revolver strapped to his ankle. She tiptoes back to me and gestures for me to open the door, so she can shoot. It's a good plan – she's a tremendous shot – but we need to know precisely where Tunde is. I gesture for her to lie on the ground and wait.

'He's no king,' I say.

'That you, yeah?' Tunde asks. 'Just wait, Pretty Boy. You think you're a legend, yeah? When Israel's mandem leave their posts to come up here and kill you, we'll finally take these tower blocks and run all of Hackney. That's a legend's plan.'

'A legend and a king are two different things, Tunde,' I say.

He doesn't respond, but I know he's engaged.

I slowly pull down the door handle, and, as I expect, he shoots. The bullet pierces the door, and I loudly fall to the ground.

'That you, yeah?' he asks, and chuckles. 'Pussio!'

Rebecca sees this as our moment to pounce, but I stop her. If Tunde thinks I'm wounded, he can't miss the opportunity to kill Pretty Boy, who killed his king.

I loudly drag myself away from the door, and Tunde takes

the bait. He runs towards the door, kicks it open, and Rebecca shoots him twice in the chest. He collapses in the doorway, and Rebecca walks over to shoot him once more in the head.

'Clever,' Rebecca says, and tosses Tunde's gun to me. 'But I think we'll have to shoot our way out.'

'I don't want that,' I say. 'Can't you talk to Israel's boys?'

'I think it'll be shoot on sight at this point.'

'Okay, let's at least get out of here.'

We hurry down the steps, and Rebecca grabs the two guns from the tray before we run out the door. She hands me one, and we make the stairwell just before the lift doors open and Israel's boys run towards the flat.

We're approaching the seventh floor when we hear people burst into the stairwell on the twelfth and hurry down after us. It's a race to the bottom, but we'll get there well before them. The issue is what we'll meet . . .

There is an explosion of gunfire from multiple shooters on the ground floor, which causes me and Rebecca to instantly stop. The gunfire lasts for roughly ten seconds before it abruptly ceases, like a coordinated strike.

'Must be Jamal's boys taking out Israel's,' Rebecca whispers.

I nod. 'And they'll be waiting for us,' I say. 'I think we need to find a place to hide till the police arrive.'

'Police?' she asks, and chuckles. 'No one here's calling the police till this is over.'

'Why?'

'We need to go back up to the eighth floor,' she says, and runs before I can react.

I follow Rebecca up the stairs, but before we get to the door leading to the eighth floor, Kofi and another man who was guarding the lift open fire from the ninth-floor landing. A bullet hits Rebecca, and she falls, but she shoots back and hits the man in the chest. I shoot and hit him in his chest and neck. He collapses, and Kofi retreats. I turn to Rebecca, and she's already back on her feet, hurriedly limping through the door. I follow her.

'Where are you hit?' I ask, concerned.

'My thigh,' she says, and continues ahead. 'And don't fucking cry, I'm a big girl. And the squats in the gym have made my quads indestructible.'

'I don't think that's how it works,' I say, and walk backwards so I can keep an eye on the stairwell.

Kofi opens the door – I shoot the wall by his head and he retreats. I toss Tunde's gun and raise the one Rebecca gave me.

'You hit him?' she asks, and tosses the small revolver.

'No.'

'Fuck are you doing?' she scolds and raises the second gun. 'I've seen you shoot. We can't talk our way out of this.'

'I know. But I can get through to him.'

'What?' she says and stops at the door to flat thirty-seven. 'He's just going to tell his friends where we are.'

'I think his friends are dead.'

'Fucking hell,' she says, and pushes the doorbell. 'This is not the time for your Robin Hood shit. These guys are loyal to Israel. He'll kill us the first chance he gets.'

Rebecca keeps her hand on the buzzer, and I tiptoe back towards the stairwell door.

'Kofi,' I call. 'We didn't do it. It was Jamal. And his people are killing your people all over this tower block. Call them, you'll see.'

Kofi doesn't respond.

I turn to Rebecca, and she still has her hand on the buzzer. Whoever is in the flat is not responding. I hear Kofi approach and turn to the door. He's trying to be quiet, but his footsteps are naturally heavy.

'I can hear you, Kofi. There's no need—'

Kofi shoots through the door three times, and Rebecca glares at me.

'Stop it, Kofi,' I say, and he shoots three more times.

He has one more bullet, but I'm sure he's not been counting like I have.

'I'm going to give you one more chance, Kofi. I—'

He shoots, and I immediately open the door. He tries to shoot again, but there are no bullets.

'We really didn't . . .' I say.

He charges towards me, and I shoot him in the forehead. He drops at my feet, and I curse underneath my breath, but I hear the lift stop on our floor. Shit. Kofi must've told someone we're here. I'm right beside the lift, so I can't see inside, and whoever's inside can't see me either. But Rebecca is in the direct line of sight. She raises her gun to the lift, and I watch her eyes as it opens. Her eyes widen, but she hesitates, and someone in the lift shoots her. She falls, and I slide into the lift to see Shadow and another of Jamal's boys using a young woman as a shield. I shoot the young man in the head, but don't shoot

Shadow because his hostage is blocking me. Shadow shoots over her shoulder, and then *she* raises a gun towards me. I shoot her in the head and ram her dead body into Shadow. He continues shooting over her shoulder until I snap his wrist and his gun falls. I drop her dead weight onto him, and he crumples. I watch as he wriggles from underneath her body to scurry towards the other guy's gun. Shadow is frantic. He might be a killer, but he's still a child. He grabs the gun with his left hand and raises it to me, and I shoot him in the head.

I drag the woman's body to the lift's doors to trap the lift on this floor, then walk backwards towards Rebecca with my eyes on the stairwell door.

'I'm okay,' she says, and sits up.

I glance at her – she has a bullet wound in her left arm, but she's raising her gun towards the stairwell door with her right.

'Fucking hell,' she says. 'Are you invisible or something? Nothing's hit you.'

'Lucky, I guess,' I say, and want to apologise for not dealing with Kofi straight away.

'Oh, fuck off,' she says. 'She was in on it?'

I glance at Rebecca, and she's staring at the young woman's body. 'Yes,' I say.

'That'll teach me,' she says.

'Not really . . .'

'Shut the fuck up and grab my phone from my pocket,' she orders.

I pick her phone.

'Call Kenya and put it on speaker,' she orders.

'Who's she?' I ask, and call.

'My cousin. Israel's daughter.'

'Hey, Rebecca!' Kenya answers. 'Long time!'

'Yeah,' Rebecca says, trying to feign excitement. 'I need a very quick favour.'

'Okay . . . no checking in, just straight favour, yes?'

'I need you to reach out to your brother. It's urgent.'

'Chad is in prison.'

'I know. I spoke to your dad, and he said you can reach him.'

'Dad can reach him. Why don't you ask Dad?'

Rebecca hesitates. 'He's out of reach at the moment.'

'Out of reach? Is everything okay, Rebecca?'

'Yes. Just call Chad and get him to call me back right away.'

Rebecca gestures for me to end the call, and I do.

'African countries, then?' I ask.

'Nothing gets past you. They had a brother that died a few years ago. His name was Mali.'

'Why are you calling Chad?'

'He'll get us in,' she says, and gestures to flat thirty-seven.

'Why are we trying to get in?'

'You'll see.'

The phone rings, and I show her the caller ID.

'Answer it,' she says. 'Speakerphone.'

'You okay, Rebecca?' Chad asks.

'Not so much, Chad,' Rebecca says. 'Israel's dead.'

'Went to shit, didn't it? Warned Dad not to trust the fucker. They'll be coming for me first thing tomorrow morning, then.'

'Not necessarily. Jamal's dead. I killed him.'

'Sweet, cousin. I heard Bash was going to be there . . . he's a tough fucker. What happened there?'

'Pretty Boy.'

'Ah, man still alive, then?'

'Say hello,' Rebecca says to me.

'Hello, Chad.'

'Hey, brother. Taking care of little cousin?'

'She's taking of me, brother.'

Chad laughs. 'No doubt, brother!'

'Sorry about your dad.'

'It's the life, brother. Jamal's dad's in here. That's why Jamal agreed to leave the towers to Israel. But his dad's getting released in a couple years, so this was always going to happen. Jamal's a heartless fucker to make the move now, though.'

'He was going to put it on us,' Rebecca says. 'After he killed us.'

'Who'll believe that shit, though?'

'Lots of Israel's crew at the towers. But they're all mostly dead now, too.'

'Shit. I been in too long. The streets out there are wild. Okay. What you need?'

'We need to get into flat thirty-seven.'

'Done,' he says. 'Good luck, yeah. Text me when it's over.'

Chad ends the call, and a moment later, a seemingly frail old lady opens the door to flat thirty-seven. I help Rebecca to her feet and support her into the flat.

'I'm sorry, Rebecca,' the old lady says. 'Just needed to be sure, you know. Israel warned everyone to stay in and lock up till morning, and he didn't say you . . .'

'It's okay, June,' Rebecca says.

June nods and leads us into a bathroom. She picks a tile out from the wall and pulls open a hidden door to a small armoury. I help Rebecca into the armoury and start searching the shelves.

'What are you looking for?'

'A first aid kit.'

'Fuck that. We don't have time for that. If we don't make it out soon, I'm going to die in here, anyway.'

'I'm quick with it. Just need to stop the bleeding, clean the wound, and—'

'Stop—'

'I have one,' June says, and picks a first aid kit from underneath the sink.

I place Rebecca on the floor and open the kit.

'Can I get a towel?' I ask June.

June hands me every towel in the bathroom. 'No one uses this bathroom,' she says.

I smile, and she smiles back.

'This might hurt,' I say to Rebecca.

'Shut up and do it already.'

I carefully pull her left arm out of her leather jacket, tear the sleeve off her t-shirt, and carefully wipe the blood with a towel. I apply several sterile gauze swabs to the wound and wrap a bandage around her arm several times and just tight enough to stop the bleeding.

'I'm going to have to cut your jeans,' I say.

'Stop talking to me . . . just do it.'

I cut her jeans with scissors from the first aid kit, and there is more blood around her thigh than her arm, so I use several towels to wipe the blood. I apply several more gauze swabs to the wound and wrap it with a bandage just as carefully and tightly as her arm.

'Happy?' she says.

'I could do better.'

'Seems to me you were watching too many survival You-Tube videos in the cottage.'

I laugh. She's correct. I grab a bulletproof vest and fasten it around Rebecca, and then fasten one around myself.

'This isn't how I thought I was going to die,' Rebecca says. 'But this is exactly how I thought you were going to die.'

'No one's dying today.'

I grab three handguns and check the clips are full and there's a bullet in the chamber of each of them.

'Unless you want to share your invisibility cloak,' Rebecca says, 'I think this might be it for me. And I was really enjoying the penthouse.'

'What?' I say, and pass two handguns to her. 'You've moved in already?'

'Err . . . yes,' she says, and tucks the guns away. 'Picked my room and everything. You're lucky I'm not kicking you out of the master bedroom. You and Alan put my home out of commission.'

'Fair,' I say, and tuck the last handgun into my waistband. 'And you're not fucking dying . . . not until Franka gives us that tour, anyway.'

I pick up an AK-47 and an extra magazine.

'I want one of them,' she says.

'You can't use it. You need both hands for that.'

'Well, I can use one hand for that,' she says, and gestures to the MAC-10 submachine gun.

'Sure,' I say.

I help her to her feet and hand her the submachine gun. I reach out to help her out of the room, but she glares at me.

'You're not fucking carrying me. I'll be fine.'

'We're going to be walking down the stairs.'

'And?' she challenges, and gestures to the AK-47. 'Plus, you need both hands for that.'

I nod, and we walk out of the bathroom.

'Good luck,' June says.

I peek out of the flat in both directions, and the hallway is empty. I lead Rebecca to the lift and step over the young woman to push the buttons for every floor going down to the ground floor. I step out of the lift and move the young woman in, and the lift descends. I lead Rebecca to the stairwell and listen carefully, but there are no sounds from the landing. I peek in, and it's empty.

I lead Rebecca down the steps, trying to stay just a few steps behind the lift. The tower block is eerily quiet, like Jamal's boys are just waiting for us at the bottom of the stairs. There is only one way in and one way out, so I'd probably do the same.

The lift arrives at the ground floor, and we're a few steps behind, but we hear nothing. Until steady footsteps approach the door to the stairwell. I aim the rifle at the door and focus my breathing. It's time.

'Jamal!' a female voice calls.

I recognise the voice; it's Priyanka.

'Priyanka? That you?' I ask.

'Pretty Boy?' she asks.

'Yeah.'

Priyanka laughs. 'I should've known you wouldn't die. Come out. We've taken care of Jamal's people.'

I drop the rifle and reach an arm under Rebecca's shoulders.

'Who's Priyanka?' Rebecca whispers.

'One of Alan's collective members. The lady has no love for Jamal.'

Rebecca chuckles. 'LL Cool J,' she says.

I support her down the stairs. 'What's that?'

'The ladies love cool Jamal.'

'That's weak,' I tease.

'Fuck you, I'm weak.'

We walk through the stairway door, and Priyanka stands proudly with several of her associates in front of the tower block's only exit. And they are surrounded by dead bodies.

'I'm here for Jamal,' Priyanka says. 'Where is he?'

'Dead, flat fifty-nine, top floor,' Rebecca says. 'I killed him with his fucking chain and then crushed his throat to be sure.'

Priyanka and Rebecca smile at each other. 'I think we're going to be fast friends,' Priyanka says.

DAY 22, 01:00

'I'm done. You're done'

Jack Moore sits in a car he'd rented under a fake name earlier in the evening, opposite a dilapidated house in a south-east London council estate. He's been watching the house for over an hour.

The moment Alan left the makeshift police station in Battersea, Jack began searching for Pretty Boy. He checked the systems to see if there was any information about Pretty Boy's reappearance, but there wasn't. There is information on the attack on Tyrone's fortress, which has all the hallmarks of an incident that would be falsely attributed to Pretty Boy. That must be what Alan's referring to, Jack thought. Alan probably organised that attack to get Jack to chase his tail and lose focus on Valentin's murder . . . Alan is panicking. Either way, Jack called Lucas to confirm, but Lucas's phone was switched off. Which wasn't surprising.

After Jack recovered from the Wapping Massacre, he'd kept Lucas on a tight leash, because he knew when Pretty Boy returned, he'd go after Lucas. But that leash loosened over the decade he's been waiting. Nowadays, Lucas just calls in when he needs something . . . money or getting a minor arrest squashed, mostly. And those check-ins were Jack's way of knowing Lucas was alive and Pretty Boy hadn't returned.

Jack assumed, like always, Lucas was just sleeping off his inebriated state in a police station, and that's why his phone was off. He checked the police station registers in the locations Lucas frequents, but Lucas wasn't there. Jack widened his search to all the stations in London, but Lucas wasn't there, either. That worried him, and he thought for a moment that maybe the prostitute that Lucas entrapped and has been exploiting for months finally snapped. But Jack knows she couldn't have killed Lucas, because he researched her record to know what sort of person she was, and she had no arrests other than a couple for loitering a couple years ago. He searched his notes and found her name – Sade Phillips – and checked if she'd been recently arrested. Again, there was nothing.

Next, he searched for any incidents on the street where Lucas always meets Sade, and was taken aback by the latest one. A car explosion six days ago. The blast was so violent that forensics haven't been able to identify the sole occupant yet. But Jack recognised the remnants of the car . . . it's Lucas's. Sade must've been there, because Lucas always arrives at the location after her. But there is no mention of a witness. There is a good chance Alan also killed Lucas to further his distraction scheme, and if he did, he'd have also killed and disappeared Sade's body. But Jack needs to confirm. Sade has no regular home address on the system, but he knows she lives in her deceased older sister's house, helping to raise her sister's daughter. Jack knows the address – he's sitting outside it.

In the hour Jack has watched the house, there has been no sign that anyone is inside, which isn't bad news because it means Alan has disappeared Sade. But then the light in what looks like the upstairs bathroom switches on, and he can see a figure for a couple minutes before the lights switch off again. She's in, Jack thinks. He steps out of the car.

Jack quietly breaks in through the back door and sneaks through the house towards the stairs, assuming the bedrooms are upstairs. But he hears a television in the living room. He pulls out a gun and heads towards the door. He peeks in, and although there are no lights switched on, the glow from the television is bright enough for him to see that the room looks lived in. But he can't see if there is a person on the long sofa facing the screen. He approaches the couch and feels a sting on his neck, and before he can react, he loses feeling in his limbs and collapses. But he's wide awake to see a tall and formidable figure loom over him. It's Franka.

Jack watches Franka grab his leg, and he's helpless as she drags him to the sofa. He tries to protest but can't, and she stares at him without an ounce of emotion as she places him on the cushions. She pulls out a smartphone and makes a video call.

Alan answers. He's in a bedroom, and you can hear a lot of

activity outside the room. He smiles at Jack. 'Hello, Jack,' he says. 'Sorry about the injection. I needed to keep you calm so we can have this conversation. Didn't want Franka to kill you before I told you how fucked you are. Also, sorry about the noise. I'm at a house party . . . needed to get my alibi in order. You understand.' He chuckles. 'And yes, Franka's going to shoot you in the head in a couple minutes . . . painless, supposedly. The least I could do for a former colleague.

'Anyway, I'll get to it because this party is great. The gun used to kill Valentin is now in your safe. And we planned to put a lot more evidence in there. But there was no need because I hear you've kept all the correspondence between you and Viktor in the lead-up to the Wapping Massacre. I gather it spells everything out, from the number of bodies you and your boys were supposed to clean up that night when Viktor was done, to how much he paid. Then there's the correspondence between you and Gennady from then on, trading favours and whatnot. Fair enough, I suppose. But even more juicy – what's going to get the press involved – is the correspondence between you, Gennady, and the former deputy commissioner who's now running for mayor of this fine city. I understand all that is insurance, which is vital considering the wolves you're dancing with. But why put it in your house? Especially once you started coming after me. I know we had to use scanners and whatnot to look through your walls and floors, but this isn't ground-breaking tech. And you know I'm thorough. Anyway, thanks for that.

'But I did add one thing. A hard drive containing correspondence between you and Gennady planning to stitch me up for Valentin. I can't have that hanging over my head. You've also helped the other part of my plan with the way you're dressed, how you gained entry to the house, and that you have a weapon, which I'm sure isn't police-issued. I'm sure you don't have any ID on you, but if you do, Franka will remove it, so your body enters the system as a gangland hit gone wrong before anyone realises it's you. It'll be difficult to bury the investigation then. Your reputation will be tarnished. All the officers you pulled up through the ranks, tarnished.

'I'll give this a few days, but if they don't find your safe, I'll call in an anonymous tip to Caroline Maguire. And we both know she'll follow it up all the way through. That's it. I'm done. You're done. Goodbye, Jack.'

Alan ends the call, and Franka shoots Jack in the head.

DAY 22, 07:00

'That sounds ominous'

The buzz from the intercom wakes me up, and I roll out of bed. I'm exhausted, but I know it's Alan at the door. And he won't stop ringing till I let him in, or might even use his card to come up.

I walk to the intercom and sure enough, Alan is impatiently waiting.

'Where's Franka?' I ask.

'What?' he responds. 'Are you okay?'

'Where is she?'

'In the car.'

'That's not on,' I say. 'Go get her, and you can let yourself up with your card.'

I end the call and walk to the kitchen to make some tea. Sometimes, like right now, I wish I drank coffee, but I never acquired the taste. Green tea will have to do.

I sip from the cup and watch Alan and Franka step out of the lift and head towards me.

'Why didn't you call?' Alan says, concerned. 'And why's your phone off?'

'I was tired . . . needed to sleep.'

'I mean at the tower block,' he says. 'I could've sent people to come get you and Rebecca out.'

'Morning, Franka,' I say.

She nods.

'A lot more people would've died if you did that,' I say.

'More than Priyanka killed?'

'No. But I didn't call her. And it seemed personal for her.'

'How's Rebecca?' Franka asks.

Franka's concern surprises Alan. 'Yeah,' he says. 'How is she?'

'She's being taken care of,' I say.

'Where? By who?' Alan asks.

'As far as I know, it's not A&E, but the facilities are more than decent.'

'How bad was it?' he asks.

'One in the thigh and one in the shoulder. Luckily, neither hit anything major.'

Alan hesitates, because that's not what he was asking about. 'Good,' he says. 'But what happened in there?'

'Jamal had no intention of making a deal. He brought us there to kill us and Israel, and then take over the towers.'

'That's just senseless,' Alan says, frustrated. 'Tyrone's territory, Callum's territory, and the towers . . . with no product?'

'He has product.'

'What?'

'You want a coffee or something?' I ask, and gesture to the state-of-the-art coffee maker Rebecca was going on about yesterday morning. 'I hear that's awesome.'

'It is,' Franka says, and walks to the coffee machine. 'Alan gifted me the same one.'

'Nice of you, Alan,' I say.

'Thanks,' he says. 'You said he has product.'

'He does. And I was trying to work out how in my dream before you woke me up.'

'What do you think?' Alan asks me.

'How exactly was the network destroyed?'

'The Lenkovs knew all the routes, so they hijacked the deliveries and burnt them. They also knew the location of our emergency stash. A month's worth of product. Burnt that as well.'

'Burnt?' I ask, and smile. 'They're smart.'

'What?'

'I imagine the delivery points are CCTV blind spots?'

'Yeah.'

'Where was the emergency stash?'

'In an abattoir in Kent. Secluded. Secure . . . I thought.'

'CCTV?'

'None around the abattoir.'

'You said secluded . . . how are the roads leading to the abattoir?'

'Why?'

'Roads, Alan.'

'Only one road.'

'What time did they raid the abattoir?'

Alan hesitates.

'Between six and seven a.m.,' Franka answers, and hands Alan a cup of coffee.

'Good,' I say.

'Good?' Alan asks.

'All warfare is based on deception.'

'What?'

Alan certainly didn't read *The Art of War* after all. 'They didn't burn any of the product,' I say, getting straight to the point. 'They burnt something. But not the cocaine. They have it, and that's what they were supplying Jamal. And what they'll use to incite the next person – collective member or an upstart – to come after you and your network.'

Alan is furious with himself – clearly he hadn't considered that.

'Relax, Alan. They are billionaires with a grudge, so it's very believable that they'd burn millions of pounds' worth of cocaine.'

'It's tens of millions,' Alan says. 'No one does that. Especially not a billionaire.'

I move on, not wanting him to dwell on what now seems obvious. 'But we'll find them,' I say. 'They must have used a sizeable vehicle to bring whatever white-powder substitute they used to the abattoir and take away the month's worth of product. We need the CCTV for all routes leading to that one road during a four-hour window around the raid. There won't be many vehicles that size at that time, so they'll be easy to spot. We can then follow the truck to wherever it ends up.'

Alan nods. 'I'll get that for you.'

'Okay. We'll discuss what we do next when we see the video.'

'I'll bring it in a couple of hours.'

'Okay,' I say. 'Faster than I thought possible, but I don't doubt you. I'm going back to bed to continue *thinking*. Let yourself back in, okay?'

Alan nods, and I walk back towards the bedroom.

'Wait . . .' Alan says.

I stop and turn to him.

'Jack Moore isn't a problem anymore,' he says. 'So one less thing to think about.'

I want to ask what he means by *isn't a problem anymore*, but I know. I nod and walk to the bedroom to sleep. I never dream about Jack anyway.

The smartphone Oleg gave me rings and wakes me up, and I answer straight away.

'Hello,' I say.

'Were you sleeping?' Rebecca asks.

I check the time on the phone, and it's 08:15. 'No. I was just thinking really hard.'

'Fuck off,' she says, and laughs.

'How are you feeling?'

'Good. The bullets are out. The bleeding's stopped. The painkillers are working. I'm fine.'

'No,' Oleg says over the phone.

'I don't know where Oleg got his medical degree from, but he wants me to stay for twenty-four hours' supervision.'

'Forty-eight,' Oleg says. 'The doctor said forty-eight!'

'She didn't say that to me,' Rebecca says.

'You understand Pashto, eh?' Oleg asks.

'Whatever,' Rebecca says. 'I would've left already, but this place is sweet.'

'Of course it is,' Oleg says over the phone. 'It's Oleg's place.'

'And I think Meiling needs the company,' Rebecca says.

'She's awake?'

'Yes. Supposedly my screams woke her.'

'How is she?'

'She looks okay . . . just a little wary.'

'Okay, I'll get Franka to come over soon as.'

'And you, I want to see you. We need to talk.'

'That sounds ominous.'

'Whatever that means, it's not that. Just get here,' Rebecca says, and ends the call.

I consider going back to bed, but I'm sure Alan will return soon. I head to the shower.

I'm just finishing a plate of eggs when Alan and Franka step out of the lift and walk towards me with purpose. Alan is holding a laptop.

'Your phone is still off,' he says.

'Oh, yeah. My bad,' I say.

'No problem,' Alan says, and he's excited. 'Just couldn't wait to share the news.'

He pushes my empty plate to the side and places the laptop in front of me. He opens it, and the screen is filled with a video paused on an image of a small truck.

'You were correct,' he says, and presses play. 'And this is it.'

The truck drives quickly on a secluded road.

'We followed it,' he says, and opens another video. 'Here's where it stops.'

Alan plays the video, and the truck drives through a nondescript automatic gate and then into a warehouse.

'It's a storage facility owned by the Lenkovs. It might look unremarkable, but it's highly fortified from what I've heard. Legally too. Because the company that directly owns the warehouse acts as custodian of many high-value assets that are used as security for loans – mostly art, precious metals, and gemstones. And that's all from their website.'

I smile.

'Why are you smiling?' he asks.

'This has me written all over it, doesn't it?'

'I think this place is a lot more fortified than any job you've done before.'

'I'm sure. But I know just the people to help.'

'Who?'

'Don't worry about that. Just leave it to me. Actually . . . could you get the building plans for the warehouse? I'm sure the one on the council website is bullshit.'

'I can do that,' he says.

'Okay,' I say. 'I need to meet someone to get the ball rolling. And I'll need Franka for that.'

The request surprises Alan and Franka.

'Is this going to be dangerous?' Alan asks.

'Not if Franka is there,' I say. 'And honestly, I need her more for her charm on this one.'

Franka smiles.

'You can wait here till we get back,' I say to Alan.

'It's okay,' he says, and chuckles. 'I still know how to drive.'

'We won't be more than a couple of hours,' I say.

'Call me when it's done,' he says to Franka.

She hands him his car key, and he walks to the lift.

I wait for the lift door to close. 'Meiling's awake,' I say to Franka.

'No one dodges bullet'

Franka and I walk towards the back door of Oleg's place, and it opens as we approach. We step in, and another door further down the small hallway opens when we close the first door.

Through the second door, Rebecca sits on the sofa in the office with her leg elevated on a stool and holding a small device that controls the doors. Oleg isn't in the room. Before I can ask, she signals for us to be quiet.

'Always lovely to see you, Franka,' Rebecca whispers, and gestures towards Oleg's clinic. 'She doesn't know you're here.'

Franka smiles. 'Thank you,' she whispers.

Franka sneaks towards the room, softly opens the door, and slips in. And a few moments later, Meiling screams with happiness, and a lively conversation erupts in German.

'That's sweet,' Rebecca says.

I nod.

'I knew Franka had some of that sweetness in her,' Rebecca says. 'But I didn't know she talked this much.'

I laugh. 'Neither did I,' I say. 'Where's Oleg?'

'Stepped out for a meeting,' Rebecca says, and switches the display on the television to *Judge Judy*.

'Didn't know you were a fan,' I say.

'She's the best,' Rebecca says. 'I want to be her when I grow up.'

'Best start with law school.'

'Best start with watching your mouth before I smack you.'

I laugh. 'I don't think Judge Judy would take kindly to that. Sticks and stones . . .'

'You watch it?' Rebecca asks, excited.

'Of course. After I'm done with the survival YouTube videos . . . it's the best thing on daytime television.'

'I agree,' she says.

'What do you want to talk about?'

'I'm taking Jamal's territory.'

That stuns me, but I try not to show it.

'Spoke to Chad. I have the support of what's left of Israel's crew.'

'What about Jamal's?'

'I'll handle them.'

'Wha—'

'Don't lecture me. I've bled for this. It's mine. I'm going to take it by whatever means necessary.'

'Okay.'

'Priyanka will introduce me to the collective members at

the next meeting. Can't have you or Alan do it because then it might look like I was hand-picked.'

'Okay. Seems all sorted, then.'

'Not really. I need something from you.'

'Sure. Anything.'

'I need your support. And I don't mean out there backing me or fighting my battles. I mean between us. I need you to be there for me. I need to know I can call you and bitch or ask for advice or whatever, and you never question if I'm in over my head. I want you to treat me like I treat you.'

'I will. And if I stray, smack me.'

'I would smack you anyway, but now I'll smack you twice.'

'Good luck,' I say, as heartfelt as I can muster.

She laughs and tries to hit me, and I leap away from her grasp. 'Shit like . . .'

Rebecca stops, and we turn to Franka and Meiling walking out of Oleg's clinic.

'Hello, *Pretty Boy*,' Meiling says, and gestures to the bracelet in her hand. 'Thank you for bringing this back to me.'

'I don't—'

'No,' she says, forcefully. 'I don't want to hear that. Just please accept my gratitude.'

I nod. 'You're welcome.'

She puts the bracelet in her pocket; I'm not sure she'll ever wear it again. 'I think it's only fair that I tell you this,' she says. 'And I've also told Franka. I'm going to kill Alan. But I'll do my best to make sure no one else gets hurt.'

I don't know what to say in response, so I nod to acknowledge. She and Franka walk back into Oleg's clinic.

Rebecca smiles. 'That was fucking cool,' she says.

'I know. But I think she'll die trying.'

'I think she'll be happy with that,' she says. 'Sit down, let's enjoy some *Judge Judy*.'

I nod and sit, and Rebecca smacks me twice on the back of the head. 'You can't run away from me,' she says. 'You love me.'

Oleg walks into his office an hour later, and I pop off the sofa to hug him.

'How are you feeling?' he asks me.

'Why are you asking him?' Rebecca says. 'He didn't get hit once.'

'I trained him well, eh?' Oleg says, proud.

'Fuck off,' Rebecca says. 'That's not training. That's luck. Or some matrix shit.'

'It's matrix shit,' I say.

'What the fuck is matrix shit?' Oleg asks.

'Magic,' Rebecca says.

'It's a movie,' I say. 'Keanu Reeves dodges bullets.'

'Dodge bullets?' he asks, and frowns. 'Why you watch this nonsense?'

'It's good . . . trust me.'

'No. No one dodges bullet.'

'Well, it's an alternate reality . . .'

'No, no,' Oleg says, and raises his hands to stop me. 'That's enough.'

Rebecca and I laugh.

'Franka inside?' he asks, and gestures to his clinic.

'Yeah.'

'Good,' he says. 'Want something to eat?'

'Not yet. But I need something else . . .'

'Ask Oleg, and you will receive,' he says with pride.

'I need Tosin and Jide for a job.'

Oleg grins.

DAY 23, 22:00

'Your father!'

I step out of Green Park station and head straight to Berkeley Street. The quintessential Mayfair street is even more vibrant at night, with flashier cars lining the street and more interesting pedestrians.

I walk down the street to the spot where I met Tosin and Jide a week ago when I needed their assistance to wipe out Tyrone . . . and Farrukh.

'Fresh guy!' Jide calls.

I turn, and their black Mercedes saloon has slowed to a walking pace on the road beside me. Jide pops his head out of the window, and even at night, he's wearing a pair of large flash sunglasses, which are different from the ones he wore last week.

'Oya now, get in!' he says with his unique blend of American and Nigerian accents.

I hurry to the car and step into the back seat, and Jide turns to me as Tosin speeds up. Tosin is also wearing flash sunglasses, and both look straight out of a *Miami Vice* dinner party. Not the way you'd expect extremely skilled and sought-after mercenaries to dress in their everyday lives. But none are as special as Tosin and Jide, and none can pull it off like Tosin and Jide.

'Fresh guy!' Jide says, and we bump fists.

'How you dey?' Tosin asks with the same blended accent, and bumps my fist without taking his eye off the road.

'I'm good,' I respond. 'How you dey?'

'Ehen!' Jide exclaims, and they laugh. 'Speaking pidgin now, abi, fresh guy?'

I laugh. 'I'm trying . . . I prepared something in Yoruba, but it sounded awful even to me!'

'I'm sure we've heard worse,' Tosin says. 'It's the thought that counts, so let's hear it.'

'You sure?'

'Of course, fresh guy,' Jide says. 'It's the thought that counts.'

'O dara lati ri ọ lẹẹkansi,' I say.

They glance at each other and nod. But don't speak.

'Okay, you can laugh,' I say.

They burst out laughing.

'Jesu!' Jide says. 'What was that?'

'Supposed to be "good to see you again", according to Google Translate.'

'Which Google are you using, oh?' Jide retorts, and laughs.

'It's "eku ijo meta",' Tosin says. 'But it's not a straight translation.'

'And where is your leather jacket?' Jide asks, and gestures to my mac coat.

'It was a little drizzly when I left, so I wore this.'

'Don't mind Jide, he has just been looking for it all over the place. That's why he's asking.'

'Dake!' Jide says to Tosin. 'Where did you get it?'

'About twelve years ago from a vintage store, so it's probably twelve years older than that.'

'On top fresh guy, you dey do vintage cool guy too, abi?' Jide says.

I'm not precise about what Jide said, but I think I understand the sentiment. 'I don't usually shop at vintage stores, but I had to . . .'

'Don't explain yourself to this idiot,' Tosin says.

'Baba rẹ na idiot!' Jide responds.

'Iya rẹ!' Tosin says.

They laugh, and it's infectious, even though I don't know what they are laughing about.

'I scouted the warehouse from 1400 hours yesterday to 1600 hours today , . . while Jide was finally eating Flora's pussy.'

'Ah ahn,' Jide protests. 'How does that one concern fresh guy?'

'I just want him to know you're a real man now. Remember last time, he and I agreed that only real men eat pussy.'

'And only the realest eat pussy for twenty-six hours straight,' I say.

Tosin bursts into laughter.

'Ah!' Jide exclaims. 'You don join abi, fresh guy? Oya now!'

'Shut up, jo,' Tosin says to Jide. 'You have the plans, right?'

'I do,' I say.

'Okay,' Tosin says. 'I've prepared a good spot around there where I can brief you, and we discuss strategy. We're heading there now.'

'Okay,' I say.

'And for the record, we didn't ask for double our rates,' Tosin says. 'That was Oleg.'

'No,' I say. 'It was me. And I'm not the one footing the bill, so don't worry.'

'Good for you,' Jide says. 'But Tosin even wanted to do it for free. And now I know it's because he found another professional pussy-licker that can join him to be abusing me. Twenty-six hours, abi?'

Tosin laughs.

'No, I didn't—' I say, trying not to laugh.

'Didn't what?' Jide interrupts. 'It's too late, oh. Twenty-six, abi? Chai! It peppered me, sha!'

Tosin's laugh intensifies, and I try not to laugh, but I do.

'Enjoy, fresh guy!' Jide says. 'I will get my own back!'

'Shut up!' Tosin says.

He turns up the Nigerian song playing on the stereo, and he and Jide erupt into a singalong, which makes the song even more enjoyable. I glance at the stereo display for the title; it's 'Don't Dull' by Wizkid. Mustn't be dull, then. I bump along to the song and watch them dance as much as one can in the front seat of a car.

Tosin leads Jide and me to the top floor of an abandoned office building across the street and a few buildings away from the warehouse. We step into an office and remain in darkness as Tosin walks us to the window with the best view of the warehouse. We observe the warehouse, and it looks even more unremarkable at night.

'It's fairly active during business hours. Trucks come and go. Staff as well. But things get lean from about 1900 hours. One particular vehicle is of most interest to us. It arrived at 1530 hours and left at 1610 hours, then arrived again at 2330 hours and left at 0010 hours, then 0730 hours and left at 0810 hours. That's the changeover for the security team, every eight hours, and the vehicle is large enough for twenty people. And that's different from the regular security guards that handle the day or night duties. We don't need to worry about them because they aren't armed, but the twenty will be.'

'Twenty guards in there,' Jide says, uncertain. 'Let's see the plans.'

Tosin leads to a desk furthest away from the window. I place the plans on the desk, and Tosin switches on a flashlight so we can examine them.

'This is wrong,' Tosin says, after examining for just a second.

'Yeah,' Jide concurs. 'Too small for that amount of security.'

'Too small for the amount of cargo that went in just in the last twenty-four hours,' Tosin says.

'Who gave you this?' Jide asks.

'The person footing the bill.'

'Not Oleg?' Jide asks.

'No.'

'Ask Oleg to get you to the real plans,' Jide says. 'It'll be expensive. But you're not footing the bill, abi?'

'I'll do that.'

'Okay,' Tosin says, and hands Jide his car key. 'I'm going to stay to do some more recon. Jide—'

'Ma so nonsense,' Jide interrupts.

'Kini nonsense?' Tosin asks.

'O mo,' Jide.

Tosin shrugs. 'Jide will drive you back and get all the equipment we need,' he says. 'And if Oleg can get you the real plans. We meet here again at 2026 hours tomorrow.'

'Your father!' Jide says, and they laugh.

'Say your name'

I park in a secluded corner behind the abandoned office building and spot Tosin's car across the road, away from any streetlights; they're already here, as expected. I pull a duffel bag from underneath my seat and head to the building. I step into the dark office, and Tosin and Jide calmly watch the door because they must have heard me approach.

'Bawo ni?' I ask.

They chuckle. 'A wa daadaa,' Jide says.

That wasn't the response the internet told me to expect, and they read my confusion even in the darkness. They laugh.

'We're good,' Tosin says.

'I've got the real plans,' I say, and pick out an iPad from the duffel bag.

They approach, and I show them the three-dimensional plans of the facility. The ground level is identical to the building plan Alan provided, but there is an underground bunker with two levels that can only be accessed through a secret cargo lift.

'This makes more sense,' Tosin says.

'How does the cargo lift work?' Jide asks.

'I don't think we need to worry about that,' I say. 'I've got a plan.'

They nod without hesitation; they trust me.

'The bunker is sealed, so it uses an industrial on-site oxygen generator and industrial air conditioning unit. Lucky for us, that has to be on the ground level to release all the heat,' I say, and navigate the plan to a large room on the ground level. 'It's there.' I address Tosin. 'We spoke earlier today about the cleaners, and unsurprisingly, they're mostly black. All from a cleaning agency.'

I pull out an employee ID with my picture and a liquid gas canister that looks like a small tea flask and place them on the table.

'I'll go in for my shift as a cleaner tomorrow morning just before nine a.m. The security and the other staff members won't pay much attention to me because I don't imagine they are the type to notice there's a new black cleaner. The other cleaners will, but they won't care much . . . initially.' I gesture to the canister. 'I'll attach this device to the oxygen generator and leave before anyone registers my presence.'

Jide picks the canister to examine it, and Tosin examines the ID card. Tosin chuckles and shows Jide the card, and Jide chuckles.

'You just want to be Nigerian, sha,' Jide says. 'Oya, say your name.'

'Do-la-po Fa-ni-mo-kun,' I say.

They burst into laughter.

'You need to work on your accent,' Tosin says. 'But just say it faster and with your chest.'

'Dolapo Fanimokun,' I speed through.

'Okay . . . not that fast,' Jide teases.

'It's okay,' Tosin says. 'But if there are any Nigerians there, just give them a random English name and say you prefer they call you that.'

I nod.

'But really, you're too fresh for a cleaner,' Jide says. 'Tosin was born for this.'

'Your father!' Tosin says.

We laugh.

'Looks good,' Tosin says, and gestures to the ID card. 'How reliable is it, though?'

'Very reliable, according to Oleg,' I say. 'I trust his judgement.'

They nod.

'Oleg got the best hacker he knows to sort it,' I say. 'The cleaning agency is a legitimate company, so putting me in their system was easy. Same with the company that operates the warehouse – Oak Custodian and Depositary Services . . . Oak, for short. The entire ground level is legitimate. All the staff and the assets held on that level are documented in agreements in Oak's systems, which are secure enough, but not for an "exceptional hacker" – the hacker's words, not mine. He's broken into their system and can include whatever we want.

And that card will give me access to every room on the ground level.'

'What about the bunker?' Tosin asks.

'The bunker doesn't exist apart from on these plans,' I say. 'The assets in the bunker are not recorded anywhere . . . intentionally, I'm sure. Neither are any staff members or the twenty security guards that change shifts every eight hours.'

'What does this do?' Jide asks, and gestures to the canister.

'We have a remote for it that'll work from here. Once we release the liquid into the oxygen generator, it'll react with the oxygen in under a minute and put everyone in the bunker to sleep for three hours at least. Supposedly, you only need to be exposed for three to five seconds for it to affect you, so we'll need to go in with gas masks.'

I pick three gas masks from the duffel bag and place them on the table.

'How do we get into the warehouse?' Tosin asks.

'If all goes well tomorrow morning,' I say, 'the hacker will put a delivery in their system, which will get us into the warehouse. Can either of you drive a truck?'

They both nod.

'How do we get into the bunker?' Tosin asks.

'That, I'm not sure about yet,' I say, and take out what looks like a pen. 'But I just need to drop this anywhere in the warehouse with a Wi-Fi connection. Then we'll have administrator access to their Wi-Fi and security camera feeds on the ground level. We watch, and, hopefully, we find out how to get in the bunker.'

They smile at each other.

'What?' I ask.

'That's the first uncertain point in your plan,' Jide says. 'Last time, you had a lot more.'

I remember; I did. Just more confident around them now, I suppose.

'What happens to the security and the staff in the warehouse?' Tosin asks.

'We're going to go in when it's lean . . . and I'll leave it up to you guys how we subdue whoever's in then.'

'Subdue? You mean kill, right?' Tosin asks.

Last time, I meant kill. Not today.

'No. I mean subdue,' I say. 'The people on the ground level are normal working people. They have Facebook profiles, and some even have profiles on LinkedIn. I'd prefer we don't kill them.'

'Prefer?' Jide asks.

'Strongly prefer,' I say.

'Unless we have to,' Jide says.

'Yes. Unless we have to.'

They nod.

'Leave this us. It's what we do'

I'm thirty minutes early for my shift as I approach the ware-house on foot. I'm a few steps behind a car that drives through the gate, but I wait for it to close before I use my card to open the pedestrian gate. I'm sure someone's watching me, and I want to test the card as soon as possible – it works.

I walk through the pedestrian gate and remain a step behind the man that drove in as we head to the staff entrance of the facility. He doesn't even acknowledge me. We step into the building, and the security guard standing by the door greets the man but also doesn't acknowledge me. The two people sitting behind the reception desk do the same. I place my card on the turnstile reader and notice one receptionist take a quick glance at the screen in front of her. But she doesn't react or look my way as I make my way through.

I wait a step behind the man as he places his briefcase, his watch, and his phone on a tray before he walks through a metal detector. The detector beeps, and the security guard on the other end quickly waves a hand detector around the man. The hand detector beeps again, but just around the man's belt. The guard then gestures for the man to collect his belongings from the tray, which has passed through a scanner.

I take off my bag – which has a home-made sandwich and the canister that looks like a tea flask inside – and place it in the tray. Then I drop a battered cheap smartphone and my belt in the tray beside the bag. I step through the detector, and there is no beep, and the security guard doesn't make eye contact as he waits for my tray to pass through the scanner. Once it has, he gestures for me to take my stuff and move on.

I nod to thank him, but he ignores me.

I know exactly where the cleaning staff go to start their morning. But I need to get to the secluded room with the oxygen generator first because my morning here ends when I step into the cleaning staffroom. I walk through the hallways, showing just enough hesitance, so if someone is watching me through the cameras, it'll seem like I don't know my way around. I walk past a few people and greet them with a sheepish smile, and each of them greets me back with a polite smile.

I turn into the dead-end hallway where the room with the oxygen generator is located, and to my surprise, there are no cameras. Which makes sense in hindsight, because they don't want the regular security guards watching the cameras to be curious about the room. I hurry to the nondescript door and place my card on the reader, and it unlocks instantly. I step into a vast room with an industrial heating, ventilation, and air conditioning unit and an equally large oxygen generator. I scan the room for cameras, but there are none. Just many exhaust fans, air ducts, and louvres to keep the room cool. I attach the liquid gas canister to the back of the oxygen generator tank and hurry out of the room.

I step out and hear footsteps approaching around the corner. I gently shut the door and then knock on it twice as the footsteps turn into the hallway.

'Do-la-po,' a woman calls, and I turn to her as she walks to me. 'I'm so sorry, this place is a maze when you haven't had your induction. And even for some time afterwards.'

'It's okay, madam,' I say with the Nigerian accent Tosin and Jide tried to teach me.

'Please don't call me that,' she says, and smiles. 'I'm India, your supervisor.'

'Good morning, India,' I say.

'Good morning, Do-la-po. Is that how I pronounce it?'

'Yes, India.'

India smiles. 'I'm sorry, Dolapo, but there has been a mix-up. We have you down to start tomorrow. But I've just checked with your agency, and they have you down as starting today. Unfortunately, your induction is scheduled for tomorrow, so you can't work today. But we'll pay you for the day.'

'Thank you,' I say.

'Just come back same time tomorrow.'

A large man rounds the corner and approaches us, and I can

see the outline of a weapon holstered around his shoulder. He must be one of the twenty guards.

'What are you doing here?' he asks us both.

'He's new,' India says. 'He was lost.'

He glances at her with contempt. 'Give me your card,' he says to me.

'Why?' India asks him. 'Every—'

'Shut up,' he says to her, and opens his palm for me to hand him the card.

India bites her tongue, and I place the card in his hand.

'Don't move,' he says to us.

He walks to the door leading to the oxygen generator room and places my card on the reader, but the door doesn't unlock. He walks back to us and hands me the card.

'Give me your card,' he orders India.

'No. I'm not doing that.'

'Give it to me, or I'll take it, and then get you sacked.'

'You can't do that.'

He glares at her, and she hands him her card.

He walks to the door and places her card on the reader, but the door doesn't unlock. He walks back to her and hands her the card.

'Okay, off you go,' he says, and focuses on me. 'And next time, ask somebody where to go. Don't just wander about like you're in your village.'

'What?' India exclaims. 'That's unnecessary.'

He glares at her like he'd knock her unconscious at any moment.

'It's okay, madam . . . India,' I say to her, and turn to him. 'It won't happen again, sir.'

'Just fuck off,' he says.

India leads me back towards the staff entrance, and she's fuming.

'I'm sorry about him,' she says. 'We all try to avoid them. So I suggest you avoid them too.'

'Them?' I ask.

'Err, yes,' she says, and hesitates. 'They are security, but different; they don't wear the uniform. I think they are the supervisors or something. But there will be one of them around each time, and they will be easy to notice because they never smile and don't talk to anyone. Unless to be rude, like you just saw.'

'I will avoid them,' I say, and spot a toilet ahead. 'Please, can I use the bathroom?'

'Oh, please, don't ask. I'll wait for you here.'

I walk into the toilet and step into a cubicle. I pull out the beat-up smartphone and search for a wireless signal, and there it is – 'Oak Staff', password-protected and with full signal strength. I place the pen behind the toilet and flush. Then wash my hands and step into the corridor.

India leads me to the staff entrance.

'See you tomorrow,' she says.

'Sorry, India, how do I get in?' I ask, and show her my card, which I'd cracked before giving it to the large security guard. 'The man broke my card.'

She shakes her head in disgust. 'It's okay, Do-la-po,' she says. 'We'll have another one for you tomorrow.'

It's 20:24. Tosin drives a cargo truck to the warehouse gate, and we wait for it to open. Jide sits beside him in the passenger seat, and I'm in the empty cargo container behind.

The gate opens, and Tosin drives through, and then the warehouse opens for Tosin to drive in. I watch the security feed on my phone as a middle-aged man leads the truck to an unloading bay like he's done several times today.

'You took your time!' the middle-aged man says.

'Sorry about that,' Jide says with a note-perfect East London accent. 'Hold up at Customs.'

'Yeah. We know. And they pay double for overtime here, so we didn't mind.'

'Double?' Jide exclaims.

Like clockwork, three men head to the cargo container with trolleys, and two security guards approach to supervise the unloading. It's time. I click the button on my phone to disable the Wi-Fi and the security cameras, and I wait for Tosin to let me out as planned.

A minute later, Tosin opens the container, and I see the men with trolleys and the two security guards unconscious and tied up. I step out and spot the middle-aged man unconscious by the passenger door, also tied up. I didn't hear any of it.

'Where are the others?' Tosin whispers.

'Two regular guards in the control room with the armed guard,' I whisper. 'Last guard is in the toilet.'

'Stay here,' he whispers.

I try to object.

'You've already done your part,' he whispers. 'Leave this us. It's what we do. What you're paying us for.'

I nod.

'Sixty seconds,' he says. 'And if we're not back, come find us.' He gestures to the military-grade electroshock weapons the three of us wield. 'But not with this.' He points to the assault rifle slung over my shoulder. 'With that.'

I nod again.

Tosin walks to Jide and whispers to him, and they run in different directions.

I count, and as I approach fifty seconds, I holster the electroshock weapon and switch to the assault rifle.

But then Jide arrives and smiles. 'Ready to come save us, abi?' he says.

'Least I could do,' I say.

Tosin arrives and smiles as well. 'Masks,' he says. 'I've called the cargo lift.'

We wear the gas masks, and a security guard groans as he wakes up. He tries to wriggle to sit up, but he sees us and is overcome with fear. Tosin gestures for him to go back to sleep, and he closes his eyes and places his head on the ground.

'Grab the trolleys,' Tosin says. 'Let's go.'

We race across the warehouse to the cargo lift and select the first underground floor. The lift descends to a vast open space that resembles a museum. It's filled with encased pieces of art and jewellery. And four armed men are sleeping on the floor.

'Drugs aren't here,' I say. 'Tosin and I will go down to the next level. Jide, take a few of the most valuable paintings you see. And—'

'That's a Basquiat,' Jide says. 'Wow.'

'And a Picasso,' Tosin adds.

'Cézanne over there,' Jide says.

'Okay,' I say. 'I get it. You guys know your art.'

They laugh.

'Take those,' I say. 'And whichever you think the owner will miss the most . . .'

'All of these,' Jide says. 'That's a fucking Lichtenstein.'

'Okay,' I say and laugh. 'We'll leave it to you. But we need to travel light with them, so we don't damage them in any way.'

'Oh, I would never,' Jide says, and steps off the lift.

'Grab some jewellery as well,' I say.

Jide shrugs, and we laugh before I push the button to go down to the next level.

The next level is similar in layout to the first, and we quickly spot the neatly arranged parcels of cocaine between the stacks of gold bars, antique furniture, and other collectables. Two men sleep on the floor, and another two sleep on a desk in a control room in the corner. We look round for the last man, and he's asleep on his feet against the wall.

'He has strong legs,' I say.

Tosin nods and turns to the parcels of cocaine. 'That's a lot of coke,' he says.

I nod.

We pack the cocaine onto the trolleys as quickly as possible and take the lift back up to the first level, where Jide is waiting. He rolls his trolley into the lift, and it's filled with four carefully arranged pieces of art, three necklaces, and a diamond the size of my fist. And he's also holding an ivory mask.

'This fucking belongs to the Benin people,' he says. 'Not whoever kept it in there. We're sending it back home.'

Tosin nods, and Jide gently places the ivory mask on top of Tosin's stack of cocaine.

The lift rises to the ground level, and we race through to the truck. As we approach, all the people in the unloading bay, who are clearly awake and have tried unsuccessfully to free themselves, pretend to be unconscious.

We push the trolleys into the cargo container and I strap them down as Tosin drives through the gates and away from the warehouse. I step into the cabin and fist-bump both of them. That was even more smooth than I'd hoped. But I shouldn't be surprised by Tosin and Jide anymore.

'That was fun,' Tosin says.

'And we didn't kill anyone,' I add.

'Well . . .' Jide says. 'What happened was . . .'

He glances at my shocked stare, and they both burst into laughter.

'I told you I would get you back,' he says. 'No one died!'

Tosin connects his phone to the stereo and plays a song called 'Oleku' by Ice Prince, and as always, they dance to the music like there's no tomorrow.

'Enjoy the last days of your life'

Alan walks down to the lower tier of the Emirates Stadium to Marat, alone at a seat almost dead level with the halfway line.

'Enjoy the game?' Alan asks and sits beside Marat.

'Yes,' Marat says, and nods.

'I'm sure you'll miss it,' Alan says.

Marat chuckles. 'I'm sure,' he says.

'I have to say, your moves were clever,' Alan says.

Marat glances at Alan and bites his tongue.

'But storing the drugs with things you're safekeeping for some of the most dangerous people in the world was just too stupid,' Alan says. 'If I had my way, I would've burnt it all to the ground.'

'When do my people get the items back?'

'The moment I receive confirmation that you've left this island.'

'Which ones are you keeping?'

'The Picasso, the Cézanne, and the necklace.'

Marat shakes his head – those are the ones that'll cause him the most trouble. Which Alan somehow knows, which is why he's keeping them.

'And when do I get *them* back?' Marat asks.

'Haven't decided yet.'

Marat nods.

'I heard Gennady went ahead of you, because he's being investigated for Valentin and Jack Moore's murder. Sad, isn't it? Who can you trust nowadays?'

'Why should I trust that you'll send the items to my people when I leave?'

'*I?*' Alan asks. 'Not just you . . . Veronika, too.'

Marat nods. 'When *we* leave.'

'Well, this wasn't my plan. Veronika killed my brother . . . so I wasn't going to rest till I killed you both. But he talked me out of it. And he wants to talk to you as well. You might not like what he has to say. And I don't think it's necessary. But he does. And I think it'll make you trust him. Want to talk to him?'

Marat nods.

'I'll let him know, and he'll walk down to us. So, you best let your shooters know.'

Franka and I watch Alan and Marat chat from Alan's box in the Emirates Stadium. My phone rings, and it's Alan. I answer.

'He's happy to talk to you,' Alan says.

415

I walk down the tier, and as I approach, Alan climbs to a seat behind Marat. I sit beside the Russian, and he glares at me.

'Pretty Boy?' Marat asks.

I nod.

'This is your plan?' he asks.

'I didn't think any more of us needed to die to end this,' I say.

Marat doesn't respond.

'I had no intention of killing Viktor—'

'Don't you dare say his name!'

'I have to, and you have—'

'Sparing my life will not make me forgive you!'

'I don't want your forgiveness. I want to tell you what happened. Because sometimes that's more important than vengeance.'

'Not for me.'

'Not yet.'

Marat shakes his head with anger.

'Your son tried to kill me. It was a drug deal, but he didn't want to pay. Which is a trait of his I'm sure you'd noticed before. And he underestimated me. Another trait I'm sure you noticed. He left me no choice. I had a choice with you, I had a choice with your people at Oak – and I hope my choices tell you the sort of man I am. And I also hope that the fact that I'm right here beside you telling you I killed your first son tells you the man I am. I give you my word, Marat – when you and Veronika leave, you will receive your items in exactly the same condition as when I took them. Except for the Benin ivory mask. You should tell whoever thought they owned it that it's best they forget about it.'

'You're a good man, Pretty Boy,' Marat says. 'The sort of man I hoped Viktor and Valentin would grow up to be.'

'Thank you,' I say.

'But I still hate you. And I dream of your death every night.'

'I understand, Marat,' I say. 'Take care.'

I stand.

'You should teach Alan some things,' Marat says. 'You can be a criminal. You can be a murderer. But you can still be a man of integrity.'

Alan stands, chuckling, and walks away.

'He's still not going to admit he killed Valentin. Even though he sat here and watched you admit to killing Viktor.'

'I didn't do that,' Alan says, turning back. 'And will not admit it because I don't need you chasing after me for ever.'

'I won't have to,' Marat says. 'Because you will not survive much longer. You must know Michael wasn't Gennady's source in your organisation. Gennady tells me that this person will not stop till you're dead. And as you can tell, this person is willing to work with whoever to make it happen. Enjoy the last days of your life, Alan.'

Alan dismisses Marat with a wave, but I can tell he's unnerved by what Marat said.

We walk up the tier to Franka, and I realise I know who Gennady's source is.

AUTUMN 1997

'A genius and a thief'

Pretty Boy, dressed in his school uniform, skips down the steps and heads to the kitchen counter where Alan and his wife, Hannah, are having breakfast.

'Morning, Hannah!' he says.

'Morning,' she says. 'Your eggs are on the table, but you're going to scoff 'em quickly if you want Alan to drop you in school today.'

'Morning, Alan,' Pretty Boy says, and pours himself a glass of orange juice. 'Why so quick this morning?'

'He's got a raid,' Hannah says, and teases Alan with feigned excitement.

'We're just making the arrests on the case I've been doing all-nighters on.'

'Congratulations,' Pretty Boy says.

'Not yet. The arrests are all scheduled to happen simultaneously in London, Amsterdam, and Ibiza . . . And I'm overseeing that, so it's going to be a busy morning and afternoon till it's done.'

'That's big!' Pretty Boy says.

'At least someone's happy for me,' Alan says.

'Oh, I'm happy for you,' Hannah says. ' I just get worried when your phone's off for so long. And that's what always happens when these arrests come up.'

'I'll be fine . . . just coordinating. I'll be far away from any bullets, which probably won't happen, anyway. And I'll call you soon as it's done.'

'That's what you said last time, and it was almost twelve hours! I almost came to the station.'

'That was a shitshow. But then that's why I'm coordinating now, so some good came out of that.'

'Don't worry,' Pretty Boy says. 'I'll walk or take the bus.'

'Sure?'

Pretty Boy nods.

'I can drop you,' Hannah says. 'I'll just open the shop early.'

'It's okay. I enjoy walking around here.'

'Okay,' Hannah says.

Alan hides a smile. It took a while to get Pretty Boy out of his shell, but he's out now, and fucking worth it. He takes the last gulp of his coffee and stands.

'See you guys later. But it might be a late night for me.'

'You see?' Hannah says. 'Get out!'

Alan kisses Hannah and leaves the house.

'I'm off to get ready,' Hannah says. 'What do you want for tea when you get back?'

'Whatever you're having,' Pretty Boy says.

Hannah smiles and walks up the stairs.

Pretty Boy finishes his breakfast, grabs his schoolbag, and steps out of the door. He walks through the pleasant South London neighbourhood with his head up and a pep in his step.

He arrives at school about fifteen minutes early and spots Mr Ingles, the PE teacher, stepping out of his car.

'Fuck,' Pretty Boy mutters.

He's forgotten his PE kit again, and Mr Ingles has said he isn't getting a spare anymore and will do theory PE for three weeks straight next time he forgets. Pretty Boy enjoys PE, especially because he hasn't been able to pursue his first ambition to become a footballer since moving in with Alan. He spots the bus back home approaching the stop in front of the school. It's ten minutes at most to get back home; if he races in, grabs the kit, and catches the bus back to school, he'll be five minutes late at most. And he might get a pass because he's never been late. He runs to catch the bus.

He's home in eight minutes. Luck is on his side. He quickly unlocks the front door, and the moment he steps in, he hears sounds he recognises that provoke fury out of him he thought he'd buried for good. He softly closes the door and listens for a few moments to confirm it's not the television. It isn't: Hannah is in the bedroom upstairs having animated sex with someone who isn't Alan.

Pretty Boy walks to the kitchen, sits in a corner, and waits.

Thirty minutes later, Hannah and her lover walk into the kitchen, naked and giggling, and don't notice Pretty Boy. Pretty Boy recognises her lover – it's Dave, Michael's nephew. Dave grabs the orange juice carton from the fridge and necks it.

'Don't finish it,' Pretty Boy casually says.

Hannah spins to Pretty Boy and is almost overcome with shock, and Dave grabs a knife.

Pretty Boy has no fear of the blade. 'I came back to get my PE kit,' he says. 'But didn't want to disturb you.'

Pretty Boy walks past them and skips up the stairs to his bedroom.

'What the fuck, Hannah?' Dave asks.

Hannah shrugs.

'What should I do?' he asks.

'I don't know. Threaten him, deal with him, I don't know. He just can't tell Alan.'

'I fucking know that. Threaten him or deal with him? Which one?'

'Whatever. And do it fast!'

Dave races up the stairs with the knife and kicks in Pretty Boy's door, but he's not in the bedroom. He checks Hannah's bedroom and the bathroom, but Pretty Boy is not there, or anywhere upstairs.

Dave races back to the kitchen, where Hannah is pacing.

'Did he come down?' Dave asks.

'What?' she asks.

'He's not up there.'

'What the fuck do you mean he's not up there?'

'He's not. Is it some fucking black magic or something?'

'Oh, shut up, Dave. He probably jumped out the window.'

'Jumped out the window?'

'Yeah. Alan said he used to be a skilled thief.'

'He's, like, fucking fifteen. What the fuck is *used to be*?'

'He's either gone to school or the station.'

'To school? After what just happened?'

'Yes. He loves school. He's a genius or something. Aced some test to get into that school on a scholarship. You didn't think I was paying for it, did you?'

'Facking hell. A genius and a thief. No wonder Alan took him in.'

Hannah nods.

'Okay. I'll head to the school and wait for him, and you go to the station and make sure you get to Alan's phone before he does, in case—'

'Stop telling me what to do!' Hannah says. 'Fucking go! Maybe you can get to the school before him.'

Dave speeds to the school and parks outside to wait for Pretty Boy to arrive, but he soon gets a call from Hannah. The school have called her to confirm Pretty Boy's reason for being late – he witnessed an accident and had to stay to give a statement. She confirmed it.

Dave waits outside in his car till the school closes, and he watches all the kids leave. But Pretty Boy isn't one of them. He waits for an hour, guessing Pretty Boy was put into detention because he was late, but then a bunch of kids come out of the gates, and Pretty Boy isn't one of them. Dave jumps out of the car to ask the kids if they know Pretty Boy. They all do, but he wasn't in detention with them. He left school at the normal time, as far as they know.

Dave calls Hannah.

'Where are you?' he asks.

'At home!'

'The kid's not there?'

'You think I'd leave you waiting out there if he was?'

'No. But he's not in school.'

'What? I thought you were watching the school?'

'I was. But I don't even know if he was there.'

'You think he got the school to lie for him? You missed him. Stop the excuses.'

'I didn't miss him. And why's he not home, then?'

'I don't know. But I need to go to the station in case he's there waiting for Alan.'

'Alan's phone's not on yet, then?'

'No. And I'm calling every minute,' she says. 'I'm going now. Come here and wait outside in case the kid comes home.'

'Okay.'

Hannah parks in front of the police station and takes a moment to get into the right mood to play the worried wife. She knows Alan would be unhappy she came, but if she plays it right, he'll be too preoccupied consoling her for his irritation to last. But before she steps out of the car, her phone rings, and it's Alan.

She panics, wondering if Pretty Boy has gotten to Alan before her. She takes a deep breath and answers.

'Hey, darling,' Alan says. 'Sorry about the late call.'

'It's okay. How did it go?'

'Success. We got everyone. One person scaled the fence and rolled down a mountain in Ibiza, but we got them anyway.'

'Good. So now I can tell you I'm outside.'

'What?'

'Yes. Charlene said she heard—'

'Never listen to Charlene. And her brother is uniform, so he gets in a lot more bother than I do.'

'Well, I was incredibly worried. I closed the shop early.'

'Sorry . . .'

'It's okay. I'm here now. Let's catch a meal or something. Can you do that? Oh, don't worry, I'm sure you have celebratory drinks . . .'

'I'm already on my way down to you.'

Hannah and Alan enjoy a fun meal in the fish and chip shop, and Alan buys a takeaway for Pretty Boy, so Hannah doesn't have to cook. Throughout dinner, Hannah is in constant contact with Dave . . . but Pretty Boy never arrives home.

Alan offers to leave his car at the station, but she asks him to drive hers because she's tired. He does. She keeps an eye on Alan's phone as he drives and worries about Pretty Boy.

She knows Pretty Boy won't run away, but she doesn't know where he could be and why. Maybe he's at a neighbour's and watching for Alan's return from there. All the neighbours seem to like him, so it could be any of them. Maybe she could talk to Pretty Boy. Offer him something . . . money, perhaps? To be a more affectionate mother? He must miss his mother. As crazy as she was.

She texts Dave to leave as she and Alan approach the house. Alan parks and stares at the house, concerned.

'He's not home?' Alan asks.

'No. I think he said he was staying with friends for a bit tonight.'

'He's making friends,' Alan says, excited. 'That's good!'

Alan and Hannah step into the house and walk to the kitchen. He switches on the light, and Pretty Boy is there, calmly sitting at the kitchen counter. Pretty Boy's presence shocks but amuses Alan. But Hannah faints and falls head first to the floor.

It's 9 a.m. the following day, and Pretty Boy sits alone in a waiting room in the surgical ward. Alan had asked him to go home, but he refused. He knows what's coming next and doesn't want to drag it on.

Alan steps into the waiting room, looking exhausted but relieved, and sits beside Pretty Boy.

'How is she?' Pretty Boy asks.

'Good. A small bleed in the brain. But she'll make a full recovery.'

'That's good.'

Pretty Boy glances at Alan and senses his unease. 'She wants me out before she comes home, right?' he asks.

Pretty Boy's perceptiveness surprises Alan, and he wants to deny it and couch it some other way. But there's no point. The kid knows. 'Just until she feels more comfortable,' Alan lies. 'You gave her a serious shock.'

Alan tried to beg Hannah. He didn't want to abandon the kid like his mum did. But Hannah gave him an ultimatum — the kid or her. And not just till she feels more comfortable. She doesn't want Pretty Boy around ever again. And it's not because of the shock or her injury. It's because of what he saw. What he'll have over her for ever.

'It's okay,' Pretty Boy says.

'What do you mean, *it's okay*?' Alan asks. 'You're a child. I shouldn't expect you to understand and forgive so quickly.'

'There's nothing to forgive. You took me in and made me happy. I'll never forget it.'

'Calm down, you're talking like it's over. I said till she feels more comfortable.'

Pretty Boy nods. 'I just don't want you to feel sad. You did a good thing for me.'

'And I'm not done with that. I'll take you home now, and we'll make proper arrangements. The owner of your school has a boarding school in Kent or something, so I'm sure we can move you there . . . and make arrangements for when you're on holiday. I know loads of people who will be happy to have you. Sheila from quiz night is always going on about how she wants to steal you . . . although I think you'd be expected to provide some benefits there.'

'Eww . . .'

'I mean to join their quiz team . . . and occasionally give her a warm bath.'

'Stop it!'

They laugh.

DAY 28, 19:00

'I have a plan'

I thought Alan knew – or at least had suspicions – Hannah was cheating on him, and that's why they divorced. But the look on his face as I reveal what happened in the autumn of 1997 tells me he didn't know.

He sits by the kitchen island in the penthouse, speechless and consumed with fury and embarrassment. And Franka and I quietly watch him.

'I'm sorry,' he says, breaking the silence.

'No need,' I say.

'There is plenty need. I abandoned you for a whore.'

'You didn't abandon me . . . you stuck to your word. It's not your fault I hated Kent so much.'

I laugh, but he isn't amused.

'Dave's certainly Gennady's informant,' he says.

'And he hates you that much because of Hannah? You divorced her.'

'Yeah, and I paid off the mortgage on her shop and her home,' Alan says, and shakes his head. 'It's not all about Hannah. I let Dave go to prison for a couple of years when everyone knew I could help him out. I'd helped lots of others in tighter spots. The network was supposed to be his, too. But I stepped in when he went inside, and when he got out, it was too late. Michael didn't want him anywhere near it because of how successful it was . . . paying for his political dreams.'

I nod; that makes more sense.

'I have a plan,' he says. 'And you won't like it because they're going to die.'

DAY 31, 08:00

'What does love have to do with it?'

Alan parks in the driveway of a beautiful detached home in Hampstead. Hannah's home. He steps out of the car and approaches the front door, but before he rings the buzzer, Hannah pulls the door open.

'To what do I owe this early morning pleasure?' she asks.

They kiss each other on the cheek, and he steps into the house.

'You want anything?' she asks. 'I'm just fixing myself a smoothie.'

'I can't stay long,' Alan says, anxious. 'But I need a quick favour from you.'

'Of course, Alan.'

'I'm looking for Dave,' he says, and watches for her reaction, but there is nothing out of the ordinary – she's good. 'I hear he's hiding somewhere with his ex – Beth. I know you're friends with Rachel, Beth's mum. I need you to call Rachel and ask about her daughter and Dave. Mention something like you heard I'm looking for Dave. Hopefully, Rachel calls or texts Beth to warn them . . . we're on Rachel's phone, so if she does, we have Beth's number and can track them down. Because we've been sitting on Dave's burner for a day, and it's not been active at all. So maybe he's tossed it.'

'What did Dave do?' she asks.

'The less you know, the better.'

She nods.

'I need you to call right now,' Alan says.

'It's eight in the morning.'

'I have people watching her house, and I hear she's awake. Sorry about this, but I need to find him fast.'

She nods and pulls out her phone to call.

'Hey, Rachel.'

. . .

'I know! Been too long. When next are you going to come to the shop? I have the new . . .'

. . .

'Oh, sorry, I didn't know about that.'

. . .

'I hope Beth is taking care of you.'

. . .

'Oh. That's no good.'

. . .

'She got back with him?'

. . .

'I know. Girls and bad boys.'

. . .

'I hope she has nothing to do with what's happening with him.'

. . .

'I don't know much, either. Just that my ex is looking for him.'

. . .

'They left town together? I understand why you're worried.'

. . .

'I try to stay away from talking about these things with my ex. But I'll try to have a word. Don't know if he'll listen, though. That's why he's my ex, you know.' She laughs.

. . .

'I understand. I understand. I'll do my best, Rachel.'

. . .

'Okay.'

. . .

'Okay, I'll call you back after I speak to him.'

Hannah ends the call. 'She's scared,' she says to Alan. 'Beth left with Dave a few days ago, and she doesn't know where they went. Doesn't have a number either.'

Alan curses underneath his breath.

'She wants me to put in a good word with you. Tell you not to harm Beth if you find them, just because she's been swayed by the charms of a bad boy.' She rolls her eyes.

'Thanks. Will find another way,' he says, and heads for the door.

'You really don't want to try my smoothie?'

'Not today, Hannah. Soon.'

He smiles at her, and she smiles back before he walks out the door. She watches him through the window as he hurriedly gets into his car and reverses out of her driveway.

Hannah is furious as she marches to her kitchen. She pulls a burner phone from a cabinet and tries to call Dave, but she remembers Alan is sitting on the number, so she doesn't and screams in anger. She's going to cut his dick off if he went with Beth to the hideout she paid for, when he told her he had to go alone. No wonder he asked her not to come – 'in case she was followed', he said. Bullshit, he just wanted to be alone with Beth.

She can't contain her rage and marches out of her house to check if any unfamiliar cars are parked nearby, but there are none. She grabs a knife from her kitchen, grabs her jacket, and jumps into her car to drive to the hideout.

A couple of hours later, she approaches a small cottage surrounded by tall trees, and the time driving has only made her more furious. She parks and jumps out of the car with the knife in her pocket, but before she gets to the front door, Dave opens it.

'What the fuck are you doing here?' he asks.

She barges past him and races around the tiny house. 'Where the fuck is she?' she barks.

'Who?'

'Don't fucking "who" me!' she says and pulls out the knife.

'Facking hell,' he says, and retreats. 'What are you talking about?'

She runs back into the bedroom and uses all her energy to lift the mattress, but Beth isn't there.

She runs back to him in the living room. 'Stop fucking playing me with me!' she screams. 'Beth!' she calls.

'Beth? What?'

'Beth! Get the fuck out here, or I will fucking cut you!'

A car approaches the cottage, and both are consumed with fear. Dave rushes to check the window. It's Alan's Jaguar.

'They played you!' he screams, and runs to the bedside table for his gun, but when he opens the drawer, it's not there.

'Where's the fucking gun?' he asks.

Hannah doesn't respond. She's stunned, watching Alan and Pretty Boy step out of the car and walk towards the front door.

Dave lifts his mattress to check if the gun fell underneath, but feels a muzzle pushed into his neck.

'Are you looking for this one?' Franka asks.

Hannah is transfixed by me and doesn't move. Alan gestures for her to sit on the sofa in the small living room, but she doesn't respond.

'Sit!' Alan commands.

Hannah sits but doesn't take her eyes off me. Franka leads Dave back into the living room and gestures for him to sit beside Hannah; he does.

'Here we are,' Alan says. 'And I gather it took me long enough.'

Hannah attempts to protest, but she's a spent force and can't muster the words.

'Don't faint again,' Alan says to her, and forces laughter.

'Just kill me,' Hannah says. 'I'm—'

Alan shoots her in the head, and blood splatter explodes onto the sofa and Dave's face. The suddenness of the kill stuns me, but then this was inevitable once I told him about autumn 1997.

'Why did you do it?' Alan asks Dave.

'Why do you think?' Dave says.

'I'm asking the questions,' Alan says.

'Fuck you.'

'I'm out of patience,' Alan says, and gestures to Hannah. 'As you can tell.'

'You're going to kill me anyway, but all right,' Dave says. 'Because you killed Charlie.'

I wasn't expecting that. Charlie is Dave's younger brother, and he was the nice one by a long mile. Why would Alan do that?

'No, I didn't,' Alan responds, offended by the accusation.

'You killed my brother. Just like you killed yours.'

Alan is indignant.

'You want to say you didn't kill Michael either? Because that's your natural reaction. To lie. But everyone in this room knows you did, so why bother?'

'I killed Michael. His time was up. But I didn't kill Charlie,' Alan says.

'Fuck off! We know you did. Mum, me . . . even Michael.

Michael acted like he didn't believe me and even benched me because I kept going on about it. But he didn't need to believe me because he already knew. And he protected you anyway because you were making all that money for him with the fucking network that was supposed to be mine . . .'

'That's what this is about, isn't it?'

'Of course, jump on that, Alan. Yeah, that's good enough for me to want you dead, but that's not what this is, and you know it. What makes it even worse is that you didn't kill Charlie because your life or your freedom depended on it . . . you did it to save your job as police. You didn't trust Charlie to stand up to Marbella police or Interpol, so you killed him.'

'What are you talking about?'

'I read the Interpol report you tried to bury. Mum re-mortgaged the house to pay for it because Michael refused to. It turned out Michael didn't want to pay for it because he'd already read it. You distancing yourself from the Downings . . . claiming Charlie was just an informant. But you lost your job, anyway!'

'Exactly. I took the risk of going to Marbella to close the deal with the 'Ndrangheta for the family. And it blew up in my face!'

'Why are you still fucking lying? You're going to kill me, anyway. You lost your job because Interpol didn't believe your story, and that was the only way they were going to stop the investigation. Again, I read the report.'

'You keep mentioning this fucking report. That's the bloody version Interpol wants on the record to cover themselves. You think if they had any shred of evidence that a high-ranking British police officer murdered a British national on Spanish soil, all they'd want to stop that investigation is the officer's resignation? It became a pissing contest, with Interpol looking to blame someone else for their dead agent. I took the blame, but it wasn't me. Interpol or their agent fucked up somehow, the 'Ndrangheta found out, and it all went to shit. I tried to protect Charlie. I really did.'

'You can't be trying to convince me with that bullshit. Maybe you're trying to convince yourself . . . or Pretty Boy. Cos I know this German dyke couldn't give a shit.'

'Michael knew that's what happened, that's why he didn't kill me. It was never about money with Michael. But you're looking for someone to blame too for your part in this. Because it was supposed to be you in Marbella closing the deal, until you stuck a pool cue up a university student's arse!'

Dave doesn't respond.

'And your mum is looking for someone to blame for letting her sons follow her brother into the life. But leave me out of it—'

'Stop . . . just stop!' Dave shouts. 'I went to Marbella. I asked around; they all loved Charlie.'

'What does love have to do with it? I loved Michael. I loved Hannah.'

'Not everyone is you, though, Alan. You're different. Mum said you were always different. You're probably going to kill her now, too, right?'

'No.'

'Are you sure? Because this was all her idea. Destroy the network so Michael would have no choice.'

'I think it's enough for her to know she killed her brother.'

'No, you did.'

'I pulled the trigger, sure. But your mum killed Michael. And your mum killed you.'

A bang reverberates around the tiny cottage as Alan shoots Dave in the head.

DAY 31, 23:58

'Where are you?'

It's approaching midnight, and Alan's impromptu celebratory house party at his penthouse flat in Clapham is in full flow. He and his guests are having so much fun that he didn't notice Franka slip away about thirty minutes ago to go visit Meiling. But then I don't think Alan would care that Franka isn't here, because he doesn't believe anyone would or could come after him today. He's the king, and he's taken care of all the contenders and pretenders. And Alan's guests, a lot of them Michael's former soldiers, believe Alan's the king as well. They are his people now. They'll give their lives for him.

Whoever's in charge of the music plays 'Power' by Kanye West, and the conceitedness of the party has reached its peak — that's my cue to leave. I'd been waiting to ask Alan a question, but it doesn't matter. I walk towards the door, but Alan notices and hurries towards me.

'You're off?' he asks, disappointed. 'I arranged company for you.' He gestures to two beautiful young women. 'The one that looks a bit like Rebecca.'

She does look a bit like Rebecca, and I smile because I'm impressed by Alan's attention to detail. She smiles back.

'Not tonight,' I say to Alan.

'Sure?'

I nod. 'I'm going.'

'Okay. See you tomorrow, yeah?'

I've done my part and it's time for me to live free of all this shit, so I want to say no. But I know he won't let me go if I do. And I'm staying in London anyway, so he could probably see me tomorrow if he tried hard enough.

'Yeah,' I say.

He grins.

'I have a question,' I add.

'Go ahead.'

'Did you kill Charlie?'

'No,' he responds almost immediately. Like he'd been expecting me to ask.

And for the first time, I can't read him at all. I'll have to take his word for it.

'Thanks,' I say.

'For what?' he asks.

'Answering.'

'Come on,' he says. 'Least I can do.'

I nod and walk out of the flat.

I step out of the building and head towards the car. The

smartphone Oleg provided rings, and it's a withheld number. Probably Mint. I ignore the call. Then the phone pings with a tracking attempt from Victoria Embankment . . . Scotland Yard. The phone rings again, and I answer.

'Where are you?' Mint asks.

'Why?' I ask.

'If you're in Clapham, get out. Now. Veronika is on her way with an army.'

ACKNOWLEDGEMENTS

I'm incredibly thankful to my wife, the Quercus team and the Greene & Heaton team for making the process of writing and perfecting (as much as we could) this novel, being a new father and training to be a solicitor so seamless. I try to explain how it all works to people, but I can't because it's just magic.

Lastly, many thanks to UK literary community for welcoming the boy from Lagos with open arms.